The Glory and the Wonder

A Novel

Book Two in the St. Michael Trilogy

Michael L. Sherer

PublishAmerica
Baltimore

First printing

At the specific preference of the author, PublishAmerica allowed this work to remain exactly as the author intended, verbatim, without editorial input.

ISBN: 1-4241-2064-0
PUBLISHED BY PUBLISHAMERICA, LLLP
www.publishamerica.com
Baltimore

Printed in the United States of America

Dedicated to the Staff and members of the Board of Directors of *Metro Lutheran* Newspaper, an independent monthly publication bridging the Lutheran spectrum in the Twin Cities area of Minnesota and western Wisconsin, with special gratitude to and affection for the journal's founding president, the Rev. Norman D. Kretzmann.

Soli Deo Gloria

Chapter 1

In the cool interior of the great gothic nave, the pure voices of youthful teen-agers combined in exquisite harmony. To a casual listener, the sound would have resembled near-perfection. But *near* was not close enough for Lillian Fischer. The Director of Music at the Lutheran Church of Saint Michael and All Angels stopped the members of her high school choir in mid-note. For five seconds their last phrase could be heard reverberating off the high stone walls of the enormous worship space.

The three dozen singers, all of whom were actively involved in the growing congregation's burgeoning Luther League program, were showing signs of restlessness. Lillian had been putting them through their paces for the past fifty minutes. It was a Saturday morning, and many of them were eager to be on their way. Still, they paid attention. They knew Lillian was a perfectionist, and the sooner they gave her what she wanted, the sooner they would be released.

"People," she said, with the trademark impatient intensity she always used at rehearsal, "I know you've sung these words a hundred times at Bible camp. And that's the problem. You're too confident, and that can make you careless when you sing them in a formal setting." She paused, and studied the enormous stained-glass window behind the choir. It showed Jesus surrounded by small children. The rainbow of color that came streaming through would have blinded her, had she decided to stare at the artwork. Instead, she studied the faces of her young singers.

She was not sure why she'd consented to let the youth choir sing a camp song at Sunday worship. Maybe it was because Pastor Jonas had suggested it to her. Twice.

"I want you to imagine you're sitting way back there in the last row at worship tomorrow. If people can't understand the words you're singing, your message will be lost on them. So sing-them-clear-ly-and-e-nun-ci-ate." The last sentence came out in near staccato, a demonstration of what she had in mind.

So they sang it once again, this time with feeling and precision.

Living for Jesus a life that is true,
Striving to please him in all that I do,
Yielding allegiance, glad-hearted and free,
This is the pathway of blessing for me.
Oh Jesus, Lord and Saviour,
I give myself to thee;
For thou, in thy atonement,
Didst give thyself for me;
I own no other master,
My heart shall be thy throne.
My life I give, henceforth to live,
O Christ, for thee alone.

Lillian dropped her arms. Her young singers looked warily at her, not sure what she'd say next. What she said was, "That was perfect. Do it that way tomorrow. Don't forget, we're singing at both services. Be on time."

IN THE PARKING LOT, seventeen-year-old Hannah Ruth Jonas waited for her classmate, Jenny Langholz to catch up. Hannah had known Jenny her entire life and considered her to be her best friend.

"You want to come over to my house and fool around this afternoon?" Jenny asked.

Hannah Ruth sighed. "Can't. Have to practice."

"You know what? You're gonna wear that piano completely out if you're not careful."

They headed north, along tree-lined Anderson Avenue, toward the Jonas home. Hannah Ruth said, "I have to work on my scales. I've had one lesson since taking the summer off. Lillian says I've been a slacker."

"Lillian's a slave driver," said Jenny.

"Easy for you to say. You're not taking piano lessons."

"Choir rehearsals are bad enough. You can hardly ever do it good enough for her."

"That's why she's such a great organist, though," Hannah Ruth replied.

"You know, she's getting to be one of the best ones in the Twin Cities. Every time she gives a recital, the church is packed."

"And now she's thrown her spell on you," said Jenny.

"Why do you say that? Just because she wants me to be one of her star pupils?"

"I know where this is leading. The next thing, she'll be starting you on the organ. Then you'll be playing substitute for her."

"I'm only seventeen, silly."

"Am I wrong though?"

"Jenny, I like music. I think I could be pretty good at it."

"You're already pretty good. Slave-driver Lillian wants you to be great. Sensational, even. I'll bet she thinks you're going to end up on the concert stage or something."

"Well, I think she actually does hope I'll become a church musician some day."

"Did she say that?"

"She told me I should think about the Conservatory of Music at Capital University."

"But that's in Ohio."

"My parents went to Capital."

"So, if I wanted to stay best friends with you, I'd have to go to college in Ohio?"

"Well, it would be sort of keen if we ended up on the same campus. We could be roommates!"

They reached the Jonas residence. Climbing the front steps, they sat down together on the porch swing. Jenny sighed and said, "Must be nice, being able to go to college where your parents went." She listened to the swing chain creak as they glided back and forth. "My mom never went to college. My dad's college doesn't even exist anymore."

"St. Paul Luther, over in St. Paul, right?"

Jenny nodded. "How can a college just run out of money and have to close?"

"Well, that was the Depression. Everybody was running out of money."

"Yeah. I know. My folks keep talking about how tough it was. Glad I didn't have to live back then."

"It was only about fifteen years ago."

"Well, when you're just seventeen years old, it might as well have been 150."

They glided back and forth in silence. Hannah Ruth said, "Maybe I could come over after three o'clock. I should be done practicing by then."

Jenny scowled, then grinned. "I guess it's better than nothing."

"And we can talk about boys."

Jenny's eyes lit up. "Any boys in particular?"

"There are only about six in the Luther League alone I'd like to have dates with. What about you?"

Jenny offered a thoughtful scowl. "Yeah. About that many, I guess."

"Well, all I've got to say is, we're already in our senior year in high school and so far neither of us has anybody to go steady with. At this rate, we'll both end up old maids."

ANDREAS SCHEIDT walked along the alley, behind the church building, gesturing toward the residences that backed up to Saint Michael Church. The carpenter-turned-contractor said to the congregation's senior pastor, "The main thing right now is, we have to figure out where to put all the cars on Sunday mornings. We're getting complaints from some in the neighborhood about how our members are lining the curbs for blocks around. It's causing traffic jams. And some people don't like strangers parking in front of their houses."

"Guess we should just get all those people to join Saint Michael Church then," said Pastor Daniel Jonas good-naturedly. "Then they'd stop complaining."

"Actually, quite a few of them already belong, as you know. But it's never going to happen that everybody's going to join Saint Michael Church."

Daniel realized his congregational president was right. He said, "So, what's the big idea you have for me to consider, Andy?"

"Well, as you know, we've got purchase options on all the houses on the other side of the alley. So we could probably take them down and pave that side of the block."

"Wouldn't that look sort of bad, all that pavement in the middle of a residential area?"

"It's only a couple blocks from Bloomington Avenue, and that's zoned commercial. But, anyway, I wasn't really thinking about paving it."

Daniel waited for the next sentence.

"What I think we could do," said Andy, stopping and studying the garages that backed up to the alley, "would be to buy all these properties outright. We could keep about half of them—the ones behind our parish house—as rentals, at least for now, and then take down the ones right behind the church building itself."

"That wouldn't add enough parking to give us what we need, Andy."

"I realize that. But, here's the deal. We'd build a parking ramp. A basement level, a surface level, and then two levels on top of that."

"And you think that would make the neighbors happier than having pavement to look at?"

"I'm in construction, remember? We'll face the whole structure with really nice stone, the kind that matches the church building. It will look like it all belongs together. It would be really classy. And, we could have skyway on the second level, going right over the alley and into the second level of the parish house. For people who come to night meetings, in case they're afraid to be outside after dark."

Daniel felt caught off-guard. He said, "That sounds expensive. And the stonework would make it even more so."

"Have I ever done a project for St. Michael Church without giving the congregation a break on the price?"

Daniel remembered how it had been Andy who headed up the construction of a first chapel for Saint Michael Church, with donated lumber, eighteen years before. The labor had been donated as well. In fact, Daniel himself had helped build the chapel, which Andy later disassembled and rebuilt at Camp Saint Michael, north of the Twin Cities. That had come several years later, after the magnificent new stone church building had gone up.

Andy continued, "And don't forget, we have a million dollars in the endowment fund. The interest has to be spent on capital projects. A parking ramp would fit that. Besides, since we haven't taken anything out of the fund for several years, I think we might have almost enough in there to cover this."

"The council and the congregation would have to approve it."

"Of course they would. But the first thing is, do *you* approve?"

"Well, it's a new idea, Andy. I hadn't imagined putting up a parking ramp. Even Central Lutheran, downtown, doesn't have one. And Mount Olivet, with all its thousands of members over by Lake Harriet, has surface parking.

"This is Saint Michael and All Angels, Pastor. We do things different around here."

Daniel realized his congregational president was right about that. What other congregation, anywhere in the Twin Cities, had ever received a bequest of four-million dollars, donated just to build an enormous new worship facility, and another million in an endowment fund, set aside to keep it in good repair or for additional construction? He wasn't sure it had happened before, perhaps anywhere.

"So, tell me your thoughts, Pastor. Is this a good idea?"

Daniel mulled it for a moment. "I think so. Yes, I actually like the sound of it. Of course, we'd need some drawings, something to show the council."

"Of course we would. And when you come by my office tomorrow morning, they'll be ready for you."

"They're already done, aren't they," Daniel said dryly.

"Well, you can't sell a plan if you don't draw up plans."

Spoken like a construction company entrepreneur, Daniel thought.

Chapter 2

It had been Lillian Fischer's idea to hold a special evening worship service every year on the Festival Day of St. Michael and All Angels. She'd reminded the senior pastor that it was the actual day of the parish's organization, back in 1927. That was, in fact, the reason for the congregation's name. Part of Lillian's argument for a worship service on what the old church hymnals called "Michaelmas" was compelling to Pastor Jonas. She'd reminded him that every extra worship service was another opportunity for evangelism, because you never knew who might wander in, if only out of curiosity.

Daniel had agreed to an annual worship celebration on the 29th of September, partly to keep his director of music happy. Another reason was the fact that Lillian wanted the service to consist of music, Scripture and Holy Communion, but not preaching. That saved Daniel, as well as the other two pastors, from having to come up with a sermon.

The problem was that, in 1946, the Festival Day of St. Michael and All Angels fell on a Sunday. Who, he wondered, would show up for Sunday night worship? Lillian had evidently considered that reality. She'd told the members of all four of her choirs she expected them to sing during the service. That pretty much guaranteed that the parents of her three children's and youth choirs would be there. And, with her growing reputation as an excellent organist, Lillian had a way of drawing music lovers from all over the metropolitan area. That included a lot of professional musicians, who were free to attend since it wasn't a Sunday morning service.

There were almost 300 in the pews when the service began, which Daniel had to admit was pretty remarkable. Still, with seating for over 800, the pews at Saint Michael and All Angels Church were far from full.

A dozen years earlier, for the dedication of the present enormous stone worship facility, Lillian had written a complex choral fugue based on an ancient hymn text. She had since decided to make it her senior choir's signature anthem for the St. Michael's Day service. The congregation had grown fond of it and always waited with anticipation until time for the offering. That's when the senior choir would rise from their seats in the balcony and voice the words penned more than 1,100 years before by a medieval churchman named Rabanus Maurus.

Lillian's husband, Luther, introduced the piece with a first-stanza solo, his strong tenor voice reaching the far corners of the nave:

Jesus, brightness of the Father, life and strength of all who live!
In the presence of the angels, glory to thy name we give:
And thy wondrous praise rehearse, singing in harmonious verse.

As the worshipers left the service, they encountered a curious phenomenon. Standing on the sidewalk, just below the bottom step, in front of the great front doors, stood a man of perhaps forty. He was immaculately dressed, wearing a suit, white shirt and conservative dark tie. His hair was carefully combed, and a handkerchief was tucked into his breast pocket.

His proper appearance made what he was holding seem all the more remarkable. The stranger, whom nobody could ever remember having seen before, was holding a large placard, fastened to a flat lath. He held it solemnly with one hand, keeping the other tucked into his suit coat pocket.

The message, carefully lettered in elegant type, and coated with plastic laminate, read, simply, "Just Tell the Truth."

That, thought Adam Engelhardt, when he saw the sign, seemed peculiar. Adam, one of the founders of the congregation, lived a block and a half north, on the same street. The owner of a thriving printing business, Adam, at age 56, thought he had seen just about everything. But the stranger with the sign made him wonder. Did the gentleman realize there hadn't even been a sermon at this service? Or, wasn't that his point? Was it a message for the worshipers instead?

Heading up the sidewalk along Anderson Avenue, he thought about it. The message, it seemed to Adam, was fairly appropriate, no matter how strange the circumstance in which it was shared.

"DO YOU HAVE any fear of flying, Pastor?"

Thirty-year-old Arnold Elliot sat facing Daniel Jonas in the senior pastor's commodious office. The extroverted businessman, only recently a member of Saint Michael Church, wore golf slacks and a polo shirt, which was stitched with the words "Elliot Charters."

Daniel looked with admiration at the young aviator. He liked optimistic people, and Arnold was clearly one of those. He thought back to the day in August the year before. Arnold had just returned to Minnesota, following service as an army pilot in the Second World War. He'd walked into the church office and announced, "I want to belong here. Where do I sign up?"

Arnold had spent his post-high-school years doing crop-dusting in western Minnesota and South Dakota. That had guaranteed him a spot in the Army Air Corps, which led to a military career with distinction. When the war was over, Arnold had moved to Minneapolis and was busy building a charter flying business.

Daniel also appreciated Arnold's candor. The businessman admitted that, even though he lived near Powderhorn Lake, he'd joined St. Michael Church because it was large and rapidly growing. "It can only be good for business," he'd explained.

Daniel was hoping there was more to the aviator's membership than that, or at least that there would be as time went along.

"You know, Arnold, I don't really know if I'm afraid of flying. I've never been off the ground."

"Well, we need to get you up there into the wild blue. You'll love it! I guarantee it!"

Arnold's style reminded Daniel of a longtime member of the congregation, Joe Pavelka, who had once tried to sell him an Oldsmobile. Joe had used almost identical language—which had finally resulted in his selling the pastor a Chevrolet.

"I think I'd have to check with my wife," Daniel said, grinning. "She doesn't like me endangering my life without consulting her first."

"No danger, believe me," Arnold replied cheerfully. "I've never lost a passenger."

"What about your fiancee?" Daniel prodded. "Does she worry about your safety?"

"It was part of the agreement when we decided to get married," Arnold replied. "I don't tell her how to run her restaurant. She doesn't complain when I go flying. Anyway, it's the only honest work I know."

"So, just when did you want to do this wild blue yonder stuff with me?"

"Well, any time, Pastor. Business hasn't exactly caught on. Not yet. So I have some time on my hands. How about sometime in the next couple weeks?"

"Where do you keep your plane, Arnold?"

"Crystal Airport, up on the North Side. I could swing by and pick you up sometime. And then I'll show you Minneapolis like you've never seen it."

"All right. I'll let you know. In the meantime, just when are you and Sandra thinking of getting married?"

"Well, I would've done it the first weekend I was back from overseas. But she's more practical than I am. She wanted one more year of independent living. But I think she's about ready now. So, maybe around Thanksgiving? That work for you?"

"I suggest you stop in the church office on your way out. Janet Fenstermacher, our office manager, has the master calendar. She'll tell you what's available."

"Gotta check with the boss, huh?" he said mischievously.

"When it comes to scheduling, you're quite right. She really *is* the boss."

"Well, maybe not where picking a date for this wedding is concerned. I think the real boss is probably going to be Sandy."

JOHN BAUMGARTNER gripped the sides of the podium and cleared his throat. The handsome young seventeen-year-old looked out over the crowd of perhaps three dozen teen-agers, took quick note of the adult sponsors sitting at the back of the room, and began his Luther League topic presentation.

"Who's your first love?" he asked. He saw puzzled looks and a few grins. Eddie Calvert, a far-from-shy sophomore boy seated in the fourth row blurted out, "Emily Jacobs." Emily, seated across the aisle in the same row, turned three shades of crimson. The room exploded in laughter.

John held up his hands, as if in surrender, and said, "Okay, folks. Let's get serious here. That's not exactly what I meant."

"Well, I thought God made pretty girls for good-lookin' guys to admire," said Eddie.

"Guess we'd better find Emily somebody who's halfway good-lookin' then," said Ralph Schmidt, seated two rows behind Eddie. There was more laughter.

John was beginning to look exasperated. One of the adult sponsors spoke up. In a loud, no-nonsense voice, he said, "Listen, people, John's worked on this topic just for you guys and gals. Pay attention, or we'll just cancel refreshments tonight."

That seemed to do the trick. John, confident he had the group's attention, started over. "Who's your first love?" This time there was no response. The topic unfolded predictably, with a dissertation on the importance of giving your first allegiance to God, so that your priorities will fall naturally into place.

In spite of their best efforts, Jenny Langholz and Hannah Ruth Jonas were not getting much out of the topic. They sat next to one another in the second row, where they had a great view of John. In their "girl-talk" sessions they'd come to the discovery that both of them were head over heels for John Baumgartner. He was, they decided, a certifiable dreamboat, and neither was ready to give up on him as a favor to the other.

So, instead of listening to what John was actually saying, they concentrated on his easy way with words, his comfortable demeanor in front of the group, his attractive, dark brown, wavy hair and eyebrows to match, and his handsome face.

"How can he be a senior this year and not have a steady girlfriend yet?" Hannah Ruth whispered.

"Maybe he's holding out for the right girl. We've got to find a way to get acquainted with him."

"Maybe he's too busy for girls. The list of his activities at high school is about a mile long."

"Maybe he's shy."

"That's doubtful. Maybe he's not planning to get married."

"Maybe he has a girlfriend and nobody knows it."

"How likely is *that*?"

Suddenly both girls realized the room had fallen silent. John had stopped talking. In fact, he was looking straight at the two of them.

"Hannah Ruth?" he said.

"Yes?" she replied, embarrassed.

"Do you have an answer to my question?"

She panicked. Had he actually asked one?

"I asked you what you thought was the best way to handle impure thoughts when thinking about dating somebody."

"I…I never have impure thoughts." *Wrong answer*, she realized. She was the pastor's daughter, after all, and here she was, implying she was better than anybody else. Besides, she really *had* had a few impure thoughts—about her and John Baumgartner, in fact.

"Well, not to get smart about it or anything," John replied, smiling, "but if you never have impure thoughts, then you'd be the first."

There were snickers and some polite laughter behind Hannah Ruth. She felt her face and neck growing warm. Why did she ever decide to sit in the front of the room?

"Anybody else?" asked John, looking elsewhere. A few hands went up and the conversation moved to a junior boy in the fifth row.

Hannah Ruth looked straight ahead but whispered out of the side of her mouth, trying not to move her lips, "Criminy, Jenny, I feel like a real idiot."

"You still think this guy's a dreamboat, now that he's humiliated you?"

"Truthfully? I actually do. Is that weird or what?"

"Nope. Not weird. I still think so too."

THE LAST PERSON Hannah Ruth Jonas wanted to talk to during refreshments was John Baumgartner. But he made a point of hunting her down and asking her to sit next to him while they ate.

"Sorry I wasn't listening during your topic," she muttered. She thought, *He sure does have a handsome face. I wonder if he stares at himself in the mirror a lot.*

"Actually, I wanted to apologize for embarrassing you. That wasn't my intent. I just thought you'd be a good person to answer the first question. You know how these guys and gals are. Nobody wants to talk, until somebody else does first."

"Next time I'll try to pay better attention," she said. She thought, *I wonder what it would feel like to have John kissing me, in the back seat of somebody's car.* Immediately she realized that was probably a perfect example of the kind of impure thoughts he had been talking about. But, since she hadn't really paid attention, she couldn't be sure.

"Listen, you want to go with me to the movies sometime?"

Her heart began to race. "Excuse me?"

"You *do* go to movies, right? Preacher's kids do actually go to movies?"

Her heart was thumping. This was John Baumgartner. Drop-dead-gorgeous John Baumgartner. The same John Baumgartner that Jenny Langholz wanted to date in the worst way. And he was asking *her* out instead.

"Would it be a date?"

"What, going to the movies? Yeah, I guess so. Sure."

"Well, what about your steady girl. Will she mind?"

"Clever, Hannah Ruth. Very clever. You know as well as I do that I don't have a steady girl. Because, if I did, I wouldn't be asking you to go to the movies with me."

Actually she had known no such thing.

"Well, ahh, sure. Except..."

"Except?"

"I think I might want to ask my folks first."

"They screen all the people you date?"

"No. Actually, I haven't done any dating yet. Well, okay, I went to the prom last spring with a guy who moved to Indiana last summer. I'll never see *him* again."

"Too bad for him, I guess."

"Excuse me?"

"Well, he went away and left an attractive young lady like you behind."

Hannah Ruth blushed. She really liked what she'd just heard, but didn't want to let on. "So, why are you asking me out? Are all the other senior girls already taken?"

"I'm asking you out because I like you. You're smart and funny…"

"How do you know I'm funny?"

"I've heard you joke with your friends."

"No kidding."

"I've had my eye on you for a while."

"Really."

"Does that surprise you?"

She thought, *I've had my eye on you for longer than you've had yours on me, I'll bet.* She said, "Well, I guess I'm flattered. A little bit."

"Good. So ask your folks if it's okay, then."

"They'll ask me where, and when, and what movie."

"I'll leave all that up to you."

"Would we walk someplace?"

"We could. Or, I could borrow my dad's car. He lets me sometimes. Then we could do a matinee some Saturday, and finish off at Porky's Drive-In, on Lake Street."

She felt a wave of excitement and confusion washing over her. She said, "I have to practice the piano on Saturday afternoons. For at least an hour."

"We could go after that."

"Okay, John. I'll ask my folks."

"Let me ask you something."

"What?"

"If your folks didn't care either way, what would *you* say? I mean, do you really want to go to the movies with me or not?"

She thought about it. *Was he completely stupid or what?* She said, in as calm and even a voice as she could manage, "I'd be delighted to go to the movies with you, John Baumgartner."

A broad smile spread across his face. He growled, "Great."

She thought, *Even his voice is dreamy. I wonder if he realizes how he sounds.*

When he got up to leave, Hannah Ruth looked around for Jenny. Suddenly she was overcome with a feeling of foreboding and dread. How was she going to explain all of this to her best friend?

Chapter 3

The drone of the Cessna four-seater made conversation difficult, but Arnold Elliot was used to shouting when aloft. Pastor Daniel Jonas found himself doing the same, and soon it seemed natural, practically yelling at the pilot.

"You own this plane, Arnold?"

"Hope to. Making payments. Jens Jorgensen greased the skids for me at his bank."

Daniel remembered how he'd first met Jens. The trust officer had been assigned to manage the five-million-dollar bequest for Saint Michael Church. One thing had led to another and the unchurched Dane, along with his wife and daughter, had become solid members of the congregation.

"How often do you take this thing up, Arnold?"

"Whenever I can find an excuse. Thanks for providing one. Now, stop trying to make conversation. You're gonna lose your voice. Just look down there and enjoy the view."

Daniel peered out the window. What he saw took his breath away. As the four-seater slowly circled the sprawling metropolitan area, the pastor traced the meandering path of the Mississippi River, from somewhere north of Anoka, south all the way to Fort Snelling, then around the bend to downtown St. Paul, and off toward Hastings, on the Wisconsin border.

As they flew across the center of the city, they passed directly over the spike-like Foshay Tower. Daniel remembered with regret how the congregation's benefactor, a stockbroker who once gave the congregation an enormous bequest, ran out of money when the Great Depression hit, and ended his life by jumping from a balcony near the top of the 25-story-high office tower.

The plane glided over south Minneapolis, then circled twice around the block-long campus where the Lutheran Church of Saint Michael and All

Angels sat, anchored at the corner of Anderson Avenue and Caldwell Street. In spite of its massive size, Daniel was amazed at how small, how compact and how insignificant it seemed from the air. That, he thought, must be how this 5,000-member congregation really looked to God. It was, he decided, a good dose of reality—and humility—to see it from this perspective.

"There's your house," Arnold shouted, gesturing to a residence further north on Anderson Avenue. Is that your wife, Rosetta, waving from the yard?"

Daniel studied the street. "There's nobody there, you rascal."

"Just having a little fun with you, Pastor," said Arnold, heading back toward the airport.

WHEN THEY HAD LANDED, Arnold said, "You have time for coffee?"

"Sure. Why not?"

"Come on. I think Sandy will treat us if we ask her nicely."

"I can certainly pay for a cup of coffee," said Daniel.

"I'm talkin' about what goes with the coffee. Have you ever had one of Sandy's famous cream puffs? She makes 'em herself."

"No. I've never been to The River's Edge."

"Well, it's about time you got there. Come on. Afterwards, I'll take you back to church."

SANDY ENGSTROM'S CREAM PUFFS were, Daniel had to admit, something to die for. Deciding in advance not to confess it to his wife, he ate two of them.

After she'd assured herself the rest of her staff had things under control, the owner joined the two men at the table. They had a commanding view of the Mississippi River, flowing below their cliff-side perch. "So you got to see the city from the top," she said, smiling.

Daniel admired the 28-year-old businesswoman's drive. She had a determination about her that convinced him she could succeed at anything she set her mind to. He wondered who would really be in charge after the two of them were finally married.

"I think I could get addicted to this flying stuff," Daniel admitted.

"It really is great," Sandy replied. "I always think the world looks cleaner from up there. You know, even the junkyards look tidy when you're up in a plane."

Arnold chuckled. "Tidy trash. Now, there's a concept for you."

"So, what are the two of you thinking about, in terms of a wedding date?" Daniel prodded.

"How about a week from Saturday?" Arnold said, joking.

Sandy was obviously not amused. She said, "Not before we get some serious premarital counseling. I think Arnold needs a few lessons in maturity." She half grinned at him, but it was clear she was serious.

Arnold offered her an inscrutable look. He said, "What's that supposed to mean?"

"Life isn't just a thrill a minute, Arnold. It's hard work. You spend all your time flying around in that plane of yours. Some of us have to manage serious businesses, with all the nuts and bolts that go with it."

"Oh, as if setting up a charter service isn't serious business? As if it won't require doing the nuts and bolts stuff?"

"Well, that wasn't quite fair, I suppose. But so far, you're having a pretty good time, I've noticed."

Daniel was getting uncomfortable with the direction the conversation seemed to be headed. He could see that Sandy was dead serious about wanting counseling. So, he finally jumped in. "Yes. Counseling. A very good idea. As a matter of fact, we require premarital counseling before a wedding can be solemnized at Saint Michael Church. Several sessions, in fact."

"Good. Why don't you schedule us then," Sandy said.

Arnold looked uncertainly at his intended. "Yeah. Sure. Go ahead and do that."

"A PARKING RAMP! What do we think this is, the Honeywell Corporation? We're a church, for crying out loud. Why do we need a parking ramp?"

Harvey Schoenherr, Saint Michael Church's curmudgeon-in-residence, was holding forth in predictable fashion. Others around the table, in the parish hall's stained-glass-walled Reformation Room, were waiting him out. The pattern, ever since Harvey had gotten himself elected to the parish council, was a split of eleven to one on almost every vote. Harvey's contrary views were always accompanied with colorful commentary.

"Now, just relax, Harvey," said Andrew Andersen, the congregation's resident diplomat. Nobody smoothed ruffled feathers with more skill than did Andrew. "Nobody's saying we have to do this. But it's a creative option, you have to admit."

"Creative!" Harvey exploded. "It's pretentious. What will the neighbors think? And don't you have to get a special permit or something for a project like this?"

"Look, Harvey, we're in a residential neighborhood. The fewer houses we have to tear down to get the parking we need, the better," said Peter Tressel.

"And Andy's figured out a way to make the ramp look really nice. It will blend right in."

"And another thing," blustered Harvey, as if he hadn't heard Peter's comment, "it's going to make us look stupid, building a skyway across an alley, just so people can get into the church building without going outside."

"Well, my wife wouldn't feel that way, if she was worried about having somebody snatch her purse after the sun went down," replied Reid Peterson. "Anyway, I think it's an ingenious idea." He paused, but only for a second. "I also think we should call for the question. We've been hashing this over long enough."

"Okay, then," said Andy Scheidt, trying to take back control of the meeting, "who has a motion to offer?"

"I'll offer it," said Paul Stone. "I move we recommend to the congregation we accept Andy's proposal, and that we fund it with money from the interest that's built up in the endowment fund. And, if that's not enough, we should cover the rest with a special fund appeal."

Gene Hennig quickly offered a second.

"All in favor say aye…and also raise your hand," said Andy.

Eleven hands went up.

"All opposed?"

"Aye," shouted Harvey.

"SO, WHAT DID YOU THINK of the movie?" John Baumgartner steered his father's Dodge along Lake Street.

From her vantage point on the passenger's side of the front seat, Hannah Ruth Jonas had an excellent view of John's handsome profile. She wasn't sure exactly how to answer. "It was okay. It was a little hard to concentrate."

"Really? I thought it was an interesting plot. There was some really good acting."

Hannah Ruth had pretty much missed the plot. She'd been busy trying to absorb the fact that the best-looking boy in high school was sitting next to her in a movie theatre. And, that her best friend hadn't spoken six words to her since she'd heard about this date. How, she wondered, was she ever going to get that all sorted out?

Then there was the fact that, halfway through the movie, without any warning, John had reached his arm around the back of her seat and smoothed his fingers down along her shoulder. She'd loved it when he did that, but she could hardly believe it when it happened.

"So, how hungry are you? We can get burgers, or just shakes. Whatever you want."

He steered the Dodge into one of the drive-in stalls at Porky's, cranked down his window, and waited for a waitress to appear. He turned to Hannah Ruth, grinned, and said, "I don't know about you, but I'm starved."

"I'm hungry too," she said. "A burger and a coke for me."

A teen-ager in a Porky's uniform stepped up to the car, pulled out her pad and pencil, and took their order. When she was gone, he said, "This place is always busy. Teenagers just seem to flock to this place. Why do you think that is?"

Hannah Ruth shrugged. "I guess I never thought much about it."

John looked at her. She waited for him to say the next thing, but he didn't. She felt uncomfortable, as though he was staring at her. She said, "I still can't quite believe I'm on a date with you."

"Well, maybe I can't either."

"Tell me honestly, John. Don't you have a lot of girls wanting to go out with you?"

"Probably," he said, grinning. Then he said, "I'm not trying to sound cocky about it. I just know girls stare at me sometimes."

Do tell, she thought.

"But, like I told you at League, I've had my eye on you for a while."

She looked down self-consciously.

"I hope you didn't mind when I put my arm around you during the movie."

She looked up. "I was...a little surprised."

"Did you mind?"

"No. I liked it."

"So did I," he said.

The server came to John's side of the car and hooked a tray onto his window. He fished his money out of his trouser pocket and paid her. When she was gone, and they were unwrapping their sandwiches, he said, "I wasn't going to tell you this, but I was a little nervous about asking you out."

"*You* were nervous asking *me*?" She thought he had to be kidding.

"Yeah. Actually, I was. See, you're the pastor's daughter."

"So?"

"So, you don't want to mess with the pastor's daughter. You know what I mean?"

"No. Not really. The pastor's kids aren't any different from anybody else's."

"Well, I'm sure that's the way *you* feel about it. But look at it from my side. Your dad is, well, he's really a special person. People look up to him. They respect him. In fact, some people think he's kind of a legend in this town."

"You're embarrassing me, talking like this."

"My point is, Hannah Ruth, it can be a little bit intimidating, going out with you."

She mulled the comment for a moment. "Well, I never quite thought of it that way."

"The fact is," he said, "that's why it took me over a year to get my nerve up, enough to ask you out."

"Well, that may explain a few things," she said.

"Like what?"

"Like the fact that I'm a senior in high school and no boy has ever asked me out before. Now I understand it. They're all afraid of my dad."

John laughed out loud. Hannah Ruth was so surprised with his reaction, she laughed right along with him.

He collected her empty coke glass and sandwich wrapper, setting them on the window tray. He turned on the lights, signaling for the waitress to come back and take it all away. As he waited for her to return, he said, "Hannah Ruth, what's going to happen to you?"

"Excuse me?"

"What's down the road? Where are you heading?"

"I'm still not sure what you're asking."

"Are you planning to go to college or anything?"

"My folks hope I'll go to Capital University, where they went."

"Columbus, Ohio, right?"

"Yes."

"I'm going to Ohio State. I'll be right across town."

"Really. Are you sure you'll be going there?"

"Absolutely. I have a scholarship. I plan to study chemistry."

"Really. I know almost nothing about chemistry. Except that chemicals are smelly."

He chuckled. "If you get a good job as an industrial chemist, then they'll smell like a lot of money."

"Is that what you're after, a lot of money?"

"No. Not really. It's like I said in that Luther League topic. You know, the one you weren't paying attention to..."

"Don't remind me."

He grinned. "Like I said in that topic, you have to know where your first love is. My first love is God. My second will be my career."

"So, I guess that means whoever you end up marrying will be your third love then."

He thought about it. "Nope. Then my wife and family would come second. But that's assuming I get married."

"So, is that a fair assumption then, or not?"

He thought some more. "I'd hope it would be. Of course, it would depend on if I find the right person."

"How will you know?"

"The same way you will."

"What does that mean?"

"It means you'll get sick to your stomach and you won't be able to think straight or breathe properly or sleep at night. And you won't be able to get that special person out of your mind."

"How do you know so much about all of this, John?"

"That's the way it was with my older brother. He told me all about it, when he was dating the girl he finally married."

She studied the handsome contour of his face. She wondered if she wasn't feeling some of those symptoms herself, right now.

John said, "You want to do this again sometime?"

For a split second, a vision of Jenny, looking extremely jealous, flashed through her mind. But she said, "Sure. I'd like that. I'd like that a lot."

Chapter 4

David Engelhardt was running out of room. When he'd begun the *Bloomington Avenue News,* he'd thought the space once occupied by his father's printing operation would be large enough for his weekly journal. And, for a couple years, it had been.

But now, with the addition of an office manager, two reporter/writers, and a director of advertising sales, he was almost out of floor space. His archive of back issues was beginning to crowd out space he needed for everyday operations. He'd thought of moving the stacks of back issues to the basement. But it was dingy and damp down there, and he knew the archive would never survive in a climate like that, over the long term. He needed someplace that was dry.

There was, of course, the upper level. David had long resisted letting his newspaper business encroach on what had once been a compact apartment. It held good memories for him, and he wanted to keep it off-limits. In fact, it was those memories that had led him to persuade his father not to sell the building when Engelhardt Printing had moved to a larger space further down the street.

David and his young bride, Molly, had lived in the upstairs apartment when they were first married. And, their firstborn had been delivered there, one warm Fourth of July fourteen years earlier. Before he and Molly had moved in, it had been the first residence for Pastor Daniel and Rosetta Jonas. And, after David and Molly had moved to a home of their own, the apartment had become the residence, for a few years, of Pastor Jonas' assistant pastor, James Darnauer and his new wife.

After the Darnauers had accepted a call to serve as missionaries in New Guinea, the still-furnished apartment had been closed up. David hadn't been sure what to do with it, so had draped the living and dining room furniture with old sheets and left things the way they had been the day the Darnauers departed.

As he stood now, in the compact kitchen, looking down at the traffic on Bloomington Avenue, David thought he heard Molly speaking to him. The last time he'd discussed the apartment with her, she'd said, "Don't be so sentimental, David. Get rid of that old furniture and turn the place into something useful. Or else, rent it out."

David didn't want to rent it out. Somehow, it didn't seem right. Besides, whenever he wanted to get away from the newspaper office for a relaxing interlude with a book, or to take a short nap, he'd simply go upstairs and stretch out on the living room couch. He was the only person with a key to the apartment, so he could always count on the space being available to him.

He walked into the bedroom and studied the scene. The bed had been removed over a year ago, donated to a homeless shelter that had been looking for one. The other furniture had been secondhand when he and Molly moved in. It had since been discarded.

He ran his hands over the faded wallpaper. It was a dull green, a shade he'd never liked much. And he noticed it was starting to crack and come loose around the edges.

He walked into the middle of the room and turned slowly around. Without any furniture, the space seemed smaller to him. Still, he realized, with deep shelves on the east and west sides of the room, he could archive a lot of back issues of the paper.

He walked to the doorway, took hold of a corner of peeling wallpaper and gently tugged. Ragged strips of it pulled free. He realized there was another, older layer beneath it. That, he decided, was going to be a problem. Before he had somebody build storage shelves in here, he really ought to get the paper off the walls. But that was going to require a work crew.

Two hours later, as he sat at his desk downstairs, a thought came to him. He could recruit the four teen-agers he'd sometimes employed for odd jobs. David had hired the four high school sophomores, all of whom were in his Sunday school class, to deliver copies of his free weekly to homes and businesses all over the Powderhorn neighborhood. They were all good kids, and excellent workers besides. They seemed to go everywhere together. David wondered whether they'd all head to the same college once they were out of high school.

One thing he was pretty sure of. They'd all be glad to have a chance to earn some extra cash.

ROSETTA JONAS sat in her favorite rocking chair, listening to her teen-age daughter practice a selection by Chopin. She marveled at the precision and fervor with which the seventeen-year-old executed the piece.

When Hannah Ruth had finished, and turned on the piano bench to face her, Rosetta said, "Lillian Fischer must love it when you show up for piano lessons."

Hannah Ruth grinned. "Well, she does keep telling me I'm headed for greater things. As long as I don't slack off."

"She's really counting on you going to the Conservatory at Capital."

"Yes. She keeps mentioning that."

"Your father and I are very pleased, knowing you're planning on that, honey."

"Well, anything to keep Lillian happy." There was irony in her voice.

"You're not just doing it for Lillian, Hannah Ruth."

"I know. I'm just joking. A little."

"How do you feel about going to college in Ohio?"

Hannah Ruth suddenly found herself thinking of John Baumgartner. "Actually, I'm looking forward to it. If they'll let me in."

"They'll let you in. Your father will see to that."

"What do you mean? Daddy isn't going to pull strings for me, is he?"

"No, of course not. But he'll put in a good word for you. And he already told me they're hoping you'll enroll."

"Who's *they*?"

"Well, the Dean of the Conservatory, for one."

The teen-ager got up from the bench. "I'm going to go out for a while. Okay?"

"With John again?"

"Well, yes. I told him I'd save some of the afternoon for him."

"Can we talk about him for a minute?"

"About John?"

"Yes." Rosetta smiled at her daughter, but there was something in her eyes that Hannah Ruth wasn't able to interpret.

She sat down on the piano bench again. "He's coming in a few minutes. How long did you want to talk?"

"A few minutes is enough," Rosetta replied.

"So...what about John?"

"You really like him, don't you."

"Golly, Mother, that should be fairly obvious."

"Yes. It is. Are you getting…you know…serious, the two of you?"

"Oh, I don't know." She knew perfectly well. "We just…well…we just like spending time together."

"I don't want to pry, Hannah Ruth, but…"

"But what?"

"But, what do the two of you actually do when you're together?"

"Are you worried about us?"

Rosetta looked affectionately at her daughter. She weighed her words carefully. "No. I'm not worried. But I want the two of you to be careful. Do you understand what I mean?"

"Mom, we're just friends."

"Pretty good friends, I'd say, judging by how much time you spend together."

"Don't you trust us?"

"I trust you. I just want you to be careful."

"Well, Mom," she replied, trying to mask the exasperation she was feeling, "John put his arm around me during a movie once. And we hold hands a lot. He's kissed me twice. For about three seconds both times. Is that careful enough?"

"I don't want you to think I don't trust you, Hannah Ruth." She paused, looked out through the window for a moment, and then back to her daughter. She said, "I remember how exciting it was to be young. There were some really strong temptations."

"Did you give in to any of them?"

"No. I didn't. But some of my friends did. Later they wished they hadn't."

"Do you want me to stop seeing John?"

"No. I'm not saying that. In fact, I like him a lot. Your father and I couldn't have picked anyone better for you if we'd done it ourselves."

"Mom, we're not getting married or anything." *At least, not now*, she thought.

Her mother grinned. "Well, maybe some day you will. But try to get through college first, okay?"

"I'll do my best, Mom."

Her mother smiled and nodded.

The doorbell rang. Hannah Ruth jumped up. "That's John. Gotta go. See you later, Mom."

After Hannah Ruth had gone out, Rosetta sat alone, slowly rocking. She remembered the day seventeen years before, when she'd brought her daughter home from Fairview Hospital. Now that tiny infant was a seventeen-year-old who could play Chopin like a professional. And planning for college.

And, no doubt, thinking about giving her heart away. To John Baumgartner.

JOHN DROVE along East Hennepin Avenue, then turned north onto Stinson. Soon they were on the Parkway, the beginning of the great greenway that circled Minneapolis like a belt. As they rolled along the wide boulevards of the city's "Grand Rounds," John said, "Some day I'd like to live in one of these fancy homes, with all this grass in my front yard. The best part would be, the city would have to mow it."

"You want to come back to Minneapolis after college, John?"

"Sure. Why not? I mean, if I can get a good job here." He wondered why she'd asked. "What about you, Hannah Ruth?"

"Oh. Naturally. My family's here. I like Minneapolis."

"Of course, I might end up living somewhere else."

She realized that was possible.

"Gets pretty cold here in the wintertime," he said, stating the obvious.

"But we Minnesotans are tough," she said. Then she started giggling.

"What's funny?"

"I've heard a lot of people say that. Then they move to someplace warmer."

He didn't reply.

"John?"

"What?"

"How long are you planning to wait before you get married?"

"I...umm...well...I don't know. Why?"

"My parents don't want me getting married before I graduate from college."

"Makes sense. I guess."

"Would you be able to wait that long?"

He thought about it. "Are you, umm, suggesting anything?"

"What do you mean?"

"Are you maybe hoping we'll get married. The two of us?"

She looked at him and grinned. "Well, it wouldn't be the worst thing in the world that could happen."

"It sure wouldn't," he said, grinning back at her.

THEY LEFT the parkway system at Lake Street and headed along the busy thoroughfare, to their favorite restaurant. John pulled into a vacant spot at Porky's and cut the engine. "I'm ready for a chocolate shake. What about you?"

"Strawberry for me, please."

A car backed out from the space next to Hannah Ruth's door. A minute later another pulled in.

John whistled softly through his teeth. "Well, take a look at that chariot."

Hannah Ruth looked to her right. It was a sleek new red and white Chevrolet convertible. Even though it was late October, the day was unusually warm. The driver, who looked like a high school kid to her, had the top down. But that wasn't what interested Hannah Ruth the most. He was sliding across the seat, circling his arm around the girl sitting next to him. He gave her, what appeared to Hannah Ruth, a fairly passionate kiss, which he made sure he took plenty of time delivering.

When he came up for air, Hannah Ruth gasped.

"What's the matter?" John asked.

"Look at who's in that car."

"I don't know him."

"Not him. *Her*."

"Do I know her?"

"You should. She's my best friend. Jenny Langholz."

"Who's the guy?"

"I've never laid eyes on him. Ever."

Chapter 5

On Sunday evening, John Baumgartner walked the six blocks from his home to the Jonas residence. Before he got to the top step, Hannah Ruth was out the door. Sliding her arm inside his, she walked with him the block and a half south, along Anderson Avenue, to Saint Michael Church.

"Your best friend's doing the topic at League tonight, right?" said John.

"My *former* best friend, maybe. I still can't believe I saw her in that car yesterday."

"Well, maybe you can ask her about him tonight."

"If she'll even *talk* to me."

When they arrived at the meeting, Jenny Langholz was standing at the podium, organizing her notes. Hannah Ruth decided not to bother her. Instead, she made sure she and John were seated eight rows back, where she wouldn't be in as much danger of having Jenny ask her a question.

She needn't have worried. Jenny didn't look at her once. Nor did she ask any questions of anyone near Hannah Ruth during the discussion period. When she was finished and had sat down, it occurred to Hannah Ruth that she hadn't heard a single word of the topic. She realized that if her dad asked her for a report when she got home, she'd be sunk.

During the business meeting, she began plotting how she was going to make conversation with Jenny. She wondered if she would even stick around.

To her amazement, Jenny approached her when the meeting was over. The fellow she'd been with in the convertible was now standing beside her. He had a rugged, athletic look about him. Hannah Ruth tried to act normal, but wasn't sure exactly what that would look like just now.

Jenny said, in a voice Hannah Ruth thought sounded artificially cheerful, "Hi, you two. I want you to meet my friend."

John stuck out his hand and grasped the stranger's. "Hi. I'm John. John Baumgartner."

"Buzz Winslow. Nice to meetcha." John thought, *This guy seems a little too cool and casual for his own good.*

Jenny said, "Buzz, this is my best friend, Hannah Ruth Jonas. Her dad's the senior pastor here." Hannah Ruth almost fell over. So, things were still okay between the two of them, in spite of everything? She felt ashamed, having jumped to conclusions.

Jenny continued, "Buzz is on junior varsity basketball. He's probably going to make senior varsity this year."

"Really," said Hannah Ruth. "Well, that's...nice."

"Saw you guys at the drive-in yesterday," Jenny said.

"Yeah, we saw the two of you, too," John replied. He thought, *Boy, did we ever.* He added, "So, are you a guest at League, Buzz, or you thinking of joining?"

"Jenny belongs. So I'll join too."

"Well...great," said Hannah Ruth. She didn't know what else to say.

"See you guys," said Jenny, steering Buzz toward the beverages.

John looked at Hannah Ruth and said, "Well, if he sinks baskets the way he kisses, he's gonna be one crackerjack varsity basketball player."

JENS JORGENSEN pulled into the parking lot at the Lake Street Sears complex. Getting out of his new Oldsmobile, he looked up at the impressive tower capping the enormous structure, then headed inside.

In the men's shoe department, he stood studying the merchandise until the clerk he had his eye on was finished with his customer. Then the banker approached him.

When Tom Pavelka had finished stacking the unpurchased boxes of shoes, he looked up in surprise. What was his father-in-law doing in the Sears shoe department? He knew he could easily afford to patronize any of the best shops downtown.

"Hi, Tom," Jens said, smiling. "I need a new pair of shoes."

"I'll just bet you do," Tom replied, dryly. He knew Jens didn't approve of him clerking in a department store. Jens seemed to think the man who'd married his daughter ought to aspire to higher things.

"I'm looking for some work shoes, to wear up at my lake home."

Tom winced. He hadn't thought about Lake St. Michael much since he'd given up his job running the summer youth program for Camp St. Michael. His eleven-year-old daughter, Jens' granddaughter, had drowned there four years before. Neither of them had ever gotten over it.

Jens sat down. He said, "Show me what you've got, Tom."

His son-in-law looked dubiously at the older man, then went to get some merchandise to display for him. When he returned, he said, "You might be more comfortable having one of the other clerks help you, Jens."

"No, no, it's you I want. Just show me a nice pair of work shoes."

Tom opened three boxes before Jens found what he wanted.

"These will do just fine. I'll take them."

Tom put the shoes back in the box and handed them to Jens. "Pay over there."

"You have a minute? I don't see any other customers right now."

"What? Well…yeah, I guess."

"Sit down, Tom."

The clerk sighed and dropped into the next chair.

"I haven't seen you for three months."

"Sonja's at your place all the time."

"She's my daughter. But she's married to *you*. I'd like to see more of you, Tom."

"Been busy, Jens."

"Too busy to come to Sunday dinner with your wife once in a while?"

"Tired. Sunday's a day of rest."

"You must be sleeping a lot on Sundays. You haven't been to church in a year."

"Sonja goes for the both of us."

"That's nonsense and you know it."

"Jens, before you joined St. Michael Church, your family didn't go to church at all. And now you're judging me?"

"I'm not judging you, Tom. I'm telling you I miss you. We all do. I wish you'd come back to church."

Tom looked at the carpet. He said, "There's just too many painful memories." He paused. Jens waited. "You know, in my mind, I can still see that huge crowd that showed up at church for Greta Ingrid's funeral. Every time I went back, after that, I just kept thinking about her. It just got too difficult."

"You know, the church can be a place of comfort."

"Yeah. Right."

"I'm serious."

Tom exhaled heavily. "I know. People say that. Pastor Jonas told me the same thing. But I'm just having a hard time."

Jens looked at his son-in-law with compassion. He wished he could find a way to get through to him. He said, "Your dad just sold me a new Oldsmobile."

"Another sore subject," Tom groused.

"That's one fine automobile he sold me."

"I don't doubt it. But I'm sure he wishes I'd have been the one to have sold it to you."

"No, I don't think so. He's pretty much accepted the fact that you don't want to sell automobiles."

Tom hesitated. "I don't know if it's exactly that. Of course, I don't really like selling of any kind. Which probably makes you wonder why I have this crummy job, selling shoes at Sears." Jens didn't reply. "The thing with my dad is, I just don't want to work with him. I have to do something on my own. Working with him, I'd always be in his shadow. Always trying to measure up. Even when he never said anything about it, I could always tell he had high expectations for me. So I had to get out of there." He dragged the heel of his shoe across the carpet, leaving a depression that quickly faded. "But I know he's not happy about me having decided that."

Jens said, "There's a new position opening up down at the bank."

"Jens, I told you, back when Greta Ingrid died, I can't work for you. I don't know anything about banking. And, how do you think my dad would feel, with me turning him down and then saying yes to you?"

"This isn't really a banking job in the normal sense of the word." Tom looked uncertainly at Jens. "We're looking for a consumer counselor."

"I have no idea what that is."

"Well, how would you? We just invented the position."

"Not just for me, I hope."

"Oh, no. Somebody will get this job. We've found we need to do this. You see, the war's been over for more than a year now. And a lot of people are getting married and buying houses, and new cars...from people like your dad, actually...and generally getting in over their heads. So now we have customers starting to default on their loans. That's bad for them, and bad for the bank. The last thing we want to do is get into the real estate business. Because, if we have to repossess somebody's house, we have to figure out what to do with it."

"So, what does this counselor do then?"

"He helps people figure out how to manage their money better. Or he will. Like I say, we just decided to create the position. This person would sit down with a customer who's getting into financial trouble and help him—or her, or them—find new ways to manage their money. It might involve showing them how to organize a budget and stick to it."

Tom furrowed his brow. "You think that's something I could do?"

"I'm positive you could. You managed the budget for Camp Saint Michael when you were running the place. And, if I may say so, you did a darn good job of it."

Tom looked around the department. Why weren't there any customers to rescue him from this conversation? He said, "I can just hear my dad if I took a job with you."

"It's not with me. It's with the bank. I'm in the trust department. I wouldn't even be your supervisor. And, besides, I already told your dad I might mention this to you."

"What did he say?"

"He said, 'Go for it, Jens. It would be a good opportunity for him. And he sure as the devil isn't going to come work for me.'"

"That's what he actually said?"

"His exact words."

Tom stretched out his legs and crossed them at the ankles. He said, "Actually, I'm starting to get the hang of this shoe-selling business. I'm not too bad at it."

"Tom, this position would let you do what you like doing best. Helping people, just like you helped all those Luther Leaguers when you gave them advice up at church camp. Except, in this case you could possibly save a marriage. Or a life."

"Doesn't sound like a life-saving kind of job, Jens."

"We had one fellow whose wife had to talk him out of suicide when his bills got so far out of hand. He's the guy, in fact, who convinced us to create the position."

Tom mulled it. "You really want to get me out of here, don't you."

"Not that it's the main consideration, " Jens continued, "but it would pay three times what you're getting here."

"How do you know what I'm getting here?"

"I don't. But if this new job doesn't pay you three times as much as this one, I'll eat my hat."

For the first time in the conversation, Tom grinned. "Might be worth taking it, just to see you do that."

"You'll think about it then?"

There was a long pause. Finally Tom said, "Yeah. I'll think about it."

THE FOUR fifteen-year-old boys were ripping and scraping with a vengeance. They'd each taken one of the four walls in the abandoned bedroom of David Engelhardt's upstairs apartment. They were having a contest to see who could get a clean wall, all the way down to original plaster, before anyone else. In spite of their enthusiasm, it was slow going.

"Boy, we're really gonna earn our pay, getting this nasty stuff off," said Alex Kleinhans.

"You can say that again," retorted Paul Bauer. "Whoever put all these layers on used really good paste. Or else, too much."

"How old do you suppose this building really is?" said Skip Warner.

"Well, a lot older than Saint Michael Church, that's for sure," replied Josh Jonas.

"Weren't you born in this apartment, Josh?" asked Paul.

"Naah. My sister was born when my folks lived here. But she wasn't actually born *here*. I think it was at Fairview Hospital."

"But she was conceived here, right?" said Alex. He snickered.

"You're getting a little personal, buddy," said Josh, petulantly.

"I wasn't trying to embarrass you or anything. I just think it's kind of neat, thinking about where people get conceived." He paused. "I think I was conceived in the back seat of somebody's car."

"Holy shamoley," Skip retorted. "How in heck would you know *that*?"

"Well, my dad keeps sayin' stuff to me like, 'Don't go getting some girl in the family way in the back seat of somebody's car.' You know what? I never even thought of the possibility before he said that. So, draw your own conclusions."

"Naah," said Paul, pulling off a long strip of dusty wallpaper, "that doesn't mean anything, necessarily. He's just trying to keep his little man out of trouble."

"I'm not his 'little man,' smarty," Alex shot back.

"Sure you are. To your dad, at least. He's just worried you're gonna do somethin' stupid and have to get married before you get out of high school."

"Well, that's not likely. Not unless I find somebody to do it with."

"How about that cute Francene Young. She's a real fox."

"Already taken. Probably. I'm not sure."

"You ask her?"

"Naah. But she hangs around with Eddie Winston."

"She's a Lutheran. He's Catholic. She'd never be interested in him."

"Well, he carries her books to classes for her."

The conversation seemed to dry up. The four boys kept peeling and scraping.

Suddenly, Skip said, "Pay dirt!" The other three looked his direction. "I'm down to ground zero. Original plaster."

"Yeah, sure, in one little place," said Paul. "Look how much you haven't gotten off yet."

"I know. But there's something weird here."

"What's that?" asked Josh.

"There's something written on this plaster."

"What's it look like?"

"Like…part of a message of some sort."

"What's it say?"

"Well, I have to get more wallpaper off first. But so far, it says '…constructed in the year…'"

Chapter 6

"He's such a dreamboat!" Jenny Langholz lay flopped on her stomach, on her bed, her knees bent, her stocking feet sticking up in the air.

Hannah Ruth, also shoeless, sat crosslegged on the bed, next to her best friend. "So, let's have the scoop. How did you meet Buzz? And who is he? And what's he like?"

"Slow down. One thing at a time," Jenny said, pulling herself up. She sat cross-legged, facing Hannah Ruth. There was excitement in her eyes. "I already told you he's a basketball player. He's a guard, and he has a wicked jump shot. And, he's definitely going to be on senior varsity. He just found out."

"I never thought of you going with a basketball player."

"Why not? Varsity players are extremely popular. And I landed one!"

"Yeah, I guess you really did. So, what's he going to do next year?"

"What do you mean?"

"After high school. Is he going to college?"

"Are you kidding? He's only a junior."

"What!"

"Yeah. Didn't I tell you that?"

"You most certainly did not!"

"Well...he is. What's wrong with that?"

"What's wrong with it is that you're a senior. You're older than *he* is!"

"So what? My uncle was a year younger than my aunt when he married her. It can work just fine."

Hannah Ruth seemed confused. Why would her best friend start dating a junior boy? She said, "You know what they say: girls mature faster, emotionally, than boys do. That's one reason girls like to date older guys."

"Well, what about you and John? He's the same age you are."

"I know. But he's really mature."

"And you think Buzz isn't? You don't even know anything about him." She had an edge in her voice.

"Okay. Sorry. You're right. I don't. Not really."

The stern look on Jenny's face seemed to soften. "Anyway, I wouldn't care if he was a freshman. He's just the sweetest guy."

"So, how did you meet?"

"In Collins' Drug Store."

"Really?"

"Yeah. I was looking for some cough drops and he was..."

"He was what?"

She held back momentarily. "I shouldn't have mentioned the drug store."

"Something embarrassing?"

"Well, actually, I overheard him asking the clerk how old you had to be to buy birth control. For guys."

"You're *kidding*!"

"No. I'm not." She giggled. "Anyway, he was too young and the clerk said so. I could tell he was really embarrassed being told that. They keep all that stuff locked up behind the counter, you know. So, anyway, he turned around and I was the first person he caught sight of. I think he wanted to change the subject pretty badly, so he just turned on the biggest, brightest smile and said, "Well, hello, Sunshine, where have *you* been all my life?"

"And you fell for that?"

"Not for *that*. It was a pretty sappy line, I'll admit. But then he offered to buy me a coke. I figured, why not. So we ended up in a booth at Collins' Drug Store, just talking."

"What did you talk about?"

"Everything. Him. Me. Us. High school. Why we hadn't met before. Well, it's pretty obvious why. He's not in our class."

"What attracted you to him?"

"He has beautiful brown eyes."

"That was it? His eyes?"

"He has a gorgeous physique."

Hannah Ruth realized that John was gorgeous in his own way, but a muscular frame wasn't part of it. That didn't bother her. What bothered her, just a little bit, was that muscles seemed important to Jenny. "You know, when John and I first saw you with Buzz, he was, well...really going at it with you. Right there in front of everybody."

"He's really eager, I know. I have to slow him down."

"You think you can do that?"

"Have to. My parents'd kill me if he got me pregnant."

"That's not likely, is it?"

"Well, I'm certainly not planning on it."

Hannah Ruth was at a loss for words. She traced a circle on the bedspread with her index finger. Finally she said, "What's the deal with the fancy convertible?"

"It's brand new! Don't you just love it?"

"Well…I don't know." Truthfully, she'd thought the red and white finish made it look like Buzz was showing off, but she resisted saying it.

"You're just a little bit jealous, aren't you. I mean, come on, John's got to borrow his dad's boring old Dodge."

"Don't make fun of John." There was hint of irritation in her voice.

"Sorry. I didn't mean anything like that." Jenny looked apologetic, but only for a second. "Here's the weird thing about the convertible. Buzz' dad gave it to him when he got on junior varsity, sort of as a reward."

"Now, let me get this straight. Your kid gets on the basketball team, and you reward him with a new convertible?"

"I know. It sounds crazy. But, see, Buzz' parents are divorced. He lives with his mom. Down on Minnehaha Parkway. Pretty nice house, actually. His dad's the president of some labor union. Turns out, they pay him a lot of money. His mom gets support from him. But his dad wants to keep close to Buzz, so he does stuff for him, like…well…like buying him the car."

"What does his mother think about that?"

"I don't know. I haven't met her."

"Don't you think you should?"

"I will. We just started going together."

"What about *your* folks?"

"They haven't met him either."

"They know you're seeing him though, right?"

"They just know I met this guy from high school, and he doesn't have a church or anything, and I'm getting him to join Luther League. My dad thought that was pretty neat. In fact, he said, 'Well, aren't you quite the evangelist.' I don't even know what an evangelist is."

"What did your mother say?"

"She said, 'When do we get to meet him?'"

"What did you tell her?"

"I said, 'One of these days. He's not ready yet.'"

"So, you haven't met his parents, and he hasn't met yours, and yet he's already...you know...kissing you like you're almost engaged!"

Jenny's voice dropped to a mysterious level. "You know what? When Buzz kisses me, he does amazing things with his tongue." She looked at her friend and screwed up her mouth into an uncertain expression. "Probably shouldn't have told you that."

Hannah Ruth reflected on her experiences with John. He'd been pretty circumspect with her. Four kisses so far. She'd been keeping count. They'd all been fairly chaste, polite, brief ones on the lips. That was all.

Jenny looked uncertainly at her friend. "So, what do you think? Do I have a real catch here, or what?"

Hannah Ruth offered as kind an expression as she could manage. She said, "Well, Jenny, I just hope the two of you know what you're doing."

"You don't think we do?"

"I really don't know, Jenny. But, for your sake, I hope so."

WHEN PASTOR DANIEL JONAS walked to church early on Reformation Sunday, he noticed the man with the sign had returned. For the first time since the special evening service on the Festival Day of Saint Michael and All Angels, more than a month before, the stranger was back on the sidewalk in front of the church building. "Just Tell the Truth," his placard read.

One of these days, Daniel promised himself, he was going to get acquainted with the fellow. But there were too many things to do before this morning's first worship service. He simply didn't have a spare five minutes.

And later, as he shook hands with members of the departing congregation at the church door, he noticed the man was no longer there.

AS THE SOPHOMORE high youth class was breaking up, following first service, David Engelhardt asked the four members of his wallpaper removal crew to stay behind for a minute.

"How's it going up there in the apartment? You four making any progress?"

"Yeah," said Paul Bauer. "We found something really weird, though."

"What's that?"

"Well, some guy left a message on the plaster. We're having a really hard time getting the paper covering it all the way off."

"Really. What does it say so far?"

"Something about how the building was originally built to be a..."

"A what?"

"It's not a complete word yet," Skip Warner said. "So far it's a-p-o-t-h-e..."

"Apothecary," said David.

"What's that?" asked Alex Kleinhans.

"It's an old word for 'drug store,'" said Josh Jonas, before David could reply.

"I'm impressed," David said, looking at Josh. "Is that in your vocabulary?"

Josh looked sheepish. "Yeah. It was the word I spelled to win the spelling contest, back in the eighth grade." The other three looked at him, puzzled. "You guys weren't in the spelling bee," he said, as if explaining himself.

"You always were the brains of the operation," said Paul grudgingly.

"Look, guys," Josh said, it's not my fault if I'm good at spelling."

"So, you were the champion speller in eighth grade," said David. "Good for you." He grinned at the pastor's son. "Tell me. Did you get a prize or anything?"

"Nothing you could take to the bank," Josh replied. "Just a blue ribbon."

"Just like a prize turkey at the county fair," Alex chided good-naturedly.

"You're just jealous because you can't spell apothecary."

"*Spell* it? I can barely *pronounce* it."

ARNOLD ELLIOT and Sandra Engstrom sat in the senior pastor's office, facing him across a low table. Daniel Jonas said, "All right. We've locked in the date. The church has been reserved. Lillian Fischer has agreed to play for your wedding. Now, let's talk about how ready the two of you are to take this step."

"Well, we've rented a hall," said Arnold.

"Not quite what I meant."

"Excuse me?"

"I'm sure you've taken the steps you need to make sure the reception works out. And we'll talk more about the details for the service itself next time we meet. This session, I want to talk with the two of you about...well...the two of you."

Sandy straightened in her chair. She said, "What exactly did you have in mind, Pastor?"

"I want both of you to help me discover just how well you really know each other."

"Pretty darned well, I'd say," said Arnold, cheerfully. He took Sandra's hand and held it affectionately.

The pastor said, "I'm sure you feel a strong romantic connection."

"There's more to it though, isn't there," volunteered Sandy.

The pastor nodded. "For example, how do the two of you handle disagreements?"

"Oh, we never fight," Arnold chimed in.

"Never?"

"Heck no. We're just a couple of love birds."

"Sandra, do you agree with what Arnold just said?"

She hesitated. "Well, we haven't had any real fights. But we've disagreed on a few things."

"What for example?"

"Well, for one thing, what's going to happen to my supper club after we get married."

"You haven't come to a decision about that?"

"Well, I don't know about Arnold. But I sure have."

"And how much did Arnold have to do with your decision?"

"Not much. I just told him, if he can't get used to the idea of me continuing to run the place, there won't be a marriage."

The pastor looked at Arnold. He was still holding Sandy's hand, but his brow was wrinkled. He said, "I can understand her point of view. But what I want to know is, how is she going to keep running that place after we start having children. A mother's place is at home with her children."

"And have you and Sandy discussed that?"

"The trouble is," said Sandy, "Arnold hasn't even asked me if I *want* children, or how many. He just assumes it. How does he think..."

"Hold it right there," said Daniel. "Turn to Arnold and ask him what you were about to ask me."

She looked uncertainly at the pastor. "Well, actually, I already have. He told me if there aren't any kids, there won't be any marriage."

Daniel shifted in his chair. He looked from Sandy to Arnold, then back to Sandy. He said, "Are you telling me, both of you have drawn a line in the sand, and neither of you is willing to budge?"

Arnold let go of Sandy's hand. He folded his arms across his chest. "Here's the deal, Pastor. I want kids. I don't know if Sandy does or not. She won't exactly say. How do we get to a resolution on this?"

"Sandy?"

"Look, Pastor, I'm not ready to make a commitment about children. I don't say we can't have...or won't have...children...sometime. But right now, the supper club is doing great. I don't want to put any of that at risk. Having children would be a distraction to me right now."

"Arnold?"

"See, Pastor, here's the deal. The wife is supposed to obey her husband. If we can't agree before the wedding, how is this going to work afterwards?"

"The wife is supposed to obey the husband when he's *reasonable*," Sandy shot back.

Daniel waited a moment before saying, "Are the two of you finally having your first real argument?"

There was silence in the room. Arnold and Sandy looked at each other. Arnold said, "No. This isn't an argument. It's a serious disagreement."

Sandy didn't say anything.

Daniel continued, "So, how do you get to a place where you can both feel good about this…disagreement?"

There was no response from either one. The pastor said, "Here's what I want the two of you to do. Before we meet the next time, I want each of you to sit down and make your own list. Rules you want to use for how to handle disagreements with the other person. And then, I want the two of you to sit together and read your lists to each other. After that, I want you to come up with a combined list, one you can agree on, maybe based on items from both lists. Unless, of course, you both come up with the same things in the first place.

"As if that would happen," Sandy said ironically.

"And then, when you come to see me next session, bring the list with you. We'll have a practice session. We'll see if your rules work when you deal with a disagreement you already know you have."

"Homework, huh?" said Arnold dubiously.

"Sounds fine to me," said Sandy. But give us a hint. What might go on the list?

Daniel said, "Well, for starters, you could agree that neither of you will use sarcasm when you're having a disagreement. Or call the other person an insulting name."

Arnold nodded. "Okay. I got it. We'll make our lists."

Sandy had a doubtful look on her face. She said, "I just hope we can find a way to combine our ideas—without getting into a fight about it."

Chapter 7

"This is pretty amazing," said Adam Engelhardt, studying the pale inscription. He smoothed his fingers over the fading black ink message, carefully lettered onto the original plaster. "Somebody named Martin Thornbury, a native of Northampton, Massachusetts, built this place in 1880. It was constructed as an apothecary shop."

The older man looked at his son, who was studying the bare plaster wall with great interest. "David, you would have thought the shops on Bloomington Avenue might have been established by Norwegians and Swedes, not an Englishman from Massachusetts."

"Oh, I don't know," the newspaper publisher replied, "The English were really the first ones to settle Minneapolis."

"Well, we know that by 1880 the Scandinavians were already here in big numbers."

"Sure they were," said David. "But they would have been the newcomers. Whoever built this place was here earlier."

"How do you know?"

"I spent a couple hours down at the library a day or so ago. I wanted to find out about Martin Thornbury. This wasn't his first location in Minneapolis."

"Really?" Adam said, wide-eyed. "Where was he before?"

"Over on the other side of the Mississippi River. In St. Anthony. That was the name of the original town at St. Anthony Falls. The St. Anthony people thought their city would be the main deal, and that Minneapolis, which probably wasn't much more than a crummy collection of shacks on the opposite side of the river, would never amount to anything."

Adam grinned. "Just goes to show you how wrong you can be."

"I'll say," said David. "St. Anthony is slipping into oblivion. There are people in Minneapolis who don't even know it was ever a separate town."

"But the interesting thing to me, David, is that Thornbury had a shop over there, and then closed it up to move down here."

"He saw the handwriting on the wall. This was the direction the population was moving. He wanted to be in on that. So he came over here instead."

"Where he left some of his *own* handwriting on *this* wall," said Adam, chuckling. His son winced at the bad joke.

"Wonder when he gave up his business," Adam said, looking at the wall again.

"Probably got tired of running it. The old book I found says he sold out in 1910. Then it became a print shop. The fellow who ran it was the owner until just before our family came here from Ohio. Remember what happened to him?"

"How could I forget the story? He died of a massive heart attack, sitting at his worktable, right downstairs."

"Which enabled you to buy the building, and the business, at a better price than normal."

Adam looked philosophical. "I sometimes wonder if I should feel guilty about profiting from someone else's misfortune." He paused. "On the other hand, his widow was going to sell out and close it down. So, I suppose I did the good folks of south Minneapolis a favor by keeping the place going."

David sighed heavily. He said, "I'm not sure what to do with this, Dad."

"With what?"

"With this message, inked onto the wall of my newspaper archive room."

"What do you think you *should* do with it?"

"Well, preserve it somehow. I'm not sure exactly how to do that. You can see how the wallpaper paste has already destroyed some of the density. It's sort of fading away. I suppose I should just cover it up again."

"Maybe you should tell somebody at the historical society."

"Yeah…well…maybe."

"You don't want to do that?"

"Actually, I do. But…"

"But what?"

"I'm afraid they'll send somebody over here to look at it, and they'll tell me I have to keep the wall open for display or something."

"Oh. I see your point. You really planned to have shelving on that wall, didn't you."

"Well, that *was* the original idea."

"Tell you what, David. Make a careful copy of what the inscription says. I'll take it over to the historical society. I'll tell them the wall is covered with a shelf now, but that the message is still there. That way, they'll have it for their records. And you'll have your storage room."

"I'm a step ahead of you. I already had Paul Bauer make the copy. It's on my desk downstairs."

"You sure you want to cover up this wall, David?"

"Well, no. Not if you want to give me a spare room, down at your print shop, to store back copies of my newspapers."

Adam considered the options. "Cover it up," he said.

NEW SNOW had fallen as members streamed into the Lutheran Church of Saint Michael and All Angels for Christmas Eve worship. As she had the previous year, Lillian Fischer prepared worshipers for the seven o'clock Eucharist with a performance of Bach's Christmas Cantata. Her senior choir held forth from their place in the balcony, the great pipes of the enormous Reuter organ rising behind them.

As the 800 seats began to fill, church council member Andy Scheidt, leaned closer to his wife and said, "We're not here a minute too soon, Lorene. Some of these people are going to end up standing."

"There's the 10:30 service," she replied.

"But Lillian's cantata is only being performed once. This is the one people like to come to."

"I just hope you and the rest of the council can get that parking ramp approved. We've got cars up and down ten different streets."

"The annual meeting's not for three more weeks. But don't worry. We'll get it passed."

"You sure about that?"

"Absolutely. I've been checking around. Everybody…well, everybody except Harvey Schoenherr, of course…thinks it makes perfectly good sense. And it's practically paid for. Most of the money's in the set-aside account."

Worshipers crowded in next to Andy and Lorene on either side were beginning to stare at them with irritation. Lorene looked at her husband and said, in a low whisper, "Enough. Just listen to the Bach."

SEVEN PEWS UP, Jenny Langholz cuddled up next to Buzz Winslow. She said, "How did you like my folks?"

Buzz shrugged. "I felt like I was getting the third degree."

"Well, it was their first chance to meet you."

"Why did we have to do it on Christmas Eve?"

"They knew you and I were coming to this service. Our family always has Christmas Eve supper. It just made sense."

"I'm not sure they like me much."

"They have to get used to you."

"What do they say about me?"

"You mean, before tonight?"

"Yeah."

"Well, they're kind of suspicious."

"About what?"

"About the fact that it took this long for you to show up and get acquainted."

"What do you think they think about me now?"

"Well, I think my mom noticed you were holding my hand all through supper."

"Was that bad?"

"Depends."

"On what?"

"On what your intentions are toward me." She paused. The Bach cantata continued to swirl overhead. "Exactly what *are* your intentions, Buzz?"

"To get a lot better acquainted with you," he said huskily. "A lot better."

WHEN THE ORGAN began to play "O come, all ye faithful," the great congregation arose from their seats, turned to face the door, and watched as the crucifer began to enter. As Paul Bauer lifted the richly-carved wooden cross high on its pole, all eyes were upon it, following its progress and turning with it as it passed. Next came Alex Kleinhans and Skip Warner, carrying the torches, followed by Josh Jonas, lifting the lectern Bible above his head. Behind him came the three robed pastors. The last in the procession was Daniel Jonas.

Daniel had gradually introduced the idea of a worship procession, so that now the congregation was used to the idea of following the cross as it moved through their midst, toward the altar. A few members had grumbled about how 'Catholic' the practice seemed, but others had explained to them that the custom was very old. And, besides, Episcopalians did the same thing.

In his Christmas Eve message, Daniel said, "We are a large, prosperous congregation. We worship in an expensive church building with beautiful stained-glass windows. I want to talk about one of those windows tonight, even though there is no light shining through it just now. I want to talk about the window that shows angels announcing Jesus' birth to Mary and Joseph."

He paused, studied the vast throng, and said, "We dare not keep the Holy Family tucked away in a stained-glass world. And we dare not pretend that Christmas is only for decent, respectable, prosperous people such as we Americans have become. Remember, Jesus was born to poor people. If he had been born in Minneapolis, he might have been delivered in a cardboard box in the alley behind the Leamington Hotel."

There were some tilted heads and puzzled looks. But many nodded their understanding. Daniel said, "We have become one of the leading congregations in this city. Our members have comfortable homes and drive nice cars."

Snuggling up next to Buzz, Jenny Langholz thought, *And some of us even have nifty convertibles.*

Daniel continued, "We are now a metropolitan church. Some of you drove here tonight from Richfield, and others from Edina and Bloomington and St. Louis Park. Some of you are living in Golden Valley, others in Robbinsdale, and still others in Brooklyn Center and Columbia Heights. Perhaps half of our congregation is now in the suburbs."

As she sat next to John Baumgartner, Hannah Ruth Jonas wondered where her father was heading with this logic. Was he saying it was wrong to live in the suburbs?

Daniel said, "It's easy for us to get into our cars when worship is over, and drive away to parts of our metropolis where there are fewer problems. We can leave the poverty and crime behind—or simply avoid dealing with it, because it all seems to be up in north Minneapolis, or downtown along Hennepin Avenue."

He paused, as if to organize his thoughts. "The next time you're at worship, when you can see that stained-glass window, think about the world in which Joseph and Mary lived. And, sometime, take a ride through the poorest sections of our city. Think about the people who live there. Remember that Jesus came at Christmas for each of them, just as he came for us. And ask yourself, 'How can we love those people?' Because God already does love them."

AT THE CHURCH DOOR, as members were coming through, Daniel shook each hand and offered each worshiper a Christmas greeting. When the recently married pair came through, he said to Arnold Elliot, "How's the happy couple?"

"So far, so good," he said cheerfully.

Sandy grinned and said, "Good thing you made us write out those rules for having a civilized disagreement. We've already had to use them."

Arnold looked at her with consternation, then saw that she was laughing. "Yeah," he said, "a couple times. Nothing serious."

"Well, keep listening to one another. And keep talking."

"Yeah. We do. I listen. She talks." She nudged him in the ribs. "Joke," he said. "It was a joke."

THE LAST TO COME through the doorway were Tom and Sonja Pavelka and their children. Daniel almost dropped his jaw.

"Don't have a heart attack, Pastor," said Tom. "I know it's the first time in over a year for me. But at least I showed up on Christmas Eve."

Daniel squeezed the young man's hand so hard it made him wince. "I'm truly glad to see you back at worship, Tom. Don't stay away until next December, though. Promise?"

Sonja replied, "We're taking this one step at a time. A year ago Tom told me he might never come back. But my dad had a good long talk with him. At least, that's what Tom says."

"Good for Jens," said Daniel. "We've really missed you here, Tom. And I know it's hard, coming back to where your daughter's funeral was. But..."

"I'm dealing with that, Pastor. It just really helps if you don't bring it up."

"All right." He smiled at Tom.

"Did Jens tell you?" Tom asked.

"Tell me what?"

"He got me a job at the bank."

"Really? You're not selling shoes any longer?"

"That was a dead-end job."

"So you're a banker now?"

"Well, not really. I just work there."

"How's it going?"

Tom shrugged. "Not sure. Maybe you better ask Jens."

JOHN AND HANNAH RUTH walked along the snow-covered path, beside frozen Powderhorn Lake. He liked the way it felt, having her arm linked with his. They listened to the crunch of snow beneath their shoes.

"Your folks going to worry I didn't walk you right home?"

"I doubt it," she replied. "They trust you and me. Anyway, they'll both be at the late service. They probably don't even have time to think about what I'm doing right now."

They walked in silence. Finally, John said, "I've really grown fond of you. You know that, don't you?"

She pulled him closer to her as they walked along. "Mom says I'm lucky to have found somebody like you. My dad too."

"But they want us to take things slow and easy, right?"

"Well, yes. How did you know?"

"That's what my parents keep telling me. I figured yours were the same."

She giggled. "We're not even in college yet. How are we going to behave ourselves until we get to the end of that?"

"Well, at least we'll be on separate campuses when we get to Columbus."

She sighed. "When you really care for somebody, and it's only a bus ride away, it might get kind of hard."

"I just keep thinking about that Bible story. You know. In the Book of Genesis. Jacob and his uncle. He wanted to marry Rachel. He had to wait fourteen years. I figure, if he could do that, I can hold out for just four."

They walked some more in silence. Suddenly, Hannah Ruth said, "That might not have been the best Bible story to bring up."

"Why not?"

"Because. Before he married Rachel, Jacob also married her sister, Leah."

John stopped walking and turned to face Hannah Ruth. He said, in a voice of mock seriousness, "Well, it's just lucky for you that you don't have any sisters."

Chapter 8

The Rev. Marcus Fangmeyer stood at his office window, looking down into the courtyard. The fountain dedicated to the memory of Frieda Stellhorn, a congregational founder and longtime member, had been turned off at the end of September. Now, in late January, the basin into which the water ordinarily splashed was filled with snow. To Marcus, the sight seemed bleak. A native of Dayton, Ohio, he was used to milder winters. But, when Pastor Jonas had asked him to come to Minneapolis to join the ministry team, he'd been forewarned.

Still, the chill of the north country had taken some getting used to. He knew he hadn't yet fully acclimated. Just thinking about the Winter Carnival, being celebrated across the river in St. Paul, gave him shivers.

He turned back toward his desk and picked up his copy of the annual meeting agenda. As a pastor in Ohio, he'd been through plenty of annual meetings. But this one was going to be different. For one thing, Pastor Jonas was usually on hand to answer questions. But tonight the congregation would be meeting without their senior pastor. He was home in bed, trying to shake a persistent cold. That meant Marcus would be overseeing the session.

He studied the agenda. He'd be offering the opening prayer. Then Lillian Fischer would direct her cherub choir. That seemed odd to Marcus. Who had ever heard of a children's choir singing at an annual meeting in an assembly room? But, he'd been informed, Lillian always took every opportunity to let her singers hold forth. Besides, Pastor Jonas had reminded his associate, with all those young people at the meeting, their parents would have to show up too. And that would more nearly guarantee a quorum.

Marcus doubted achieving a quorum would be a problem this time. After all, a major building project was on the agenda. Even though the money was all tucked away in a separate account, just waiting to be spent, you never could tell what might or might not happen during the question period.

He was just glad Andy Scheidt would be running that part of the meeting.

"AND NOW," said Andy, gripping the podium confidently and surveying the large crowd, "We come to the last item on the agenda. Your church council is proposing we construct a fine new multilevel parking ramp across the alley behind our sanctuary. You've all received information about this in advance. The drawings have been on display in the Reformation Room for a couple months. We have possession of the property. And the money is in the bank. All we need now is a motion and a second."

He paused. Gene Hennig raised his hand. "I move we proceed with the project as proposed."

Andrew Andersen was quick to second the motion.

"Any discussion?" Andy asked. He waited. To his surprise, nobody's hand went up. He persisted, "Anyone at all?"

There was another pause. George Kleinhans stood up and said, "I think this all looks pretty straightforward. I think we should vote."

In the split second between George's last word and the next one that would have come from Andy's mouth, another voice was heard. It came from a gentleman wearing a conservative suit, with a handkerchief tucked into his breast pocket, standing behind the last row of chairs. "Excuse me!"

Andy squinted. He didn't recognize the voice, or the face. "Do you have a question? Or a comment?"

"I wonder if you've thought about how the neighbors will feel."

Andy said, "Which neighbors would those be?"

"The ones living around the church building."

"If I'm not mistaken," Andy said, "we ran a story and an explanation in the *Bloomington Avenue News*, asking for response from the community, back when we first proposed this." He looked for David Engelhardt, the publisher of the weekly newspaper. "That is right, isn't it David?"

"Yes. We ran it. And we published several letters to the editor commenting on it. None were negative."

"Well, I don't read the *Bloomington Avenue News,* " the stranger replied. "And I only found out about this recently."

"Excuse me, but are you a member of this congregation?" asked Andy. He was still puzzled about the man's identity.

"No. I don't belong here."

"Well, this is a voters' meeting. You need to be a voting member to participate."

There were murmurs in the room. Adam Engelhardt raised his hand. "Mr. Chairman, with all due respect, if the gentleman lives in the neighborhood, it would be the charitable thing to let him speak to us. I'm sure he has no intention of trying to vote on the proposal."

Andy looked uncertainly at Adam, then back to the stranger. He said, "All right. But why don't you come up here and speak from the podium. It's hard to hear you."

The visitor walked to the front of the room, turned and faced the crowd. He said, "My name's Edward Cunningham. I live directly across the street from where this proposed new parking ramp is supposed to be constructed. I don't relish the idea, let me tell you, of going out the front door of my house every morning and looking at some big stone monstrosity. After all, this is a residential neighborhood."

"We have permission from the city to move ahead," said Andy, trying not to sound defensive.

"Doesn't matter," the man replied with a tone that bordered on petulance. "Just because it's legal doesn't mean it's ethical."

There was a buzz in the room. Andy felt the discussion slipping out of control. He looked at Pastor Fangmeyer. Marcus offered a wry smile, and then approached the stranger, who moved away from the podium. The young clergyman said, "I think we have a situation here that may need more attention than we can give it right now. I wonder if we might do ourselves a favor by postponing this vote, perhaps for a month. In the meantime, perhaps I can have a conversation with Mr. Cunningham. There's no point in making a neighbor angry over something we're about to do."

There were nods of agreement. Andy looked visibly disturbed by the prospect of putting off the vote. But, before he could say anything, a half-dozen voices said, almost in unison, "So move!" A second was quickly offered, and the item was tabled, pending a reconvening of the annual meeting a month hence. Andy kept his feelings concealed as he adjourned the meeting.

Lillian's children's choir rose to sing one more time. And then the crowd began to disburse.

Pastor Fangmeyer turned to the visitor, who was now standing on one side of the room, not sure whether to remain or depart. He said, "Would you like to have me, or Pastor Jonas, come by for a visit with you?"

"No. Not Pastor Jonas. It should be you." Marcus nodded, even though what he'd just heard made him feel a little disloyal to the senior pastor.

"Sometime this next week?"

"The sooner the better. But not at my place."

Marcus didn't know what to make of the comment. "In my office, here at the church, then?"

"Fine. Tomorrow afternoon? Two o'clock?"

Marcus nodded. He turned to say a word to Andy, only to discover he had left the room. He turned back to the stranger. But he was already on his way out the door.

MARCUS SAT in a comfortable chair in his spacious office, facing Edward Cunningham, who was seated nearby. He noted the trim, tidy appearance of the visitor, who appeared to him to be about his own age, 34. Cunningham had a lean look about him. His dark brown eyes seemed to burn with intensity.

"How long have you lived over on the next street?" the pastor asked.

"Three, four years. Before that I was in a place over by Powderhorn Park."

"You realize, of course, that if we don't build the parking ramp, the city could always rezone the block for some other purpose. That might end up being even less appealing to you than a parking ramp, dressed out with attractive stone."

"But the city isn't doing this project. Your church is." He said the word 'church' with a hint of disdain.

"This is a large church, Mr. Cunningham. We've over 5,000 members. Our congregation needs more parking."

"Maybe your congregation has gotten bigger than it needs to be."

"Well, I guess that's the Holy Spirit's business."

Cunningham snorted.

"You doubt what I just said?"

"The Holy Spirit dwells in communities where the truth is told."

Marcus studied the man's pocket handkerchief. Something clicked. This was the man who sometimes walked back and forth in front of the great front doors of the church building, carrying a sign reading, "Just Tell the Truth." He said, "You don't think we tell the truth in this congregation?"

"I seriously doubt it."

"Have you been to worship here?"

"Never."

"Then how would you know?"

"'Neither on this mountain, nor in Jerusalem, will you worship the Father, but those who worship truly, worship the Father in Spirit and in truth."

"The Gospel of John, chapter four."

"That's right. You know the words. Unfortunately, you don't believe them."

"Excuse me?"

"Look at this place. You've built an empire here on this block. And now you're taking over the next block. You're as bad as Solomon."

"This isn't exactly Solomon's temple, Mr. Cunningham. It's a parish church."

"It's an empire that won't stop until it takes over the neighborhood. How do you think the little churches around here feel, with your great big high-and-mighty church building and all your members, who don't have enough parking, coming in here from all the suburbs, just to act holy and important? And people like me, who live in quiet little houses on quiet little streets, get pushed out of the way because you need your almighty parking ramp?"

Marcus was taken aback. He had been unprepared for the intensity with which the man poured out his feelings. He said, "God can work through small congregations or big ones. There's room for both."

"That's what the first Christians thought. But what happened to that big Jerusalem congregation that baptized 3,000 new members on the Day of Pentecost?"

"It...continued for a while...and then..." Marcus felt as if he was being quizzed by a seminary professor. It irritated him, at least a little.

"And then God sent the Romans to destroy it. They smashed the Jewish temple, and scattered the Christians. Why? Because they'd become big, and proud, and unable to discern the Spirit any longer."

"You know that for a fact?" asked Marcus, trying not to sound churlish.

"Where did the Christians worship after that? You know as well as I do. In people's living rooms."

Marcus grinned.

"Did I say something amusing?"

"You don't know much about the history of this congregation, do you?"

"I know it's gotten too big for its own britches."

"This congregation started out in people's living rooms. That's how they worshiped for almost a year."

"Well, they should have stayed in their living rooms. Like they did in the New Testament. How will the Spirit ever speak to a mob like you have going in and out of here every Sunday? Where two or three are gathered together..."

"Where do you worship, Mr. Cunningham?"

"In a living room."

"With a small group?"

"Small enough to discern the Spirit in our midst."

"And what does the Spirit say to your community?"

"All manner of things. 'Do not be unequally yoked together with unbelievers.' 'Let your light shine before others.' 'Don't cast your pearls before swine.' 'Test the prophets, to see if they are from God.'"

"All of those ideas are from the Bible. Our congregation teaches all of them."

"But you don't *believe* them. You don't *embrace* them. You don't *practice* them."

"The Bible also commands us not to judge one another."

"Except when there's an obvious falling away from truth. 'First take your complaint to your brother. Then bring two or three others. Then take it to the entire congregation.'"

"Matthew 18."

"Of course. And, 'When the Spirit comes, he will lead you into all truth.'"

Marcus was feeling exasperated. He took a deep breath and said, "Do you believe you have all the truth, Mr. Cunningham?"

"The Spirit is leading me into it."

"And how does the Spirit help you discern truth from falsehood?"

"What do you mean?"

"The founder of Christian Science believed she had the truth. The founder of the Jehovah's Witnesses believed the same thing. How do you know they were wrong and you're right?"

"How do you know *you* are?"

"We teach at Saint Michael Church that the sign of a true fellowship is love for one another."

"How are you doing so far?"

"At loving one another? We're working at it."

"If you truly had the Spirit, you'd be achieving it."

"That doesn't sound very loving to me, Mr. Cunningham."

"The truth can hurt."

"How do you know when your beliefs wander into error?"

"The Spirit leads us into all truth."

"Yes, I know. You already said that. But how do you know when the Spirit has done that for you?"

Cunningham paused. He said, "The Spirit speaks to our fellowship."

"How, exactly?"

"Through signs and wonders. Visions. Revelations. The impartation of wisdom. 'Your young men will see visions and your old men will dream dreams.'"

Marcus sighed. He said, "We're pretty far apart, you and I."

Cunningham nodded. He said, "But we'll pray for you."

"Oh, and you'll be in our prayers as well."

"Why would you pray for us?"

"Well, for starters, I think you and your community could do with a healthy dose of humility. We're going to pray that you receive it."

THE FOLLOWING AFTERNOON, Andy Scheidt came by the church office. Pastor Fangmeyer welcomed him inside, and motioned him to a chair. When they were seated, Andy said, "I was really pretty steamed about how that guy came waltzing into the annual meeting and sabotaged the agenda the way he did. And he wasn't even a member!"

Marcus nodded.

"So I did a little research yesterday. Turns out, he actually does live across the street from where we want to build. But he's renting. He doesn't actually own the place."

Marcus arched an eyebrow. "Renters have rights too, Andy."

"Yeah. Sure. But this guy's lease is up. He's moving in another week."

"Really. Where's he going?"

"Landlord didn't know. But I asked the owner what he thought about our project. He said, 'Fine with me. Maybe it'll get some of the cars off the street and away from the curbs in front of the rentals I own.'"

Chapter 9

Pastor Daniel Jonas folded his linen napkin and laid it down. He looked around the room, with its rich paneling and leaded windows, and marveled that he'd never been inside the Minneapolis Club before. He looked across the table at his host and said, "Harry, that was a delicious meal. More than I normally eat in the middle of the day, I have to say."

Forty-year-old Harry Broadman smiled and nodded. "Glad you could join me today. We'll have to do this often. I'm a member here. You can come as my guest any time."

"Well, I hope you know how pleased I am that you're also a member of Saint Michael and All Angels Church." Harry had, in fact, been a member of the large congregation for exactly eight days. "If I may ask, how did you select Saint Michael Church?"

"It's simple. It's a thriving congregation. I like big, active churches. They give me energy. I love being in that gorgeous building with those beautiful stained-glass windows. I love how your organist plays. And I really appreciate your solid, thoughtful, energetic preaching."

Daniel tried to control the pride he felt welling up inside. He focused, instead, on the energy he was getting talking to this high profile businessman.

"I have to make a confession, though," Harry continued. "I haven't always been a Lutheran. Well, I *was* growing up. But when I went off to college, I joined a big Methodist congregation. The preacher was amazing. And when I got to Denver, Colorado, I became a Presbyterian. They had a large, exciting congregation. While I lived in Omaha, I was an Episcopalian. And now I'm in Minneapolis, and back to being a Lutheran."

"Well, I'm glad we were able to coax you back into the fold. But tell me something, how does a small town boy from someplace in Kansas end up in the executive suite at General Mills?"

Broadman smiled. "Part of it came fairly naturally. See, I grew up in this tiny little town way out by the Colorado border. Everybody grew wheat. My dad was one of them. I remember sitting at the dinner table on many an evening, out there in Bird City, Kansas…"

"You're kidding, right?"

"Excuse me?"

"About Bird City. There isn't really a town with such a name, is there?"

"Oh, absolutely. I'm not making this up. Get a map of Kansas and check it out. Look way up in the northwest corner. Of course, make sure it's a pretty good map. It won't show up on some of them."

"How did it get a name like that?" Daniel asked.

"Never researched it," said Harry. "Anyway, my point is, I used to sit at supper, listening to my dad complain about how the big grain firms and the food merchandisers make all this money and the farmers don't get a fair shake. I knew I wasn't going to stay on the farm, so I decided to go into an occupation that works with farmers, and see if I could change some of that."

"And that's how you got to General Mills?"

"Well, eventually. I got a degree in corporate marketing. I turned out to be pretty good at it. I worked for several other firms before coming to Minnesota. But the thing I wanted to share with you is this: a company like General Mills isn't necessarily getting more than their share. I mean, one thing I learned is that big companies have big expenses. Their actual profit margin may not turn out to be that great."

Daniel nodded, but wondered about Harry's comfortable lifestyle.

"Sure, some of us get big salaries. But when you figure the return the company gets for the skills they're paying for, it makes sense."

"What exactly do you do at General Mills, Harry?"

"I'm a visionary." Daniel's eyes grew large. Harry chuckled. "An idea person. New products. Better ways of marketing the old ones. Outmaneuvering the competition. Stuff like that. It turns out, I'm pretty good at it. So, I end up with a nice car and a house in Edina and a boat on Lake Minnetonka."

Daniel nodded. "One thing I've been wanting to ask you, Harry."

"What's that?"

"Where, exactly, does Betty Crocker live?"

Harry laughed out loud. Then he leaned across the table and whispered, "We keep her locked up in a closet, down the hall from the test kitchens."

"She's not real, is she?"

"Oh, try telling that to all our customers who swear by her cookbooks. She may not *exist*, but she's *real* all right."

Daniel got the distinction. He said, "Harry, just because we have over 5,000 members at Saint Michael Church doesn't mean we're going to give you a free ride. We really want you to get involved somewhere. A man of your obvious gifts will have a lot to offer."

"What?" he replied, feigning shock, "You mean I can't just hide in the crowd?" Then he offered a broad smile and said, "I'm a busy man. But I want you to plug me in where you can use me. I'll do my part."

"What in particular would you most like to do in the congregation, Harry?"

The businessman leaned back in his chair and thought about it. He said, "You told me the congregation began in 1927, right?"

"That's correct. In somebody's living room."

"That's just amazing, when you think about it." He continued, "So, I've been doing some arithmetic. The congregation will be 25 years old in 1952. That's not far off."

"Five years isn't far off?" Daniel said, puzzled.

"Not when you're planning an extravaganza."

"Excuse me?"

"What are you thinking about for the 25th anniversary year?"

"Well…I don't think we've thought about it much."

"You know, at General Mills, when we launch a new product, we start years before the item finally hits the shelves. You really have to do it that way, if you want the right results."

"So…you think we should be planning our 25th anniversary celebration now?"

"We should be starting to think about it. We should be getting a planning team together. We should be visioning and dreaming. It's a wonderful big congregation. It should be a big celebration."

"You've been thinking about this, haven't you?"

"Well, only since you told me how old the congregation is."

"I told you that three months ago, when you first walked in at worship."

"And I have some ideas. Not that they're the only ones, or even good ones. But I'd be glad to head up a planning team for the celebration."

Daniel nodded.

"Give me the names of three other people who know the congregation intimately, and whom you'd recommend to work with me."

Daniel realized the businessman had just appointed himself to head a task force that hadn't even been created yet. He replied, "Adam Engelhardt. He's practically the founding father of the congregation. Andreas Scheidt..."

"He's the president of the congregation, right?"

"That's right."

"Not a good idea. We'd overload him and distract him from his primary task. He could be ex officio. But let's find two others who aren't already in leadership positions."

Daniel realized his new member was making good sense. "I'd also suggest...Tom Pavelka. He's a longtime member who left the church for a year and is just now coming back. He needs a place to plug in."

"Excellent. Who else?"

"Well, she'll keep you on your toes, and challenge you now and then, but you can't do better than our director of music and choirs, Lillian Fischer."

"She's a genius, you know that?"

"Lillian?"

"Absolutely. She's one of the best evangelism tools you've got. People come to this church because of her music. You know that, don't you?"

Daniel nodded.

"That and the preaching." He didn't give Daniel time to respond. "Lillian's an excellent suggestion. Why don't you appoint all three of them and let them know I'll be wanting to meet with them."

"You want me to do that outside the church council?"

"Do you need their permission?"

"Well..."

"I'm talking like a corporate executive, aren't I. But, you know what? This congregation is the size of a corporation already. And you're the chief executive. Oh, I know, you think you should defer to the elected governing body. But, I have to tell you, that's not the way we'd do it at General Mills."

"I'm sure it's not. But consulting the council is more my style."

"Great. I don't want to tell you how to do your job. Just let me know when they appoint the four of us, and we'll get going on this."

Daniel wondered if he'd just hitched his wagon to a galloping stallion. He realized there was going to be no holding Harry Broadman back. Maybe, he decided, that wasn't such a bad thing. At least things would get done.

"Glad you could join me for lunch, Pastor," Harry said, getting up. "You let me know when you're ready to take a boat ride on Lake Minnetonka."

Daniel nodded. "I'll let you know. But for now, I need to go down to the library and check out a book of maps."

"What for?"

"To see if I can find Bird City, Kansas."

JOHN BAUMGARTNER and Hannah Ruth Jonas sat on the swing, inside the front screened porch. They glided gently backward and forward. John glanced surreptitiously toward the front door, assuring himself there was no fear of discovery, before he reached over and slid his hand into Hannah Ruth's. She clasped his with an eagerness that pleased him a lot.

"I'm sure lucky I found you," he said, squeezing her hand.

"I wasn't lost, you know."

"You know what I mean."

They glided in silence. Suddenly Hannah Ruth said, "Have you ever actually *been* lost, John?"

"What do you mean?"

"When you were a little boy. Did you ever wander away from your parents by accident or anything?"

"Gosh, no. That would be scary for a little kid."

She nodded toward the center of the porch. "Your family didn't live in Minneapolis when I was just a little girl. I don't think I ever told you this. My brother, Josh, once got stolen right off this porch."

"What!"

"He was just a baby. Mom had him in his playpen, out here on the porch. She was sitting right here on the swing. She thought the screen door was hooked, but it wasn't. She went into the kitchen to make some tea. When she came back, he was gone."

"Holy blazes! What happened?"

"He was missing for a week. I don't remember it very well. But my folks have talked about it different times. My Mom said she almost lost her faith in God."

"Was he hurt? Josh, I mean."

"Well, I'm not sure. Sometimes I think he acts pretty weird. Probably affected his brain or something, you know?"

He looked at her, incredulous. Then he realized she was having fun with him. "That's nothing to joke around about, Hannah Ruth."

She grinned. "I know. Sorry."

"What would happen to us if somebody stole our baby off the front porch?"

"Are we having one?"

"What? A baby?"

"Yes."

"Well, after we're married. You know."

"Are we getting married?"

"Are you giving me a hard time, Hannah Ruth? Of course we're getting married." He paused and thought about what he'd just said. "Well, I hope we are." He hesitated. "Aren't we?"

She laughed softly. "Just don't make assumptions. You've never brought it up before."

"Gosh, you're right. Well, I'm bringing it up. Are we going to get married? I mean, we *are*, aren't we?"

"Since we're not even out of high school yet, I take it that's not a proposal."

"Well, not in so many words. But you're not going to go running after a bunch of other guys when you get to college, are you?"

"I should be more worried than you. Ohio State is fifty times bigger than Capital University. Think of all the pretty girls *you're* going to meet."

"We'll just be across town from each other. I'm planning on sticking with one girl. From Capital."

"Well," she said, looking out toward the street, "that sounds…I don't know…I guess…pretty nice, actually."

He circled her shoulders with his arm and pulled her close to him. He nuzzled his nose in her neck until she squirmed. Then he planted a warm, lingering kiss on her lips, the most sensuous one he'd ever delivered.

She said, "John, the neighbors could be watching."

"Hope they are," he said, kissing her again.

Chapter 10

"Where'd you learn to kiss like that?"

"I've had lots of practice."

"Well, maybe I've let you have a little too much."

"It hasn't just been with you, Jenny," said Buzz, looking smug.

Jenny backed away from him and slid over on the front seat of her boyfriend's convertible. She scowled at him. "So, there've been others?"

Buzz moved over toward the middle of the seat and slid his arm around her. She folded her arms defensively, looking irritated. He tried to pull her close. She resisted. "Listen, Punkin..."

"Don't call me that. It makes me feel fat."

"It's not an insult. It's a cute little nickname for my cute little girlfriend."

"Just don't call me that anymore."

"Punkin, I've been calling you that for six months. You never said anything before."

"Well, I'm saying it now. So, stop it, okay?" There was intensity in her voice.

"What's the matter with you tonight?"

She sighed heavily. "I'm just feeling a little bit used by you, that's all."

"What do you mean?"

"You've had other girls. You never told me. How do I know what you ever did with any of them?"

"It's probably none of your business," he said matter-of-factly. He noticed her eyes were beginning to slant. He pulled harder on her shoulder, as if to force her toward him. She shook free of him. "Boy, you're one feisty little wildcat tonight," he said.

She pushed him away from her. "Tell me about these other girls," she demanded.

"Why should I? They're ancient history. They have nothing to do with us."

"They'll have everything to do with us, if it affects our relationship," she retorted. She stared out through the windshield, watching the last of the sun fade from the surface of Lake Nokomis. She wondered why she'd agreed to let him bring her here to park. Suddenly she wished she was somewhere else, anywhere except alone with Buzz.

He looked at her with an expression she couldn't interpret. It was as if he was trying to decide whether to be gentle or rough with her. Finally he said, "Look, I'm a basketball star, okay? The girls like my looks. They like to see me in action. They like to flirt. Some of them do. Sometimes."

"Who lately?"

He looked at her but said nothing.

"And don't tell me it's none of my business, or you can find somebody else to take to the movies and the drive-in."

He said, "What is it with you women, anyway? So a guy sows a few wild oats. It's what guys do. Get over it."

"Take me home, Buzz," she demanded.

"Like heck, I will. We're gonna talk this through."

"I'll walk then."

"You're fifteen blocks from home. It's almost dark. You don't want to do that."

"Buzz, I *mean* it. Take me home."

"Not until we talk this through."

Jenny considered her options. She tried to calm herself. The sun was now almost gone from the sky, and the lake was starting to look murky. She said, "Tell me something, Buzz. Have you been making out with other girls while you've been dating me?"

"No. It was before we met."

She looked dubiously at him.

"You asked me where I learned to kiss like I do. I told you. I just didn't tell you when."

"I still want to know how many other girls you've kissed."

He was silent. It was as if he was counting them up. Finally he responded, "Six."

"Six!"

"Of course, that's counting Ellen Samuels, back in junior high school. That was no big deal."

"But the other five were, right?"

"No. Not really. It was just smooching. I only kissed three of them one time each."

"That leaves two."

"Yeah. Okay. A couple cheerleaders. Last year. I went with one of them about a month. She dumped me for a senior varsity guy. I wasn't on the first team yet." He noticed her face seemed to soften. At least, he thought he noticed that. It was getting so dark it was hard to tell. "There, you feel better now? The big basketball star gets dumped."

"That leaves one," she continued.

"Yeah. Julie Bjornson. She was hot." Immediately he wished he hadn't said it. "But not as hot as you are, Punkin."

"Buzz..."

"Sorry. I won't call you that again. What should I call you?"

"Sweetheart. Darling. Something like that."

"How about Sugar?"

She sighed. "Okay."

He moved closer on the seat. "Don't be mad at me...Sugar. I'm really keen on you. You're just...just the best."

She looked at him in the gloom. "Do you understand why I'm upset?"

"Yeah. Of course. You think I'm treating you like just one more trophy. Right?"

"I'd say that's pretty accurate."

"Well, you're not just one more trophy, Jenny. You're special. I've never stayed with a girl this long in my entire life."

She breathed out slowly. He moved closer on the seat. He tried once again to slide his arm around her shoulders. This time she let him do it.

"Jenny...Sugar...I don't want us to fight. We're too good together to be doing that." He squeezed her shoulder with his hand, while with the other he reached for her knee, then moved slowly upward along her thigh.

She put her hand on his wrist, as if to stop him, but his hand kept moving, up to her waist, then to her breast. He leaned close and said, in a husky whisper, "There's more than kissing we can do, you know."

She wanted to pull his hand away, but somehow she lacked the will. She opened her mouth as if to speak, but he smothered it with his own.

"I WANT YOU TO UNDERSTAND," said Adam Engelhardt, "that the original is no longer available for inspection. This faithful copy will have to do."

He laid the inscribed page on the table in front of the research assistant.

Alexander Cartwright studied the lettering. He said, "This is really quite interesting. It's not often we find a building here in the Twin Cities where the key to its origins is part of the building itself."

Adam nodded. "I thought you'd be interested. You might want to put this in your files."

"Yes. Thank you. This is very interesting indeed." He leaned back in his chair and looked at Adam directly. "You have an interest in things historical. That's good. We need to cultivate more of that."

"Well, it wasn't difficult, taking interest in this inscription. I own the building, and I used to run a print shop there. My son once lived in the upstairs apartment, where we found this. He's running a newspaper on the main level."

"I understand all of that. But some people would have said, 'Oh, some old scribbling on the wall. Let's just paint over it.' You didn't do that—which sets you apart from a lot of people."

Adam sat enjoying the compliment. Cartwright noticed and said, "I'm not saying this to flatter you. We have a real crisis with many of our historic buildings here in Minnesota. A lot of people see them differently than you do. They want to get rid of them, or change them so much that they'll be scarred beyond recognition."

"Well, I don't know much about that," said Adam. "I only know about this one building."

"Come here," said Cartwright. "I want to show you something." He got out of his chair and led the way to a bookshelf, from which he pulled an oversized volume. "Here's a pictorial record of all the famous old houses built in Saint Paul and Minneapolis between 1880 and 1920."

Cartwright laid the book on a worktable and began to turn the pages. As he did so, he seemed to mumble, half to himself, half to Adam. "Saint Paul...Summit Avenue...Selby...Grand...amazing old Saint Paul houses. This one here's been torn down...this one's also gone...this one became an apartment house; then they ruined the exterior; might as well demolish it." He kept turning pages. "This section is for Minneapolis. Look at these wonderful old palace...Park Avenue...Third Avenue...Kenwood Parkway... Ridgewood...LaSalle...Pillsbury...Franklin...First Avenue South..."

He stopped turning the pages. "You know, half of these houses are already gone or badly compromised. Another quarter of them are at risk."

Adam said, "I can imagine their owners found them too expensive to keep up any longer."

"Exactly. The people with money are out in the suburbs now. They don't want to live in a city house with a small yard. And most of these neighborhoods are changing. The former owners all ran away from social problems, and took their money with them."

"So, who owns all these houses, then?"

"Well, this one here is a group home. Here's one that's been converted into a bank. Imagine! Here's one that's become offices for a group of lawyers. These two, over by the Art Institute, actually became a Lutheran theological seminary. Some of these are owned by people who simply can't afford them any more. They're running down pretty badly. Before long, they'll disappear."

"That does seem sad," said Adam, stroking his chin with two fingers. "On the other hand, some of those houses were bigger than they needed to be in the first place. I mean, how many bedrooms and fireplaces does one family really need?"

"Well, of course. That's exactly true. But still, they're remarkable architectural treasures. It would be good to see at least some of them preserved." He closed the book and returned it to the shelf. "Have you ever been inside any of those old mansions, Mr. Engelhardt."

Adam chuckled. "Sorry. I've never moved in those circles."

"Well, of course. Most of us don't. But I've been in some of them, just as a matter of historical curiosity. You can't believe the interiors in some them—beautiful wood paneling, gorgeous central staircases, parquet floors, leaded windows. It's just a tragedy how people treat them when they get hold of some of those places."

"Maybe the historical society should consider buying some of them."

"Don't think we haven't thought about that. But where would the money come from? It's not even a matter of being able to afford some of those old houses. I mean, the values, in real terms, are going down now, year by year. The big problem is, how would you maintain them? In some cases, restoring them to their original condition would be enough to bankrupt an organization like ours. And doing anything less would show a lack of integrity."

"I suppose it's just a matter of time when they'll all disappear from the scene," Adam said.

"What we need," said Cartwright, "are people who have your interest in history, but who have the means to buy and care for these properties."

"I guarantee you, I'm not one of those people."

"You don't know anybody who might be, by any chance."

"Well, I'm not sure."

"Because if you did, you might want to convince him—or her—to consider saving this one." He pulled out his center desk drawer and retrieved a newspaper article. Laying it on the desk top, he said, "This house is coming up for auction in the next month. It's on Frankin Avenue. Elegant, isn't it?"

Adam admired the Tudor style of the three-story, brown brick mansion. He couldn't remember ever having seen it. He'd been up and down Franklin Avenue plenty of times, but had rarely paid attention to the decaying old homes, except when he saw a wrecking ball taking one of them down.

"This house has a curious history," said Cartwright. "And that's one reason why I'd especially like to see someone keep it intact."

"What's the history?" Adam asked.

"The owner was a real high-flier. He was one of the richest men in Minnesota in the 1920s. Some say he was the richest one in the state for about a year. At least on paper."

"When did he sell this place?"

"Oh, he never did. It was taken for unpaid debts, after the Great Depression set in."

"He lost all his money?"

"That's not all."

"What else?"

"He took a swan dive off the 25th floor of the Foshay Tower."

Adam's eyes grew wide. "I know who that was."

"If you lived in Minneapolis in 1929, which I understand you did, you'd have known his story very well."

"Michael Morgan-Houseman," said Adam.

"Very good," said Cartwright. "You have an excellent memory."

"Not really. He's the man who gave my Lutheran congregation five million dollars once, to construct a new church building."

"Michael Morgan-Houseman did that?"

"Yes. In memory of his five-year-old son. The little boy was struck down in traffic, and died a few days later."

"And he gave all that money to your congregation?"

"Our pastor had helped Mr. Morgan-Houseman deal with his grief."

Cartwright looked fascinated. He said, "Too bad you don't have some spare cash. This could be your house."

"Oh, no. Not mine. My wife would never live in a palace like that."

"Well, maybe your congregation could buy it and make some use of it."

"I don't think that would be in the cards. We're in the middle of building a multi level parking ramp. Besides, what would we do with a decaying old mansion on Franklin Avenue?"

"Actually, it's not decaying. It's in very good condition. But the problem is, the only person who's come forth so far, showing any interest in the place, has announced he intends to turn it into apartments. Now, if that isn't obscene, I don't know what is."

Adam nodded. He marveled at the passion in Alexander Cartwright's voice. He tried to envision what the Morgan-Houseman mansion looked like inside—and what it would look like after someone had gutted the interior. He said, "Not that I have even the slightest interest in buying the place, because I absolutely don't have, but..."

"Yes?"

"Is there any chance I could get a look at the inside of it? Before they go in there with crowbars?"

Cartwright returned a hopeful expression. I can get the owner's name for you. He's pretty eager to find a buyer. I'm sure he'll be happy to walk you through the place."

Chapter 11

"Who needs more coffee?" asked Polly Broadman, circling the dining room table.

"I think everyone can use a warm-up, Dear," said Harry, looking from one to the other of their guests. There was no dissent, so Polly proceeded to refill all the cups.

"Great meeting, folks," Harry said expansively. "Pastor Jonas certainly knows how to assemble a task force. There's nothing but quality here. And, I've just made three new friends."

"It's great to get to know you," said Tom Pavelka, sipping his coffee. "I think we're going to have a good time putting this celebration together. Although, I have to admit, I wouldn't have thought of starting quite so far in advance."

"Big events take time to plan properly," said Harry. "Let's make this a celebration to remember."

"Oh, I think it's going to be just that," said Lillian Fischer. "Although, I must say, renting the Minneapolis Auditorium for a festival worship service sounds a little ambitious to me."

"We have 5,300 members now. We need to find a way to let them all celebrate together. Just imagine what sort of choir they'll make when they sing the hymns, Lillian."

"It sends shivers down my back, just thinking about it," she replied. "But where will we find money to rent that big barn of a place?"

"We'll have a special fund drive. Just for this event. We can kick it off this fall and build it for the next five years."

"Are you going to head that up, Harry?"

"No. But I know just the fellow. I had lunch with him yesterday."

"Who's that?" asked Tom.

"Your father-in-law."

"Jens Jorgensen?"

"Who better than a banker? Jens is very excited about the idea. He said he'd do it if the task force wants him to."

"Well," said Adam Engelhardt, "I can't imagine why we wouldn't want him to. As long as the church council knows what we're doing. And, as long as people don't start redirecting their regular offerings into the special fund."

"I promised Pastor Jonas we'd keep him up-to-date on our plans," Harry said. "He's already instructed me to show up at church council meetings and keep them abreast of everything we recommend as a task force. That should keep everybody happy."

Lillian set her empty cup down. "This has been delightful. But I have five young boys at home, and my husband is probably rough-housing with them on the living room floor right now. So I should be going."

Adam grinned. It was common knowledge at Saint Michael Church that Lillian and Luther Fischer had tried to give birth to a daughter, only to end up with five boys. The persistent rumor was that they'd quit having children when a girl arrived. But with Christopher, John, Michael, Timothy and Peter in tow, how many more times would they really want to try?

"It's really good to have you on the task force," said Adam. "Everybody knows how busy you are."

"Oh, piffle," she said, getting up. "I would have been offended if I hadn't been asked. Besides, how often do I get an excuse to have coffee and dessert in a nice Edina home?"

"We'll have the next meeting here as well," said Harry. "If that's all right with everybody." Nobody objected. "Great. I'll let you know when."

When the others had departed, Adam held back. Harry wasn't sure exactly why the last guest hadn't gone out with the others, so he waited a moment, and then said, "I'm especially glad to have you as part of this group, Adam. I understand the congregation was actually organized in your living room."

"On the Feast Day of St. Michael. September 29, 1927."

"You're our resident patriarch, then. Did you ever think this flock would grow so large?"

"Honestly? No."

"Well, if it hadn't, I probably wouldn't be a member." He paused, grinned, and said, "No offense. Nothing wrong with worship in a living room. But I've grown to appreciate large congregations. They're exciting places to be."

Adam nodded. He hesitated, as if he was weighing his words. He said,

"Did Pastor Jonas tell you how we got the money for our present building?"

"Yes. Some wealthy businessman gave it. In memory of his little boy. He gave five million dollars in one big chunk. Amazing."

"Could I talk with you for a few minutes about him?"

"About the wealthy businessman?"

"Yes. Michael Morgan-Houseman."

Harry looked quizzically at his guest. He offered an almost imperceptible shrug. "Sure. Come on into the living room. Let's sit and chat."

When they were seated, Adam said, "Our discussion tonight, about celebrating the congregation's twenty-fifth anniversary year, reminded me that we might want to take some steps to remember our heritage, in fairly specific ways."

"I'm sure we'll want to do that."

"Even though he was never a member of St. Michael Church, Michael Morgan-Houseman had a key role in our early history."

"That seems pretty obvious."

"Well, about a week ago I learned that the mansion he used to live in, back when he gave the bequest, is coming up for sale."

"Really. Where is it?"

"On Franklin Avenue. Not far from the Art Institute."

"And...who owns it now?"

"A real estate company. They've been trying to sell it. It's still in what you could call mint condition. Which helps explain why the real estate company can't sell it. It's too expensive for its neighborhood now. Nobody with that kind of money wants to live there anymore."

"So...what are they planning to do with it?"

"They've pretty much decided to cut their losses and get rid of it."

"How will they do that?"

"They're going to sell it at auction. Sealed bids. A week from Friday."

"In other words, somebody could get it at a steal."

"The problem is, the only known interested party wants to buy the place, tear out all the gorgeous wood on the inside and turn it into a four-plex. They'll keep the exterior looking like it always has, but the inside will be gutted."

"Ouch," said Harry. "Do they have to do that?"

"I think the buyer figures it's the only way to get his money back if he buys it. Of course, if he buys it cheaply enough, he'll come out doing very well for himself."

Harry crossed one leg over the other. "And you think, maybe, the congregation should show some interest in this piece of property?"

"Well, it does have a significant sort of tie to Saint Michael Church."

"But what would the church do with an old mansion?"

Adam smiled. He chose his words carefully. "I've only known you for a very short time, Harry. But I've already discovered what it is I think makes you such a successful businessman. You're a visionary. You imagine things other people don't. That impresses me. Quite a lot."

The corporate executive nodded with appreciation.

"So, maybe a little of that has rubbed off on me." He cleared his throat. "It occurs to me that our congregation has accumulated a lot of historical material over the past twenty years. There are photographs and memorabilia. Some of them are stacked away in cabinets in the Reformation Room at church. There's really no good place to put them out for people to see. Wouldn't it be grand to turn the Morgan-Houseman residence into a sort of history center for the congregation? We could have displays in the very house where the idea was first proposed for the church building we're using today."

"A history center in an historic old house," said Harry, mulling it. "That's an interesting idea." He thought about it, slowly drumming the fingers of one hand against the upholstered arm of his chair. He said, "We have no way of knowing how much the other party will bid, of course." Adam nodded. "And if we'd want the place, but bid too low, then it gets turned into apartments."

Adam said, "Whoever owned the house over the years kept it up meticulously. You really should see the place."

"No need for that," said Harry, waving his hand. "You've described it perfectly well. I'm sure it looks just as you say." He studied the cluster of framed pictures on the wall behind Adam, as if he'd just discovered they were there. Then he said, "You want me to put a bid on the place, right?"

Adam offered a sheepish grin.

"The city of Minneapolis might not appreciate my buying it for the church." Adam cocked his head, puzzled. "It would take it off the tax rolls." He drummed his fingers some more. "Of course, when they knocked down some of the other big old houses over there, they ended up with ugly parking lots. Not much taxable value there either."

The host got out of his chair and began pacing. Suddenly he stopped and looked at Adam. "If I bought it and gave it to the congregation, I'd get a tax write-off." Adam opened his mouth to speak, but Harry wasn't finished. "But the congregation would be stuck with another piece of real estate."

"I was sort of thinking you might like to buy it and keep it yourself. As an investment. Just to save it from who knows what might happen to it otherwise."

Harry thought about it but didn't reply.

Adam said, "I apologize for bringing this up. It really is a little presumptuous, now that I think about it."

Harry shook his head. "No. Not at all. In fact, I'm glad you did. If I found out later about the history of the house, and that it had been torn up by some speculator, I'd have been really upset. You've done the right thing."

Adam said, "Well, whatever comes of it, thanks for thinking about it anyway." He got up to leave.

"How about another cup of coffee?" said Harry.

"Thanks. But, no thanks. I need to go. I told Elsa I'd be home by nine. It's already half-past. She'll think I've been kidnapped."

"I'll have Polly phone and tell her you're on your way."

"One more thing."

"Yes?"

"I'd like to invite you and Polly to come to our home for dinner some evening."

"Really?"

"Absolutely. I think you might enjoy visiting in the home where the congregation was organized."

"It would be our distinct pleasure. Just call my social secretary and set it up."

"Ahh...okay. Who would that be?"

"Why, Polly, of course."

IT HAD BEEN an idyllic summer. John and Hannah Ruth had spent the entire three months at Lake Saint Michael, serving as junior camp counselors. They'd jokingly told each other it would be a good way to save some money for college while not being tempted to spend it. The truth was, both loved working with the young people who came to Camp Saint Michael, week after week. And, it gave them an excuse to spend time near one another all summer long.

On the last weekend, after the campers had departed, the two of them repeated a Sunday afternoon ritual. Pulling on their swimming suits and taking one of the camp canoes, they paddled their way across the smooth surface of the lake, toward the four small islands, each with its thick stand of trees.

This time they paddled more slowly, fully aware that this would be their last chance together on the lake. Seated behind Hannah Ruth, John dipped his oar smoothly in the water, then moved it to the other side, where he repeated the motion. He said, "We really work well together, you and I."

She didn't reply, but matched his motions with her own oar.

"The kids seemed better behaved this week," he said. "They seemed more subdued. Did you notice?"

"They were all in mourning."

"What?"

"School is starting next week. They don't want to face up to it."

"School is starting for you and me, too. Ohio, here we come."

"I'm a little nervous about going so far away from home."

"I'm going with you, remember."

"I know. But I've never been away from home for very long."

"Hannah Ruth, you're eighteen years old. You can handle it."

"I know. But don't you feel just a little…I don't know…sad about finally leaving home?"

"After college we can come back."

"If we get jobs in Minnesota."

"We're bound to. Lots of opportunities in the Twin Cities."

"John?"

"What?"

"Suppose I get a job in one state and you get one somewhere else."

"That won't happen. After college we're getting married. Where one of us goes, the other one will, too."

"What if I get a better job than you do."

He dipped his oar and suddenly sent a scoop of lake water splashing onto her mostly bare back. She shrieked, turned around and glowered at him. "What was *that* for?"

"To remind you who's in charge. I'm the guy. The guy gets the best job. He decides where they'll live. The gal obeys."

"Says who?"

"Says the New Testament. 'Wives, obey your husbands.'"

"You're not my husband."

"Will be."

"You're pretty darn cocky."

He grinned. "I'm yanking you around. Can't you tell that?"

"And another thing," she said, turning back to face the front of the canoe and beginning to paddle again, "I'm not so sure about that 'Wives obey your husbands' stuff."

"You don't believe what the Bible says?"

"The Bible also says women should be quiet in church. Does that mean we can't talk, or sing, or speak the responses? You can't take everything in the Bible at face value."

"That Bible verse means women can't preach."

"Then why does it say they should keep silent?"

"You probably have to read the verses connected to it. And we don't have a Bible with us, so I guess we can't figure it out right now."

"Well, if you think I'm going to obey you blindly on everything, you can just think about finding a different girlfriend."

"Not a chance. I'm not changing girlfriends now that I've found the perfect one."

"Then watch what comes out of your mouth, Mister Smarty Pants."

"Okay, boss, I'll watch it."

"Don't get ridiculous. I'm not your boss."

He chuckled. He didn't know why, exactly, but he loved teasing her, and getting her to react.

They circled to the far side of the four small islands and glided past the one called Matthew. As they approached the Isle of Mark, John deliberately let go of his paddle, gently pushing it toward the shore. "Oh, oh," he said, just loud enough for Hannah Ruth to hear.

She turned around, then saw the oar, floating toward the island. "Go get it!" she shouted impulsively. He dived in and began swimming with powerful strokes toward the little beach, against which the oar had become lodged. But instead of swimming back with it, he sat down on the shore and leaned back on his palms.

Hannah Ruth looked at him in disbelief. Every summer camper knew the rule. Nobody was permitted on any of the four "Gospel Islands." It was a time-honored rule. She wasn't sure why it was forbidden, but she knew that, as a counselor, she had warned every one of the campers in her care, all summer long, that if they set foot on one of them, they'd be sent home immediately.

And now, there was John, sitting on the shore of the Isle of Mark, blatantly flouting the rule.

"You take the canoe on back!" he shouted. "I'm staying here."

"No you're not. Get back out here."

"Nope. I'm staying."

"John, what's the matter with you?"

"It's your fault. You called me Mister Smarty Pants. My feelings are hurt. I'm just gonna stay on this island and nurse my wounds."

"Oh, for crying out loud," she said, turning the canoe. Alternating her strokes on either side, she steered it toward the shore. He reached for it and pulled the end up on the beach, which was no more than two canoe lengths long.

She climbed out and sat down next to him. "We're not really supposed to be here, you know."

"Camp ended today. It's the end of the season. Nobody's going to know. Unless you blab it to somebody."

She punched him on his bare shoulder.

He said, "We could just stay here, you and I. Our own little kingdom."

"Who'd feed us?"

"Nobody. We'd die in each other's arms, a pair of starved lovebirds."

"You're just crazy," she said with mock disdain.

He studied the distant shore, where a series of lake homes stood. Further down, out of view, was one that the Jonas family owned. He sighed and said, "Have I told you lately that I love you?"

"Not for at least a week."

"Well I *do* love you. And I'm gonna have a devil of a time waiting four more years before we get to have sex."

Chapter 12

Hannah Ruth looked at John. He was gazing at her with an eagerness she'd not seen before. She said, "Is that why you coaxed me onto this island? So we could have sex?"

"Huh. Gosh, no. Nothing like that."

"Sounds like you don't want to wait four more years, though."

"Well, no. I don't. But I'm going to. What do you think I am, anyway? You're my girlfriend, for crying out loud, not some sex object."

She was taken aback. She said, "Thank you. That's what I was hoping you'd say." Then she said, "To tell you the truth, I've been wondering lately what I would do if you tried to get me to do it with you."

"Why? You think I'd try to force you into it or something?"

"No. Not really. It's just that…"

"What?"

"Well, I haven't told you this, but I've been getting mail all summer long from Jenny Langholz."

"Your best friend. Except for me, of course."

"Yes. Dear old Jenny. You know what? I really worry about her sometimes."

"Because of Buzz, right?"

"Yes. Because of Buzz."

"So, what's she telling you about her and him?"

"Well, it sounds like things have gotten pretty hot and heavy between the two of them. She tells me she wants to wait until they get married. But he's an athlete, you know, and I think he could force her if he wanted to."

"Has he tried?"

"She says he's gone quite a ways with her. Farther than I'd ever let you go with me at this point. The thing is, she says he wants to convince her that she wants it, so he can do it with a clear conscience."

"So far, no dice though, right?"

"That's what she says. But, I really wonder about those two."

"What do you mean?"

"She automatically assumes they're going to get married. I wonder if they really should."

"I know what you mean. He's not a very good match for her. I mean, he goes to church and League with her, but sometimes I wonder if he's just doing it to get what he wants from her." He paused and studied the ripples washing against the canoe. "You think I'm right about that?"

She sighed. "I think he has her pretty confused. I mean, she once talked about going to Capital University with me. Now she's given all that up. She says she's going to Augsburg College instead, with all those strict Norwegians. She says she 'has to,' because she needs to be close to Buzz. He has another year of high school. She's ready for college."

She traced a circle on the ground, then put a dot in the middle. "What if she meets some other guy at Augsburg? Will that make Buzz mad? What will he do then?"

"Boy, Hannah Ruth, we can't solve all Jenny's problems."

"I feel kind of responsible for what's happened to her, though."

"Why should you?"

"She really wanted to date you. Instead, I got you."

"You're kidding!"

"I'm serious."

"Well, don't feel responsible for five seconds. I would never have dated Jenny Langholz in a million years."

"Really? Why not?"

"Well, for starters, because she's not you."

"That's a nice thing to say. But what's the real reason?"

"That's actually it. I've never had any interest in her. I've been thinking about you for...well, for a long time."

"That's sweet."

"That's the truth."

They sat in silence. Hannah Ruth said, "In one of her letters, Jenny told me she and Buzz entered the jitterbug dance competition in the Minneapolis Aquatennial."

John almost snorted. "Can you see Buzz doing the jitterbug?"

"I guess he's pretty good," she said. "They almost won a prize."

"Holy cow. There they are, at the Minneapolis Auditorium, dancing up a storm, and here we are, stuck away on a lake, counseling a bunch of summer campers."

"You'd rather have been in the dance competition?"

He grinned. "Never in a million years. This has been one great summer. The kids have been great. And I've been up here with you all summer long. It's just been unbelievable."

She studied the mainland, across the water. "We better get the canoe back. We still have to drive back to the city."

"Not yet."

"What?"

"Come on. We have to explore this island." He jumped up, and then pulled her up with him.

"We're barefoot. We might step on something in there. Let's not."

"Come on. This is our one and maybe only chance ever."

She sighed and followed him through the trees, watching the ground at every step, avoiding sharp rocks and protruding roots.

At the center of the small island there was a clearing. When John saw what was in front of him he let out a long, low whistle. "What the devil is *that*?"

"It's...a tombstone!" she replied.

"Sure as heck is. Look at this." He knelt in front of the stone and read:

GRETA INGRID PAVELKA
1933-1944
Now she is with the angels

"Greta Pavelka," said Hannah Ruth in a near whisper. "That's...Tom and Sonja Pavelka's daughter. She died when we were in ninth grade. Remember that?"

"Yeah. Everybody remembers that. She drowned up here at camp somewhere. But you told me they buried her in Minneapolis."

"Well, I thought they did. My dad had her funeral. He went to the graveyard with the family. I'm positive that's what he told us afterwards."

"So, what's her grave doing up here?"

"I have no idea." She smoothed her fingers gently across the carved letters. "But I guess it explains why nobody's supposed to be coming on any of these islands."

"At least this one," said John.

They stood up and looked around the rest of the clearing. "Look at this," said John, pointing to a bare patch on a nearby tree. "A couple of lovebirds left their calling card." They walked toward the tree, close enough to see a heart carved where bark had been pulled away. Inside its shape appeared the fading message:

Tom + Sonja
July 4, 1932

John said, "This is just unreal. Tom and Sonja Pavelka carved their initials here in 1932. And eleven years later they buried their daughter, right next to the same tree."

Hannah Ruth drew her arm around John's waist. She said, "You and I were two years old the year they left this message."

He turned to face her. "Hannah Ruth, suddenly I feel a little bit like we're trespassing."

She nodded. "We should go."

As they paddled back toward the camp, Hannah Ruth said, "I was going to ask my dad about Greta Ingrid's burial. But maybe I won't."

"Really?"

"I don't exactly want to admit I was on the island. You know?"

"Yeah. I know. I think you're right. I don't think I'm going to tell anybody either."

"IT SEEMS STRANGE not having Hannah Ruth at home any longer," said Rosetta Jonas. She passed the casserole dish to her husband.

Josh said, "I don't know. I kind of like it. I always wanted her room. Now I can see the street. And climb out the window onto the front porch roof if I want to."

"Don't you even *think* about it, young man," his father said sternly.

"Just kidding, Dad."

"It's going to be a lonely Thanksgiving," Rosetta said. "The first one with her away."

"She'll have a good time visiting in Fremont," Daniel replied. "The relatives will all spoil her."

"Is she taking John Glamour Boy Baumgartner along?" Josh chided.

"Yes, John's going with her," said Rosetta. "And don't talk with food in your mouth."

"The other guys and I were talking about college," said Josh. "Skip's planning to go to police academy, like his dad."

Daniel suddenly experienced an uncomfortable flashback. Fourteen years before, in the spring of the year, Skip Warner's father, Sam, a member of the Minneapolis police force, had sat in this very room, at this same dining room table. He had come to assure Daniel and Rosetta that their infant son, who had been stolen out of a playpen on the front porch, would surely be found and brought home again. The entire incident, which had dragged out for a week, had plunged Daniel into a dark night of the soul. He marveled, over the years, that Joshua Daniel had not seemed to demonstrate any traumatic symptoms. Perhaps he had been too young to remember any of it.

"So Skip's following in his father's footsteps, then?"

"Yeah. Says he wants to. He'll be good at it."

"I'm sure he will," said Daniel. "His father's an asset to the force."

"What about the other two boys?" Rosetta asked.

"Well, Alex isn't sure. Maybe he'll join the Army or something. Paul wants to go to the University of Minnesota. Maybe major in chemistry or physics or some other boring science thing." He paused. "Man, I can't believe anybody would want to study anything like that."

"I thought he might follow in his father's footsteps and become a building contractor," said Daniel.

"That's his fail safe. In case he hates science," said Josh, grinning.

"So, what about you, Joshua Daniel? What are you thinking about?"

"Dad, why do you keep calling me that? All the guys call me Josh."

"Because that's what we named you. And because part of your name is *my* name. I'd think you'd be a little bit proud of that."

"But everybody at school calls me Josh. Everybody."

"Well, around here, I'm still going to call you Joshua Daniel. Okay?"

Josh scowled. "A guy can't even choose his own name."

His mother began laughing silently to herself. Josh looked at her. "What's so funny?"

"A guy can't choose his own parents, either. Did you ever think of that?"

"Yeah. Actually, I did." He looked sideways at his mother. "Not that I'd choose anybody else for parents. Necessarily."

"Well, that's a comfort," Rosetta replied. She barely concealed a smile.

"You still haven't answered my question," said Daniel.

"About what?" Josh replied.

"What you're thinking about after high school."

"Well. College. Naturally."

His father nodded with appreciation. "Capital University?"

"No, no, no. Never. Not Capital."

"What's wrong with Capital?"

"Well, for one thing, both of you went there. And for another, Hannah Ruth is there."

"Is that bad?"

"Well, criminy…"

"Joshua Daniel." His mother looked sternly at him. "Criminy is not a word."

"Sorry, Mom." He poked at his casserole. "Would you want to go to college where everybody knew your parents and your sister?"

"You were in the same high school with your sister. Was that a problem?"

"Well. Okay, maybe not. But you guys went to college there. I can't go where you went."

"Nobody will remember us by the time you get there," Daniel said.

"Sure they will, Dad. The professors will. The ones that knew you."

"There aren't so many of those left by now."

"Well, anyway, I think I want to go to Wartburg."

"Really?" his parents responded in unison.

"Yeah. Anything wrong with that? Tons of kids go there from our church."

"Well…I know…and that's fine," Daniel said. "I just hadn't realized you were thinking of going there."

"Well, I hadn't either. Until a couple weeks ago."

"Really," said Rosetta. "What happened a couple weeks ago?"

"I found out Sarah Engelhardt might go there."

"David Engelhardt's daughter?"

Josh grinned sheepishly. "She's kinda cute."

"Well…yes, I guess she is," said Rosetta. "But when did you start getting interested in Sarah Engelhardt?"

"Oh, about five minutes after Pete Fenstermacher did."

"What's Pete Fenstermacher got to do with it?" asked Daniel.

"I heard him bragging, about a month ago in the locker room at school, about how he was going to go after her and make her his girl. So, I sort of went after her myself."

"How did you do that?" asked Rosetta, looking amused.

"Well, if you must know, Mom, I saw her at Luther League the next Sunday night. I asked her what she thought of Pete Fenstermacher."

"Sort of indirect, wasn't it?" said Daniel, whose amusement now matched that of his wife.

"Okay. Maybe. But you don't want to come right out with this kind of stuff, you know? So, anyway, she said, 'Pete Fenstermacher? I couldn't possibly be interested in him.' So I asked her, 'Why not?' She said, 'Because I'd never be able to marry him, not in a million years.'"

Rosetta was almost dissolving in mirth. Trying not to laugh out loud, and marveling that her son was being so candid about the subject, she said, "And why couldn't she marry Pete Fenstermacher?"

Now Josh was grinning. He said, "She said, 'Because I can hardly spell his last name. Why would I want to be stuck for the rest of my life with a name that has thirteen letters in it?'"

Daniel was grinning. Josh was discussing the son of the highly efficient executive secretary at Saint Michael Church. "So, what happened after that?"

"Well, I was fairly casual about it and all. I just said, 'You know, the name Jonas only has five letters.'"

His parents both broke out laughing. Josh looked at them in surprise, secretly enjoying the fact that he'd evoked such a response. Even he was amazed at his own cleverness.

"So, that really impressed her, I suppose," said Rosetta, regaining her composure.

"Well, not completely. She said, 'With your last name, I'd have to learn to pronounce the J like a Y. That's kind of a bother.'"

Daniel looked at his son in disbelief. But Josh delivered the clincher. "Then she said, 'But I think I could get used to it.'"

"Well, wasn't that good of her," said Rosetta dryly.

"Sure was," said Josh matter-of-factly. "I'm having dinner at her house on Sunday." He paused and looked uncertainly at his parents. "I mean, if it's okay with you guys, that is."

Chapter 13

The shoes of three men echoed on the bare wood floor of the empty mansion. As they walked through the richly-paneled den, with its elaborate stone fireplace and leaded stained-glass bay window, Adam Engelhardt said to Harry Broadman, "You don't know how thankful I am that you won the bid on this house last spring."

"It was the least I could do for a friend," said Harry, admiring the stone lions gracing the ends of the fireplace mantel. "Besides, it may turn out to be a good investment for me. One way or another."

The young man, who stood listening to the older two talk, finally cleared his throat. Twenty-one-year-old Michael Edwins clasped his hands behind his back and rocked up onto the soles of his shoes and back again. It was his way of suggesting, *You people are ignoring me.*

Adam said, "I'm sorry. Harry, I haven't introduced you to Michael."

"No. You haven't. I thought maybe he was a friend of yours from church."

"You're half right. He's a friend. A brand new one. We met the other day at the Art Institute. He was admiring a display by classical Swedish painters. I just happened to bump into him."

"Well," said Harry, furrowing his brow, "Not to be rude, but why are you here with Adam Engelhardt this afternoon, young man?"

"He didn't tell you?" Michael responded, looking genuinely surprised.

Adam said, "Michael needs something, Harry. And so do you. I think I have a solution to both problems."

"Didn't know I needed anything, Adam. What is it?" asked Harry, looking puzzled.

"Your problem is, you've owned this lovely, deserted, empty mansion for over three months now, and nobody's living in it."

"Well, I thought you and I agreed that I'd own the place and the church would use it for historical displays in the 25th anniversary year."

"That's right. On the first level, anyway. But the displays won't go up for three or four more years. And you can't just let the place sit empty."

"I can't? Why?"

"This isn't Edina, Harry. It's Franklin Avenue. Maybe you haven't noticed, but this neighborhood is changing. If you leave this place deserted and unattended, the neighbors just might be tempted to come by one of these nights and start removing the doorknobs and the shutters."

Harry pondered it. "Nothing's happened to the place so far."

"You've been lucky. An empty house down on Pillsbury Avenue, not so far from here, had a break-in last winter. I think whoever got in might just have wanted a place to keep warm. But they decided to build their fire in the dining room, where there isn't even a fireplace. You might have heard that the entire first floor was gutted before the fire department could put it out."

"So we're really living on borrowed time, you think."

"I'm convinced of that. And that's where Michael, here, comes in."

"He's going to sit sentry on the front porch for me?"

"No. He's willing to live here. For a couple years, at least. If you'd like him to."

Harry looked Michael up and down. "Really!"

Adam said, "He's a first-year student at Northwestern, the Lutheran seminary over by the Art Intitute. You could give him free lodging here. He'd keep an eye on the place, keep the lights on in the evenings, make people realize somebody actually lives here. And it wouldn't cost you a nickel, Harry." The executive looked as if he still needed convincing. "Besides, if you can't trust a seminary student, then who *can* you trust?"

The executive looked at the younger man. He said, "And you'd want to live in this drafty old building all by yourself?"

Michael shrugged and offered an affable grin. "Beats paying rent. Besides, I sort of like this place. It's really quite stunning—the architecture, the staircase, the wood paneling, the fancy fireplace, the colored glass panes set into the downstairs front windows. I could pretend I was a duke or an earl while I was camping out here."

"You'd stay upstairs in one of the bedrooms, I assume."

"After you furnish one of them," volunteered Adam. He hastened to add, "It would be a good investment."

Harry nodded. "You won't leave the kitchen a mess, right?"

"He's actually something of a gourmet cook."

"At his age?"

"Well, that's what he told me. Why should I doubt him?"

"So, we'd need a kitchen table too, and some chairs and some dishes and utensils."

"I could pick out all of that," said Michael.

"If I pay for it," Harry said, offering a look of irony.

"It's your house," Michael replied. "Think of it as an investment."

IN JANUARY, 1948, the congregation's annual meeting was less well attended than it had been the previous year. The issue of whether to construct a new parking ramp had been peacefully resolved with an overwhelmingly positive vote the previous February and, by the following November, it had been dedicated for use.

This year's meeting did, however, have one significant item on the agenda. In response to a recommendation from the 25th Anniversary Year Task Force, the church council had agreed to a major initiative to establish a vast network of living-room cells, all over the congregation. It was intended to remind the congregation of its origins. But, more important, it was designed to help members, who tended to get lost in the large worship throng on a Sunday morning, connect more intimately with some of their fellow members.

That project had led the church council to believe another pastor would be needed, someone who could launch the program and administer it. So, a motion came to the annual meeting proposing that a fourth pastor, one responsible for "family life ministries," be added. The motion was approved without debate.

Daniel Jonas had been given the task of identifying the best candidate for call. He conducted the interviews himself, narrowing a field of six, recommended by the district president, to one. After his second conversation with the Rev. Aaron Ward, he was convinced this was the person the Holy Spirit was leading him and Saint Michael Church to call.

Aaron was serving a congregation in Saginaw, Michigan. He had developed an effective system for dividing his membership into smaller units for prayer and service. Daniel was impressed with the model, and also with Aaron, who struck him as a servant with a pastoral heart and with good sense about parish ministry.

THE CHURCH COUNCIL ratified the senior pastor's recommendation at their March meeting. On the first Sunday in April the congregation voted without dissent to call the Rev. Aaron Ward. By mid-May the 30-year-old clergyman, his wife Alice and their two small children had arrived in Minneapolis. George Kleinhans had headed a committee of three to locate a suitable parsonage for the new clergy family. They found a large, comfortable two-story home on Cedar Avenue.

The congregation quickly fell in love with Aaron and Alice, and proceeded to spoil their children. Aaron was engaging, thoughtful and funny. He enjoyed listening to other people's jokes, and told his share of them as well. Alice made it clear she had no intention of looking for a job. She knew that many younger women had entered the work force during the Second World War and had kept their jobs after their husbands came home. In spite of that, she devoted herself to her children and busied herself in the life of the large and still-growing congregation.

AT THEIR FIRST staff meeting following Aaron's arrival, Daniel explained to the other three pastors on his team how he wanted to have them serve. Looking at seventy-year-old Pastor Martin Schultz, he said, "Martin, we called you to tend to our older members. We want you to continue doing that. But there are so many of them now, we'll allow you to ask the others of us to step in when you need us."

Aaron Ward leaned forward in his chair, a look of eagerness on his face. Daniel noticed and nodded toward him. "Actually, Pastor Jonas…"

"We're colleagues, here, Aaron. The members of the congregation can call you 'Pastor.' But when we're meeting like this, you should call me 'Daniel.' And, unless you're uncomfortable with it, I intend to address you by your first name."

Aaron found it temporarily disconcerting, facing the prospect of addressing the clergyman he'd admired from afar with such familiarity. But the other two men at the table were nodding, indicating it was the pattern. He said, "All right then, Pastor…I mean, Daniel…I just wanted to suggest that, since we'll be organizing these small cells for our members, some of the older ones may be taken care of that way."

Martin eyed him carefully. "You mean, you're going to work me out of a job?"

Aaron was taken aback. But he realized there was no animosity in the older man's words. "No. Not at all. I just think it could become the case that we'll be able to lighten your load some."

"How might that work?"

Aaron looked at Daniel. He said, "Am I getting us off the topic?"

"No. Go ahead. I'll get us back on track soon enough."

Aaron said, "Well, in the cells we organized in Saginaw, members of the small groups prayed for each other. If someone was sick, they took it on themselves to visit them. We didn't give anybody the responsibility of taking communion to homes or the hospital, but I suppose that might have been possible as well."

Martin was weighing it. He looked at Daniel. "I'm old-fashioned. But I'm also a realist. Some days I've been running out of energy, trying to keep my schedule of home visits. I think Aaron might be onto something."

Daniel grinned. "We'll explore that some more. Now, back to the discussion with which I began. I was going to explain to all of us what Aaron's assignment will be. I think he's already begun to tell us."

Aaron said, "Well, we don't have to do here what we did in Michigan."

"That's right," Daniel replied. "You may find a totally different situation here. We're already committed to developing the cells. That's why we called you. But they don't have to look exactly the way Harry Broadman envisioned them."

"One of the members has already decided what the cells will look like?"

"No. Not really. Harry just likes to take matters into his own hands. He makes a suggestion and you can tell, pretty easily, that what he really wants you to conclude is that he's got it all figured out already." Aaron's eyebrows went up. Daniel said, "Don't let Harry Broadman intimidate you. He's a dreamer. He's full of ideas, almost all of them very good. But stand your ground with him. I think you'll find him to be a good friend and one of your best cheerleaders."

Aaron nodded uncertainly. He had met Harry Broadman, but hadn't yet had an extended conversation with him. He wondered what their relationship was going to be like.

"And," said Daniel, looking at Pastor Fangmeyer, "that leaves Marcus—and me. The two of us have functioned pretty much as generalists, doing whatever needed to be done. But now that Aaron is here, with a fairly specific assignment, I think that you, Marcus, might want to focus more on parish education and evangelism."

"Not to do all of that myself, I hope," he said in a hesitant voice.

"Of course not. All of us will help with anything you decide we ought to. And, of course, there's a lot of good lay leadership in this congregation. Get the members involved. A lot of them are eager for a meaningful ministry assignment. I've heard as much from many of them."

Marcus said, "Stewardship? Youth ministry? What about those?"

"Stewardship will be my focus," said Daniel. "Youth ministry is being handled very well now with our lay volunteers. Although we may want to think about hiring someone to do that on salary."

"What about preaching?" Marcus asked.

"I'm not saying this to be egotistical," said Daniel. "But the council, and many of the members, are telling me they want to hear their senior pastor preach about half the time. Some of them have said they want me in the pulpit *all* the time. That's not going to happen, believe me." There were chuckles. "I want the others of you to take your turns. Let's do this. I'll preach every first and third Sunday. Marcus, you take every second week. Aaron, you take every fourth."

He looked at Martin. "Do you want to be included in this rotation, Martin?"

"Yes. Every fifth Sunday."

The others looked at him with puzzlement. Then Aaron said, "Four times a year, right?"

"That's just enough for me," said Martin.

Daniel said, "Good. Let's see how that works. Now, on to other business. Lillian Fischer wants to compose an oratorio for the 25th anniversary celebration. She wants all the choirs to be involved. She would like to know that all the pastors will be behind the effort. Anybody here have a problem with Lillian creating an oratorio for the congregation?"

"Oh," said Marcus, looking at the new arrival, "I wonder if anybody has warned Aaron not to tangle with Lillian Fischer. Or, if they do, to be sure they're wearing armor?"

Chapter 14

Jenny Langholz sat next to her mother, on the living-room couch. Georgianna looked at her daughter with an expression that suggested she was armed for battle. “Sweetheart, I haven’t wanted to bring this up…well, that’s not true. I’ve wanted to. I just haven’t done it.”

“It’s about Buzz and me, isn’t it?” Jenny replied defensively.

“Yes. It’s about Buzz and you.”

“Well, what about us?”

“Jenny, you don’t have to use that tone.”

“Mom, I already know what you’re going to say.”

“All right. Tell me. What am I going to say?”

“You’re going to tell me Buzz is no good for me, and I’m wasting my life with him, and I can do better, and if he gets me pregnant it’s going to break your heart, and you and Daddy will probably never speak to me again.”

Georgianna was taken aback. She’d expected a shovelful but had gotten the entire wagonload instead. She wasn’t sure what to say, partly because a lot of what her daughter had just said to her was right on target. She cleared her throat. “Look, I know you’re out of high school now.”

“Mom, I’ve finished a whole year of college.”

“All right. And that’s probably all the more reason you probably think you don’t need advice from your parents any longer.”

“Daddy isn’t here. Are you speaking for the both of you?”

“Well, now that you mention it, yes. He and I pretty much agree about all of this.”

“All of what?”

“Jenny, Buzz is out of high school. He doesn’t want to go to college. He doesn’t have a job. To hear you talk, he isn’t looking for anything. What kind of future are you going to have with some young man who has no ambition?”

"He…he's not lazy, Mom."

"So what sort of prospects does he really have?"

"He…doesn't really know…yet."

"He lives with his mother. His father gives him money. He drives around in that…convertible…" The last word came out with disdain.

"Mom, you told me when Daddy got out of high school, *he* rode around on a motorcycle."

"He rode it to his job. Where he earned money until he could afford to get married."

Jenny slumped back into the couch, folded her arms defiantly across her chest, and went into a sulk. She said, "There's nothing I could say to you or Daddy about Buzz that would make you like him."

"Actually, Jenny, this is not about Buzz. This is about you."

"Mom!" she practically shouted. "This is about Buzz *and* me. You know perfectly well it is!"

"Jenny, lower your voice."

"Why? Why should I? You're making me really angry. I feel like I'm in front of the grand inquisitor. Why do I have to listen to any of this?"

"Well, because for one thing, you may be attending Augsburg College, but you're still living at home. And we're not charging rent. So I think you owe your parents some consideration."

"Fine," she barked, "I'll just move out then."

"Where would you go?"

"Buzz has a spare bedroom at his place."

"Jenny, you know that's foolish talk."

"What's foolish about it? Are you afraid he'll end up in bed with me? How do you know he hasn't already?"

That stopped the conversation cold. Georgianna looked at her daughter, with what Jenny perceived to be an almost hateful expression on her mother's face. She frowned, then scowled, then found herself losing control. Her eyes began to flood and she covered them with her hands. She wept deep, soulful sobs.

It caught Jenny completely off-guard. Her expression melted away and she began to look, at least faintly, contrite. She sighed heavily. "Okay, Mom. I'm sorry. I wasn't trying to be cruel to you."

Georgianna pulled her hands away from her face and, with tears staining her cheeks, moaned, "What kind of daughter have we raised? Whoever taught you to talk and act like this? And whatever happened to honoring your parents? I thought you learned that in catechism."

For once, Jenny was speechless. She felt like firing back a rejoinder. But she really didn't want to be responsible for further antagonizing her mother. And, she was absolutely not interested in seeing more tears flow. She studied the pattern in the couch upholstery, trying to figure out how the conversation had gone so terribly wrong.

Her mother had found a handkerchief and was drying her eyes and face. She sniffed and said, "Jenny, the problem your father and I are having with all of this is that we love you so much. We don't want you to get hurt. We know you're old enough to make your own decisions. But, Darling, you're breaking our hearts. Can't you see that?" She looked beseechingly at her daughter.

Jenny took a deep breath and let it out slowly. She said, "Listen, Mom, I love you and Daddy, too. You know I do. It's just that...I don't always feel like you trust me very much. I mean, hardly any of the decisions I've made since I started my senior year in high school have been acceptable to you. How do you think that makes me feel?"

"Well, Jenny, if you let Buzz Winslow get you pregnant before you're married, and before he can support you, how do you think that would make *us* feel?"

"Mom, he's not going to get me pregnant."

Her mother looked at her uncertainly.

"He uses protection."

"Jenny!"

"What?"

"Buzz is having sex with you?"

"For God's sake, Mom."

"'Thou shalt not commit adultery.' Jenny, we believe that! I thought *you* believed that! And, by the way, why are you using the Lord's name in vain?"

Jenny jumped up from the couch. She marched across the room and stared out the window, toward the street. She waited for a moment, then turned and said, "You know, Mom, maybe I really *should* just move out."

Georgianna didn't get up. She stared at her daughter with a look of panic. "No. You shouldn't. You should stay right here. Until you're out of college."

"That's three more years, Mom. We could end up doing a lot of shouting in three years."

Her mother looked vacantly at her daughter. She said, quietly, "I really wish you had gone to Capital University. With Hannah Ruth Jonas."

"Well, Mom, I didn't. And that's past history. There's nothing wrong with Augsburg College." She realized her mother wasn't convinced. "Except, of course, that Buzz knows how to get there." There was thinly-veiled sarcasm in her tone.

Her mother returned a defeated look. She said, as kindly as she knew how, "Jenny, please, come and sit down next to me."

Jenny hesitated, but then did as she'd been asked. When she was seated on the couch, a safe distance from her mother, Georgianna said, "Now I'm going to ask you a question. And I promise not to judge you or ridicule your answer. I'm just going to listen to what you tell me."

"What's the question?"

"What do you see as Buzz' best qualities, and what do you most appreciate about him?"

Jenny was surprised at the question. Her first impulse was to reply, *He's an incredible kisser, and he really knows how to satisfy a girl.* She decided that was absolutely not what she should tell her mother. Then she considered the possibility that the question might actually be a trick. But the expression on her mother's face convinced her otherwise.

The trouble was, she'd never been asked the question directly before, at least not by an adult. And, thinking it over, she realized she hadn't really had a chance to make a proper list.

She said, "Well, Buzz is…really, really nice to me…most of the time…"

Her mother's eyebrows went up, but she held her tongue.

"Okay, I'll admit, sometimes he gets a little nasty. When he doesn't get his way." She wished she hadn't had to admit that. She said, "You and Daddy fight sometimes, right?"

Her mother nodded, but almost imperceptibly.

"And…well…Buzz is…" She wanted to say a real catch. Instead, she said, "a really attractive guy. That's important to me, Mom. You don't want me going out with somebody who looks like a slob." She thought about it, and decided to say more. "He's really dreamy looking in just his swimming trunks." Immediately she realized that was far from the substantial sort of answer her mother was looking for.

She wracked her brain. "And, well, Buzz is…" She stopped. Nothing else on her mental list would impress her parents—certainly not his convertible, nor the fact that his main vocational fantasies involved sky diving or professional basketball or becoming a bartender.

True to her word, Georgianna Langholz held her tongue. Even though she sensed her daughter's monologue had likely come to a dead end, she waited.

Jenny screwed up her face in a philosophical grimace. She finally said,

"You know what, Mom? When it comes right down to it, there really isn't that much to Buzz. The guy likes shooting baskets and driving around in his convertible and bragging about himself. And, to tell the truth, the only thing he's really passionate about is trying to get me to take my clothes off for him." After her mother's shocked expression began to fade, she continued, almost in a confessional tone, "I guess that's not a whole lot to build a relationship on, is it?"

Her mother offered a hopeful, sympathetic look.

"You know what? You've helped me a little bit. See, lately, the way things have been going, I've been getting really, *really* tired of all the arguments I've been having with Buzz. Every time we go anywhere, he wants to know when we're going to do it."

"'Do it'?"

"You know. Go to bed together. Mom, I've never let him get me into bed. Never. But he's come pretty close a few times. The way he kisses me, it just takes all my resistance away. I'm really afraid one of these times we're going to end up doing it. Maybe even in the back seat of his car." She paused. Was she really saying all this to her mother? "The thing that scares me the most is, he says he has protection, and I know he carries one of those things around in his billfold. But, if we got really close to—you know, actually doing it—how do I know he'd remember to use it? Or, if it would even work?" She looked at her mother, who had an almost frightened look about her. "The thing is, I don't want Buzz getting me pregnant. Not while I'm still in college. And, the way things are going, I don't know if I can fight him off for three more years."

Georgianna was crying again. This time the tears came silently, running down her face in rivers. When she looked up and realized what was happening, Jenny moved close to her mother, took her hands in her own, and said, "I've been sort of thinking of breaking it off, actually. Sort of wanting to."

She paused. "But I've been too stubborn. I didn't want to give you and Daddy the satisfaction of knowing that you were right and I was wrong." She hesitated. "And, anyway, I didn't have the nerve. I've always worried that, if I broke it off, he'd do something sudden, maybe try to get even, or hurt me or something. I look at those big muscles on him, that I've always really liked a lot, and I realize that, if he got really mad at somebody, he could be a scary guy, using them."

Georgianna said, "Jenny, I don't want you to get hurt."

"I know. I don't want to hurt you either. Even though I think I probably already have."

"Just be careful, Darling."

Jenny sighed so heavily her mother wondered if there was any breath left in her daughter. She said, "I will, Mom. I will. But, I got myself into this—and I have to figure out a way to get myself out of it."

"WHAT'S THE MATTER with you?" demanded Arnold Elliot. He had rolled over in bed, to face his wife, only to find, for the tenth night in a row, that she was lying with her back to him.

"Go to sleep, Arnold," she mumbled. "I've had a long day at work. So have you."

"Sandy, when are we gonna make love?"

"Go to sleep, Arnold."

"Dammit, Sandy, we're married now. Stop putting me off!"

She rolled over and faced him. "I told you when we got married, I'm not giving up the supper club. And, if you got me pregnant, I'd have to. So just get over it, all right?"

"So this means no lovemaking, then? Ever?"

"We've been over this, Arnold. You take care of birth control, and we'll make love. But you keep telling me, 'That should be the woman's responsibility.' Well, this woman is using the most responsible kind of birth control ever invented."

"In other words, no sex."

"As long as you're going to behave like a stubborn cuss."

Arnold lay staring at her in the gloom. He said, "If I'd known you'd be such a jerk about this, I would never have married you. There were plenty of girls in Europe when I was over there. I could have had any one of a hundred."

Sandy sat up in bed. She said, "Listen, Buster. You didn't marry one of those, did you?" He didn't reply. "*Did you*!" Her volume had doubled.

"Sandy, why are you yelling at me? And in bed, for God's sake!"

"Because you're talking like an infant. I gave you an alternative solution. You refuse to take it. Evidently, because you don't think it would be manly or whatever. Well, that's the best I can do for you. You're not getting me pregnant. Not now, anyway. And that's that."

She turned her back to him again and pounded her pillow forcefully, then settled down into it.

Arnold sat propped against the bed's headboard. Any desire he'd felt for Sandy in the last five minutes had completely evaporated. He was frustrated and angry. And now he was feeling humiliated. Something inside of him told him that protection against pregnancy was something that soldiers were supposed to use with prostitutes. It didn't seem proper for a husband to have to do that with his wife. He didn't know why he felt that way, but he knew he did.

After five minutes of staring into the darkness, brooding and sulking, he suddenly threw back the blankets, half uncovering his wife. Grabbing his pillow, he growled, "Obviously you don't want to sleep with me. Have it your way. I'm going to the guest bedroom."

He walked out the door and slammed it behind him.

Chapter 15

Josh Jonas stretched out on the beach towel, tucked his hands behind his head, closed his eyes and began soaking up the late afternoon sun. "Boy, this is the life," he sighed.

Sarah Engelhardt, who was lying next to him, said, "Enjoy it while you can. School starts again in three weeks."

"Don't remind me."

"We're going to be big-shot seniors when we go back. How do you feel about that?"

"I don't know. It only lasts for a year. Then you go off to college and you end up at the bottom of the heap again."

"Let's enjoy being seniors before we turn back into freshmen."

"Mmmmm," he murmured contentedly. He was losing interest in the conversation.

She sat studying the surface of Lake Nokomis. "There's a sailboat out there, Josh."

"Mmmmmm."

"You lazy bum. Open your eyes, sit up, and look at it."

"Can't a guy just relax once?"

"I think we should get a sailboat."

His eyes came open. He adjusted momentarily to the sun before replying. "We? Who's 'we'?"

"You and me. We should get a sailboat."

"You mean now, or just in case we get married some day?"

"Well, we could wait until after the wedding."

She waited for him to contradict her whimsical comment, and took significance from the fact that he didn't.

"Sarah, where the heck would we keep a sailboat?"

"At your folks' lake place. Up at Lake Saint Michael."

"Then we'd have to run up there to use it. And who'd pay for it?"

"You would. After you get out of college and start getting rich."

"Just exactly what do you expect me to do with my life in order to earn this big pile of money you're itching to get your hands on?"

She grinned. "I don't know. I'm kidding, actually. I just like to dream about it sometimes."

"Having a sailboat?"

"Having lots of money."

"A fool and his money are soon parted."

"But a clever man uses his money to build a fancy house over by Lake Calhoun."

"So, in other words, you didn't learn a single thing in catechism, or Sunday class, or Luther League. You still think collecting a pile of money's what it's all about."

"Josh, I didn't say I actually wanted to be rich. I just said I like to dream about it once in a while." She looked at him, admiring his tousled brown hair and his brilliant blue eyes. "And, I should have known a pastor's kid would give me a sermon about my misplaced priorities."

"It wasn't a sermon. I'm just saying, there's more to life than money."

"What's on your list, Josh?"

"Huh?"

"What are the really important things for you?"

"You pretty much know already."

"Well, let's see. As I recall, it's finding your purpose, and living it out."

"And…?"

"And…serving God, whichever way you're best able to."

"And…?"

"And…" She frowned. "And, I'm not sure what else."

"And helping other people. And leaving the world a better place than we found it. And using our God-given gifts as fully as we can. And living with integrity."

"Okay, okay. Don't dump the whole load on me!"

He grinned. "Your turn."

"Excuse me?"

"What's on your list?"

She returned an impish grin. "Same as yours."

"So, is that the way it's going to be? Whatever I say, you're just gonna agree with it, and never do any thinking for yourself?"

"I can't help it. I like your list."

"And I like...*you*!" he said, rolling over and planting a warm kiss on her mouth.

When she pulled free, she said, "Josh, people are probably watching us."

"So?"

"So the preacher's son is going to get a reputation."

He pulled himself up into a sitting position, looked out at a canoe on Lake Nokomis, and said, "You know, I really get tired of that sometimes."

"Being a preacher's kid?"

"Being reminded of it. And having people expect things of me they wouldn't for anybody else."

She nodded.

"Do people think I'm going to be perfect, just because I grew up in a parsonage?"

"Well...I guess I never thought much about how that would feel."

"And then there's my 'perfect' older sister. I'm sure everybody compares me to Hannah Ruth. She's off in Ohio, getting accolades for her piano and organ recitals." He paused. "You know what? I took piano lessons from Lillian Fischer for three years. She finally told me to save my money and take up the clarinet or something."

Sarah laughed softly. "Not everybody has the same gifts. You shouldn't try to imitate your sister."

"Oh, I never would. Never in a million years."

The sun was tipping. Sarah said, "We should go pretty soon. They're going to close the beach."

"Not until we say they can," said Josh, as though he were somehow in charge of City Parks Administration. He said, "What do you think my gifts are, Sarah?"

"You feeling the need for a little affirmation?"

"No. I just want you to tell me what you see in me. That's all."

She tucked her legs up close to her and clasped her hands together, in front of them. She studied a gull, standing near the shore. "I think you have the gift of inquisitiveness. You never let things lie. You always want more answers. I like that about you."

"Anything else?"

"Lots of things. You have the gift of charity. And compassion. And imagination. And a natural love for people. A lot like your father, actually."

"There. You see what I mean?"

"What? You don't like that I'm comparing you to your Dad? Don't be so thin-skinned, Josh. I mean it as a compliment. Everybody admires your Dad, and how he interacts with people. And I see those same qualities in you."

"The next thing you're going to tell me is that I should go to seminary like he did, and follow in his footsteps."

"Not necessarily. But you could if you wanted to. You'd make an excellent pastor, Josh. You know that, don't you?"

He sighed. "I guess. But how am I ever going to be my own person if all I ever do is follow in the shadow of other people?"

"There's nothing wrong with imitating greatness."

"Boy, you really have my Dad on a pedestal, don't you."

"I wasn't thinking of your Dad, actually."

"Who, then?"

"Christ. 'When you're in Christ, you're a new creation.' Remember that?"

"Of course. We had to memorize that."

"It's my confirmation verse."

"Really."

"Yes, really. What's yours?"

He didn't respond.

"You don't remember your confirmation verse?"

"I remember it."

"So, what is it, then?"

He hesitated.

"Are you ashamed of it?"

"No. Just a little afraid of it, actually."

"Why?"

"Because I want to live a long life. If I can."

"What's your confirmation verse got to do with that?"

"'For me to live is Christ. To die is gain.'"

"Oh." She was silent. Then, "Of course, it doesn't say *when* you'll die. That verse could be just as meaningful if you lived to be a hundred."

"Yeah. Maybe."

"Are you worried about dying?"

"Not exactly. But I still remember, back when we were in confirmation, that time when Tom Pavelka got a letter from the government, telling him his brother had been killed in the war. That really spooked me out. He was only about twenty. I remember thinking that was way too young for anybody to die. He never got to have a wife and kids or a career or anything. And, what do you suppose it was like for him when that bullet got him."

Sarah sighed. "This is getting a little morbid."

"And then I got that confirmation verse. I almost thought of trying to trade it in for a different one."

"Well, nobody ever knows when they're going to die."

"And remember Tom and Sonja Pavelka's eleven-year-old daughter who drowned up at Lake Saint Michael? That was around the same time his brother was killed in France. Man, that must have been rough for them."

"Josh, I know. But there aren't any guarantees."

"I used to think there should be. I mean, if you were really faithful and everything."

"Well, there *is* a guarantee with that."

He looked at her, puzzled.

"You know. 'Be faithful unto death and I will give you a crown of life.'"

He looked at her with admiration. "I'm impressed. You're just full of biblical wisdom, aren't you."

She grinned sheepishly. "That was the Bible verse I was really hoping to get when I was confirmed."

ON THE SCREEN, Gregory Peck was trying to convince somebody that he was not really such a bad guy. But Jenny Langholz had missed almost all of the plot so far, and wasn't concentrating now. She was sorting things out in her mind. In the next seat, Buzz was leaning close to her, holding her hand, while his other arm was around her shoulders. She wondered why he didn't have a backache by now.

This was the fourth time out with Buzz since she'd decided, sitting in the living room with her mother, that she was going to break it off. But there hadn't been a good time to tell him. Not on any of those other three dates. This time, she was determined to do it, no matter how awkward things got. She was due to return to college in a couple more weeks, and she wanted everything settled before then.

Why had she let Buzz convince her to come all the way out to Columbia Heights just to watch a movie? She wished she hadn't told him, almost a year before, that her parents used to come out here to the Heights Theater. For some reason, Buzz thought that made it romantic, bringing her back to the same movie house.

Why had she let him talk her into sitting in the very back row? It was too easy for him to get fresh with her, sitting behind everybody else. And, it didn't help that there were scarcely twenty people in the theater tonight, none of them seated within four rows of the two of them.

Buzz let go of her hand. Having freed his, he moved it up to her breast, and began stroking it. She grabbed his hand and tried to pull it away. He whispered urgently, "Don't stop me, Sweetheart. I want this, and I know you do."

"Buzz! Cut it out! We're in a theater!"

He seemed not to hear her. She realized his fingers were unfastening the top button on her blouse. She began rebuttoning it, but he was busy with the third and fourth buttons, opening both of them before she could stop him.

"Buzz! Don't. I don't want this!" She thought she saw others in the theater beginning to turn and look their direction. But she didn't care.

He said, "Dammit, Jenny, you won't let me do it anywhere else. It's dark in here, and there's plenty of time, and I've been more patient with you than most other guys would have been. So, just relax and enjoy it." There was an almost ominous tone in his voice.

Suddenly she jumped up and hurried down the empty row of seats, then out into the lobby. By the time she reached the sidewalk, she had refastened all the buttons. But her heart was racing.

Buzz caught up with her. "What's the matter with you? I paid for that movie. We're missing half of it."

"You haven't seen five minutes of it and you know it," she retorted.

He looked at her with impatience. "Come on," he commanded. "Let's get in the car." He gestured with his head toward the parking lot.

She looked uncertainly at him, but then demanded, "Take me home, Buzz."

"Let's go get in the car," he said firmly.

Hesitantly, she began to move toward the lot. He took her arm and practically dragged her to the convertible. "Get in the back seat," he ordered.

"The *back* seat. Why?"

"You know why."

"Buzz, I'm not getting in the back seat."

He yanked the back door open and practically shoved her in. He scrambled in behind her, but he wasn't quick enough for Jenny. She had opened the door on the other side and quickly scrambled out. When she slammed the door, she heard a dull thud, suggesting Buzz' head might have been in the way. She heard a muffled obscenity. But she wasn't intending to stick around to find out what had actually happened.

She ran so fast that, first one, then both of her shoes came off. She felt the asphalt pavement through her socks as she raced across the parking lot and onto the sidewalk. She looked both ways in desperation. There was not a car in sight. She began running south, along Central Avenue. She reached the railroad tracks, passed the city limits sign and realized she had crossed back into Minneapolis.

Her feet were getting tired. She was running out of breath. She wondered why Buzz hadn't caught up with her yet. She turned around and saw what she thought might have been his car, finally coming out of the parking lot.

Where could she hide? Had he seen which way she'd gone? Would he come after her?

A southbound bus came into view, heading into the city. She ran across the street and, even though it wasn't a bus stop, flagged it down. As she dragged herself aboard, the driver said, drolly, "You don't have any shoes."

"I know. I'm sorry."

"No problem for me, but maybe for you."

She dropped her fare into the box, took a seat on the driver's side, and began watching, out the window, for sight of Buzz' convertible. Suddenly she realized he was driving parallel to her window, in the next lane. Her blood froze.

She moved to the other side of the nearly-deserted bus. As the blocks went by, she wondered how far the bus was scheduled to go. She hadn't even bothered to find out.

The driver stopped for a red light at Lowry Avenue. Out her window, Jenny saw a police car, sitting at the curb, across the intersection. She yanked the bell. The driver opened the door and she scrambled off. She ran toward the squad car, only to discover that there was no one inside. She crouched behind it, waiting for the traffic on Central Avenue to move along. When the bus departed, there was no sign of the convertible. She stood up and tried to calm herself. She realized there had been standing water in the gutter where she crossed the street. She now had soaking socks and feet. She was beginning to feel like a tramp.

A uniformed policeman came out of a cafe and approached his vehicle. He saw her standing next to his patrol car.

"Officer," she said in a shaky voice, "I need your help. I need to get to south Minneapolis. Can you help me?"

"My assignment is Northeast. What's the problem?"

"I'm...there's...somebody is after me. I just need to get home."

"You know this person?"

Should she tell him? "He used to be my boyfriend. I'm just really afraid of him right now."

"Where is he?"

"He was right there, at that intersection, a couple minutes ago."

He looked her up and down. "You don't have any shoes. And your socks are filthy."

"I know. Could you...could you possibly...please, *please*, take me home."

Chapter 16

"Daddy, I think he was going to rape me."

Will Langholz sat at the kitchen table, watching his daughter pull her sodden socks off her feet. She had just escaped from a nasty encounter with the young man he'd once praised her for bringing to Luther League. He'd called her 'quite the evangelist' for doing that. How had it come to this?

"You know you can't see him again," he said quietly.

"I have no intention *ever* seeing Buzz again."

"The problem is, how are we going to keep him away from you? We could get a restraining order from the police. But he might not obey it."

Jenny looked at her mother, who had gone down on her knees, and was washing her daughter's feet. Jenny felt ashamed, allowing her to do it. It was almost like her mother was Mary Magdalene or Jesus or somebody like that.

She also felt ashamed for everything that had happened, and for having misjudged Buzz. Most of all, she was ashamed for what she'd put her parents through.

"Daddy, I can't go back to Augsburg College. I need to get out of the city for a while."

Her father sat studying the patterns in the kitchen wallpaper. He said, "You could go down to Iowa and enroll at Wartburg. There are a lot of your friends from Saint Michael Church attending there."

"I don't know if my credits would transfer."

"That's not the main thing right now. Your safety is."

"They might not have room. Augsburg starts in two weeks. Wartburg must be almost ready to start, too."

"I'll talk to Pastor Jonas. He knows the college president. He can arrange it, if anybody can."

She sighed. "What if Buzz finds out I'm at Wartburg?"

"We'll make sure he doesn't."

"How can we do that?"

"Let's just take this one step at a time, Jenny."

BUZZ WAITED until the new school term began at Augsburg College. One day, at midmorning, he drove to the campus. In the registrar's office he asked which classes Jenny was taking and which ones she had that day. He was informed that such information wasn't available to strangers.

"But I'm her *boyfriend*, for God's sake."

Said the clerk, "Well, if you're really her boyfriend, then you should know that information without having to ask me."

Buzz returned a stupefied look, then scowled and pushed his way out of the office. On the campus, he began stopping students, asking if any of them knew Jenny Langholz. He finally found one who did.

"Why are you looking for her?"

Buzz hesitated. "I'm her boyfriend. I haven't seen her for awhile."

The student looked dubiously at him. "She hasn't been telling you what she's up to then, right?"

"What do you mean?"

"She's not coming back here this year."

"She dropped out?"

"No, she wouldn't do that. I heard she transferred to another college."

"Where?"

"Not sure. Out of state, I think."

As he drove toward south Minneapolis, Buzz muttered, "You think you can just dump me and run, Jenny? Well, you can run, but you can't hide." He cruised slowly by the front door of her house. He thought briefly of going to the door. But he realized, even if one of her parents was home, he'd probably get a frosty reception. He kept on driving.

He went, instead, to Saint Michael Church. Maybe, he thought, the youth ministry director could tell him something. But that office door was closed and locked. He headed to the room where the Luther League held its meetings. Since Jenny had gone off to Augsburg, the two of them hadn't been here together. But he still felt a connection to her in this place.

He prowled about the room, looking at announcements fastened to the bulletin boards. Then something caught his eye. There was a sheet of paper fastened to one of the boards, with a big "Congratulations!" lettered at the top, in red. It was a list of all the kids from Saint Michael Church who were attending Wartburg College, down in Waverly, Iowa, this year. To his amazement, Jenny's name was typed on at the bottom. It was the only one not in alphabetical order. Obviously, it had been added at the last minute.

"WELCOME TO RIVER FALLS," the dorm monitor said, smiling at the newcomer. "Glad you're here. How come you waited so late to enroll?"

"I...ah...had a change of heart. About my old school. I wanted a change of scenery."

"Well, it says here you're planning to become a teacher. This is a great place to study for that."

"Yes. I know. That's why I came here."

"So, which part of Wisconsin are you from?"

"Oh, I'm from Minnesota. Minneapolis."

"Really. So, why didn't you just go to the University of Minnesota then?"

Jenny Langholz hesitated. "Too big. And, I wanted to get away from home."

"Well, this place will be your home away from home. Here's your room key. Come on, I'll introduce you to your roommate."

IT HAD TAKEN BUZZ five hours to drive from Minneapolis to Waverly, Iowa. When he arrived in the small county seat town, he followed the signs to the college campus. He climbed the steps and went into Luther Hall. As he had done at Augsburg, he sought out the registrar's office.

"I'm trying to find my...fiancee."

The middle-aged woman studied him, over the top of her glasses. "You don't say. Engaged to a college girl. Isn't that just a little bit previous?"

"Excuse me?"

"We don't encourage our students to get married while they're in college. It causes far too many problems."

"Oh, we're not married. Yet."

"And, what is the name of the lucky lady?" she asked, with thinly-veiled sarcasm.

Buzz felt irritation welling up, but held it in check. "Jenny Langholz. From Minneapolis, Minnesota."

The registrar began flipping through a stack of cards. "Which class?"

"Second year."

She flipped through more of her cards. "No. Nothing. There's no one here by that name."

"She enrolled at the last minute. You must have her on another list or something."

The registrar got out of her chair and went to find another roster. She studied it for a moment. "We had a Jennifer Langholz enrolled here for about a week. But she never arrived. I have a note saying she withdrew her application."

"Jesus," Buzz whispered softly.

"I beg your pardon?"

"Sorry. I'm just...really confused. It's almost as if she's trying to run away from me."

"I thought you said the two of you were engaged."

"Well...we will be. If I ever catch up with her."

The registrar arched one eyebrow.

"You don't know where she is, then?"

"Young man, I haven't the faintest idea. Perhaps you should contact the Bureau of Missing Persons."

SARAH ENGELHARDT sat straight up in bed. It was a cool night, and yet she was soaked with perspiration. She tried to calm herself. It was as if an urgent message was crowding her brain, and she needed to tell someone. But what was the message?

She sat listening to the silence. She wondered what had just happened to her. Something vivid had flashed through her mind. It wasn't exactly a dream. She rarely remembered her dreams, and none of them were vivid. This had been like a visitation from an angel or something.

She lay down again. What was it she had just seen. Or heard? Why had it seemed so real, and yet so elusive? She lay still, trying to calm herself, trying to concentrate. Finally she slipped back into unconsciousness.

Twenty minutes later she awoke a second time. She sat up, stared at the pale outline of her bedroom window, and whispered. "Uncle Martin. It's Uncle Martin!"

She crept from bed and looked at the luminescent hands of the ticking alarm clock on her dresser. Eight minutes past four. It was too early to awaken her parents. She put her hand on her chest and felt her heart racing. She wished she could talk with someone. But there was no one with whom to talk. So she climbed back into bed, where she tried to go back to sleep.

But sleep didn't come. She lay thinking about what she'd learned...or imagined. Finally, at seven o'clock, when she heard movement in the hallway, she pulled herself from bed. She found her mother in the kitchen.

"Mom, have you heard from Uncle Martin lately?"

"No. Not since last Spring. Why?"

"I think something may have happened to him."

"Why do you say that?"

"I don't know. I just...kind of sense it."

Molly Engelhardt looked carefully at her daughter. It was the oddest thing she'd ever heard her say. She thought about her brother. Martin Lundgren had graduated from Gustavus Adolphus College a dozen years before, then had earned an advanced degree in Forestry from the University of Montana. Now he was working in a national park in Colorado. The last time Molly had seen him was at the family's annual holiday reunion at Christmas time, in Litchfield, Minnesota.

"How did you get this sense, Sarah?"

"It just...sort of came to me."

"When?"

"At four o'clock this morning."

"While you were asleep?"

Sarah pondered it. "I think so. But it wasn't a dream, exactly."

"What was it then?"

"I don't know. Sort of like a...gosh, Mom, I can't really say this to you."

"Say what?"

"It seemed like a really bright vision."

Molly looked at her daughter in puzzlement. "Well, what did your...your vision say about Uncle Martin?"

Sarah sighed. "I don't exactly know. Except that I have this really strong feeling that something serious may have happened to him."

AGAINST HER OWN best instincts, Jenny Langholz went home for Thanksgiving weekend. On Friday afternoon, while her parents were at the big Sears store on Lake Street, buying Christmas presents for her, she sat on the front porch of their home and turned the pages of a book she was supposed to be reading for a class at college.

It wasn't until she heard him on the front steps that she looked up to see Buzz standing on the outside of the screen door, trying to open it. But she had made sure it was latched, which meant he had to talk to her through the screen.

"Hey, Sugar, where in hell have you been for three months?"

"Buzz, go away. I don't want to see you."

"Well, I want to see *you*."

"Go away. Or I'll call my dad out here." She wondered if he could tell she was bluffing.

"You and I have some unfinished business."

"You and I have nothing to finish, Buzz. Now get off our property."

"Open this door, Jenny. I don't want to have to break the latch."

The hairs began to rise along the back of her neck.

Buzz began yanking at the screen door, as if somehow he could jimmy the latch into the open position.

Suddenly a police car pulled up in front of Buzz's convertible. An officer got out and headed up the sidewalk, toward the porch. A second policeman got out and stood by the passenger door, watching, as his partner approached Buzz.

"Are you Edward Winslow?"

Buzz released the handle of the screen door and turned around. It took him a second to realize that someone was actually addressing him by his given name. "Yeah. Why?"

"Is that your convertible?"

"Yeah."

"I have a warrant for your arrest."

"For what?"

"Statutory rape."

"Must be mistaken identity."

"The complaining party described your convertible. Not many cars in the city look just like yours."

Buzz whirled around, stared hatefully at Jenny and barked, "You dirty little slut. This is your doing, isn't it."

Jenny was thunderstruck. But the policeman solved the mystery. "Charges have been filed against you by a Maria Gonzales. She says you forced yourself on her, sexually, last Sunday evening."

Buzz looked back at the officer, a look of wild panic in his eyes.

"Come with me please."

As the officer handcuffed and led Buzz down the sidewalk, Jenny felt her heart begin to race. She wondered what would become of her former boyfriend.

And, she wondered, who would come to take away his convertible.

TWO WEEKS AFTER her daughter's nighttime epiphany, Molly Engelhardt received a letter from her brother. It was written from a hospital bed in Denver, Colorado. Martin Lundgren explained he'd been called out in the middle of the night, to help fight a fire started by a careless camper, when a burning tree had come down on him. He had ended up in the hospital with a broken arm and leg.

Almost as an afterthought, he mentioned the day and time of the accident. It had been the same night Sarah had awakened so suddenly from her sleep, at just after three o'clock in the morning.

In the time zone for Minneapolis, Molly realized, that would have been a few minutes past four.

Chapter 17

Daniel settled into his chair and smoothed his fingers across the linen tablecloth. The River's Edge had always been a class act, especially since Sandy Elliot had inherited it from her parents and turned it into an upscale restaurant. Through the large, plate-glass window he studied the Mississippi River, as it flowed swiftly past, down below the bluff.

Sandy arrived with two cups of coffee, and a cream puff on a plate. Daniel wondered whether any other customers ever got such service from the owner herself.

Sitting down opposite him, she smiled and said, "Sorry I didn't make the cream puff. I've given up doing that. But everybody says they're still sensational."

"You're not having one?"

"Look at me. I need to take off ten pounds. I'm a victim of my own cooking!"

"Thanks for taking a few minutes to talk," Daniel said. "It's become impossible for one pastor to visit all our members now. We have nearly 6,000. They just keep streaming in from all over." She nodded, a look of admiration in her eyes. "Do you realize we now have members driving all the way from Anoka? Just imagine!"

"They really love you, Pastor Jonas. And that music director of yours. And...well, a lot of things. There's just a lot to like about Saint Michael Church. It's no wonder people come."

He inhaled. "I was sort of hoping you and Arnold would be coming. More than you have been."

She looked at the tablecloth, pretended to brush away crumbs that weren't really there, and sighed. "Yes. I know. When you married us, we promised to be faithful." She looked up. "We really intended to. Honestly."

He returned a look of understanding, but said nothing.

"Well, for one thing, both of our lives have become just crazy. Arnold's air charter service has finally taken off...excuse the bad pun. A lot of weeks, he isn't even home on weekends. He's getting lots of corporate people using him now, for business trips. Especially from here to Chicago. Sometimes they stay two or three days. One guy from 3M stays down there a full week at a time. Can you believe it? His company pays Arnold's lodging and meals while he's hanging around, waiting to bring the guy back."

Daniel tried to imagine what sort of life that must be for Arnold.

"And, as for me," she continued, "I know this place has kept me busier than it probably should." She furrowed her brow. "But I promised myself, when my father died, that I wouldn't let The River's Edge go down. He built it up. I want to keep it going. And, well, so far, I guess I have."

"Sandy, the place is thriving. Every time I've been here for supper with Rosetta, it's been packed."

"Yeah. Especially on weekends. That's part of the problem. I work so late on Saturday nights, I just can't drag out in time for church on Sunday mornings."

"We have four services now. Are you aware of that? You could come as late as 11:15 in the morning if you wanted to."

She nodded. "I'm going to work on that. I'm also cutting back the hours I put in here. Business is so good, I've hired a manager. He does a lot of what I used to do. That frees me up a little. And, look around. You see how quiet it is in here right now?"

"Is that a good thing?"

"Yes, actually it is. We've stopped being a full-service, three-meals-a-day restaurant. Now we're just a supper club. The doors don't officially open until four o'clock in the afternoon. That takes a lot of pressure, and work, off the staff."

"So, how did I manage to get in before business hours, then?"

"I just made sure of it. Nice to be treated special, isn't it?"

"Yes. I guess it is."

She returned her gaze to the tablecloth. Her brow was furrowed again.

"Is there something else we should be talking about, Sandy?"

She looked up. "I...ahh...might need some advice. Or maybe some counseling."

"What about?"

"About Arnold and me."

He tilted his head, waiting for the next sentence.

"You know, back when we were taking those classes with you, before we got married, you told us to work on communication?"

Daniel nodded, apprehensive.

"Well, that hasn't worked out too well."

"What's the problem, do you think?"

"The problem is, we never talk. And, when we do, it isn't pleasant." She sighed. "We've been married a year and a half now, and it seems like we have less to say to each other with each passing week."

"When you do talk, how does it go?"

"Like I said, it's usually not pleasant. Arnold is...well, calling him headstrong would be putting it kindly. Pastor, he's bullheaded."

"What about?"

"Well, for one thing, about when to have children."

"As I recall, the two of you disagreed about that when you were meeting with me, before the wedding."

"Here's the thing. Arnold knows I don't want kids until the supper club is really secure, and can function without me on site all the time. Well, I'm just about at that point now. But Arnold wanted to start having kids right out of the box. I mean, I think he'd have been happy if he'd gotten me pregnant on our wedding night."

"Obviously you talked him out of that."

"Well, fought him off would be more like it. The thing is, he's so darn stubborn. I told him I wouldn't have sex unless he used protection. He thinks that's my responsibility. Why should it be? He's the one that wants it. Shouldn't he take a few precautions? Why should I have to do it?"

"You still haven't settled this."

"And I think it's ruined our relationship. I mean, think about it. We've probably had sex ten times in fifteen months. Arnold sometimes complains about having to accommodate to my wishes. Sometimes he gripes about it even while we're in the act. Can you think of anything more romantic than that?" Her sarcasm was tinged with bitterness.

"Have the two of you considered a therapist? Or a marriage counselor?"

"Can you imagine the nightmare we'd have, trying to schedule something like that? Besides, Arnold would never consent. Like I said, the man is bullheaded. He's convinced all our marital problems are my fault. Why should he have to submit to the humiliation of counseling when he's the perfect one?" The word *perfect* was spoken with a sneer.

"Would it help if I spoke with the two of you together?"

"You'd have to find a way to bring the topic up as if you'd thought of it yourself. If he even suspected I'd shared this with you, I'd never hear the end of it." She looked at him with an expression that suggested frustration and defeat.

Daniel looked out the window. "That river's been flowing through that valley for a long, long time. It will still be flowing, long after you and I have left the scene." He looked at Sandy and smiled. "It reminds me of God's faithfulness. It just keeps on flowing. It's greater than we are. It outlasts us. Even when we feel like we can't make things work, God stays with us, always faithful."

Sandy offered a wry smile. "Well, that's hopeful, I guess. But when I look at the river, it reminds me of Arnold."

"In what way?"

"No matter what I say to him, no matter how logical or reasonable I try to be with him, he just keeps on going, with that Johnny-one-note argument of his. It's always the same damn thing…I'm sorry, Pastor. I'm feeling kind of bitter about this. It's always the same with Arnold. He's the husband. He should get his way. I'm the wife. I should do what he wants. Getting married, in his mind, is an unspoken agreement that we'll try to have kids, evidently on his schedule. On his terms."

She glared at Daniel. "What is it with men, anyway?" He shifted uncomfortably in his chair. "Present company excepted, I mean." He offered a weak smile.

She sat up straight in her chair, inhaled and let it out heavily. "Still, I'm ready to admit, some of this is my fault. I've been putting him off. I've probably convinced him we don't have a real marriage. And, it occurs to me, I could drive him into the arms of a prostitute if I'm not careful."

An image flashed into Daniel's mind, from more than fifteen years before. An attractive young woman, who later turned out to be a professional escort, had once tried to seduce him, first in his study at church, later in her well-appointed apartment. He had almost succumbed to her wiles.

Sandy continued, "So, I've decided the next time Arnold says he wants to have us start a family, I won't put him off."

"You're finally ready?"

She nodded.

"Why do you have to wait until Arnold suggests it?"

"Excuse me?"

"Why don't you suggest it yourself."

The thought had, evidently, not occurred to her. She offered a wry smile. "There's at least one problem with doing it that way."

"And what would that be?"

"Arnold might just have a heart attack and drop dead from surprise."

"DAD?"

"Yes, Joshua Daniel?"

"Are you going to be upset with me if I don't go to Capital University, like Hannah Ruth did?"

Daniel looked at his son, across the dining room table, and smiled. The meal was over, the dishes had been cleared, and Rosetta was busy in the kitchen.

"You already told me you were going to Wartburg. And, anyway, why would I be upset?"

"Well, you and Mom went there. And Hannah Ruth is going there."

"Hannah Ruth went to Capital because Lillian Fischer thought she should go to the Conservatory of Music there."

"I know. But isn't it some sort of legacy if you go to the same college your parents went to?"

Daniel shrugged. "I suppose. But that's not important, really. You should go to college where you'll be happy. And, where you can learn what you'll need for whatever it is you decide to do with the rest of your life."

"That's another thing. What if...what if I...you know...decide not to...not to go on to seminary...to become a pastor?"

"Were you considering becoming one?"

Josh hesitated. He realized he didn't really know the answer. "Sarah Engelhardt thinks I should consider it."

"Does she."

"Yeah. But, here's the deal. I don't want to become a pastor just because you did."

"That sounds reasonable."

Josh returned a hopeful expression. "You mean you don't care if I become a pastor or not?"

"If you decided to become a pastor, I'd be very pleased. And proud. But, what I meant was, if you become a pastor, you shouldn't choose that just because I did."

That didn't seem to settle the question for Josh. "But, what if I decided to do something else?"

"Joshua Daniel, I think Martin Luther had it right. He said any vocation can be God-pleasing, if it's one that matches your gifts. Nobody should despise a farmer or a factory worker or even a garbage collector. You can do any of those things to the glory of God." He paused. A wry grin crept into his face. "Of course, given your gifts, I certainly hope you don't decide to spend your life collecting garbage."

Josh laughed. "That's not going to happen, Dad." He mulled what he'd just heard from his father, then said, "The problem is, I don't know how to decide what I *should* do. How did you know what you should do with your life?"

Daniel leaned back in his chair, stroked his chin with his thumb and forefinger, and reflected on his son's question. "Well, choosing your father's career might be the easy way out. And the wrong choice. I didn't do that, as you know."

"Of course not. Grampa ran a lumber yard. But how come you didn't?"

"Well, I went away to college and…you know, Joshua Daniel, you're the first person in about thirty years to make me think about this."

"Here's what I want to know mostly. Did you have some big moment of discovery? Or was it a slow, gradual process? I mean, discovering you could probably be a pretty good pastor, if you wanted to."

Daniel grinned. "The official answer, of course, is that it was a slow process of discernment. And I truly believe that the Holy Spirit was tugging at me to consider it. Besides, the seminary was right across the street, so that option was always right in front of me."

"And what's the unofficial answer?"

Daniel had a faint smile on his face. He leaned across the table, toward his son, and said, in a low, almost mysterious voice, "The unofficial answer is that your mother told me I had all the qualities a good pastor would need, and that I should think very seriously about it."

Josh looked wide-eyed at his father. He'd never heard that bit of information before. He said, "So, in other words, I should be paying attention to what Sarah is saying to me."

Daniel sat up straight. "Well, I don't know. Are you planning to marry her?"

"Why do you ask?"

"Because your mother and I were engaged when she told me that."

Josh thought about it. "What would you think if I married her? Sarah, I mean."

"She's a delightful young woman. But don't start making any wedding plans just yet. You need to wait until after college."

"And after seminary too, then, right?"

"Are you planning to go to seminary?"

"Well, actually, no. At least, not now. I don't know. I'm not sure."

"What do you think you really want to do with the rest of your life, Joshua Daniel?"

His son sat thinking, for perhaps half a minute. Then he said, "I want to do something that will help people. I want to make the world better. Maybe as a pastor. Maybe not. Maybe I'll know by the time I get out of college."

"Good plan," Daniel replied. "Just don't forget to let me know when you finally decide."

Chapter 18

Lillian Fischer set her coffee cup down. Harry Broadman looked at her, waiting for an answer to his question. She said, "Well, since you asked, the oratorio I'm planning for the twenty-fifth anniversary celebration is on schedule. I'm beginning to compose the sections. And, it now has a name."

The other members of the planning task force perked up.

"It will be called 'The Glory and the Wonder.' It should run about forty minutes. I plan to incorporate all four choirs, and provide solos for soprano, alto, tenor, and bass. There will be a half-dozen hymns included, all from our church hymnal, so the congregation can participate as well."

Jens Jorgensen, who had joined the group at Harry's invitation, flashed an impish grin. "I don't suppose any of us dare guess who will get the tenor solo parts."

Lillian looked at him impatiently. "The best tenor voice should get them," she replied sardonically.

Jens said, "And that would be Luther Fischer, right?"

Tom Pavelka jumped in. "I'd be mad as the devil if Luther *didn't* sing those parts."

Lillian looked appreciatively at Tom for coming to her rescue.

"Didn't I hear you say there was going to be a small orchestra as well?" Harry prodded.

"Yes," Lillian replied. "Some friends of mine from the Minneapolis Symphony. Only about ten players." She looked at Jens. "If we can afford them, that is."

"The fund-raising is going great," Jens assured her. "Don't worry about paying the musicians."

"I'm getting kind of excited about the neighborhood cell groups starting up," Harry said rubbing his palms together. "By next fall they should be ready to go. At least, that's what Pastor Ward tells me."

"I'm trying to imagine this," said Tom. "Three hundred living room groups, all over the metropolitan area. That's a lot of living rooms."

"Pastor Ward had better hurry up and get this thing launched," said Harry. "Janet Fenstermacher told me last week that the congregation has reached 6,300 members. If we don't get moving, we're going to need even *more* living rooms."

"ARNOLD, LET ME ask you something."

"Mmmm?" Arnold Elliot's nose was buried in the Minneapolis *Tribune*.

"Put that paper down. I want to be sure you're listening."

He sighed and dropped the paper into his lap. "What?"

"When are we going to start having children?"

Sandy Elliot had expected disbelief, or possibly even enthusiasm. Instead, what she got was stony silence.

"Did you hear me?"

"Wha...? I...Yeah. I heard you."

"Well?"

"Children? You want children?"

"I know you think I'm making this up, but I'm finally ready to start having kids. You've been nagging me about it since the day we got married. So, are we going to start having them or not?"

"Well...you mean now?"

"Arnold, what's the matter with you?"

"Children! Holy blazes." He seemed to weigh the suggestion, as if it were a brand new idea. "Can I think about this for a couple days?"

"What's to think about? I'm cutting back at the supper club. I have time to raise children now. This is the right time."

Arnold gave her a look she couldn't decipher. She returned one of her own, a scowl that made it abundantly clear she was getting irritated.

He finally said, "It's just that...you know...you always said no before. You caught me by surprise."

"Well, get over it, Arnold. Because I want a baby."

JENNY LANGHOLZ leaned back against the headboard and tucked her legs up close. Facing her, Hannah Ruth Jonas had assumed a similar posture.

"It seems like a lifetime ago since we sat here like this, Jenny."

"I know. It was back in high school. We were talking about boys. You were trying to talk me out of going out with Buzz." She offered a rueful look.

"Boy, I should have listened to you."

"Is he still in jail?"

"I don't know. I just know that, if he comes near me, the police will put him away for a long, long time. So I guess that's the good news."

"What's the bad news?"

"I don't have a boyfriend. Probably never will have."

"Aren't there any nice young men over there at the Teachers' College in River Falls?"

"Plenty. But nobody I'd want to get serious about."

"Why not?"

"I'm giving up on boys...men...whatever you want to call them."

"Don't give up, Jenny."

"You know what? I tried double dating with my roommate a couple times. I found it almost repulsive."

"Why?"

"I don't know. I just don't trust guys anymore. They talk polite to you. Maybe they're even sincere. But I keep remembering, that's how it started out with Buzz. Look how it ended up."

"It wouldn't be that way again, Jenny."

"How do you know that? How can you tell?"

"You just have to trust people."

"I trusted Buzz."

Hannah Ruth sighed heavily. This was going nowhere. She decided to change the subject. "John and I are going back to Camp Saint Michael to be counselors again this summer. We leave on the weekend."

Jenny frowned.

"Why don't you come with us? They can always use more help up there."

"No. I'd be like a fifth wheel on a four-wheel cart. You two are so perfect together. Why should I spend the summer watching the two of you enjoy each other's company?"

Hannah Ruth looked compassionately at her best friend. "You still haven't forgiven me for taking John away from you, have you?"

Jenny's face showed alarm. "What? No. That's not true. Anyway, John chose you, not the other way around." She hesitated. "At least, that's what you told me originally."

Hannah Ruth nodded. "I told the truth. It was John's idea."

Jenny said, "I think I'll spend the summer babysitting in the neighborhood. Mom knows a family that needs some help. I've already asked them."

"They need a sitter during the day?"

"Both parents have jobs to go to. A lot of women are going off to work these days. They need somebody to help with their children. I don't know how they manage during the school year, but during the summer it's an opportunity for somebody like me to make some money."

"You sure you want to spend your summer hanging around home?"

"Positive."

Hannah Ruth said, "I wish you'd have come to Capital University with me."

Jenny said, "Well, what's done is done. River Falls is a perfectly good school. I've decided to be an elementary school teacher. I know I'd be good at it."

"You will. You'll be a great teacher."

"What about you, Hannah Ruth? What are you going to do with that music degree of yours?"

"I don't know exactly."

"Weren't you going to come back here and get a music position after you graduated?"

"Well, yes, I was, but..."

"But, what? You're not coming back?"

"I just don't know yet."

"What's changed?"

"Well, John has. He's rethinking his future."

"Wasn't he going to become a chemical engineer or something?"

"He wasn't sure for the longest time. But now he thinks he wants to study medicine."

"What?"

"Yes. He wants to become a doctor."

"Well," said Jenny, arching an eyebrow, "how does that make you feel—the wife of a future M.D.?"

"It's going to take a lot longer for him to get finished. By the time he gets through medical school, we'll probably both be in the poor house."

"No. It's perfect. He can study at the University of Minnesota. You can give organ lessons and teach music in public school, maybe in the same school I'm teaching in."

"Well...it might not work out like that."

"Why not?"

"He's thinking about attending Hahnemann Medical School in

Philadelphia. He found out it was a really good place to go."

"Philadelphia! You might as well be moving to Europe!"

"He hasn't definitely decided to go there. Not yet."

"But he will. I can tell. I can see it in your eyes."

"He really hasn't decided yet."

"Well, I know I should be excited for you. But I'm not."

"You're upset, aren't you?"

"I think the whole idea stinks."

"Jenny, I'm sorry. We might still come back to Minnesota. Eventually."

"What, in ten more years or so?"

Hannah Ruth was silent. She desperately wanted to change the subject. She said, "My baby brother's going to go to Wartburg College."

"No kidding."

"He just got accepted."

"What do you think of that?"

"It's fine with me."

"At least you won't have him underfoot at Capital."

"I'm really glad he's made that choice. He needs to make his own way. He doesn't need his big sister checking up on him for the next two years."

"Your folks okay with him going there?"

"My dad's fine with it. My mom...well, I think she wishes he wasn't leaving home."

"Why not? He's out of high school. He has to go somewhere."

"I know. But..."

"But what?"

"Well, my mom's sort of strange about Josh. I think it's because of that time when he was a baby. She almost lost him when that creep stole him off the front porch. I think she's afraid of losing him again."

"Criminy. You can't hold onto your kids forever."

"I know that. And Mom knows that. And she'll be brave about it when he finally leaves. She's just having a hard time with the whole thing."

"PASTOR, HERE'S ANOTHER IDEA for you to chew on, along with your salad."

Harry Broadman grinned at Daniel Jonas, across his favorite table at the Minneapolis Club.

"You're just full of ideas, Harry," Daniel said. "Doesn't that well of yours ever run dry?"

"I'm an idea person, remember? That's what General Mills pays me for—great ideas."

"Okay, what's your latest brainstorm, Harry?"

"The congregation buys a full-page advertisement on the back page of the first news section of the *Tribune*. It appears the week before the celebration service at the Minneapolis Auditorium. It invites the entire city to our big event. And there can also be something in there about Lillian Fischer's new oratorio. In fact, we could use the name of the oratorio as a big headline across the top of the ad."

The businessman held his hands apart, as if framing a newspaper page. He announced grandly, "The Glory and the Wonder! Twenty-five Years of Amazing Growth in South Minneapolis!" Then, underneath, we can print the full schedule of what's going to happen during the celebration week. And maybe a map, to show people how to find exactly where Anderson Avenue and Caldwell Street is. We'd print photographs of all the pastors. Yours would be bigger than the others, of course."

"Harry! Slow down! Too many ideas, coming too fast. I can hardly digest all of this."

"Just respond to the general idea, Pastor. Do you like it or not?"

The waiter came and took away the salad plates. When he was gone, Daniel said, "It sounds pretty grandiose to me. Do we really want to brag to the whole city about our success?"

"It's not bragging. It's taking pride in our assets, and inviting people to share them with us."

"You know what they say about pride, Harry."

"That's only if it's pride-*full*. This wouldn't be."

"What would the difference be?"

"Well, like you said. Bragging. We don't need to brag. We just tell. And invite."

"But won't people see it as bragging?"

"People read newspaper advertisements and they think all sorts of things. Some people might think General Mills brags when it advertises that Cheerios and Wheaties are better than any other cereals. It does the job, though. Those two are the best-selling brands in the country right now."

"But this is a Christian congregation, not a product you can peddle with advertising."

"'Don't hide your light under a bushel.' I learned that growing up in Bird City, Kansas. It's in the Bible, you know."

"I know, Harry, I know. But that refers to your faith in Christ."

"Well, that's what this ad would be about. We have this wonderful faith in Christ, and it's enabled us to grow to over 6,300 members. Why should we apologize for that?"

"We shouldn't apologize for it. But we need to think about the smaller congregations in the city. There are a lot of Lutherans who would be offended if we started shouting about how big and wonderful we are."

"It's only once every twenty-five years."

Daniel realized he wasn't making his point successfully. He changed tactics. "Harry, it's a theological problem for me."

"How's that?"

"Lutherans believe there are two ways to think about the church. One is called the Theology of Glory. That's what you've just been talking about. The other way is the Theology of the Cross."

"I don't get it. What's the difference?"

"The Theology of Glory wants success without suffering. It wants to be in charge. It wants to throw its weight around. It's like having Easter without Good Friday."

Harry looked puzzled.

"The Theology of the Cross is what Lutherans believe is the authentic way to think about God and the church and our lives. It focuses on Jesus' suffering and death on the cross. And it remembers that sacrifice and suffering and humility are really the only things that change the world for the better. That's why Jesus died. We should imitate that, and try to be like Jesus."

"So, then, what good is Easter if all we care about is Good Friday?"

"Easter is God's way of telling us that Good Friday really works. If you follow the path of humility, and maybe even suffering, you won't be sorry. You'll be a winner in the end."

Harry pondered what he'd just heard. "But our church building and our big congregation seem pretty glorious. Don't you think so?"

Daniel nodded. "That's why we have to be more careful than ever not to swagger, and not to forget to live with humility. You can still make that work in a large congregation like ours, but it takes more work."

Harry sat thinking. Finally he said, "So the full-page ad isn't such a great idea then?"

Daniel grinned. "How about a full-page ad in David Engelhardt's neighborhood newspaper?"

"Oh, we'd planned to do that all along. But, you know, we're not just a neighborhood church anymore. We have members all over Hennepin County now. I still think an ad in the *Tribune* would be entirely appropriate."

Daniel sat thinking for a minute or two. "All right, Harry. Plan to run the ad. Just don't use 'The Glory and the Wonder' for the headline." He paused. "And the photos of the pastors—you make those all exactly the same size."

Chapter 19

"You sure this is going to work okay?"

Josh Jonas looked uncertainly at Sarah Engelhardt. He had just helped her move into the student nurses' residence at Fairview Hospital School of Nursing, and was now sitting with her in the lounge. He slid closer to her on the couch.

"It's going to be fine, Josh. I'm really excited about this. In three years, I'll be a nurse. Then I can start earning money to help you finish paying for college."

"But you're going to be here, and I'm going to be way down in Iowa." Suddenly Wartburg College seemed to Josh as though it were located in a foreign country.

"We'll write. You'll be home for Thanksgiving and Christmas. It will be okay."

"Just don't fall for any of those Luther Seminary students. I understand they come prowling around here, looking for future wives."

"Don't worry about me, Josh. Just make sure you don't go after some cute Iowa girl down there in Waverly." She leaned close and kissed him on the cheek.

"I wish you were coming to college with me."

"We've been over this. I've decided I really want to be a nurse. This is a good place to train for that. I can't do that at Wartburg College."

"You know what's ironic about all of this? I first decided to go to Wartburg because you said you were planning to go there."

She nodded. "I know. But people change their minds. You have to accept that. This is really the better choice for me. Okay?"

Josh sighed. "Okay." He looked miserable.

"Look on the bright side. You'll be getting free medical care for the rest of your life." She grinned. "Isn't it the neatest thing? Your sister's marrying a medical doctor. You're dating a nurse."

The import of what she'd just said stabbed at him. "I can't afford an engagement ring. Yet. And I've never talked to you about this. But I want to make this very clear, Sarah. I plan to marry you some day. You'll wait for me, won't you?"

"Wow, that's the weirdest marriage proposal I've ever heard. Is that what it was?"

He looked sheepish. "Yeah. I guess."

"Are you saying this now because you're afraid you might lose me otherwise?"

"I'm saying it because I wish I could marry you right now. But I can't."

"Josh, I'll marry you after you get through college and…" she studied him for a moment. "Are you planning to go to seminary, or not?"

"I don't know. Yet. Would that make a difference?"

"Well, maybe. If you go, we probably should wait until you finish."

"Then maybe I won't go."

"Josh! You're not going to make me responsible for you skipping seminary!"

He offered a pensive gaze. "Life sure has gotten complicated since high school."

"You mean, in the three whole months since we graduated?"

He grinned. "I'm gonna miss you so darn much."

"I'll miss you too. Come on. I'll walk you out."

"COME ON, I'll walk you in," said Aaron, picking up his mother's suitcase at the curb. Rebekah Ward waved the taxi away, then smoothed the fabric on her trim skirt and jacket and checked to feel if her newly-coifed hair was still in place.

"Will you relax, Mother? Your grandchildren aren't going to care how your hair looks," the young pastor said, leading the way up the front walk.

"No, but your stylish young wife will notice," said Rebekah. "We can't have her spreading stories about how dowdy her mother-in-law looks, now can we?"

Aaron sighed. They weren't even to the front door yet, and already his mother was starting. How, he wondered, would they survive ten days with her?

"Gramma, Gramma!" shouted five-year-old Elizabeth as they arrived in the living room. The blond, curly-haired youngster jumped up from her dollhouse and ran into Rebekah's arms.

With an indulgent smile, the older woman said, "Elizabeth, darling, can you say 'Grandmother'? That's far more ladylike than 'Gramma.' Whoever taught you to say such a thing?"

Aaron rolled his eyes, then went away with the suitcase, down the hall toward the guest room.

Aaron's wife, Alice, appeared at the dining room doorway. "Hello, Mother Ward. Welcome to our new home."

Rebekah looked around. "Well, it doesn't look all that new, does it?"

"It's an older house. But it's new to us."

"Yes. Well, if Aaron had gone into business like his father, you could have been living in a nice upscale house in Grosse Pointe by now. But, never mind."

Alice bit her tongue.

"Where's baby James?" asked Rebekah, looking around as if she might spot the three-year-old hiding behind a piece of furniture.

"It's nap time. I've put him down," Alice replied. She hesitated before adding, "And he's not really a baby anymore."

"Well, he's *my* baby. He always will be."

Aaron reappeared and stood next to his wife. "You must be tired from the train trip, Mother. Would you like to lie down?"

"Nonsense. I'm just fine. We should have tea. You do make tea, don't you, Alice?"

"Mother, she made tea for you every time you visited us in Saginaw."

"Well, then, I think we should have some."

AS THE PLATE of freshly-baked nut bread went around, Rebekah Ward looked at Aaron and said, "I'm sorry your father couldn't come. Again. He never seems to want to come along with me. Some excuse this time about needing to finish still another project for the company." She paused, sipped her tea, and added, "If you ask me, General Motors owes him a fat bonus for all the extra work he does for them."

Aaron wanted to change the subject. "How was the train trip?"

"Oh, like all the others. The porters were rude. They never have what you really want in the dining car. And it takes frightfully long to get all the way out here to the frontier."

"Mom, it's Minnesota, not the Wild West."

"Well, it's a long way from Detroit. And how am I supposed to get to know my grandchildren if they're living so far away?"

"Maybe you should fly next time."

"And maybe *you* should come to Grosse Pointe more often."

"It's a big congregation, Mother. I'm busy. It's hard to get away."

"Well, why didn't you get a call to Mount Zion in Detroit, then? We have 5,000 members, just like your congregation..."

"Actually, we have 6,500 now, Mother Ward," Alice interjected gingerly.

"What? You're larger than Mount Zion? That's not possible."

"I know," said Aaron. "Your congregation has always been the largest in the American Lutheran Church. But it was bound to happen that some other parish might grow larger one day. And Saint Michael Church seems to have."

"Well," huffed Rebekah, "there must be some mistake in the records. Are you sure you actually have that many members? You shouldn't be counting inactives and drop-aways, you know."

"Besides, Mother, pastors don't arrange for where they're going to be called. They wait for..."

"Yes, yes, I know. The Holy Spirit has to call you. Technically speaking. But who really believes that? It's all church politics. Everybody knows it is. I'll bet you could have gotten a call to Mount Zion if you'd wanted to."

Aaron looked at his half-empty cup of tea. He thought, but did not say, *Mother, I wouldn't have accepted a position in a congregation where you're a member if it had been the last call available on the planet.*

PERCHED ON A BENCH built into the front of his classroom desk, the middle-aged professor with blazing eyes leaned forward, toward his enraptured students. He said, "Now I'm sure all of you think that a hamburger in a sandwich shop down there on Bremer Avenue is probably about the best meal a young person can imagine having."

Josh Jonas looked up from the notes he'd been furiously writing, wondering where Professor Ottersberg was heading with such a comment. This was supposed to be a lecture about the fall of the Roman Empire.

"Well, the Huns, who began moving south and west, against the borders of the empire, had their own methods for food preparation, some of which would, I suspect, raise a few eyebrows in a group like this."

A wry smirk crept into the instructor's face as he explained, "A hunnish warrior would often take a juicy slab of raw, red meat, slap it down on the back of his horse, lay his saddle on top of it, and then ride hard on it, all day long." He paused for effect. "It was a tenderizing process, you see. And, then, in the evening, he'd pull it out and devour this tasty treat for his evening meal."

There were looks of disbelief on every freshman student's face. The professor ended the vignette with a dramatic flourish. "I dare say he considered it to be every bit as delicious a delicacy as anything they'd serve up over here in the college cafeteria!"

The room exploded in laughter.

The professor hopped down from his perch, pointed to the reading assignment chalked on the board, and then walked out of the room.

AS THEY HEADED for the lunch line, Josh and his roommate, George Krantz, processed what they'd just experienced. "That Professor Ottersberg is amazing," said George. "Every lecture, he tells these stories and hypnotizes the class. And then he hits them with a zinger at the end. How does he do that?"

"Well, he doesn't hypnotize *me*," Josh replied.

"Huh? Well, if he doesn't, you're the only one."

"Can't afford to fall into a trance in *that* class. I need to take good notes. For the exam. My hand always hurts from writing after I get out of there."

"Well, you don't have to write it all down, you know. It's just an elective."

"Not for me."

"What do you mean? You're a philosophy major, right?"

"I'm changing."

"What! When did you decide that?"

"After about the fifth Ottersberg lecture. This professor is incredible. I've decided I want to major in history. I want to take all his courses."

"What's your dad going to say?"

"What's he got to do with it?"

"You told me he was a philosophy major. Isn't that why you picked that?"

"Yeah. Maybe. Probably. I didn't know what else to pick. Now I know."

"Why don't you pick something that's practical."

"Like what?"

"Like business. That's what I'm taking."

Josh shook his head. "I have no interest in that. None whatsoever."

"There's more money in it. If you get the right job."

"Money isn't everything."

"Tell that to the treasurer's office."

"You really think I'm all wet, choosing history, don't you?"

George stopped on the sidewalk, turned toward Josh and said, "What are you going to do with it? You could do research. Or you could teach it. What else is it good for?"

"It's good for...explaining how things got the way they are."

"And why does that matter?"

"Because. Once we understand how we got here, maybe we can figure out how to change things. And maybe make the world better than it is."

"ONE MORE DAY," Alice Ward whispered to her husband.

Aaron, who had been lying awake for twenty minutes, rolled over in the darkness and drew his arms around his wife. He pulled her close and whispered back, "You've been a good soldier. I don't know how you did it."

"What I just don't understand," said Alice, "is why nothing is ever right for your mother. She complains and criticizes and finds fault with everything we do."

"Now you know why I took the call to come to Minnesota and not the one to Toledo, Ohio. She'd have been on our front porch every time we turned around."

Alice giggled. "I thought you were supposed to let the Holy Spirit tell you which call to accept."

"Oh, you're right, of course. And, when Pastor Jonas wrote me that letter, the Holy Spirit gave me the best advice possible."

SARAH ENGELHARDT was sitting in her dormitory room, studying for the following Monday's classes. It was a Saturday afternoon, and the radio was playing in the background, big-band music from one of the local stations.

The first time the headache came, she thought it was because she'd been concentrating too hard on the book in front of her. She backed away from the desk, stood up, and tried to relax. Sometimes, she'd discovered, a tense headache would go away if she simply stood perfectly still, allowed herself to go limp and then let it drain out of her.

This time it didn't work. The headache persisted. She found an aspirin, and then went to get a glass of water. By the time she had swallowed the pill, her head was pounding. Not sure what else to do, she lay down on her bed and tried to relax again.

The pain began to subside, gradually, until it was completely gone.

She waited twenty minutes, then got up and returned to the desk. As she began to read, she felt the throbbing start to return. Troubled, and a little irritated, she closed the book, sat up as straight as she could, and closed her eyes.

Everything seemed to go white. And then it began. There crowded into her consciousness a vision of Josh. He was kneeling, holding onto something. He was in pain. He looked miserable.

As suddenly as the images had crowded into her head, they evaporated.

An hour later, after she'd found it impossible to return to her studying, or to sleep, she pulled a sheet of writing paper from her desk drawer and began to pen a letter to Josh.

A week after she mailed it, she received a reply.

Dearest Sarah,

Thanks for your letter. It's the strangest thing, what you wrote. Last Saturday, at lunchtime, my roommate and I decided to skip the meal in the college cafeteria. We went to a place a lot of students like. They make these amazing egg and cheese sandwiches. I watched the cook float the egg in so much grease, it never touched the surface of the griddle. It sounds like a horrible way to make a sandwich, but they sure taste good.

Of course, it helps if you have a cast-iron stomach. A couple hours later, I was on my knees in the bathroom. I lost the whole meal. I think food at Roy's Place takes getting used to. I might go back, or I might not.

What I'm curious about is how you knew I wasn't feeling well on Saturday. I didn't actually tell anybody.

You should hear this incredible history professor we have here. Last week he told about an heir to the throne of some French kingdom or another. The guy was on horseback, chasing young women who were on foot, running through the city gate, which was evidently pretty low. The professor ended the lecture by saying, "The poor fool forgot to duck. It literally knocked his block off."

I miss you. See you at Christmas. Oh, did I remember to tell you? My roommate wants me to go home with him for Thanksgiving, so we're heading to Chicago. Don't be angry. I told him it had to be Thanksgiving, because I'm spending Christmas with you.

With all my love, Josh

Chapter 20

George Krantz steered his father's automobile along the busy boulevard, all the while talking a mile a minute. "Chicago's a great place, Josh. You can't believe all the stuff that's here. We've got the Museum of Science and Industry, and the Chicago Zoo, and the Cubs. Oh, and there's that other pro-baseball team, too."

Josh laughed. "Cubs fans don't have much use for the White Sox, I hear."

"That's an understatement. If we could just figure out a way for the Cubs to win a few more games, everything would be hunky dory." He turned onto a wide residential boulevard and headed east. "And, of course, there's the University of Chicago, one of the best academic schools in the country."

"How come you didn't go there?"

"Well, aside from the fact that it's a bigger school than I wanted to go to, and the fact that we're pretty strong Lutherans, and my folks wanted me going to our church college, there's the fact that the U. of Chicago sits in a pretty rough neighborhood. My Mom wasn't too hot on me walking around on that campus for four years."

"This neighborhood we're driving through isn't the greatest either, I'm noticing."

"That's why I'm bringing you down here. Oh, by the way, don't tell my folks we were in this part of the city. Tell them we drove to the University campus. I'll make sure we go over there later, so it won't be a lie."

"So, how come you brought me here, George?"

"There's something I want you to see. It's pretty amazing."

Eight more blocks brought them to an intersection, where the car slowed to a crawl. George pointed toward the curb. "Look at that church building."

"It's...enormous," said Josh. "Must be Roman Catholic. They seem to have all the big buildings."

"No, in fact it's currently the Church of God of Apostolic Fire."

"Never heard of it."

"All sorts of churches like that down here in the rough part of town. But the reason I wanted you to see it was, this used to be our Lutheran congregation. It once had 4,000 members. Look at those huge stained-glass windows. It was a beauty."

"What happened?"

"The neighborhood changed. All the German Lutherans moved out. My folks included. That's why we're in the west suburbs now. The crime rate in this part of town started going up. White people got scared. They sold their houses for ridiculously low prices. That just drove the property values down faster. Pretty soon there was nobody here to keep this church going. They ended up with about a hundred people in the pews. That's pretty incredible when you consider, you can seat about a thousand in there. So, of course, things became impossible for them. They couldn't pay the heat, or the insurance, or the upkeep on this place."

"So they sold it?"

"At first, the building just stood empty. There was a gorgeous stained-glass window up over the altar. It showed Jesus walking and talking to two of his disciples. One Sunday morning, toward the end, a rock came crashing through that window, right during Holy Communion. Pieces of Jesus' face landed all over the altar and the chancel carpet. We weren't attending here anymore when that happened. But some of the members who were there told my folks about it. One dear old lady almost had a heart attack."

"That must have been terrible."

"It was about a month later when they voted to close. They just walked away from this big stone cathedral, and left it sitting here."

"You said the Church of God of something-or-other owns it now."

"The Church of God of Apostolic Fire. Yeah. They bought it for about five hundred dollars. But they can't really afford to keep it up either. My dad says there were almost four hundred of them in their congregation when they moved in. Maybe more now. But I guess they wear their heavy coats to church all winter long. They can't afford to heat the place. So, of course, all the water pipes froze and burst and so, now there's no plumbing in the building either."

"That's really sad."

"Well, yeah, I guess. But look at this neighborhood." George kept driving along the boulevard, past houses that had obviously once been inhabited by people of considerable means. "This whole area is going down. People don't want to live here. Trouble is, a lot of them are just stuck. They'll never get out.

And, of course, that means the young people will end up in gangs, or have babies when they're not married, or who knows what."

"Is anybody helping these people?"

"Well, I'm sure the folks at the Church of God of Apostolic Fire do their part. But it's a huge problem. Nobody really knows how to fix it." He snickered. "My dad once said he had the solution. Just bulldoze down the whole neighborhood and start over." He glanced at Josh, who looked incredulous. "Some solution, huh." He grinned ironically. "My dad wasn't really serious."

ARNOLD ELLIOT looked puzzled. Why had his wife invited him to dinner at her own supper club? And why had she arranged for a secluded table, with candlelight, and a bottle of expensive wine?

"It's a special occasion," she said. "The wine's for you. I'm not supposed to have any."

"According to whom?"

"My doctor."

He looked suspiciously at her.

"I'm giving you an early Christmas present, Arnold."

"What? A romantic dinner?"

"No, Goofy. I'm pregnant."

He stared at her, incredulous.

"Don't you have anything to say?"

"I…ahh…holy buckets, are you sure?"

"I'm positive." She waited for his next sentence, which didn't come. "Aren't you happy for us? I thought you'd be ecstatic."

"Well, Sandy, to tell you the truth, I'm a little worried."

"What? Why?"

"The thing is, I've gotten the air charter service going really well now. And my best customers are all wanting to fly to Chicago and stay over for several days at a time, as you know. I don't really want to cut back, now that it's finally working for me."

"Who said you had to?"

"Well, what kind of a father am I going to make if I'm gone all the time?"

"I guess you should have thought of that before you got me pregnant." Arnold blinked. "Anyway, what's the problem? I know you're gone a lot of the time. But you always come back. We can raise children with a father who travels. Lots of couples do that."

Arnold pursed his lips. He nodded tentatively. Then he said, "Well, somebody better drink this wine. We can't let it go to waste." He poured himself a glass and lifted it, as if to toast his wife. "Here's to...whoever we end up having."

JOSH LAY SPRAWLED crossways on the mattress, flat on his back, his hands clasped behind his neck, his legs dangling off the side. Sarah lay on her side next to him. He marveled that her parents let them spend private time in her bedroom, with the door closed.

"One more day and I have to go back to college. Rats. I wish I could stay here with you. Maybe I could transfer to Augsburg College."

"Then you'd miss all those lectures by Professor Ottersman."

"Ottersberg."

"It's been great having you home. I really missed you."

"Prove it."

She leaned close and kissed him softly on the mouth. He sighed with contentment. "Now I *absolutely* can't go back to Iowa."

"You'll be home for Easter. And, in the meantime, we'll just keep writing letters to each other."

He rolled over on his side, facing her. "I'm curious about something."

"What?"

"That letter you sent me back in October. You told me you knew when I was sick to my stomach. How did you know that, exactly?"

She returned a distant look. "I don't know, actually. I just...did."

"Did you dream it, or what?"

"It just sort of came to me." She paused and thought about how to say the next thing. "Do you promise not to think I'm crazy if I tell you what it was like?"

"You? Crazy? Never!"

"Well, it was like a vision almost. I wasn't asleep. I was wide awake. I just suddenly got this picture of you, down on your knees, in a lot of pain."

"I was in the men's room, bending over the stool. Did your vision tell you that?"

"No. Just that you were in some kind of trouble."

He furrowed his brow and looked at her uncertainly.

"Josh, I never told you this, but it happened to me one other time. Before you went away to college." His eyes grew wider. "I think that other time, it actually *might have been* a dream. I was asleep. I got this...sort of vision...about my Uncle Martin. I knew he was in danger, but I didn't know how or why. I told Mom about it. Later, when Uncle Martin wrote to us, it turned out I got the mental picture about him at almost exactly the time when it was happening."

Josh looked at her in amazement. "So, you're a mind-reader, then. Is that it?"

"I don't know. I checked a book out of the library, about premonitions and foreknowledge and things like that. I don't really understand it very well."

"Does the book say why it happens?"

"Nobody seems to know, exactly. The theory is that certain kinds of people have this ability...or gift, if you want to call it that."

"What kind of people would that be?"

"Well, as far as I can tell, people like me."

"PASTOR, CAN WE TALK?"

Daniel Jonas looked up from the sermon notes he was busy revising. In the doorway to his office stood Maggie Washington. The crusty, forty-nine-year-old redhead had run the congregation's social ministry program for the past dozen years.

"Sure, Maggie. Come on in."

He gestured to one of the chairs on the other side of his desk, as he came around to take a seat in the other one.

"I'm concerned about those six houses across the alley."

"The ones the church owns, north of the parking ramp?"

"Exactly. I think they're starting to be a problem."

"Why do you say that?"

"Well, the church council gave my ministry team permission to manage them. And we've got them all rented out, as you know, at bargain rates, to families who need cheap housing."

"And...?"

"And I think we're being taken advantage of."

"How so?"

"Well, one of the families has stopped paying their rent. They keep saying they don't have it. But I notice they have a brand new car in the driveway. There's another house where the family seems to have invited all their relatives to move in with them. I think they may be violating some sort of fire code. It's almost turned into a rooming house. And in another one, there's a family where the husband moved out and I think the wife has a boyfriend in there with her. She has three young children still living with her."

"What about the other three houses?"

"Well, at this exact moment, no problems that I can detect. But, at the rate we're going, who knows how long that will hold up?"

"What do you think we should do, Maggie?"

"Well, mainly, be aware of it. I'm not cut out to be a landlady. I realize the congregation pays my salary, but I have a lot of other stuff to do without riding herd on a bunch of people who don't know how to behave in the houses we let them use."

"It sounds as if we need to rethink the management of those properties."

Maggie sighed. "I hate to admit it, but the Property Committee might do a better job. I really thought I could handle it. I really wanted to see it work out. It seemed like such a perfect way to help out people in the neighborhood." She frowned. "Sometimes I think I'm just too idealistic for my own good."

"Community ministry is never easy, Maggie. The easy thing would be not to try doing anything at all. You always have new ideas for us to consider, and you have a good way of pushing us into new directions. Your instincts are almost always right. Don't be discouraged if, once in awhile, something doesn't work out the way you hoped it would."

"Well, thanks for the words of affirmation. And, believe me, I really do love this work. Even my husband, Henry, secular socialist that he is, thinks I'm doing a bang-up job."

Daniel thought she might be blushing, but it was hard to tell, underneath the sea of freckles that covered her face.

She said, "But we're still left with what to do with those six rental properties."

Daniel nodded. He said, "In the best of all possible worlds, what would you like to see happen to those houses?"

"You won't like it."

"How do you know? Try me."

"Well, it'll cost money." She laughed her trademark throaty laugh. "Everything I want to do, that amounts to anything, always costs money. You know that."

"Well, we're not adverse to spending money. If it's for the right thing."

She weighed his comment. "I'd really like to see us tear all of those houses down. And then build a community center. I could move the community clothes closet over there. And the neighborhood food pantry. We could open a free clinic for families who can't afford doctors. That last part might take a while, but we do have some M.D.s in the congregation. Maybe some of them would donate their time. I can imagine, eventually, a free legal clinic, too. For people who need help with that sort of stuff."

Daniel nodded. "All good ideas, Maggie. You'd need help with the two clinics."

"Yeah. I know. Stuff to work on in the future. You always want to have stuff to work on, Pastor. Keeps the congregation stretching and growing and reaching out. We need to keep doing that."

"What would happen to the families living in those houses?"

"We'd have to give them notice. There are more and more cheap rentals available around here. The neighborhood's changing. You've noticed, I'm sure."

Daniel nodded. He wondered whether the day was far off when the majority of the membership would live outside the neighborhood. The trend was unmistakable.

"One other thing," Maggie said. "And I know this is a long-shot. But, if we had room over there, and enough money, I think we should also seriously consider building a gymnasium. *Our* kids could use it. But so could the neighborhood kids. Just think what kind of outreach we could do for those young people who don't have a church home."

Daniel nodded.

"Even if they didn't end up in our congregation, it would make us a friendly place in their eyes. And it would keep them off the streets."

Chapter 21

Pastor Aaron Ward looked out over the sea of faces. All the assembly room seats were full. That meant all 315 cell captains had shown up. He was relieved. No repeat training sessions would be required.

"Welcome," he said, smiling at the throng. "And thank you all for consenting to take your turn this year at leading one of our living room cells." He looked down at his notes, realized he had it all securely in mind, and stepped confidently away from the speaker's stand. "The purpose of this meeting is to remind you of the purpose of the cell meetings, to inform you of a slight adjustment in the procedure, and then to answer any questions you may have about how to lead your small group."

The captains had all been provided folders with information about their duties. Many were poised to take notes in the margins. Aaron said, "As we've done for the first two years, we'll continue to open our meetings with prayer, then a Scripture reading. All the readings for an entire year are in the folder you've received. Then comes the discussion, based on the reading. It should be a conversation about how this portion of Scripture applies to everyday life. The members of your group will have lots of ideas. The problem is usually not finding enough to talk about, but figuring out how to cut it off."

There was mild laughter in the room.

"Here's what's new this year," said Aaron, walking comfortably back and forth in front of the assembly. "We want you to save about ten minutes, just before you break for refreshments, to talk about a possible community outreach project your cell group would be willing to adopt and carry out during the year."

A hand went up. "What sort of project, exactly?"

"Whatever you choose. Maybe you want to adopt a family that needs special help of some kind. It might be something as simple as helping them get their leaves raked in the fall. Or it could be something else."

"Like what else?" asked a young man in the fourth row.

"Well, there's a list of possibilities in your folder. But you're not limited to those."

Another hand went up. "We're having a really good problem in our cell."

"What's that?" Aaron asked.

"We're outgrowing our living room. We keep getting new members."

"Well, there's something in the folder about that, too. You need at least seven people to make a cell. Fewer than that and the sharing becomes too limited. When you reach fourteen, you're expected to divide the group. You'll need to find an additional living room, and an additional cell leader."

"We already have eighteen. But nobody wants to leave."

"Well, be gentle, but be firm. More than twelve makes a good conversation difficult. Maybe you'll have to draw straws to see who stays and who moves on."

There was laughter.

"Do we need to meet every single Monday night?" asked a young woman sitting near the back.

Aaron recognized her, and remembered she had three small children at home. "No, you can meet as infrequently as once a month. But the group will grow closer, more quickly, if you meet at least twice a month." He paused, then grinned and added, "I hate to mention this, but that was in your folder, too."

There were chuckles.

A young man in the second row said, "We've asked a few people who are members but who just don't want to get into a cell group. What should we do about that?"

"You can't force it. And we don't require it. But, if you'd do me a favor and let me know who these folks are, I'll be happy to visit with them. Sometimes they have good reasons for not wanting to participate. Of course, sometimes they're just making excuses." He paused. "It's a little bit like finding reasons for not coming to Sunday worship."

"I've noticed," the young man replied, "that every single person in our cell group is coming faithfully to worship. I think that's one of the things this program has accomplished."

Aaron nodded. "That's the way it worked when I was a pastor in Saginaw, Michigan. Our worship attendance was better than any other congregation in the city."

"So, is that really why we're doing this?" a middle-aged woman asked.

Aaron smiled. "Not really. It's just one of the wonderful added benefits. The real reason we're doing this is that, with 6,600 members, we need a way to personalize our ministry at Saint Michael Church and help our members feel connected. How many of you believe that's what's been happening with this program?"

All the hands went up.

"I JUST LOVE the fact that we've found an excuse to start meeting again as a living room group," said Georgianna Langholz. "This feels just like back when we first started the congregation."

"And here we all are, in Adam Engelhardt's living room, where it all began," said Lorene Scheidt.

"Older and wiser, all twelve of us," said Andy.

"The only person missing is good old Frieda Stellhorn, God rest her soul," added Polly Kleinhans.

"Well, enough reminiscing," said Adam. "I volunteered to lead the cell group this year, which explains why you're all in my living room, of course. So I think we should get started. Let's begin with prayer." All eyes went shut. Adam began, "Lord Jesus, we give you thanks for all those gathered here tonight. Be with us as the unseen guest. Send your Holy Spirit into this place, and into our hearts as we share our hopes and intentions for our life together in Saint Michael and All Angels Church." He paused. "We thank you especially for Pastor Daniel, and our other pastors as well. We thank you that, through your Spirit, you have grown this congregation so amazingly in our midst...and for allowing us, who are in this room tonight, to have had such an important part in its beginning."

He paused again. It was as if he wasn't sure how to end the prayer. Then he said, "May all we say and do here tonight be pleasing to you. Amen."

A murmur of Amens arose from the others.

Frances Bauer said, "Adam, before you read the Scripture portion for tonight, I want to make a suggestion."

He looked at her, not sure what was coming.

"I know it's not in the list of suggestions Pastor Ward gave us for conducting a cell group meeting, but I really miss how we used to sing hymns together, back when we were a living room church."

"That was 1927, Frances. We haven't done that for twenty-three years."

"I know. But I still remember liking it a lot. And we sang songs from the old Ohio Synod hymnal. Remember those old books with the covers falling off, that they gave us from the chapel over at St. Paul Luther College?"

Jake Bauer looked at his wife and said, "Frances, the college is gone, the

Ohio Synod is gone, and, for all I know, all those hymnals are gone. Are you trying to turn back the clock?"

Frances looked sternly at her husband. "No. I'm just saying I wish we could sing a hymn together once in a while. After all, Elsa still has her piano, sitting right over there, and she probably still knows how to play it."

Elsa smiled. "We got rid of all those hymnals a long time ago, Frances. But, I can still remember how to play one that was a favorite of yours." She got up from her seat on the couch, next to Adam, and walked to the piano bench. "Remember this?" She played seven chords of introduction.

Frances' eyes lit up. She began to sing, as Elsa accompanied. Quickly, many of the others joined in:

Savior, teach me, day by day, love's sweet lesson to obey;
Sweeter lesson cannot be, loving him who first loved me.

It seemed astonishing to Adam that everybody in the room still remembered the words, and that they were singing them with such fervor and obvious joy.

Elsa kept playing. Frances knew the second verse, but her husband, and most of the other men, were dropping out. They simply couldn't remember anything beyond the first stanza.

With a childlike heart of love, at thy bidding may I move;
Prompt to serve and follow thee, loving him who first loved me.

By the time they reached the third stanza, only Elsa and Frances were singing. The others were listening with appreciation, and a little surprise.

Teach me all thy steps to trace, strong to follow in thy grace;
Learning how to love from thee; loving him who first loved me.

But, in spite of the fact that she had always loved this hymn so well, that was all Frances could remember. She stopped singing. Elsa, however, kept playing and sang, confidently and flawlessly, the final two stanzas. It was as if she had the words in front of her, even though there was nothing at all on the music rack.

Love in loving finds employ, in obedience all her joy;

Ever new that joy will be, loving him who first loved me.

Thus may I rejoice to show that I feel the love I owe;
Singing, till thy face I see, of his love who first loved me.

Then the piano fell silent. All eyes were on Elsa. She turned and looked at the others. She smiled and said, "You're right, Frances. It was a wonderful old hymn. Sometimes I wish we still had that old *Evangelical Lutheran Hymnal*."

Adam cleared his throat. "This meeting is going to take longer than the hour we're supposed to limit it to."

"Nobody cares, Adam," said Fred Stumpf cheerfully. "Just take as long as it takes."

Adam said, "I asked Will Langholz to read the Scripture portion."

Will had the passage marked. He opened his Bible and announced the reading. "This is from Mark, chapter 1. 'Now, after John the Baptist was put into prison, then came Jesus into Galilee, proclaiming the Gospel of God, and saying, "The time is fulfilled, and the kingdom of God is at hand; repent ye, and believe in the gospel."'"

He closed the book and looked at Adam. The host said, "Just to get the discussion started, I've been thinking this week about repentance. You see, I knew in advance what the Bible reading was going to be."

"Unfair advantage," muttered George Kleinhans. But he offered the comment with a grin.

Adam said, "My experience is that people who most need to repent are usually the last ones to want to do so. It seems to me, there are a couple things that have to happen. We need to face up to what we may have done that we shouldn't have, or what we should have done that we didn't, and then say we're sorry."

"Isn't there also a third thing?" asked Georgianna Langholz.

Adam looked at her. "Excuse me?"

"Don't we also need to do something to try to fix the damage we might have caused?"

Adam nodded. "Yes. I guess that's right. We probably do."

Georgianna continued, "I really felt as though I'd sinned against my daughter, Jenny. You know, back when she was dating that..."

"That sexual predator," her husband said, cutting in. The words came out sternly, as if he still hadn't gotten over the Buzz Winslow incident.

Georgianna said, "What I'm trying to say is, I should have been more sensitive to Jenny, more open to her. For some reason, she always got the impression I was judging her when she dated that young man. So she never really trusted me to have a fair conversation with her. And that made her want to take chances with him I'm positive she never would have, if I could only have trusted her earlier."

The room was silent. But Georgianna wasn't finished. "So, I want to repent of that. And I'm thankful I have a roomful of good friends who will listen to my confession, and help me feel forgiven for it."

Myrtle Stumpf said, "I don't mean anything especially by this, Georgianna, but since you mentioned the need to do something to fix what went wrong, do you think you've been able to do that?"

Georgianna looked at her friend and said, "I hope so. I told Jenny I knew I'd been impatient with her, and hadn't trusted her when I should have. I asked her to forgive me." There were tears in the corners of her eyes. "Jenny and I have never been so close as we are now, since I told her that." She sniffed. "So, you see, repentance really does work, if you follow all the steps."

Adam said, "Well, that's probably a better application of tonight's reading than anything I could have come up with."

"But you had something prepared to say, didn't you, Adam?" Andy Scheidt queried.

"Well. Yes. I did." He hesitated. "Should I share it?"

"That's what we're all here for," said Jake Bauer.

"All right. Here it is, then. All of you know the house that the dead millionaire, Michael Morgan-Houseman, used to own, came up for sale a couple years ago."

"Sure. Harry Broadman bought it."

Adam nodded. "Well, that's not the whole story. I really…sort of…talked him into bidding on it. Because I didn't want to see it turned into apartments. Harry went ahead and did that, and ended up buying it."

The others in the room looked at him with great interest. None of them had ever heard that story.

Adam said, "After he bought the place, it sat empty for several months. I realized, and so did Harry, that he had a property he didn't really know what to do with. I'm sure it was an inconvenience for him. It probably still is. He has a student from Northwestern Lutheran Seminary living in it. But it's still a kind of albatross around Harry's neck. I felt guilty about it afterwards."

"What did you do, Adam?" asked Fred.

"Well, I finally went to him and told him I was probably out of line even to suggest he bid on the place. Of course, he acted as if there was no problem whatsoever. He was very generous with me. Harry's like that. But I needed to tell him. And I felt a lot better afterwards. In fact, I asked him to forgive me for being presumptuous."

"Did he?" Fred asked.

"Well, he told me that wasn't necessary. But then he said, 'If you feel you need that from me, I forgive you. Absolutely and unconditionally.' The truth is, I really did need that from him."

The room fell silent. Everyone appeared to be reflecting on what Adam had just said. The host finally said, "Who else wants to get into the discussion? Does anyone else have a story about repentance they'd like to share?" Nobody made a move. But Elsa looked at her husband and seemed ready to jump into the conversation. Adam nodded toward her.

She said, "I've been wanting to confess something for quite some time now. I've been wondering if I could find the right words. But this discussion is the perfect opportunity. So I want to say something directly to you..."

She looked at Polly Kleinhans, but said nothing. Polly returned an expression suggesting she was ready to hear whatever was about to come out of Elsa's mouth. But Elsa appeared to have been struck dumb.

Finally, Adam said to his wife, "Elsa, what were you going to say? You didn't finish your sentence."

Elsa said, "Can you help me, Adam? I can't remember this woman's name."

Everyone was looking at the 61-year-old hostess. Nobody could believe what she had just said.

Adam said as quietly, and as kindly, as he could, "Elsa, that's Polly. Polly Kleinhans."

Chapter 22

David Engelhardt sank comfortably down into the old upholstered chair in the small living room above the newspaper office and, stretching out his legs, crossed them at the ankles. He studied his father's face. Adam, seated in the well-worn couch nearby, had an expression David could not decipher.

"I was always glad you kept a couple pieces of furniture up here, David. It makes a nice little hideout when you want to get away from the office for a few minutes."

David nodded. "And a nice place for a private conversation, away from listening ears. So tell me, what's the big secret?"

"Did I say I had a secret to share with you?"

"You've been secretive about this meeting with me, ever since you suggested it, last week."

"Well, there are several things, actually. And they're not the sort of stuff I want everybody in the neighborhood to hear just yet."

"Okay. So what's on your list?"

"Well, for starters, how would you like to take over the printing business?"

"Take it over? I was sort of planning on that. After you retire."

"I'm thinking of retiring early."

"Dad, you're only 62. What's your hurry?"

"I want to start slowing down. And I've been doing some arithmetic. You know how well we've prospered. I'm confident I can afford it."

"But why would you want to? You always said you'd stick it out until you couldn't walk to the office anymore. Your legs look pretty healthy to me."

"My priorities have changed," Adam said, smiling. "Besides, I thought you'd like to be in charge of both the printing operation and the newspaper."

"Well, to tell you the truth, the newspaper would be too much to handle if I was running Engelhardt Printing besides."

"But Paul David graduates from the university in another year. Couldn't he run the newspaper?"

David had told his son he wanted to groom him for that position, and the twenty-year-old was now ready to step into his father's shoes. "Yes, I guess he could." But then he said, "I still don't get it. Why do you want to retire *now*?"

Adam studied the bare wall, noting the strange dark squares contrasting with the faded wallpaper, where framed pictures had once hung. He said, "I've been keeping this from you. I can't keep it to myself much longer." David tilted his head, wondering what was coming. "Your mother is...she's beginning to forget things."

"Mom? I hadn't noticed that."

"You wouldn't. It isn't all that evident to most people. But when you're around her day after day, like I am, you start to see a pattern."

"So, how bad is it?"

"Not terribly so. Yet. But I've seen this sort of thing before. Do you remember old Wilma Shaughnessy, the lady who used to be Lillian Fischer's landlady, back before Lillian got married?"

"Sure. Nice old gal. She owned the house Lillian and Luther live in now."

"Well, she moved out after she started forgetting things. Moved over to St. Paul to live with her sister. It started the same way with her. Just little things at first. Then it got worse. One day she took a streetcar to a nearby grocery store and ended up in north Minneapolis somewhere. She had no idea how she got there, and no idea how to get home. That was when Lillian knew it was getting bad."

"Is Mom getting like that?"

Adam frowned thoughtfully. "It's really very odd. It was at one of the meetings of our neighborhood cell group, one night a few months ago, when I first noticed it. Your mother couldn't remember Polly Kleinhans' name. George and Polly Kleinhans have been among our best friends for the past 25 years. And yet, during the same evening, Elsa was able to repeat, from memory, all the stanzas of an old hymn none of us had sung for years. She was the only one in the room who could do it."

David shook his head. "Long-term memory is good. Maybe even getting better? Short-term memory is failing. You're right, Dad. That seems pretty odd."

Adam said, "So you can see why I don't want to have to keep going to work every day. I want to be at home with your mother now. She needs someone to watch out for her. I'm not even sure she should be cooking, without somebody checking to see the stove gets turned off, for example."

"So, does that mean we're not having the traditional Christmas Day dinner at your place?"

"That's another thing I wanted to talk to you about. Would it be a problem if you and Molly hosted us this time?"

"Probably not. I'd have to ask Molly, of course. We'd talked about going to Litchfield to be with her family on the 26th, but I think we could still do that."

Adam folded his hands, lay them in his lap, and studied them. "There's one thing more you probably should be aware of." David tilted his head and eyed his father. What else could there be, he wondered. "I'm beginning to worry a little about your mother going up and down the stairs."

"Why?"

"Because she seems to take them more slowly than before. It's almost as if she's not confident doing the steps. I don't know why. I'm guessing it's related to her forgetfulness." He shook his head. "I know this sounds foolish, but it's almost as if she's forgetting how to climb stairs and come down again." He looked at his son with a bewildered look. "Do you think that's possible?"

David seemed not to have heard the question. He said, "All the bedrooms are upstairs. You can't have her sleeping on the living room couch, Dad."

"Well, it's not gotten terribly bad. Not yet. But that's partly why I want to give up the business. When she goes up and down stairs, I want to be there to help her."

IN THE SPRING of 1950, Sarah Engelhardt graduated from nursing school. After the ceremony, her parents hosted an open house at their home. Adam didn't let Elsa out of his sight. By this time, close friends had begun to notice peculiarities in her conversation, and to make appropriate allowances.

Sarah was distressed to see what seemed to be happening to her grandmother, but behaved publicly as though nothing was wrong. In private with Josh, however, it was a different story. After the guests had gone, and they had time to themselves, she sat with him, in her parents' living room.

"I'm really concerned about Grandma. I just hope Grandpa doesn't have to put her in a nursing home one of these days."

"Well, you're the nurse. What's *your* diagnosis?"

She shook her head. "It can only get worse. At least, it almost always does.

If we're lucky, it will go really slow. I just can't bear the thought of her forgetting who I am."

Josh put his arm around his girlfriend and gave her shoulders a gentle squeeze. He said, "Well, now your grandfather has a nurse he can call on if he needs to."

"I'll do what I can, of course. Which might not be much." She showed a worried frown. "During my training, I dealt with some patients who were experiencing memory loss. Some of them got really angry when people tried to help them. There was one man who ended up shouting profanities at everybody who came near him. His wife told me privately that he'd never said a cross word in his life, to anybody, before his memory started to go. Isn't that sad?"

Josh nodded. He said, "Let's talk about something more pleasant. You're a full-fledged graduate of the school of nursing. What's next for you?"

"I have a job offer at Fairview. For now, at least, I think I'll take it."

"This isn't working out right," Josh groused. "You're all done with school and I still have a year to go."

"Your last year will go fast."

"And then what do we do?"

"It all depends on you, Josh. If you decide to go to seminary, I'll just keep working until you get out."

"I could enroll at Northwestern. Or Luther. Then I could stay up here with you."

"That wouldn't make any sense. Those seminaries aren't even in our church. You need to go to Wartburg, in Dubuque."

"Or my dad's alma mater, in Columbus, Ohio," he said.

She flashed a look of alarm.

"Just kidding. I wouldn't do that to you."

She leaned her head against his shoulder and sighed contentedly. "We'll worry about that next year. For now, I'm just glad you're back here with me. And we have the whole summer together."

He gently stroked her hair and mumbled, "Lead us not into temptation."

She turned her head and looked into his eyes. "Why did you say that?"

"Because it would be really tempting to do something with you that we'd both regret."

"Not before we're married, Josh."

"Maybe I could drop out of college without finishing. We could get married right away. You could work at the hospital and I could..."

"Could what? Become a bum? There's no way in the world you're going to quit college after your junior year. You're too close to finishing now."

"You still can't tell when I'm kidding, can you, Sarah?"

"I don't think you were kidding."

ON THE FOURTH OF JULY, after the sun had gone down, two teen-age boys whose family was renting one of the six church-owned houses across the alley, behind the parish house for Saint Michael Church, pulled a sack of fireworks out of their bedroom closet. They opened the window of the second-story room and began lighting the rockets, sending them out and up into the air.

When the rest of the family had gone looking for the pair, in order to take them along with them to a public fireworks display, the boys had hidden themselves in a neighbor's garage. As a result, and as they'd hoped, they were left behind, unsupervised.

After the fifth incendiary device was lighted, the younger boy fumbled it, dropping it into the pile of explosives still waiting to be set off. Quickly the entire cache was aflame, shooting wildly in all directions, inside the room. The boys dashed out the bedroom door and down the stairs. Flames ignited the curtains, then spread to a pile of comic books strewn across one of the beds. Within minutes the room was an inferno. Ten minutes later, the entire house was ablaze.

None of the occupants of the other five dwellings were at home, all having headed for one patriotic fireworks display or another. As a result, the fire jumped from one house to the next, until all were burning.

By the time the fire trucks arrived, none of the six rental units was worth saving.

PASTOR JONAS and his wife, Rosetta, had taken two weeks and gone to Ohio to visit their Fremont relatives. Consequently, there was nothing for Maggie Washington to do but wait for their return. In the meantime, she walked about the charred ruins of the six dwellings, whose fate the church council had failed to decide two years before. As she looked at the disaster zone, she pondered what to do next.

When the church council met, during the second week of July, Maggie was present. She'd invited herself, and her request had met with no resistance.

Council President Robert Ylvisaker invited Maggie to address the group. She said, "Gentlemen, we're helping all six families with donations from the church food shelf, and things from our clothes closet. I've helped all of them to find other rental properties in the neighborhood. I understand our property insurance will provide us reimbursement based on the actual value of the buildings we lost. Of course, none of them were in really great shape by the time they all burned down. But the funds we receive could be the down payment on a social ministry center. You have a proposal from me that's never been voted up or down. I'd like to ask you, now, to put it back on the table."

"You know, Maggie," said Russell Tokheim, frowning thoughtfully, "we have a lot on our plate right now. We're collecting all this money for the 25th anniversary festivities. That's only two years away."

"Well, I can just imagine the congregation will want our visitors to see a bunch of charred lumber across the alley when they drive into our wonderful four-level parking ramp during the celebration," she replied sarcastically.

"Oh, we'd never do that, Maggie," replied Lyall Schwarzkopf. "We'll have to clear all that away and bulldoze the area. Maybe we could just plant some grass in there for the time being."

"I'm sure all the poor people who need medical and legal help will enjoy sitting on the lawn we plant," Maggie shot back.

"We don't have a medical clinic yet, Maggie," said Jason Scherschligt. "Nor a legal clinic. Those are just dreams of yours."

"Well, how do you think we got the food shelf and the clothes closet and the community meals program? Somebody dreamed all that up. And, in case some of you don't have a really good fix on the history of this congregation, you're looking at the person who did it. So, let's stop stonewalling and start building some new visions. We suddenly have the opportunity to use that space. Let's do something great with it."

The members of the all-male council looked warily, yet sympathetically at their feisty director of community ministries. Everybody knew Maggie had a heart of gold, and a fierce determination to get what she wanted. But they also knew she was not much good with cold facts and hard realities. Those things she always left to others.

"Maggie," Robert said, in his always calming voice, "Your original proposal called for space for the two clinics, but also for a gymnasium. Suppose we take this in two parts. We might have an easier time selling the clinic building to the congregation first. Then, later, we could propose the gym."

Maggie looked warily at the chairman. She said, "I've always said half a loaf is better than no loaf at all. I'd be happy with that. But, in the meantime, what would you do with the space where the proposed gymnasium was supposed to go?"

"Simple," said Lyall. "We can pave it and use it for extra parking." Maggie's mouth was open immediately, a ready rejoinder on the tip of her tongue. But Lyall wasn't finished. "And, we put up basketball hoops at either end, so the neighborhood kids can have an open-air gymnasium the rest of the week."

Whatever it was that Maggie Washington was about to say suddenly escaped her. She closed her mouth.

Chapter 23

Skip Warner steered the squad car slowly along Broadway, past Lyndale Avenue, toward Fremont. As he talked, he scanned the scene on both sides of the street with a policeman's trained eye.

"I can hardly believe it," said Josh, turning on the passenger seat to look at his high school buddy. "I'm not even out of college yet and you're already through training and serving on the force."

"I told you the day we graduated from high school I'd be heading for the police academy."

"Yeah. I know. But you already have your own car, and your own beat."

"Well, being the son of a career police officer didn't hurt." He spotted an African-American youngster waving from the sidewalk. He lifted his right hand, gesturing recognition to the boy. "On the other hand, when you have no seniority, you get assigned to places you might not have chosen. Like north Minneapolis."

"Things can get pretty rough around here," said Josh, studying the decaying urban landscape. "Not nearly as bad as what I saw in south Chicago three years ago, when my college roommate took me around. But bad enough."

"Gotta keep your eyes open," Skip said, turning off Broadway into a residential neighborhood. "Keep in touch with the folks. Make sure they know you're their friend." He paused, looked at Josh and grinned. "Not so different from what a good pastor would do."

Josh nodded. He hadn't thought of that.

"So, you heading to seminary after next year, buddy?"

"Oh, I don't know. I think half the congregation expects me to."

"What about your dad?"

"I know he'd like it if I did. He's not pressuring me."

"I'd say that's wise. Best way to scare your kid away from doing something is to tell him he ought to do it."

"Really. What did your dad tell you about police work?"

"Believe it or not, he told me to think twice. He told me it was risky. Man, that wasn't anything new. Considering all of the scrapes he's had over the years, you'd think he'd realize I was aware of that."

"But you became a cop anyway."

"Just seemed natural, Josh. Dad's cut out for police work. He's really good at it. Respected on the force. I felt like it was right for me, too."

The squad car came to a stop at the curb near an intersection. With the motor idling, Skip turned to Josh and asked, "So, what feels right for you, Josh? I mean, if you're not going to be a pastor like your dad, what *are* you going to do?"

Josh sighed. "I don't know. Seminary would be four more years. I really want to marry Sarah after college. Waiting one more year is bad enough. Waiting five more is...gosh, I don't know if I could survive that."

"Couldn't she get a nursing job down in Dubuque, while you went to class?"

"Seminary frowns on guys getting married before they finish." He chuckled. "This will give you a laugh. My dad told me the seminary profs don't even like their students *dating* women before graduation. Too distracting, supposedly. But immediately after the diplomas are handed out, and certainly before they get a call to a congregation, they're supposed to meet some girl, fall in love with her, get engaged and married."

Skip chortled. "Not exactly realistic."

"Those guys are called 'one-week wonders.'"

"You mean, some of them actually do that?"

"Sure. Most of them have girlfriends waiting in the wings. They just don't tell the seminary faculty about it."

Skip checked his watch, then put the vehicle back into gear. As they rolled through the intersection, he said, "You remember back in tenth grade, when we did that project for David Engelhardt?"

"You mean, ripping all the old paper off the walls in that upstairs room at the newspaper office?"

"We were just four young twerps back then, weren't we?"

"We sure didn't think so at the time."

"Time goes by so fast," said Skip. "I'm married. A baby's on the way. I'm on the police force. I've been out of high school three years. How's that possible?"

"At least you have your future figured out, more or less. Mine is still a mystery."

They pulled into the side street where Josh had parked his father's car. "You probably need to get back to south Minneapolis. Your dad's gonna need his wheels, right?"

"He said I could have the car for a couple hours. It's only been ninety minutes."

Skip said, "Look, I'm not trying to tell you what to do or anything, but just in case you're interested, Saint Michael Church is going to offer a new position starting next year sometime. You might want to consider it. You could stay in Minneapolis, earn some money, and marry your sweetheart."

"What kind of job?"

"You know my dad got elected to church council last January, right? Seems like for about the tenth time in his life. Anyway, they had a couple meetings with Maggie Washington, and she convinced them to find some money to get a free medical clinic up and running. There'll be doctors and nurses volunteering some of the time. But there has to be somebody to run the place. You always used to talk about wanting to do something to change the world, or make it a better place, or whatever. This might be a good test for you. You could see if you really wanted to do something like that."

"Funny, my dad never mentioned a new position like that," Josh said.

"Why would he? If you were him, would you want your son to drop his plans for seminary and take a job working with poor people?"

"You're assuming my dad really wants me to go to seminary."

"Well," said Skip, as if it was the most obvious thing in the world, "don't you really think he does?"

"JOSH! SLOW DOWN! I can't keep up with you."

Daniel Jonas slowed his pace to a fast walk. Then, spotting a park bench, he stopped and collapsed onto it. His son stood grinning at his father, who was trying to catch his breath.

"Gotta get back in shape, Dad. It'll keep you young."

"Or send me to an early grave," Daniel replied.

Josh dropped onto the bench, next to his father, stretched his legs out in front of him and folded his hands behind his neck. "Thanks for going running with me. I really appreciate it."

"Well, I haven't seen Minnehaha Falls for awhile. I'm sort of glad you gave me an excuse to do that again."

"Dad?"

"Hmmm?"

"What do you know about that new position Maggie Washington's going to be offering next year, in the new free medical clinic?"

"What I know about it is that the church council has approved it, and if they hadn't, Maggie would have filibustered them until they did."

"She's one tough customer."

"That's why she's good at what she does."

"Dad?"

"Yes?"

"What would you think if I applied for that job? After I finish college next spring."

"You?"

"You're not too hot on the idea, are you?"

"Joshua Daniel, would you even be interested?"

"I don't know. I'm not sure. I talked to Maggie about it."

"You *did*?"

"Yeah. Just to find out what was going to be involved. I was curious."

"Joshua Daniel, you majored in history, not social work. Or sociology."

"I know. But what can you do with a history major?"

"Well, what did you think you might do with it when you chose it?"

"To be honest, I didn't think much about it. I thought it wouldn't matter if I was just going on to seminary."

"And, so…?"

"Dad, I've thought a lot about it. I don't want to disappoint you or anything. But so far, I'm not sure the Holy Spirit is telling me I should be a pastor."

Daniel looked at his son with an expression that suggested patience, understanding and a hint of sadness. "Well, I have to say, I admire your honesty."

"You're upset. I was afraid you would be."

"Joshua Daniel, you need to do what seems right for you."

"So, if I applied for Maggie's new position…"

"It's not going to pay very much. It will be a living wage for someone, but not much more."

"Sarah's earning a salary at the hospital."

Daniel's expression changed to one of puzzlement. "I think you just lost me. Are you and Sarah planning to get married next spring? And, if you did, would she be okay with you taking that position? And, if you decided to start having children, could you do that on your salary alone?"

"We'd wait to have kids. Until we built up some savings."

"If you were one of our pastors, you'd receive a house to live in. With this job, you'd have to find the money to pay rent."

Josh nodded. "I know. We'd have to figure that part out."

"What do you think her parents might say?"

"Dad, I don't even know what *you and Mom* might say."

Daniel frowned thoughtfully. "Truthfully, at this point, I don't know what I *should* say. This is pretty sudden. I think your mother and I need to talk it over."

"Of course, you know it's my life—and Sarah's—we're talking about here."

"I know, Joshua Daniel. I know."

LILLIAN FISCHER looked from one to the other of the members of the Anniversary Task Force. As she did so, she said, "Now, I want all of you to understand that, just because I'm sharing this information with you, I'm not giving anybody here a veto over what I'm planning. This is just for your information, you understand."

Everyone in the room understood Lillian's methods. She was not one to abide contradiction. She said, "The oratorio will be developed in four sections, with parts for choirs and soloists in each. The theme for each section comes from one of the four stanzas of hymn 484 in the *American Lutheran Hymnal*, which, as you all know, we have in our pews."

"What's hymn 484?" asked Jens Jorgensen.

"It's about the presence of angels in our daily lives. Even though they may escape our awareness, they're still present with us." She paused, but only momentarily. "It should be fairly obvious why I chose that text."

Jens nodded. "Saint Michael and All Angels. Of course."

"But I'm not using the tune, just the text. I'm composing new music for the singers."

"It's going to be sensational, whatever you do," said Harry Broadman. "Everything you do is wonderful, Lillian."

"Oh, piffle." She pretended embarrassment, but it was clear she was basking in the praise she'd just received. "There will be five hymns to be sung by the congregation. One at the beginning, and one after each of the four sections. They'll all be from our hymnal. I've found a dozen and a half that would be suitable. Now I have to trim down the list."

"What do you mean 'suitable,' Lillian?" Tom Pavelka queried.

Lillian straightened in her chair. "You may have noticed that some of the hymns in our worship book are, let us say, embarrassingly subjective. They tend toward the sentimental. They seem to assume that faith is a personal arrangement, between me and God. Well, that's not strong hymnody. Methodists and Baptists may like it, but Lutherans shouldn't be using texts and tunes like that."

"I don't get it," Tom protested. "If they aren't suitable for Lutherans, why are they in a Lutheran hymnal?"

"Well, Tom, if I'd been on the hymn selection committee when they put that book together, you can bet they *wouldn't* have been."

There was laughter around the table.

Jens said, "So, if you don't want to use 'subjective' hymns, what other kind is there, Lillian?"

"A good solid church hymn turns the focus away from my personal experience and toward the community's shared confession, and God's promises. For example, 'A Mighty Fortress is Our God' does exactly that."

"Are you planning to use that one in the oratorio?" Harry asked.

"I'm not sure. Let me surprise you."

"Lillian, nothing you do surprises me," said Harry. "Even your surprises don't. Because I expect you to do the unexpected."

Lillian eyed him carefully. "Well, I'm sure you know what you meant by what you just said, Harry. Personally, I was a little confused. But let's leave it at that."

"So, Lillian, when do you expect to have the composition ready?" asked Tom.

"Well, as you will have noticed, I've had other things to think about lately."

"We noticed," said Harry. "And let me be the first to congratulate you on the birth of your newest son."

Lillian spoke unusually softly as she replied, "Thank you." She was still not used the idea that now, with six children, she had not yet accomplished her original purpose, giving birth to a daughter. That meant her husband had named all six of their progeny. The arrangement had been that he would name the boys, she the girls. So, there were now Christopher, John Mark, Michael, Timothy, and Peter running around the Caldwell Street residence, and baby Joel in the cradle.

Jens had one more question. "Are you staying with the title you started with? For the oratorio, I mean."

"Yes. Absolutely. 'The Glory and the Wonder.'"

"What exactly does that refer to?" Harry asked.

"Let me tell you, first, what it *doesn't* refer to. It's not a reference to our big church building, and our fancy organ, and the fact that we have four pastors and over 6,700 members. Even though all of that truly is glorious—and wonderful."

"Well, what then?" Harry persisted.

"It's a reference to the gifts we all have from God, day after day. The promises he guarantees to all of us. And, especially, the power and protection we have because angels are watching over all of us." She paused, studied the faces of the other members of the task force, and added, "If that isn't glorious and wonderful, then I don't know what in heaven's name is."

Chapter 24

"Come with me, Josh," said Luther Fischer, getting up and out of the wicker chair. "I want to show you something." Josh pulled himself up, then followed the history professor down the front steps.

As they crossed the lawn, dodging bicycles and wagons left lying here and there, Luther said, "Watch out for the baseball. It's coming your direction."

Josh looked to his left, just in time to duck out of the way of the flying orb, whizzing by. Beyond him, in the side yard, eleven-year-old Christopher Fischer stood, ball glove in hand. Out near the curb was nine-year-old John Mark, just having snagged the ball. He waited for the two men to move out of the way before firing it back toward his older brother.

"You know what, Luther? If you keep this up, you're going to have enough boys for your own baseball team."

Luther chuckled. "Lillian says we're stopping at seven, girl or no girl."

"So, what did you want to show me?"

Luther opened the garage door and stood back. "What do you think of her?"

"Your Pontiac? You've had it since I was in high school."

"It runs great," said Luther. "Joe Pavelka sold it to me when it was almost new. I've never had a problem with it."

"Well, I guess that's a good thing," said Josh. He wasn't sure why he was standing here, admiring the Fischer family sedan.

"Why don't you buy it from me?"

"Me? This car? Why?"

"Because, you're a college senior. You go to school down in Iowa. You need transporation, and so far you haven't got any."

"Luther, don't think I haven't thought about it. Plenty of times. But I'm a college boy. I haven't got a spare nickel to my name."

"You could buy it from me on the installment plan. And you wouldn't have to start paying me until you had a full-time job, next year sometime."

"Why are you selling it?"

"Look around, Josh. Our family is growing like everything. We can't fit eight of us in the same car. And we don't really want two automobiles. So, I've been talking to Joe Pavelka about something bigger."

"Like a bus, maybe?" Josh said, grinning.

"You're not far off the mark. We're looking at a station wagon. It would be just the ticket for vacation trips to Crawford County, Ohio, for example."

"But you have to get rid of the Pontiac first."

"Joe told me what he'd give me in trade. Not that much, as it turns out. So, I figure, I could sell it to you for what Joe would give me, and you could have a good, reliable car for a good price."

Josh opened the door and looked inside. "You have 60,000 miles on it, Luther. I guess there should be a few more years on it."

"If you take care of it, and keep the oil and the filter changed, you should get at least 100,000 out of her."

Josh said, "Can I take it for a test run?"

"Sure. Hold on." The professor stepped into the back yard and shouted, "Christopher! Tell your mother I'm going on an errand. Back in a half hour."

AS THEY ROLLED south, along West River Road, toward the Ford Parkway high bridge, Luther said, "I think this is the first time I've sat in the passenger seat in this car. Ever."

"Lillian doesn't drive?"

"Hasn't wanted to. Hasn't needed to. She walks to church and back. It's only five blocks, you know."

"Seems like a pretty nice old car, Luther."

"Talk to your parents. See if you can sell them on our little deal."

"Well, I have to agree to it myself, first."

"What are your thoughts so far?"

Josh studied the road ahead, then smiled. "I think I'd like to have this car."

He turned onto Minnehaha Parkway and headed west. Luther said, "So, tell me again, why did you want to talk to me this afternoon?"

Josh took a moment to organize his thoughts. "You're a history professor at the University. I'm a history major at Wartburg College, ready to graduate in one more year. I just wanted to ask your advice about something."

Luther said, "All right. Ask."

"When you got out of college, what were you really planning to do?"

"What I actually did. I taught high school history. In my hometown. But it didn't take me long to discover the kids in Crestline, Ohio, weren't much interested in history. Oh, they paid attention, did their homework, turned in their assignments, all of that. But none of them were really all that excited about it. After a year I discovered I could do better teaching college courses. So I came up here and got my doctorate at the U. I've been on the faculty ever since."

"The thing is," said Josh, "I'm sort of thrashing around. I have one year to go. I really like my major. In fact, I've discovered I really love history. But I don't know what I want to *do* with it. I mean, I could teach somewhere, I guess. But if I get the same kind of response from students that you did, I think it would drive me crazy."

"That's something to think about."

"I never really thought much about being a university professor, though. How's that worked out for you?"

Luther sighed. "It's good. And it's bad. Students just taking courses because they're required to aren't much of an inspiration. The ones wanting a history major are a lot of fun to teach. But, it's a big campus. Lots of bureaucracy. Faculty meetings. Committees. Required research. Sometimes I wonder why I chose this profession."

"Do you regret it?"

"No. Not really. Anyway, it's too late to change now." He paused, "Of course, I sometimes wonder what kind of pastor I could have become."

"Really?"

"Sure. At Capital University, the seminary was right across the street. I thought about it a few times."

"My dad went to Capital."

"He was a few years ahead of me. I don't think we were on campus together."

"The thing is, I sort of want to consider seminary. But, then I'd have to wait four more years to get married."

"And Sarah Engelhardt doesn't want to wait that long for you, right?"

"Well, actually, she might be willing to wait. I'm just not sure I would be."

"It's amazing how long a young man can wait if he has to. Lillian put me off for several years. Oh, she'd deny it if you asked her. But I practically had to drag her to the altar."

"Well, I wouldn't have to beg Sarah. She really wants to get married. But,

I don't want to do that and then end up in some job I'm not sure I'd be happy in."

Luther said, "If you turn here you can take the road up past Lake Harriet and Lake Calhoun, and then to the Lake of the Isles." Josh turned right and followed the next section of the parkway. The older man said, "One thing you need to keep in mind, Josh, is that, no matter what vocation you choose, there will be disappointments somewhere along the way. Nothing you choose is going to be paradise. That's why I think everybody needs a vocation and an *avocation*."

"What do you mean?"

"Well, my vocation is teaching history. And doing historical research. But my *avocation*, the thing I really like doing the most, is tinkering with cars. And, of course, selling them to other people so I can buy newer ones."

Josh chuckled. "How many cars have you owned since you've been married, Luther?"

"Don't ask."

WHEN THE PONTIAC was safely back in the garage and they had returned to the front porch, Luther said, "Have a seat. I want to get something for you."

Josh dropped down into one of the two wicker chairs and reflected on how much he'd enjoyed driving Luther Fischer's car. He wondered if his folks would object to him taking it back to Iowa for his last year of college.

Suddenly from the side yard came the shout, "Josh! Think fast!" Turning his head, he realized that John Mark had thrown the baseball in his direction. He leaped up from the chair, just in time to catch it with both hands.

"Watch that, young man," he shouted cheerfully. "Somebody's going to lose a window if you're not careful." He threw the ball back to the youngster.

John Mark looked at him as if to suggest that accidentally shattering glass was an impossible scenario. He turned back toward his older brother and fired a strike into his glove.

When Luther returned, he had a sheaf of typing paper, bound together between stiff covers, secured with metal clasps. He handed the document to Josh. "Since you're interested in history, here's a little research one of my students did. This might catch your fancy."

Josh studied the title, typed on a gummed label and affixed to the cover: "Historic Homes on Franklin Avenue." He lifted the cover and scanned the contents. There were six old mansions identified. As he studied the addresses, he realized they'd just driven past all six on their way back from the parkway.

"Hey, neat," he said, slowly turning the pages. "How accurate is the stuff in here, Luther?"

"I gave a copy of this research to the curator at the historical society, over in St. Paul. He was impressed. It's pretty carefully researched."

Josh said, "Is this your personal copy, then?"

"It is. And, if you're interested, I'll let you take it with you for the next couple weeks. Until you head back to Iowa."

"Great!" said Josh, his eyes alive with curiosity.

"Which just proves a theory of mine," said Luther, sagely. "You could probably earn your bread and butter doing any number of things. But it looks to me as if your avocation is really what you're majoring in at college."

"NICE CAR, Josh," said Harry Broadman. He was standing on the sidewalk in front of the house Adam Engelhardt had convinced him to purchase. Josh's "new" Pontiac was parked at the curb. "Looks a lot like one Luther Fischer owns, I must say."

"This is it," said Josh. "I just bought it from him." He hesitated. "Well, okay, he's letting me drive it until I can afford to start making payments. My dad has the title. He's paying the insurance on it. For now."

"Good for him. Good for you. So, tell me why you wanted to use your last Sunday afternoon before going back to college walking through my old mansion."

"Well, to tell you the truth, I'm curious to see what your place looks like inside."

"Any reason in particular? We could have done this any time."

"I just finished reading a research project a university student completed. About six houses on this street. Your house is one of the six."

"And?"

"And, I thought you'd like to know some of what I learned about this place."

"You mean, that a millionaire named Michael Morgan-Houseman owned it?"

"That part I knew. But how about the person who actually built the house, in 1907?"

Harry said, "Really? So Morgan-Houseman wasn't the original owner?"

"Gosh, no. He bought it in 1922. You didn't know that?"

"Okay. You know more about the place than I do. Let's go inside, and you can tell me what you've learned."

AFTER THEY'D WALKED through the empty dwelling, Josh made sure they ended up in the front parlor. He said, "This place is really well kept up, Harry. A lot of the old homes around here are decaying."

"It really is amazing," said Harry. "The people who bought it after Morgan-Houseman jumped off the Foshay Tower had a real appreciation for the place. Partly, I'd guess, because they thought it might bring a better resale price if they took good care of it. But they didn't count on the neighborhood changing. People with enough money to buy one of these palaces just don't live around here any more."

"You see that fireplace, Harry? Look at the ornate stone lions on either end."

"Always wondered about those," the businessman said. "Somebody must have carved them for the original owner."

"Turns out, the original owner was a wealthy lumber baron. Made his money running timber mills in northern Minnesota and selling the lumber to builders in places like Minneapolis and St. Paul and Milwaukee and Chicago. But he also loved antiquities—and archaeological artifacts."

"Excuse me?"

"He made several trips to Europe and Palestine and Mesopotamia—all over the world, in fact. Back before people were so careful about such things, he hired some guys, over in what was once the Assyrian Empire, to do some digging for him. They uncovered these perfectly matched lion heads. They could be three thousand years old."

Harry looked at Josh with narrowed eyes. "You're sure about that?"

"Positive. It's in the research."

"How does the researcher know?"

"He found a document in the basement of the Minneapolis Public Library that was evidently donated by the heirs of Lincoln Price. That's the lumber baron. Anyway, it explains where the lions were found, and how they became part of the fireplace mantel."

"This sort of thing really gets your engine revving, doesn't it," Harry said with admiration.

"This whole house has me revved up," Josh confessed. "It's like walking through a museum. Except, people actually *lived* in it." There was electricity in his voice, such as Harry had seldom heard.

"There's more," said Josh, walking toward the fireplace. "Have you ever wondered about these square blocks of stone that line the fireplace, on the sides and across the top?"

"Well, each one is different. I just figured that was the architect's way of making it look a little more interesting."

"There's a reason why each one is different. That same document I was telling you about has a chart, and it was copied over into the research paper Luther Fisher let me borrow. It identifies the origin of every single one of these stones. Evidently, Lincoln Price was on a quest to find little pieces of history everywhere he went. He brought them back to Minneapolis and put them into his fireplace."

"Okay. Tell me about the stones."

"Well, this one here was found lying loose at Stonehenge, in England."

"What!"

"I know, it seems unbelievable. But it's in the library document." He moved to another square. "This one was in a heap near one of the gates of the Great Wall of China. This one came from the Colosseum in Rome. Over here is one from the Temple of Zeus in Olympia, Greece. And this one came from the site of the Temple of Solomon, at Jerusalem."

"You're kidding!" the businessman exclaimed. Josh shook his head profoundly. "You're *not* kidding."

"Harry, you can't ever sell this place. There's just too much history here."

OUTSIDE, standing on the front steps, Harry said to Josh, "Thanks for introducing me to my house. The place is even more amazing than I, or Adam Engelhardt, thought it was."

"If I wasn't such a nut on history, I would never have discovered any of this stuff."

"Almost makes you wish you could live here yourself, doesn't it?"

Josh looked at Harry and smiled. "It's your house, Harry." He looked back out toward the street. "I just think it's great that somebody in our congregation actually owns it."

Harry took a deep breath. "I almost sold the place last spring."

"What!"

"Yep. You probably know the church council approved the funds to build a new annex for Maggie Washington's programs."

Josh knew.

"Which means, in addition to opening a new free medical clinic there, next spring sometime, she'll also move the clothes closet and the community food shelf and the community kitchen over there. And, that means that the space she's using now will be available for the historical displays we're planning for the anniversary celebration, two years from now."

Josh was putting it together. "Which means the displays won't be here, in your old mansion."

"And *that* means," Harry continued, "That I don't really need this place after all. And, even though Adam Engelhardt convinced me to buy it, I just don't know how much longer I want to hang onto it. I mean, I'm an absentee landlord. The neighborhood has, shall we say, mischief makers running around, looking for abandoned houses to rifle." He took a deep breath. "The final straw was when I was informed by Northwestern Lutheran Seminary that they couldn't find a single student to live in this place as a caretaker this coming school term. That means I've got an empty house on my hands. Of course, I might be able to find someone else, but those seminary boys were absolutely trustworthy. You know what I mean?"

"Why don't you just move in yourself, Harry?"

"Because I don't believe in divorce. And, if I made Polly move out of our lovely suburban home in Edina, into this place, that's what we'd be looking at."

Chapter 25

"Jenny! Phone call for you! Long distance!" Georgianna Langholz shouted from the base of the stairs.

Jenny laid the red pencil down on the school paper she was grading, got up from her bedroom worktable, and walked to the landing. "Who's calling me long distance?"

"Come and find out," her mother said, mischievously.

In the dining room, she picked up the receiver.

"Jenny? This is Hannah Ruth. In Philadelphia."

Jenny squealed. Then she heard laughter on the other end of the line. "Sorry. I just got excited. I haven't talked to you since…I don't know when."

"Well, you're only the second person I'm calling with the news. After my parents, of course."

"What sort of news?"

"John and I are getting married. In Minneapolis. Right after Christmas."

Jenny squealed again.

"My ears are starting to hurt," Hannah Ruth joked. "Now, listen to me. I want to ask a favor."

"What's that?"

"Will you be my maid of honor?" There was silence. "Or are you still mad at me for stealing John away from you?"

"Oh, stop it, you silly goose. I'm over that. I'm just trying to figure out…why are you getting married in the middle of the winter? What's wrong with spring?"

"Well, John and I were talking it over, and we couldn't see any reason to wait until summer. All our friends and family will be home for the holidays. We might as well do it then."

"But, John's still in medical school. Can you…you know…afford it?"

"I have a job teaching music in the schools here now. And I'm giving lessons.

And I'm playing the organ every Sunday in an Episcopal Church."

"So you two can afford to live on just your salary?"

"Well, the Episcopalians pay a lot better than most Lutheran churches do." Jenny laughed. Hannah Ruth continued, "Don't tell my dad I said that. He'll think I'm being disloyal."

"To answer your question, I'd be happy to be your maid of honor. Just tell me what you want me to wear."

"I'm putting everything in a letter. You should get it next week."

"Wonderful. I'm happy for you. For both of you."

"Jenny?"

"Yes?"

"How is teaching going for you?"

"Fine. Just fine. I love fourth graders. And my parents are giving me free rent, as long as I do a few things around home for them. So that's perfect."

"Are you…umm…you know…seeing anyone?"

"No. That's not going to happen."

"No good candidates?"

"Oh, plenty of candidates. I've just sworn off men. I'm staying single. I thought I told you that."

"Well, you did. But I thought maybe you'd change your mind."

"About as soon as we land a rocket on the moon. But not a day sooner."

"GEORGE! LISTEN to this!" Josh climbed off his dorm room bed, the letter from his mother still in his hand. He began to read to his roommate:

…Your sister called us on Saturday. She and John are planning to be married at Saint Michael Church the Sunday after Christmas Day. They want you to be a groomsman…

"Can you believe that? My sister's getting married and her boyfriend's still in school!"

"Well, it's medical school. She's probably going to work and put him through, right?"

"Yeah. Obviously. But what's the difference between them doing that and me marrying Sarah before I go to seminary? She could work and put me through, too."

"I thought the seminary didn't like that sort of arrangement."

Josh sighed. "They don't like it. But it sure doesn't seem very fair to me."

"THAT WAS SOME CEREMONY," said Sarah, leaning close to Josh in the front seat of his Pontiac. "I hope ours can be just as grand."

"My dad says he's glad he only has one daughter. He doesn't think he could afford two weddings like that."

"Well, that's why it was so grand. Your folks only have one daughter. This was their one time to really do something special."

Josh studied the frozen surface of Lake Nokomis, through the windshield, and put his arm around his girlfriend. He said, "You know I still haven't made the first payment to Luther Fischer on this car."

"Is he complaining yet?"

"No. But the thing is, that's part of the reason I haven't gotten you an engagement ring. Yet."

"We could be engaged without one. People do."

"I know. But it isn't the best way to do it, is it?"

"The main thing is, you make a promise and seal it with something special. I think that's what the ring is really about."

"Yeah. I guess."

"Of course, if you *didn't* give me something to guarantee it, I suppose I'd never really know if we were truly engaged or not."

He offered her a look of confusion. Suddenly he reached back and unfastened the chain that hung around his neck. Except when swimming or taking showers, he'd always worn it underneath his shirt. On the chain hung a silver cross with Martin Luther's colorful coat of arms in the center.

He reached over and fastened it around Sarah's neck. "There," he said, trying to sound serious, "now we're officially engaged."

She smirked. "That's a confirmation cross, Josh. I have one just like it. It says 'I am a Lutheran' on the back."

"Well, for right now it's an engagement cross, okay? And the day I give you a diamond, I expect you to give that chain back to me. Understand?"

She grinned. "You've been wearing this cross all these years since eighth grade? I put mine away in a drawer. I only wear it when it goes with my outfit."

"Shame on you," he chided in mock disbelief.

She said, "You know, if you went to seminary and I came down to Dubuque and got a nursing job in one of the hospitals there, and they happened to find out we were secretly married, they wouldn't kick you out, would they?"

"Much as I'm tempted, I don't think we'd dare try it."

"Why not?"

"Because a pastor is supposed to be good to his word. If we deceived the seminary faculty, what's to make them think I wouldn't deceive the members of any congregation that called me?"

"You think they'd make that much of it?"

"I'm not willing to find out."

She sighed. "So, where does that leave us, then?"

"It leaves us getting married next June. I'm going to take Maggie Washington's job in the free clinic. You can keep right on at the hospital. We can find a place to rent. It won't be easy, but we can do it. What is it they say? 'Love always finds a way.'"

She was silent.

"You don't like that idea?"

"I don't like you giving up on seminary. Not if that's where you really belong."

It was Josh's turn to be silent. They listened to each other breathe, and looked at the lake. Finally he said, "Remember when we laid out there on the sand and you told me we ought to get a sailboat?"

"Mm-hmm."

"I don't think we're going to get one."

She laughed. "Not too likely, is it."

"Harry Broadman has a really nice one, out on Lake Minnetonka. He'd probably let us use it once in a while."

She started giggling. "You can be so ridiculous sometimes."

He grinned at her. "What's the matter? You don't think Harry would let us use his sailboat?"

"What's the matter is, you always have an answer for everything. It doesn't matter how goofy it is, you always have a solution. Nothing is impossible with you."

"We have to be positive, Sarah. Being negative never got anybody anywhere."

"I just don't want you taking that job at the clinic and then wishing you had gone to seminary."

He stroked her hair, then leaned over and kissed her with more passion than she'd remembered him showing before. He said, "Okay, here's the deal. You told me not to drop out of college. I listened to you. But for this next part, it's your turn to listen to me."

"What do you mean?"

"I mean, I'm going to go to work in the clinic. I'll give it...I don't know...three years. If I really hate it, I'll find a different job. Maybe I'll become a history teacher. But, in the meantime...I mean, right after I graduate, I want us to get married. Okay?"

She looked at him with searching eyes. "You promise you won't tell me, three years from now, that you wish you had gone to seminary?"

"Even if I did wish it, I promise not to tell you that."

"What do you think our parents will say?"

"We'll worry about that later. Right now, I want to know what *you* say." She looked at him, not sure how to answer. "Sarah, I want us to get married next June. Are we going to do it, or not?"

She gazed at him with eyes full of love. Finally, she answered. "Yes. Yes we are."

THE DAY AFTER Josh graduated from Wartburg College, Harry Broadman phoned the Engelhardt residence, and then the Jonas home. He had the same message for both Josh and Sarah. "Meet me for lunch, the day after tomorrow, at the Minneapolis Club, half past noon. You'll be my guests."

When they were ushered into the dining room, Harry was seated at his favorite table. He gestured to them to be seated, then said, "This is going to be one heckuva wedding. Your sister's was wonderful, Josh, but this one ought to fill the church. Just think, the two leading families of the congregation are being joined in marriage."

"I'd say the Broadmans are a leading family, Harry," Josh replied.

"I'm talking about our founding pastor and the congregation's founding family. It's going to be stunning."

"You're embarrassing us," said Sarah.

"Good. I was hoping I could accomplish that. Now, tell me, how are the wedding plans going?"

"Two more weeks," Josh said. "Lillian Fischer is doing something special with the choirs, I think my dad said. At least with the singers who are still around in the middle of June."

Harry nodded. "Minnesota in the summertime. Well, I have a feeling folks will come back from the lake for this event."

"The biggest problem," said Sarah, "is that we haven't found a decent place to rent."

"Not that there isn't anything decent out there," Josh added. "But we can't afford any of those. And the places we *can* afford, well, let's just say you wouldn't want to have your friends visit you there." He paused significantly, then said, "We may end up living with my folks for a while." He looked at Sarah, smiled, and said, "We'd stay at Sarah's place, but her bachelor brother's living there for now."

Harry shook his head, a look of disdain on his face. "Never get married and then move in with your relatives. It never works out. Believe me."

Chapter 26

Sarah was going to challenge what Harry had just said, but he wasn't finished. "I didn't invite the two of you to lunch just to show off my fancy club. Although I never mind doing that with my friends."

He grinned. They looked puzzled. He continued, "I have something for the two of you." He pulled an envelope from his suit coat pocket and laid it on the table. They stared at it. "That's the deed to the house on Franklin Avenue. I'm giving it to you as a wedding present."

Their eyes were huge.

"One upstairs bedroom is furnished. The kitchen is ready to go. You might want to buy some furniture, so you can actually live in the downstairs parlor—you know, where that wonderful fireplace is, Josh. I've put a little something in the envelope to help you pay for that."

"Harry!" Josh said, astonishment on his face, "You can't...we can't...you shouldn't..."

"Why not," said the corporate executive expansively. "It's my house. I can do whatever I please with it."

HARRY BROADMAN'S PREDICTION proved accurate. The Lutheran Church of Saint Michael and All Angels was full to overflowing for Josh and Sarah's wedding. Lillian Fischer pulled out all the stops, making the great Reuter pipe organ thunder. For the second time in six months, Daniel Jonas delivered a wedding homily and then presided over the exchange of marriage vows for one of his own children.

During the reception, held in the festively-decorated community room, next door in the parish house, Luther Fischer's three older boys took delight in rigging out what had once been their father's old Pontiac with tin cans and streamers. Christopher wrote "Just Married" on a large piece of white butcher paper, which he and John Mark fastened to the back of the car.

Late in the afternoon, the newlyweds pulled away from the curb, the horn honking, a huge throng waving them off. They drove down Highway 61, to Red Wing, where they stayed in a quiet inn.

The following Wednesday they returned to Minneapolis. Josh drove along Franklin Avenue, and, when the old, brown-brick mansion came into view, he said, "My dear, do you suppose the butler will have the fireplace lit for us?"

"Sure," Sarah replied, poking him in the ribs. "About as likely as the cook will have a hot meal ready, or the maid will have turned down the bed."

Josh pulled up behind the house, and then drove along the twin strips of concrete, to the brick carriage house, with its long-vacant servants' quarters overhead. He climbed out, pulled the sliding wooden doors apart, and peered into the silent interior.

Against the back wall he caught sight of a faded poster, showing a vintage 1920s automobile, and the legend, "America's finest drive the finest—Packard."

He shook his head and thought, *We are in so far over our heads living here, who's ever going to believe this?*

AT FIRST it sounded like an innocent chest cold. But the coughing grew worse by the day, until Sandy Elliot began to be concerned about her two-year-old daughter. Priscilla Ann would awaken in the night, unable to breathe, crying pathetically. Her mother would hold her in her arms, rocking slowly in the upholstered rocking chair next to the child's bed, soothing her and singing softly.

When the condition seemed not to improve, Sandy took Priscilla Ann to the doctor. He examined her thoroughly and announced the child's lungs were filling up with fluid. He sent her to the hospital.

After two weeks of confinement, with three physicians puzzling over what to do to reverse the malady, the youngster finally stopped coughing. It was eight o'clock on a Friday evening. Sandy felt relieved. She sat next to the hospital bed, calculating the hours until Arnold would fly back from Chicago, and then dozed off.

When she awoke, sometime after midnight, the room was full of medical personnel. Her own doctor took her by the arm and guided her into the hallway. His face was ashen. He said, "Sandra, it happened so suddenly. Little Priscilla just slipped away from us. I'm so terribly sorry."

SANDY AND ARNOLD sat next to one another on the living room couch. A pall of death hung over the house. It was the morning after the funeral, and they were living on borrowed time. Arnold was contracted to transport a St. Paul businessman to Chicago later in the day. Sandy had agreed not to ask him to cancel the flight. It would have meant a substantial economic setback for Arnold to do so.

But part of her was regretting that decision, and resenting Arnold for having spent fully half of their married life living out of town. Finally she spoke. "I feel as if a great big part of me got left back there at the cemetery." She paused. "She was such a little darling. How will I live without her?"

Arnold said, "You did everything you could, Sandy."

She wanted to say, *And a big help you were, you skunk. Off you go to Chicago whenever you want to, and leave me here to handle the house and raise our child. A few words of apology for that would go a long way.* But she said nothing. Instead, she pursed her lips and stared out the picture window, toward the street. There was no traffic. There were no signs of life. It looked, outside, the way she felt inside—lifeless.

"Arnold, are you sorry about what's happened?"

"What? Of course I am? What kind of question is that?"

"You never paid much attention to Priscilla Ann. It seemed as if she was my child, but not yours."

"Well, you spent twice as much time with her as I did."

She nodded, but her expression was not kind.

"Sandy, you knew what you were getting into when you married me. I told you it would be like this. It couldn't be helped."

"Couldn't you have found some day trips to do, instead of these four-day and week-long layovers out of town? It might have helped our marriage."

He said nothing.

She sighed heavily. "It's too late for that now. We have to think about the future." She thought she saw him squirm a little. Maybe she just imagined it. "Arnold, we need to start over."

"How would we do that?"

"Do I have to draw you a picture? I want another child."

He nodded. His face betrayed nothing.

"Don't you?"

"What?" He squirmed again, then got up from the couch. "Boy, Sandy, I don't know if I could go through this a second time."

"Go through what?"

"Having a child and then losing her. Parents aren't supposed to have to bury their own children."

It was Sandy's turn for silence. Finally she got up and walked over to Arnold. "So, is that a yes or a no?"

He furrowed his brow. "Just let me think about it, okay?"

She responded with fury. "Just go back to Chicago! Go fly with your rich clients! Have a good time! As far as I'm concerned, I don't really care if you ever come back or not!"

WHEN THE PHONE RANG at the Franklin Avenue house, Josh and Sarah were busy unrolling an elegant new patterned carpet in the front parlor, another gift from Harry Broadman. Josh went into the dining room and picked it up.

"Josh? It's Adam. Do you think you, or Sarah, or both of you, could come over here?"

"Are you at home, Adam?"

"Yes. It's kind of urgent."

"Ahh...yes...I think we can come in a few minutes."

"As soon as you can. Thank you."

SARAH SAT on the top stairway step, next to Elsa Engelhardt. She was stroking the older woman's back with gentle motions of her hand. "Are you okay, Gramma?"

Elsa nodded, but didn't reply. Her face was soaked with her own tears. Sarah had found a handkerchief, and was helping her dry her eyes.

At the foot of the stairs, Adam turned to Josh and said, "It's the first time this has happened. Elsa stopped wanting to climb stairs by herself. So I've always helped her go up and down. But today, she was suddenly afraid to go down. She just stood at the top of the stairs and looked down, as if she didn't know how to navigate them. I tried to help, but she pushed me away and kept hanging onto the railing."

"You don't have a downstairs bedroom. That's a problem, Adam."

The older man sighed. "That's a problem for sure. Once we get her to come down, I don't know how I'll ever get her back up again. And, of course, then I'd have to figure out how to get her back down."

Josh said, "Your son, David, doesn't have a downstairs bedroom either."

"I wouldn't ask David and Molly to help. They have their own lives to live."

Sarah had succeeded in convincing Elsa to come down the stairs with her.

She guided her into the living room and helped her sit down on the couch. The men followed. As the four sat looking at each other, Adam said apologetically, "I tried to call David and Molly. They didn't answer."

Sarah replied, "I'm glad you called us, Grampa. We're glad to help."

"I think I need to find a nursing home for Elsa," said Adam. His eyes began to fill with tears. He said, his voice shaking, "We've lived in this house since 1923." He broke down and wept, unashamedly. Josh put his arm around the 62-year-old and gave him a solid hug.

"I don't know which place to choose. Sarah, I thought you, being a nurse, might have a good suggestion."

"Grampa, let me check on a few places for you. It's Saturday. It might take a little longer on the weekend, but let me try." She smiled and said, "Are the two of you going to be okay if Josh and I leave you?"

Adam nodded. "We'll be fine."

"Come on," said Josh, getting up and gesturing to Sarah. "Let's go see what we can figure out." He looked at Adam, who was showing relief. He said, "Whatever you do, just don't let Elsa go back up the stairs."

AS THEY RODE along Bloomington Avenue, toward the Franklin Avenue intersection, Sarah said, "It's so sad, seeing what's happening to Gramma. She's forgetting so much. And yet, Grampa doesn't want to let her go. He loves her so much." Her voice was quavering.

Josh replied, "I've been thinking. Maybe she wouldn't have to go to a nursing home."

She looked at him, wide-eyed. "What else would they do?"

"You know that paneled library on the first floor, at our place? It's on the back side, where it's sort of private. It's only about ten steps from the downstairs bathroom. There's a closet in that room. Why on earth, I don't know, but there is one. And, there's nothing in that room. Except built-in bookshelves. I think a bed and a chest of drawers could fit there with plenty of room to spare."

"Josh! You want to invite my grandparents to live with us?"

"We got the house as a gift. Why shouldn't we share it with our family? Besides, the two of us are sort of rattling around in there. We could use the company."

She looked at him, thunderstruck.

"And, you know, Sarah, Adam has gotten to be a really good cook the last couple years. He's had to. Maybe he'd cook a meal for us once in awhile."

"Josh, he's got his hands full with Gramma!"

"But he cooks for her. Anyway, I'm just half kidding. About the cooking, I mean."

By the time they arrived home, Sarah had thought it over. "You're so amazing, Josh."

"Excuse me?"

"You always have a solution. I just love you so much."

"So, you want to try this half-baked scheme of mine?"

"We'd need a bed and a chest of drawers."

"Why couldn't we just move the furniture from their own bedroom. That would give Elsa some comfort, I'd think."

"You'd need some help."

"Let's see... Your dad...your brother...my buddy, Skip Warner...any of those could help. Maybe all of them."

"I'll call them for you, Josh."

"Aren't you forgetting something?"

"Probably. What?"

"Shouldn't you ask your grandfather what he thinks about all of this?"

Chapter 27

The people began arriving at the Minneapolis Auditorium an hour before the oratorio was to begin. Chairs filled the entire floor, and were all occupied within twenty minutes after the doors were opened. Latecomers climbed the steps, finding seats in the balcony.

By the time Lillian Fischer brought down her baton, coaxing the first chords from her select orchestra, the place was packed. For forty minutes the great room swirled with the music of celebration. In choruses, solos, and hymns, the texts for which were printed in the multi-page worship booklets distributed to all, the throng shared thanks and praise for the glory and the wonder of God's promises and blessings.

For the closing hymn, Lillian had chosen stanzas by the faithful German pastor/composer, Martin Rinkart. The congregation rose to its feet and sang, full-throated, "Now thank we all our God with hearts and hands and voices!" As they did so, the singers began to file off the platform, revealing an altar, pulpit, and an enormous banner, proclaiming "The Glory and the Wonder." At the second stanza, a procession, led by 17-year-old Peter Scheidt, the crucifer, began its way down the center aisle. Behind Peter came Nick Gidmark and Brian Hinck, carrying torches. They were followed by Tom Pavelka, lifting the large book of Scripture readings high over his head. Then came the four pastors, in black cassocks, white surplices and red stoles.

The last to enter was Pastor Daniel Jonas. His mind was racing, back to the day his congregation vacated a small, white frame building at the corner of Anderson Avenue and Caldwell Street, twenty-three years before. This same hymn had been sung as he and the congregation processed from the old structure to the wonderful new stone edifice next door. The chills that had run down his spine on that day were now returning.

IN HIS SERMON to the huge assembly, Daniel said, "This is a glorious and wonderful day for the Lutheran Church of Saint Michael and All Angels. There are far too many of us here today to fit into our 800-seat sanctuary on Anderson Avenue, and that's a very good thing. In fact, I am informed by our office manager that, as of one month ago, this congregation exceeded 7,000 members for the first time in its history."

Before he could begin the next sentence, spontaneous applause broke out and continued for nearly a minute. Daniel could not remember ever having been so interrupted during a sermon.

Nor could he have known that the membership of Saint Michael Church had reached its zenith, never again to be exceeded.

He said, "I have been greatly encouraged by the success of our small cell gatherings, a program effectively developed by our partner in ministry, Pastor Aaron Ward. What we have now accomplished is a very large community of faith with over 300 intimate communities. And if anyone in this room doesn't belong to one, I hope you soon will."

There were some chuckles. He said, "I realize I just said something that doesn't really apply to all present today. Many of you are not members of this congregation. Some of you belong to other churches, and we're glad you came to share our special time. But we're not interested in coaxing you away from your own congregation. Stay there. Continue to do God's work where you are."

There were nods and smiles of appreciation, all around the room.

Daniel paused and looked out over the sea of faces. He waited until he knew that his listeners were fully tuned in. He said, "Jesus Christ is the light of the world. That's the glory and the wonder of it!" He continued, "You and I, every one of us, have sinned and fall short of the glory of God. But God, through his precious Son, Jesus, has come to love and care for us, in the midst of our broken world, in spite of everything we do. He loves us back into his open arms. That's the glory and the wonder of it!"

He was feeling a rhythm develop. The congregation was catching it. He said, "Every one of us in this room has been blessed in special ways. These wonderful gifts come from God, who just keeps on blessing us with more and more of his gifts from day to day. Brothers and sisters in Christ, that's the glory and the wonder of it."

He took a breath. His pulse was increasing. He waited a split second, then said, "It's also glorious and wonderful that the Lutheran Church of Saint Michael and All Angels has grown from a living room full of solid saints, all but one of whom are here today, into an enormous faith fellowship of over 7,000 baptized members. But the glory doesn't go to us. We didn't build this congregation. It was the Holy Spirit, the one who calls, gathers, enlightens and sanctifies the whole Christian Church on earth." He smiled. "That last phrase came directly from Martin Luther's *Small Catechism*, by the way. I hope you remember having memorized those words."

There were nods of recognition.

"So, let us go from this place, full of wonder for what has happened in our midst, giving all the glory to God, determined to serve our Lord faithfully throughout the coming 25 years."

AS THEY LEFT the auditorium, Adam Engelhardt walked slowly, making certain his wife didn't stumble. Her footing, he had noticed, had become less and less certain in recent months.

Elsa said, "That was a wonderful service. And I really liked the sermon. I wonder who that pastor was. He spoke so well."

And, inwardly, Adam wept.

IN THE EDITOR'S OFFICE at the *Bloomington Avenue News*, David Engelhardt sat chatting with his son. Paul David, tired from a long day trying to meet his weekly publishing deadline, was happy for an excuse to sit down and simply talk to someone.

"You're making this newspaper hum, Paul David. I have to admit, it's more readable and more attractive than it was when I was running it."

"You did a great job with what you had to work with, Dad."

"Don't be modest. It's better than it was."

"I'm having a good time with it."

"You're a natural. It shows in your work."

Paul David said, "Did you stop by just to butter me up for something?"

"No, I stopped by because I've been neglecting you. All week long you scramble to get the next issue together. All week long I run around south Minneapolis, trying to find new clients for print jobs. We're both doing well, but we never see each other anymore."

"Except at supper."

"That raises an issue."

"Oops. Getting tired of me living at home?"

"No. We love having you. We get free lawn mowing and snow shoveling thrown in. It's a good deal for your mother and me."

"So, what's the issue, then?"

"I need your help with something. Your grandparents' house is sitting empty."

"You haven't been able to rent it out, have you?"

"I've interviewed a dozen families. I wouldn't trust a single one of them with my own house, much less your grandparents' place. That's a really nice house. I don't want to see it torn up."

"I hesitate to suggest this, Dad, but, should you perhaps be thinking of selling it?"

David sighed. He looked at the old, framed inscription hanging on the wall. It was a German prayer, once used by one of the founding members of Saint Michael Church. Old Frieda Stellhorn always recited the words before the worship services of the living room congregation, which existed briefly 27 years before. Many of those services had been held in Adam and Elsa Engelhardt's living room.

He said, "I don't like the idea of selling it. There's just too much of our family in that place."

Paul David said," Well, if you don't want to rent it, and you're not prepared to sell it, what's left?"

David said, "I'd like to have you move in there."

His son did a double-take. "Really?"

"If you would. I'd be willing to go back to cutting my own grass and shoveling my own snow. Of course, you'd have to do it at your grandparents' home."

Paul David sat thinking. "Most of the furniture is still in there, right?"

"Your grandparents' bedroom is empty. Otherwise, yes."

"Okay. Yeah. Sure. I can do that."

David looked surprised. "That was easy. Are you sure?"

"Why not? Then I could walk to work."

"Well, that's a point."

"Dad?"

"Yes?"

"What's going to happen to Gramma?"

David wasn't sure how to answer. He said, "She still likes to have me come and visit. Of course, I'm not sure whether she really remembers me anymore. She's stopped calling me by name." He sighed. "I hate to admit it, but I think we're losing her, a month at a time."

Paul David nodded. "I'm really proud of Sis. She and Josh were good to take them in."

"It's worked out. Your grandfather is happy as a fox in a henhouse over there. He actually cooks dinner for the four of them. And your grandmother hasn't had to go to a nursing home. That's what I appreciate more than anything else."

Paul David picked up the stale remnant of a sandwich, looked disdainfully at it, and tossed it into the wastebasket. He said, "One problem with moving out, though. No more of Mom's cooking." He looked at his father and grinned. "You know what a lousy cook I am."

David studied his son's dark brown hair, his intense brown eyes, and the neatly-trimmed beard that set off his handsome square Germanic face. Had he been interested, he could probably have had any girl he'd have wanted.

"Paul David, are you going to remain single for the rest of your life?"

His son tilted back in the old wooden captain's chair and folded his arms across his chest. He said, "I'm perfectly happy the way I am."

"Except, you're a lousy cook. Wouldn't it be nice to have someone do that for you?"

"Dad, I'm surprised at you. I should go looking for a wife just so I can get decent cooking? There has to be more to it than that."

"Of course there is. Don't you want to have a family one of these days?"

"Not especially."

"You're never going to give your mother and me grandchildren, are you?"

"Sarah and Josh will take care of that."

"They haven't yet."

"You know what? That's no better reason for getting married than getting decent cooking would be. Doesn't there have to be mutual attraction, and love and...well...a desire to share your life with someone?"

"Of course. Of course."

"Well, so far, I don't feel the need for any of that stuff. I mean, look, Dad, I'm free as a bird. I come and go as I like. I can work here in the office until some ungodly hour, getting a deadline met, and nobody's waiting to scold me when I come home late." His father was looking dubious. "Dad, I love my independence. It's great! Nobody tells me what color socks to wear, or whether to pick them up off the floor. Nobody to complain if I wear the wrong tie, or if don't wear a tie at all." He hesitated. "Nobody to complain if I belch once in a while."

David shook his head. "I enjoyed my independence when I was a college boy, too. But I got to the point where I wanted some companionship." He thought about it. "Actually, I got to feeling that way before I even got out of college. But the point is, you're going to grow old some day, and there won't be anybody in your life to care for you. Have you thought about that?"

Paul David said, "Yeah. I have. But so far, Dad, I'm not all that concerned about it. Old age is a long ways away. For now, I just want to live my life, and edit this newspaper, and have free time for myself."

"Okay," David said. "I've made my case. I won't bring it up again."

"Oh, you probably will," said Paul David, cheerfully. "And I'll tell you the same thing then that I just told you now"

Chapter 28

In the weeks following the great 25th anniversary celebration, Elsa Engelhardt began to slip inexorably into her own private world. Increasingly, she did not recognize her husband, her children or her grandchildren. On one occasion, when Sarah sat with her, in the parlor of the Franklin Avenue house, the older woman asked, "How long will you be staying with us?" When Sarah smiled and replied, "As long as you'd like me to," Elsa said, "But my dear, won't they be missing you in Galion?"

The reference was to the small factory town in north central Ohio, where Adam and Elsa had grown up fifty years before. While Sarah had visited there a few times in her youth, she had never lived in Galion. For the first time, she felt as though her grandmother was slipping away from reality altogether.

One day Sarah returned from her nursing shift at the hospital, to discover the house empty. That was unusual, because Adam had found it more and more difficult to convince his wife to leave the residence, even to go to Sunday worship.

After twenty minutes, peering out the front window, she saw her grandparents walking slowly along Franklin Avenue. With some difficulty, Adam guided his wife up the front steps, then into the large front hallway.

After he had put her down for a rest, he came into the kitchen and said, quietly, "Today she thinks I'm the custodian."

"The custodian, Grampa?"

He returned a sad smile. "She and I were sitting in the front study, on the love seat. She told me she was tired of this place and wanted to go home. She said, 'Since my husband isn't here, and you're the custodian, you'll have to take care of it for me.'"

Sarah shook her head.

"I wanted to tell her that your brother is living in our home. I didn't have the heart to do it. So I said, 'Elsa, it's quite a ways from here.' She replied, 'Nonsense. It's just two blocks away.' I didn't know what to make of that, so I got an idea. We put on our sweaters and went walking. Down to the corner, around the block, and back here. When she saw your house, she said, 'Thank you for walking me home. I'm tired now. I think I need a nap.'"

Sarah grinned. "That was good thinking on your part, Grampa."

"That was desperate thinking, my dear."

"OKAY, THAT'S IT," said Lillian Fischer, looking up from her hospital bed. "Seven boys. No girls. I'm not having any more children. If you want a girl, Luther, you're just going to have to adopt one."

Luther offered an apologetic grin. "Baby Stephen Matthew is as cute as a bug in a rug. I just came from the nursery. He's sleeping like...well, you know..."

Lillian sighed. "I guess I've done my part to subsidize the diaper industry."

"Sorry," Luther said, looking repentant.

"Well," she replied philosophically, "I don't know exactly how it all works, but it can't be entirely your fault that all we had was boys."

His expression changed to one of relief. But it faded when she added, "But it can't be all mine either."

SARAH was at the free medical clinic, volunteering her services as a nurse. It was a Thursday afternoon, and she had come directly from her work shift at the hospital. Josh was down the hall, interviewing a neighborhood resident who needed something for her infant son, whose cold was stubbornly hanging on.

In the midst of a blood pressure check, Sarah stopped and said, "Excuse me, I need to sit down for a moment." The patient, an unemployed gentleman of 50, nodded and waited patiently. He was used to waiting. It had taken him an hour to get his turn at the free clinic.

Sarah felt faint. She closed her eyes and sat perfectly still. Then a vision of peace and light overtook her. She was in a great white space of some sort. It felt wonderful to be there. And then her grandmother, Elsa, was with her, smiling, laughing, putting her arm around Sarah, the way she used to do when both of them had been younger.

And then Elsa said, "Thank you, darling. You have been so good to me. Take care of Adam. And take care of Joshua Daniel." Then, turning from

Sarah, she began to walk off into the brightness. Sarah felt no eagerness, nor any need, to stop her. She watched as she disappeared into the light.

The vision ended. Sarah sat quietly, feeling at peace, a sense of wellbeing surging over her. When, at last, she opened her eyes, the first thing she saw was the clock on the wall. It was five minutes before five o'clock in the afternoon.

"Ma'am?"

She looked at the man, still sitting on the bed, nearby. He said, "Are you all right?" She nodded. But she felt as though all her energy had left her.

WHEN JOSH AND SARAH returned to their home, shortly after six, the house was quiet. When they walked into the hallway that led to the library, they heard Adam's soulful sobs. They found him seated next to Elsa's side of the bed, holding her lifeless hand, his head bowed. When he looked up at them, the tears were flowing down his face.

"She died so quietly," he said. "It was as if she knew it was time."

Sarah knelt down beside her grandfather's chair and smoothed her hand across his back and shoulders. "I'm so sorry, Grampa. But she's at peace now."

Adam said, "She didn't really know me at the end."

"Maybe she did," said Josh, reassuringly.

"No," Adam replied. "I'm sure she didn't. The last thing she said to me was, 'Tell Sarah to take care of Adam. And tell her to take care of Joshua Daniel.'"

Adam pursed his lips, fighting back tears.

Sarah felt a chill run down her spine. She said, "When did she die, Grampa?" She felt a second chill when she heard his reply.

"It was just five minutes before five o'clock."

Chapter 29

"Thanks, Mom. Great as usual."

"You know, Paul David, one of these days you're going to wish you'd learned to cook. You're not going to have me around to prepare supper for you forever." Molly Engelhardt looked affectionately at her bachelor son.

"Mom, if that ever happens, God forbid, there are restaurants out there. Or, so I've heard."

"I think you might get sick of going to those."

Paul David waited. He was positive this was the lead-in to another of his parents' familiar 'When-are-you-getting-married?' routines. But the commentary never came. Instead, his mother said, "Scott and Claire-Ellen Rankin were over here a couple nights ago. Your father and I invited them. We thought it was time we got better acquainted with our youth ministry couple."

Paul David wondered why his mother would mention that to him.

"Scott asked about you."

"What about me? I've only talked to them a couple times in my life."

"I know. They wanted us to ask you something."

Paul David shook his head. "If they think I've got time to volunteer for work with the Luther League, tell them to forget it. I'm burning the candle at both ends these days."

"That's another thing," said David, setting down his coffee cup. "Are you ever going to take a vacation, or do you intend to keep going full speed until you drop from exhaustion?"

Paul David returned a thoughtful look. "I probably should take some time off. It's just that, I really like the work. You know?"

"I know. I did your job for over ten years. But you have to take a break once in a while."

"So, Mom," Paul David said, trying to change the subject, "What did Scott Rankin want to ask me?"

Molly said, "They have almost fifty kids signed up to go to the national Luther League Convention in Indiana this summer. The two of them are going as adult sponsors. They need one more woman, and one more man, to go along. Scott thought you'd be perfect."

"Why?"

"Well, because you're single. You're young. The kids all think your beard makes you look like a 'really neat guy.' That was Scott's description, by the way. And, because your father had already mentioned to the Rankins that he really wished you'd take a vacation."

Paul David said, "So, this is really your doing, right, Dad?"

David shrugged. "Don't look at me. Asking you to go to West Lafayette, Indiana, with a trainload of teen-agers was *their* idea, not mine."

Paul David looked at his mother. "What did you tell them?"

"I told them it was up to you. They'll be calling you one of these next days."

"Gosh, Mom, I don't know. I'm 23. These kids are teen-agers. I'm already forgetting what it was like to be one. They're all probably full of the dickens. Sounds like a lot of work. Not much of a vacation, really."

"Remember when you went to one of those conventions?"

"Sure. Ames, Iowa. It was…really great, actually."

"Well, you couldn't have gone if some adult hadn't taken time off to go along as a sponsor."

"Lutheran guilt," Paul David muttered. "You're using Lutheran guilt on me."

Molly laughed. "No guilt, Paul David. It really is up to you. I just want you to do the right thing."

"Or else I start cooking for myself, right?"

"I didn't say that."

He studied the tablecloth, mulling the idea. Finally he said, "Dad, you want to edit the paper for a couple weeks? You still remember how to do that?"

David looked at his son, pretending shock. "You wound me with such a question," he replied dramatically. Then he said, "Sure. If you can trust me with the *Bloomington Avenue News* for that long."

His son narrowed his eyes, as if contemplating an applicant for a job. He said, "I'll take the chance."

FOR HIS SIXTY-THIRD birthday, Josh and Sarah took Adam to The River's Edge for a special supper. Josh had informed Sandy Elliot in advance. The owner of the thriving supper club had arranged a secluded table for the threesome, with a spectacular view of the Mississippi River. She instructed her staff to give her guests special treatment and, by the time a surprise birthday cake was delivered to the table, she had taken the empty chair, more or less inviting herself to share in the festivities.

Adam was smiling from ear to ear when the blazing confection arrived at the table. Sandy said, "I instructed the birthday singers not to serenade you tonight, Adam. I didn't want to embarrass you."

"You have birthday singers?" Adam said, surprised.

"Not really," she said, laughing. "But it might have been a nice touch. I don't know a nicer person than you, Adam. We're really honored Josh and Sarah decided to bring the patriarch of Saint Michael Church up here for this little party."

"Well, they're really too good to me," he replied. "Now that my wife is gone, I really should be moving out of their house. But they simply won't hear of it. Aren't they the best grandchildren you've ever heard of?" He took an enormous breath and blew out the dancing flames.

"Grampa is the easiest person in the world to have in our home," said Sarah. "Besides, he's a fabulous cook. Josh and I come home from work, and Adam has a tasty casserole steaming in the oven. Or, you name it. He can cook all sorts of things."

"Enough," said Adam. "Humility is a Christian virtue. I'm in danger of losing mine right now."

"It's your cake," said Josh. "Go ahead and cut it."

As the guest of honor filled the dessert plates, Sandy said, "You know, Adam, you and I have something in common."

"We both like to cook?"

"Well, no. I really don't. That's why I have a kitchen staff." She chuckled. "I like cooking well enough, but I like running the supper club a lot more. Anyway, that wasn't what I had in mind."

"What, then?"

Sandy looked tentatively at Josh, then Sarah, before declaring quietly, "You and I have each lost a loved one in the not so distant past."

Adam laid down the cake knife. He looked wistfully at Sandy. "That's right. The Lord took your wonderful little girl from you."

"I still miss her. Just as I know you miss Elsa. She was a special lady."

Adam said, "You know, I'd prefer we ended this celebration on a happy note." She nodded. "But I would really like to spend some time talking with you about that topic. I suspect you and I could help one another. Can we do that?"

"Absolutely, Adam. I'd like that very much. Very much indeed."

AS THE PASSENGER TRAIN made its way from West Lafayette, Indiana, to Minneapolis, Paul David found himself seated next to Jenny Langholz. The sun had gone down and most of the Luther Leaguers in their care had begun to settle back into their seats for the evening. The clackety-clack of the wheels on the tracks was already lulling many of them to sleep.

Jenny said, "I wasn't really planning to go to this convention. In fact, I'll have to be back in the classroom just a few weeks after we get home. But, the Rankins were really persistent. And, you know, I'm really glad I came."

"No kidding," Paul David murmured. He'd thought he might just go to sleep about now, but obviously Jenny wasn't quite ready for that.

"It brought back memories of the convention I went to, back in 1943," she continued. "It was in Dubuque, Iowa. That one was a lot smaller. But it was a really great experience." She paused, then added, "Hannah Ruth Jonas and I went together." She sighed. "Now she's off in Philadelphia, married, giving music lessons to kids." She paused again. "Seems like a long, long way from high school."

Paul David wasn't all that eager to pursue the conversation, but he didn't want to be rude. "I went to the convention at Iowa State University. That was pretty unforgettable."

"It's amazing how young these high school kids seem. Back when I was one myself, I felt like I was practically an adult. Looking back, I realize I was really pretty immature in those days."

Paul David listened to the clacking of the wheels on the rails.

Jenny said, "Did you have any trouble with James Wilson during the convention?"

He thought about it. James was a high school junior, the only one in his group of twelve who wasn't a member of Saint Michael Church. He'd come along because a Luther Leaguer had invited him. "Ahh...no, not really. I did notice he spent a lot of time with Alice Feldermann. Seems like they were sitting together at almost all the sessions. But James wasn't any trouble, really."

"The reason I asked was, Alice was sort of a loner when we started out. But once we got to Purdue University, James started paying so much attention to her, I wondered if either of them were getting anything out of the convention program."

"Yeah. They were doing a lot of hand-holding, that's true."

"Did you notice? They're sitting together on this trip home."

"No. I didn't." He thought about it. "You think that might be a problem?"

She laughed softly. "I don't know. What do you think?"

"Where are they sitting?"

"Five rows ahead, our side of the train."

"Hang on a minute," he said, stepping into the aisle. He walked through the car until he reached the seat where James and Alice were sitting. They were fast asleep. James had his arm around her shoulders, and Alice was leaning close to him. But it seemed harmless enough.

When Paul David was back in his seat he said, "They're both unconscious. I didn't detect any signs of hanky-panky."

She chortled softly.

They rode in silence, except for the sound of the train. Suddenly, not sure why he did it, Paul David said, "Whatever happened to that guy, Buzz Winslow, you used to go with?"

"I make it a policy not to think about him," she said frostily.

"I knew him in high school. Before he started going with you." She didn't respond. "He was a real showoff, I thought. Egotist, maybe, is the better word."

"I'd say that fits."

"He ever get married or anything?"

"Actually, he did. Let me correct that. He *had* to get married."

"I'd say that fits, too," said Paul David.

"He's working in a night club, out in Hopkins or Wayzata or someplace like that."

"I remember he always drove around in that two-tone convertible."

Jenny remained silent. Paul David realized that, for a conversation he really hadn't wanted to get into, he had been doing quite a bit of talking. And, it occurred to him that Jenny had volunteered some fairly significant information about somebody she really didn't want to talk about.

He said, "How do you like teaching fourth grade?"

"I love it. It's what I was meant to do. And fourth grade is exactly the right level for me."

"Does it seem strange, saying goodbye to your students every year and having to say hello to a whole new bunch of them every fall?"

"Not at all. That's part of the charm of it. Just think of all the kids who are going to graduate from high school and who will remember having had me in the fourth grade. I'm building this enormous fan club."

"Assuming they all have happy memories from your class." He realized the comment might have sounded insensitive. "Not that they wouldn't, of course."

"Oh, you get one or two a year. Usually kids who have trouble at home. They end up being trouble at school. You just have to try to help them, the best way you can. Sometimes it works out, sometimes it doesn't."

"What kind of trouble at home?"

"Broken families, mostly. You know, after the soldiers came back from the war, we had this big surge of divorces. Women had taken jobs while the men were gone. When the guys came back, a lot of their wives didn't want to just stay home and have babies. They wanted careers. It broke up a lot of marriages. I've seen some of that in the families of some of the kids I teach. It's really unfortunate."

"You know, James Wilson comes from a home like that. He lives with his mother. He hardly knows his father anymore."

"I didn't know that," Jenny replied. She added, "How terribly sad for him."

ADAM ENGELHARDT and Sandy Elliot sat drinking coffee at midmorning. The River's Edge was officially closed, but Sandy had invited Adam to come anyway. It would be, she assured him, the best of all possible times for a private chat.

"It's been two years since Priscilla Ann died," she said. "She would have been four this year. I still miss her terribly."

"You had her for such a short time," Adam said sympathetically. "It wasn't that way at all with Elsa and me. I had her for a lifetime. But, in some ways, it's just as difficult losing someone who's become your soul mate. It's so indescribably difficult to finally let them go."

"I know," Sandy said, laying her hand on his. "I felt that way when my father died. He was only 55. He had congestive heart failure. I felt cheated, somehow, when it happened. I was counting on enjoying his later years, and having him give me away in marriage, and seeing his grandchildren..." She paused and began to sob. With difficulty, she finished "...seeing them grow up."

Adam sighed heavily. "I don't know why God allows things to happen as they do. I only know that we are all in God's good keeping. We need to trust him with our lives."

"Oh, Adam, I try to. I really do." She dabbed the corners of her eyes with her handkerchief. "But, I'm afraid God and I haven't been on such good terms lately. I haven't been to church for so long, I'm not sure I'd know how to behave if I ever went back." She hesitated before continuing. "Sometimes I wonder if God was punishing me by taking my daughter away, because I had been so unfaithful."

"Bad theology," said Adam, smiling. "That isn't the way God operates."

"Oh, I know it isn't. It's just what I find myself thinking when I'm feeling sorry for myself. Still, I can't imagine God is very happy with me these days."

"You know, Sandy, there's always an opportunity to start fresh. You and Arnold could come back to Saint Michael Church any one of these next Sundays and start getting reconnected with the congregation—and with God."

"Well, that's another thing. Arnold isn't coming back to church, I can guarantee you that. He hardly even comes home anymore. That skunk is arranging his flights to Chicago so he has to stay down there as long as possible. I'm convinced of it. When he walks in the house, he seems like a stranger to me these days."

"Maybe you should go with him on some of his flights."

"I don't think his corporate clients would be too excited about that. Sometimes he has all the seats full. And, anyway, what would I do, sitting around in Chicago while he does who knows what? I have this place to run."

"It was just a suggestion."

"You're a good friend, Adam. I know you meant well."

"Well, thank you for the coffee. I think I should be getting back. I'm fixing meatloaf for my grandchildren for supper. I haven't been to the market yet."

"You're so amazing. What would they do without you?"

"Well, hire a cook, I guess."

She grinned. "Come back out here any time you like. Understand?"

"I'd like to. But only if Arnold doesn't get jealous."

"Don't you worry about Arnold. Not for a minute. What he doesn't know won't hurt him. Believe me."

Chapter 30

Paul David Engelhardt had finished his supper and excused himself from the table. Molly sat looking at her husband, who was taking his time finishing his coffee. She waited for him to set his cup down before speaking.

"David, I had a call from Sarah this afternoon."

"Is that so unusual?"

"No. But what she said to me is going to cause some problems."

David eyed his wife carefully.

"She said she's planning on having us at their place for Thanksgiving."

"Well, that might be a nice change. We always have them here. And, for once, you wouldn't have to cook."

"David, I can't go there."

"Why not?"

"You know why."

"Actually, I don't."

She exhaled heavily. "You're going to scold me for saying this, but I can't go into a house where that…that damned…"

"Molly, after all these years, I thought maybe those Morgan-Houseman demons would have been exorcised from you. Obviously not."

"It's not as easy as it seems, David. You know what that villain did to me."

David wished he and Molly could both forget. But the memory of how her one-time employer had made her his sexual victim, had threatened to blackmail her if she revealed it to anyone, and then had gotten her pregnant out of wedlock, still seared their memories. But it had all happened in 1927, and that was 26 years ago. Besides, Michael Morgan-Houseman had killed himself long, long ago.

Molly said, "I really thought I'd gotten past all of that. After you talked to me that time, out at my parents' farm in Litchfield, I tried to forget about him. I really did. But…"

"But the house he lived in is a reminder, just like that stained-glass window at church is, the one with his little boy in the design."

"The church window doesn't bother me anymore. But that house..."

"I suppose I should have tried to discourage my father from taking such an interest in the place. But you know how he is about old historical buildings."

"When I found out he'd talked Harry Broadman into buying it, I was really angry with him. But I didn't say anything. How can you be angry with Adam? But then when Harry told us he was probably going to use the place to put up historical displays for the congregation's anniversary year, I was furious." She continued, "But then he told us they wouldn't have displays over there. That made me happy. And when he said he was going to sell the place, I was really pleased. But then he gave it to Sarah and Josh for a wedding present. I almost went into a depression."

David nodded. He hadn't realized his wife had been on such an emotional roller coaster. "You never told me any of this."

"I was too ashamed."

"Molly, when you have feelings, you need to deal with them."

"I know. I probably should have said something." She looked contrite, but only momentarily. "So, I'm saying it now. You need to know my feelings about Thanksgiving Day. I really don't want to go over there."

"Well, we don't have to go. We can have everybody come here. But it may hurt Sarah's feelings. You've never told her the story about you and Morgan-Houseman, and I don't blame you. But that means you'd have to make up an excuse. Would you feel good about doing that?"

Molly showed a defeated look. "Oh, probably not. But is there anything wrong with telling a white lie once in a while?"

"I don't care what color the lie is, once you start telling them, your credibility is shot. Besides, after you tell the first one, the next one comes more easily. Pretty soon they're tripping off your tongue. That's what we taught our children, remember?"

She was silent.

"Actually, I think it would be healthy for you just to go over there once and get it over with. It's their house now. Dad is living there very happily. The place is full of the spirit of the three of them. And, you'd get to see all those amazing stones set into the wall around the fireplace. Josh can tell you where each of them came from."

Molly had a morose look about her. "I was really hoping you'd just say we didn't have to go."

"Well, I did say that."

"But you really want me to go."

"Yes, that's true. I do."

She folded her hands on the table in front of her and studied them in silence. "All right. We'll go then. But if I have a panic attack, you have to promise to bring me right home."

David returned a broad smile. "At the first sign of one."

WHEN SHE CAME HOME after a day in the classroom, Jenny Langholz found a note taped to her bedroom door. She pulled it off, unfolded it and recognized her mother's handwriting.

Jenny, there were two phone calls for you this afternoon. One was from Pastor Jonas, the second from Paul David Engelhardt. Both asked that you call them. Mom.

She went down to the dining room and called the church office. Janet Fenstermacher informed her Pastor Jonas was out making home visits. She suggested Jenny try phoning him the next day from school, during a break between classes.

She called the *Bloomington Avenue News*. The receptionist put her on hold. Paul David picked it up.

"Hi. Did you talk to Pastor Jonas?"

"No. He wasn't available. I have to call him tomorrow."

"Listen, do you have twenty spare minutes to come over here? I'll try to tell you what's going on."

THE EDITOR'S OFFICE was a blizzard of paper. There were stacks of it everywhere. Paul David had to clear a chair for Jenny, moving the clutter to a different location.

When they were both seated, he took a deep breath and said, "You remember James Wilson and Alice Feldermann?" She returned a blank stare. "The Luther League convention last summer."

"Oh. Yes. Of course. Alice was one of my twelve girls. James was one of your dozen boys."

"Exactly. Well, their mothers want you and me, and Pastor Jonas, to meet with them."

"What about?"

"Pastor Jonas wouldn't say. He said the parents weren't all that specific either. But evidently they're upset about something. And they think we're involved in whatever it is."

"Oh, my."

JOSH JONAS looked up from his desk at the free medical clinic, expecting to see the next client at the door. Instead, it was a uniformed policeman.

"Skip! What are you doing in south Minneapolis on a weekday? This isn't exactly your beat."

"Lunch break. Don't you ever take one?"

"Sometimes I just skip it."

"Well, there's a diner two blocks from here. Come on. I'm buying."

"I may have a client coming."

"We'll just tell the receptionist to inform the next one that a cop came in here and suddenly took you away."

"I don't think that would be a good idea."

"Okay, then have her tell them you were feeling faint and had to go get some lunch."

Josh frowned, looked at his watch, gazed at the empty doorway and said, "Okay. Let's get out of here."

AS HE SPREAD mustard on his bratwurst, Skip Warner said, "I wanted you to be the first to know. Karen and I are going to have baby number two."

"Have you told your parents—and hers?"

"We'll tell them tonight."

"Wow. I really *am* the first to find out."

"We've always been best buddies. I had to tell you."

"And now you want to know why Sarah and I haven't had our first one yet, I suppose."

"Well, the question had occurred to me."

"Neither of us are ready. We figured it out. If one of us stopped working, we wouldn't be able to pay our bills."

"Your house is free and clear."

"We have to pay for groceries. Taxes. Everyday expenses. And I'm making monthly payments to Luther Fischer for the Pontiac."

"I thought he gave you a deal."

"He did, you lunkhead. But, considering what I'm able to pay him, it's still gonna take about four years."

"Okay, so no babies for awhile, it sounds like."

"Probably not. I think my folks and her folks may be a little disappointed. Neither have any grandchildren yet."

"Well, you don't have kids just for the grandparents."

"I know. But you always get the feeling they wish you'd have them."

Skip nodded and grinned. "I want to show you something." He unbuttoned the sleeve of his shirt and pulled it back. There was a tender red scar, running along his forearm, from just above the wrist to just below the elbow."

"Yike. What happened there?"

"Battle wound," Skip said. "Got it ten days ago. Some lunatic on Broadway was trying to hold up a bakery. I got the call and raced over there. I walked in the door, the guy turned around and took a shot at me. Grazed my arm. Man, was I lucky."

Josh's heart was racing. "He could have killed you!"

"I'm wearing a bulletproof vest, Josh."

"It doesn't cover your head, Buddy."

"Yeah. You're right. He *could* have killed me. If he'd really known what he was doing. Turns out, he'd stolen the gun just before the holdup. I don't think he knew the first thing about how to use the dang thing."

"What happened to the guy?"

"Well, he's in the slammer, of course. I wasn't gonna let him get away, not after he shot a hole in my shirt sleeve and everything."

THE FIVE OF THEM sat around a table in the Reformation Room at the Lutheran church of Saint Michael and All Angels. The late afternoon sunlight streamed in through stained-glass scenes of Erfurt, Worms, Eisenach, Wittenberg and Augsburg, German cities central to the Lutheran Reformation.

Abigail Feldermann and Nancy Wilson, the parents of the two youth who had attended the Luther League convention, were seated on one side of the long rectangular table. Across from them, Jenny Langholz sat next to Paul David Engelhardt.

At one end, Pastor Daniel Jonas was seated. There was a serious look on his face. He turned to Abigail, a widow who had belonged to the congregation for the past three years. "Let's begin with you, Abigail. Tell Jennifer and Paul David what you told me the other day."

Abigail said solemnly, "My daughter, Alice, is pregnant."

Jenny's mouth dropped open.

"She says it happened at the Luther League convention. I understood she was being chaperoned by an adult." She looked sternly at Jenny as she said it.

"That would be impossible, Mrs. Feldermann. Those girls were never out of my sight. Never. I slept in the same dormitory annex with them. Boys didn't go in there."

"My son, James, says he's the father," said Nancy. "He claims they did it on the train trip home. In the middle of the night."

Paul David felt the hairs begin to stand along the back of his neck. He said, "Mrs. Wilson, I can't believe that. We were all riding in coach seating. They would have had to...you know...it would have to have been in full view of other passengers. Besides, I checked on them during the trip home." He realized that was only partly true. He'd only checked on them once.

"Alice said they had a blanket covering them. They did it after the sponsors were all asleep." She looked fiercely at Paul David. "What I want to know is, why were they allowed to sit together all those hours on a dark train? It sounds like an invitation to temptation." She paused. "Obviously, that's what it was."

Paul David said, "When I checked on them, they weren't using a blanket. I didn't see one."

"Are you calling my son a liar?"

"I'm saying...I don't know exactly what happened. But I think it might be good if I could speak with your son."

"I don't think so, young man. The damage is done. And I want to know what the church is going to do about it."

Jenny surprised herself by saying, "With all due respect, Mrs. Wilson, it isn't the church that caused this to happen. It was your son."

"They're just kids," Nancy shot back. "They were in your care. I'd think you'd take some responsibility for this."

Jenny thought, *What about a little parental responsibility?* But she said nothing.

Daniel finally stopped the conversation. "I think things are beginning to deteriorate," he said. "Both of you parents have shared your concerns. The youth sponsors have heard them. I'll want to speak to Jennifer and Paul David alone. And, Abigail...and Nancy...we need to talk some more as well."

Abigail dropped her eyes. But Nancy was defiant. "I don't need to talk with anybody. I'm not a member of this church. This is exactly the reason I don't belong to a church. I should have known there wouldn't be any help coming from a meeting like this." She got up to leave.

"Mrs. Wilson, your son has already admitted paternity. I don't think you can just walk away from this," Daniel said as evenly as he could.

"Oh, don't you! Well, just watch me!" She stormed out of the room and disappeared down the hall.

Daniel looked temporarily shaken. But he quickly composed himself and said, "Abigail, would you be willing to let me speak with Alice, just she and I? I promise not to scold or accuse her, or make her feel any worse about this than she does now."

"Yes. I'd appreciate that, Pastor. And, I should apologize for Mrs. Wilson's behavior."

"You have nothing to apologize for. I think maybe *she* does, however."

Chapter 31

Jenny Langholz was already seated in the booth at the coffee shop when Paul David walked in. He was ten minutes late when he slid into the seat facing her. He sighed and said, "Sorry. Deadlines."

She smiled. "Don't apologize. I needed time to think."

"Bet you never thought going on a youth outing would get you caught up in a controversy."

"I hardly slept last night. I wonder what my fourth graders thought of me. I must have had circles under my eyes." He nodded. But she continued, "During lunch hour today, I called Claire-Ellen Rankin. We had a pretty interesting conversation."

"What did she say?"

"As it turns out, she and Scott were sitting just one row in front of Alice and James, but on the other side of the aisle, on that train trip home. Claire-Ellen says she didn't sleep much that night. She had all her girls' welfare on her mind. She was sort of staying tuned for sounds, movement, stuff like that. She also says she looked over at Alice and James six or seven times during the night, mainly because they were one of only two boy-girl couples seated that way."

"And?"

"For one thing, they never used a blanket. In fact, if you'll remember, it was plenty warm on that train. She didn't remember the porters making blankets available to anybody."

Paul David stroked his chin thoughtfully. "Well, that's pretty interesting. Anything else?"

"She said if the two of them had been doing anything like they claim they did that night, she would have seen it."

"And she didn't."

"Absolutely not."

"Well, then I guess you can sleep better tonight."

"Maybe. But we still don't know what Mrs. Wilson is going to do. I'm sure she still believes her son."

The waitress finally came. Paul David ordered coffee. When she departed, he said, "I spent last night in bed wondering if one or both of us were going to need a lawyer." Jenny offered a wan smile. He said, "I've never had to do that. Ever. I know there are a few of them in the congregation. There's Gene Hennig…and Larry Crosby…and Dwight Penas. Maybe we should talk to one of them about this."

"Let's not borrow trouble. Alice and Pastor Jonas are supposed to be having their little talk sometime in the next couple days. We should wait until that's over with."

He nodded. "You know, Jennifer…"

"Why don't you just call me Jenny. I'm not your teacher, you know."

"What do they actually call you? In the classroom, I mean."

"They call me Miss Langholz."

"So, who calls you Jennifer?"

"My grandparents. And my mother, when she's really angry with me."

He laughed. "My folks have called me Paul David for so long, I've decided it's my official name. I even sign my letters that way."

She studied his handsome face. It occurred to her she hadn't ever had coffee alone with a man before. She'd never considered Buzz to be adult enough to be described that way.

"You were pretty good in that meeting at church yesterday," he said.

"You weren't so bad yourself." She began reliving the experience in her mind. "At one point, I really wanted to walk around to the other side of the table and slap Susan Wilson right on the face. She was really rude. And irritating. And downright insulting."

"But put yourself in her place. She was humiliated. And angry. And probably at her wits' end. I suspect she figured she'd done the best she could, trying to raise her son without his father around, and this was the thanks she got out of it."

"Well, if she were my mother, I'd probably have moved out by now."

"The boy's a junior in high school, Jenny. Where would he go?"

She realized he was right. In spite of that, she replied, "Well, maybe moving in with that good-for-nothing father of his might have been an improvement on what he has now."

"I'd be surprised if that were true. And, anyway, when all is said and done, the fact remains, he got this girl pregnant. He's going to have to deal with that. Somehow."

DANIEL JONAS closed the office door and sat down in the chair facing Alice Feldermann. As he did so, he said, "Mrs. Fenstermacher is going to stay in her office, on the other side of the wall, while we talk. I can leave the door open if you'd like."

The teenage girl looked like a frightened rabbit. But she said, "No. You don't need to."

Daniel chose his words carefully. "You know that your mother, and James' mother, were both here yesterday." She nodded miserably. "And Jennifer Langholz, and Paul David Engelhardt, two of the adult counselors who went with you to the convention, were also here."

Alice said, "I shouldn't have spent so much time with James. He's a really nice boy. But I didn't even know him before we got on the train. And by the time we got to the convention, he was sitting next to me and holding my hand and everything."

Daniel nodded. He said, "I know this may seem painful for you, but I need to have you tell me exactly what happened on the train coming home."

"We sat together. He had his arm around me. I liked it, so I let him."

Daniel waited. He decided to let the story come out without his prompting.

She continued, "We slept together." He sat up, surprised at what he'd just heard. But she added, "I don't mean we actually did anything. We just slept, all the way back. Everybody was pretty tired by the time we got on the train."

"You and James didn't…do anything else…except just sleep?"

Alice was silent. She fidgeted with her hands. Her gaze darted about the office walls, from one framed picture to another. Then she looked at the floor. "I know lying is a sin. I didn't want to lie. James and I agreed on the same story. We told the same thing to both of our mothers."

Daniel waited. Tears began to form in her eyes, and then to flow down her cheeks. Finally he said, "Alice, did James get you pregnant?"

She nodded, still staring at the carpet.

"Did it happen on the train?"

She shook her head slowly from side to side.

"Then tell me what really happened."

She found a tissue in her purse and blew her nose. Her eyes remained focused on the floor. She began haltingly. "After we got home, James called me. He said he had a stack of really good photographs he'd taken at the convention. I was in a lot of them. He wanted me to see them. I agreed to go over to his place one afternoon, about the second or third day after school started. His mom wasn't there. She works downtown. We were alone in his apartment. He said it was okay. He said his friends are always coming over when nobody's there except him."

She took a deep breath and let it out heavily. "We looked at the pictures. We were on the living room couch. He had his arm around me while we did. Pretty soon he was kissing me on the cheek and the neck. Then he told me he thought he was falling in love with me. He said it started happening while we were at the convention."

Daniel said, "Alice, look up. Look at me." She obeyed. "Did you feel the same way about James?"

Her lower lip was quivering. "I don't know. I really liked him. A lot. When he told me he thought he was falling in love with me, it made me feel really...well, I've never had a boy pay attention to me before. I'm sort of shy."

Daniel nodded. With trepidation, he asked, "What happened after that?"

She hesitated. "He got up from the couch. He took my hand and pulled me up too. He said, 'Come on. My mom won't be home for a couple more hours.' He took me into her bedroom. He helped me take my clothes off. For some reason, I didn't want to stop him. Then he took his off."

"This happened in his *mother's* bedroom?"

"It was his idea. I don't really know why he wanted to do it there."

Daniel sat thinking. He said, "You realize a couple of our adult convention sponsors are in some hot water because of what the two of you said."

"I know." More tears began to fall. She began to cry softly.

"Have you told your mother what you just told me?"

"No. I'm afraid to."

"Has James told his mother?"

"He never would."

"Why not?"

"He doesn't get along with her. He told me he hardly ever tells her the truth about anything."

DANIEL STOPPED BY the apartment building where Alice and her mother lived. He had phoned ahead, so Abigail Feldermann was expecting him. In the living room of her tidy apartment, he sat waiting as she poured a cup of coffee for him. He thanked her, took a sip, and then set down the cup.

"I spoke with Alice."

"I know. She told me."

"Did she tell you what she said to me?"

"No. She said I should wait to hear it from you."

"Abigail, I want you to promise me something."

"I suppose it depends on what it is."

"I want you to promise that, after I tell you what Alice told me, you won't punish her. She's going to need some love and acceptance."

Abigail had trepidation in her eyes. But she silently agreed.

"I'm not sure, really, whose fault any of this is," Daniel continued. "But Alice admitted to me she and James didn't get intimate on the train. Or anywhere else during the convention trip." Abigail returned a skeptical look, tinged with surprise. "They were in bed together at James' apartment. After they were back in school."

"How do we know they're telling the truth?"

"Alice says the two of them agreed together to make up a story and stick to it. Then she realized other people were getting in trouble because of it. So she decided to tell me what really happened."

Pastor, I'm not trying to be difficult with you, but I still need to know. How can we know for sure which version of her story is the right one?"

"That's the problem, isn't it. Once someone tells an untruth, you don't know which part of their story to believe after that." Abigail nodded. "But I'm pretty sure the second story is the right one."

"What makes you sure?"

"I spoke with the other two adults who went with the Luther Leaguers. They're confident Alice and James didn't do anything on the trip home, except sleep. One of those two adults was awake most of the night, trying to keep watch over the girls. She's persuaded Alice's original story is a fabrication."

Abigail sat quietly, staring into space. Finally she said, "Well, I'm glad the adult sponsors aren't implicated in this. For their sake." Daniel's expression was one of silent agreement. "But for my daughter's sake, and James', I don't know how to feel. James has gotten my daughter pregnant. I'm not sure if he forced her, or exactly what happened…"

"They both agreed to it, as it turns out."

She sighed and shook her head. "If Alice didn't try to stop him, I don't know how it can be all his fault."

"They both made a mistake. I just hope you can forgive your daughter."

"Oh, I can forgive her," she replied testily. "But she has a baby on the way. She's not finished with high school. She's too young to get married—and, I think we both know, she's emotionally too immature. I don't believe in abortions, and I didn't teach Alice to believe in them either. I just don't know what future she's going to have."

"Talk to Alice. Be kind. Be patient with her. Make sure she knows you love her, even after all of this. And, if I can help in any way, please let me be of assistance. For her sake. And for yours."

"YOU DID WHAT?"

"I had to tell him. You can't lie to a pastor."

"Alice, you can lie to anybody if you set your mind to it."

"Maybe *you* can. Not me."

"So where does that leave me? Your mom is going to tell my mom, and I'm gonna catch hell for this!"

"I'm sorry, James. I'm just not a very good liar."

"You can say that again!"

MOLLY ENGELHARDT cleared away Paul David's supper dishes and headed for the kitchen. She stopped, turned back and said, "Oh, by the way, your grandfather was here this afternoon."

"Adam?"

"Yes. He came for the key to your house. There was something in one of the dresser drawers, an old framed picture, he wanted to pick up."

"Did he find it?"

"Yes. And he brought back the key."

Paul David waited for the next sentence, but his mother just looked at him. "Is there more?"

"He was, shall we say, a little disappointed...with you."

"I know, Mom. The place is a real pigpen."

"Couldn't you be a little tidier? It never looked that way when he and your grandmother lived there. I think he was hoping to get a reminder of what it had been like when the two of them were still living there. It turned to be rather upsetting for him."

"He had Gramma to keep the place clean. I have no time for anything."

"Well, I'm not trying to scold you. I just thought you should know, your grandfather was disappointed—maybe even a little shocked by what he saw. Just in case you see him anytime soon."

Chapter 32

It was ten o'clock in the morning. The weekly edition of the *Bloomington Avenue News* had just gone to the printer. Paul David was enjoying one of the rare moments of peace and tranquility in his work week. He was leaning back in his desk chair, his shoes propped up on the edge of the desk, his hands clasped behind his head. In his line of sight, on the office wall, was the framed certificate proving he had graduated with a degree in journalism from the University of Minnesota.

College life was becoming for him a fast-fading memory. It had been a good four years, but he had been eager to get finished so he could start editing his father's newspaper. In retrospect, he realized that, even with the class load, homework, extra-curricular activities, and weekends working for his father, those school days had been carefree by comparison.

A gentle rapping came at the door frame. To guarantee accessibility to everyone, he'd had the door removed, so the only place for a visitor to knock was on the frame.

"A young man to see you, chief," said Tom Tozer, his advertising manager.

"Anybody I know?"

"He says he knows *you.*"

"Show him in," Paul David said, removing his feet from the desk. He pulled himself erect and watched the doorway.

In walked fifteen-year-old James Wilson.

Paul David blinked twice. It was the middle of a school day. What was this high school junior doing in his office? "James. What a surprise. Come on in."

He cleared away a stack of paper from the only other available chair in the cluttered office and gestured to the teen-ager to have a seat.

James sat down in the old wooden captain's chair and gripped the arms as if he feared he might otherwise fall out of it. He showed a brave face, but Paul David saw the uncertainty in the young man's eyes.

"What can I do for you, James?"

"I...umm...I need some advice."

"Okay."

"I...ahh...things are kind of a great big mess for me right now."

Paul David nodded. "How can I help you?"

"You know I got Alice Feldermann pregnant, right?"

"Yes. I know."

"Well, here's the thing. I didn't exactly tell my mom the whole story about that."

Paul David already knew the story, but decided to let James tell it.

"I actually lied to her. Told her we slept together on the train, coming back from that convention. Turns out, we slept together at my place. It was my idea. Alice didn't necessarily want to."

"So, I guess your mom's not mad at me any more then." Why had he just said that? He suspected it wasn't helping the situation much where James was concerned.

"The person my mom's mad at is me. Mad as hell. See, she thinks I did this to get back at her for some reason."

"Do you have some reason to want to do that?"

"I don't know. I guess I'm mad at her a lot. Because all she ever does is yell at me. I never do anything right for her. I get the feeling I'm always in her way. I don't think she really wanted to have me. And she's stuck with me. Since my dad took off, when I was little, she's been stuck with raising me. And living in that crummy apartment. I guess that's maybe why I did it. Partly."

"Did what? Got Alice pregnant?"

"Yeah. In my mom's bed." Paul David sat straight up. He hadn't heard that detail before. "I could have done it in my own room. But I did it in hers." He drummed his fingers on the arms of the chair. "I guess maybe I really hate her for how she treats me. I think that's why I did it there."

"You told your mom all this?"

"No. Alice's mom did. Alice can't keep a secret. And she can't tell a decent lie."

"I'd say that's to Alice's credit."

"Yeah, well, maybe. But it sure as hell didn't help *me* any."

"She would have found out sooner or later, don't you think?"

James seemed not to have heard the question. "When I got home from school yesterday, she was worse than ever. She yelled and swore at me. Said I was wrecking her life. Called me worse names than she's ever used before."

"I'm sorry, James. No young man should be treated like that."

"That's not the worst."

"What could be worse than that?"

"She threw me out. She said when I went to school this morning, I didn't need to bother coming back. She was having the locks changed. She told me I could go live with Alice, for all she cared. Or go live in the city park. Or in a cardboard box."

For the first time, James looked vulnerable. His head was down. Paul David heard him sniffing. He got up, carried his chair around to the other side of the desk, kicked a pile of newspapers out of the way, and set it down next to James. He sat next to him and said, "James, look at me."

James didn't look up. Paul David lifted the youngster's chin and saw that his eyes were red.

"Has she ever said that sort of thing to you before?"

He sniffed. "She used to say if I didn't change my attitude, she was going to put me in an orphanage or something. But she's never thrown me out before."

"You're sure she actually meant to do that?"

"When I got up this morning, she had already gone to work. She had my suitcase packed. It was on my chair, at the kitchen table."

Paul David was speechless.

"So, I guess I need some advice." He swallowed hard. "Do you know anybody who wants to have a stray kid come and live with them for a couple years?"

FOR SOME REASON, Paul David had chosen the same booth in the coffee shop where he and Jenny Langholz had sat, discussing Alice and James. Now, here he was, at 10:40 on a Friday morning, looking across the table at James Wilson.

The high school junior looked at the glass of coke sitting in front of him, but didn't drink from it. Paul David sipped his coffee, trying to organize his thoughts. He said, "Let's just say, for argument's sake, that your mom really did mean to throw you out."

"Even if she didn't mean it, I'm not going back there. Ever."

"You have to go somewhere, James."

"Maybe I'll just hitch a ride out of town. My dad's in Madison, Wisconsin, someplace. I could go look for him."

"What do you know about your dad?"

"Nothing much."

"When did you see him last?"

"I don't even remember him. I was about one year old when he took off."

"How do you know he's still in Madison?"

"That's where the checks come from that he sends my mom."

"There's a return address on them?"

He shook his head. "No. A post office box."

"Well, I don't think you can go live in a post office box, James."

In spite of himself, the teen-ager smiled.

"Look, I'll make you a deal. You let me take you to school. I'll explain to the principal you had an emergency at home, and they shouldn't count it as an unexcused absence or mark you late or anything like that. You go to all the rest of your classes today. Then you come here after school. You can stay at my place tonight. And then we'll figure something out. Okay?"

James looked relieved. "You sure?"

"I'm positive, Buddy." He looked at James, admiring his wavy dark brown hair and dark eyebrows. "What happened to that suitcase you said your mom packed for you?"

"It's sitting next to Mr. Tozer's desk, back at your office."

"Okay. That's no problem." He hesitated to raise the next point, but decided to do it. "What about Alice? Have you talked to her lately?"

"She doesn't go to my high school. I haven't seen her for awhile."

"Then just leave her alone. For now. Sooner or later you and she will probably need to talk."

"Yeah," James replied ruefully.

"Now, drink your coke. Then I'll take you to school. If we don't wait too much longer, you might get there in time for lunch."

"MOM? It's Paul David."

"Yes, dear. What is it?"

"Can I bring a guest home for supper tonight?"

"May I?"

He exhaled impatiently. Did she think he was still in grade school or what? "*May* I?"

"I suppose. Do I know her?"

"It's not a date, Mom. It's a teen-age boy. We're…friends. I mean, I'm trying to be a friend to him. I think he's going to be really hungry about suppertime."

"Well, all right then."

"You don't sound exactly enthusiastic."

"It's fine, really. It's just that..."

"Just that *what?*"

"It's just that I was hoping, for a moment there, that it might be Jenny Langholz."

"THIS WILL BE YOUR ROOM, James. Mine's right next door. The bathroom's at the end of the hall."

James set down the suitcase, looked around, and flashed a look of gratitude. He sat down on the side of the bed and looked at the antique wallpaper. "This sure is different from my room at home." He immediately corrected himself. "Different from the apartment where my mom lives, I mean."

"Just make yourself at home here, James."

There was an awkward silence. James said, "What should I do tomorrow night?"

"Stay here."

"Really?"

"Stay as long as you need to."

"I thought this was just going to be temporary."

"We'll see how it works out, okay?"

"You're positive you want to do this?"

"I figure it's a fair trade...if I get a little slave labor out of you."

James looked uncertainly at him.

"Surely you'll want to do something to pay your rent."

A sheepish grin crept over the teen-ager's face. "What sort of 'slave labor.'"

"Well, tomorrow's Saturday. How about you try cleaning up the mess downstairs? I've got junk lying everywhere. Just straighten it up a little bit."

James nodded. There was a look of eager determination in his eyes.

"Does that work for you, James?"

"That works for me."

THE FOLLOWING EVENING, at six o'clock, Paul David left the newspaper office and walked the block and a half to his home on Anderson Avenue. When he came in the front door, he wondered momentarily whether he had stepped into someone else's house.

The living room was immaculate. So was the dining room and the kitchen. He went up the stairs and peered into James' room. There was no one there. He headed down the hall to his own room. The door was standing open. The place was as tidy as a hotel room before the guests would arrive. He stepped over to the closet, where he found James, down on his knees, carefully arranging the shoes in a neat row.

He cleared his throat. James jumped up and flattened himself against the wall. "I hope you don't mind. Your closet was kind of a mess."

"James, this whole *house* was a mess. You've almost made it look too clean to live in."

"You don't like what I did?"

"I love it, you rascal." He tousled the young man's hair, then drew his arm around his shoulders. "Come on. My mom's got supper ready. You must be hungry, after doing all this."

"Yeah," he admitted cheerfully. "I'm starved."

THE NEXT MORNING, Paul David showed up at the last worship service, as he always did, sitting in the twelfth pew from the front on the north side, where he normally sat. This time James Wilson was seated next to him. It was part of the covenant the two of them had worked out.

The deal was that James could stay with Paul David, as long as he thought he needed to. He could eat his evening meals with his host, at Molly and David Engelhardt's dining room table. Paul David would give him a small weekly allowance, and buy him supplies he'd need for school, and new clothes as often as he needed them.

For his part, James would keep Paul David's house looking tidy. He would do his homework on time and keep his grades up. He would do any errands around the newspaper office that might be needed. He would come to worship with Paul David every Sunday morning, even though he'd never, ever, attended a church worship service before. And, he'd attend Luther League meetings once a month.

That last condition was the one that had James worried. He knew Alice was a member of the League. He didn't know whether she'd be showing up any more, now that she was pregnant. He also knew a lot of the kids who attended, and he realized they all knew what he had done. But he'd gritted his teeth and agreed to the requirement, along with all the others Paul David had set down for him.

And so, he found himself on a crisp Sunday morning, sitting in the vaulted worship space of the Lutheran Church of Saint Michael and all Angels, surrounded with stained-glass windows bearing angel themes, listening to Lillian Fischer play a complicated Bach prelude on the majestic Reuter pipe organ.

At one point, he leaned close to Paul David and said, "This is kind of an amazing place, isn't it?"

The older man smiled but said nothing.

The liturgy was a puzzle to James, but Paul David helped him find his way, singing confidently in order to set a proper example.

In his sermon, Pastor Martin Fangmeyer spoke about Jesus' parable of the Prodigal Son. He said, "All of us make our heavenly Father angry one time or another. And God would have every right to slam the door on us, lock us out and throw away the key. But God does no such thing. Instead, he opens his arms to us, welcomes us home, and gives the kind of embrace we cannot live without."

In that moment, the growing sense of security he'd been gaining for the past two days seemed to lock itself into James' soul. He felt Paul David's arm around his shoulders and felt a shudder of contentment run through his body.

"And what does God ask of us, once we've come home to his open arms?" the pastor asked. "The words are in Martin Luther's *Small Catechism*. 'Therefore, we ought to thank, praise, serve and obey him.'" He paused, smiled, and said, "Those of you who memorized those words know what comes next. Please recite the rest of it with me."

James looked at Paul David, and was fascinated to see him say the words, along with many others in the large congregation: "This is most certainly true."

For the first time in his life, James Wilson felt as if he were finally home.

Chapter 33

Molly and David Engelhardt went to Thanksgiving Day dinner at their daughter and son-in-law's home on Franklin Avenue. They were joined by Paul David, who brought James Wilson with him.

To her astonishment, Molly encountered no evil spirits in the dreaded house. When Josh Jonas explained to her that the building predated Michael Morgan-Houseman by two decades, and then described the significance of the stone inlays around the ornate fireplace, she found herself thinking completely differently about the residence.

James was overwhelmed by the scale and lavishness of the home. Never in his fifteen years, living in a simple apartment, had he experienced such elegance in a private residence. Nor had he been so unconditionally embraced by an extended family as he was when the food was passed in the ornate dining room.

On the way home, in Paul David's Ford, he said, "Do you know Mr. Pavelka?"

"Which one, James?"

"How many are there?"

"In our congregation? Two. There's Joe, the automobile dealer. And his son, Tom, who works at a bank downtown."

"It was Tom who talked to me."

"Really? When?"

"After Luther League last time. He was there to do the program."

"What was it about?"

"He talked about learning how to manage your money so you don't end up in the poorhouse."

"That's what Tom Pavelka does for a living. He helps people stay out of debt. The bank pays him to give people good advice."

"Well, he had some advice for me. But not about that."

"What did he tell you?"

"During refreshment, he came over and started talking to me. One thing led to another and he found out how I'd gotten Alice in trouble. He said I should think about writing her a letter and tell her I was sorry for what I'd done. And offer to help her any way I could."

"Well, that's not bad advice, I'd guess."

"He told me the same thing happened to him and his girlfriend when they were in high school. They got pregnant and she had to drop out. Then, after they graduated, they got married."

"Yes. That was a long time ago." Paul David decided not to tell James that the child that resulted had died at age eleven, drowning in Lake Saint Michael.

"So, I was thinking, maybe I should write to her."

"I gather she wasn't at Luther League."

"One of the other kids said her mom won't ler go out any more." He was silent for a moment. "I guess that's not very fair, is it. I'm still in school and going places. She can't do any of that stuff now."

"Do you know what you want to write to her?"

"No. Not exactly. But, if I do decide to, I was wondering if you'd read it over, before I mailed it off."

"Of course, James. If you want me to."

They rode in silence, until they were nearly home. Suddenly James said, "I did something sort of…I don't know…stupid, maybe…one day last week. I never told you about it."

Paul David steered the car onto Anderson Avenue and headed toward his home. "Okay, just how stupid was it, exactly?" As far as he was concerned, James had been living up to their mutual covenant almost perfectly. What, he wondered, had he done now?

"I went back to my mom's place after school one day. I wanted to find out if she really did change the locks on the door."

"You still have a key to that place?"

"Yeah. I didn't try using it, though."

"Afraid she'd be there waiting for you?"

"I noticed her mailbox in the entryway didn't have her name on it any more."

"Maybe she just took it off."

"I think she moved."

"Why do you think so?"

"Because one of the other tenants was taking his mail out. I asked if Nancy Wilson still lived there. He said he thought her apartment was empty now."

"Did he know where she'd gone?"

"No. Nobody keeps track of anybody else in that place."

"What if she'd still been there. Would you have tried to talk to her?"

"Hell, no. I don't ever want to talk to her again."

"You may change your mind later on, James."

"She obviously doesn't want to talk to me anymore. Why should I want to talk to her?"

ONE DAY IN FEBRUARY, as she was preparing to make rounds at the hospital, Sarah Jonas went to check the patient charts and got a surprise. Peter Fenstermacher, the son of Saint Michael Church's office administrator, was listed as having been hospitalized. Sarah remembered he had left the neighborhood after high school, and had also left the congregation. She had lost track of him.

When she had opportunity, she went to his room. He lay with a bandage on his shoulder, and a bandage strip running diagonally across his bare chest, secured to another wrapped around his midsection.

"Pete? Remember me?"

He looked at her, curious. Then he said, "Sarah Engelhardt." He grinned. "I almost dated you in high school."

"What do you mean, 'almost'?"

"I was going to ask you out. But old speedy-shoes Josh Jonas was about three steps ahead of me. You guys were still dating when I got out of high school and moved to northeast Minneapolis. Whatever happened?"

"We got married. What happened to you?"

"Still single. So, when you get tired of Josh, just let me know." He laughed, but immediately winced and grimaced. "They told me to lie still. Now I know why."

"How did you get the shoulder wound?"

"Occupational hazard. I'm on the police force. Some punk took a shot at me, outside a drug store, up on Central Avenue in the middle of the night."

"How did you end up on the police force?"

"Skip Warner told me I should think about it. So I did."

As she left Pete's room, Sarah found herself wondering what sort of life she would have had, married to someone in a high-risk occupation like his. She decided she probably ought to count her blessings.

Chapter 34

Daniel Jonas sat on the porch swing with his son and glided gently back and forth. The chains holding the swing creaked as they moved against the heavy-duty hooks secured to the porch ceiling.

"I think this thing needs oil," said Josh. He reflected silently on the times he'd sat here, in years past, reading comic books as a grade-schooler, or mixing it up with his high school buddies, or courting Sarah.

"Your mother used to sit here with you when you were just a little tyke." They continued swinging in silence.

"Long week coming up," said Josh.

"Holy Week always is. But at least we've gotten Palm Sunday out of the way." He looked at his son. "Thanks for reading the passion Gospel at church this morning. At all four services. You probably have it memorized by now."

"How come we have to read two whole chapters at one worship service?"

"We only do it on Palm Sunday."

"I know. But it takes about ten minutes."

"That's why we let the congregation sit down for it."

Josh reflected on the experience. Usually one of the pastors read the extra-long Gospel text on Palm Sunday. But the pastoral staff had, for some reason, decided the senior pastor's son should do it this year.

"You know what, Dad? It felt good."

"What did?"

"Being up there in front of the congregation. It seemed sort of right to me."

Daniel stopped the swing and looked more carefully at his son. "How do you mean?"

Josh said, "I've been thinking about this for awhile. I think I want to go to seminary."

"Have you decided for sure?"

"Pretty much. I haven't said anything to Sarah yet."

"Maybe you should."

"I wanted to talk to you first."

"Well, I appreciate that, Joshua Daniel. How long have you been thinking about it?"

Josh took a deep breath. "Ever since college. But then things started getting complicated. Like marrying Sarah. Ending up owning a house. Getting committed to my work at the free clinic."

"You've done a great job at the clinic. Everybody says so."

"I've loved doing it. But I think it's starting to wear me down. We have way too many people for the resources available. There are never enough hours in the day. People are always making demands on my time. Not that I mind the demands, but after a while you sort of run out of energy."

"Sounds a little bit like my job," said Daniel sagely.

Josh thought about it. "Yeah. I suppose." He looked out toward the street, where his Pontiac was parked. He and Sarah had come for dinner, and would be heading home in another hour or so. "You know what? Skip Warner once said something to me that sounded a little like that."

"Really."

"Yeah. He said a pastor's work sounded to him kind of like a policeman's job. You have to listen to people. You have to be a friend to them. You have to be ready for emergencies."

"Skip's a good fellow. Sounds like he's pretty wise, too."

"He told me, back in high school, that his dad helped you and Mom find me when I got kidnapped—when I was still a baby."

"We haven't talked much to you about that over the years, have we?"

"Why haven't you?"

"That was a painful experience. Maybe I didn't want to reopen that chapter, once we thought we had it closed." He began swinging again. He said, "It started right here on this porch. On Palm Sunday afternoon, as a matter of fact."

"You're finally ready to talk about this?"

"To tell you the truth, what I really want to talk about right now has to do with something I've been feeling about you, ever since that happened." Josh had learned, from his father's example, not to interrupt in the middle of someone else's unfinished paragraph. Daniel continued, "Ever since that night when Sam Warner came up those steps and told us they'd found you, safe and unharmed, I've always felt as though God saved your life for a purpose."

Josh had never heard this from his father before.

"I wasn't sure what the purpose was, and I wasn't going to presume on God by assuming I should tell you how to find your future. That's for you and the Holy Spirit to work out together. But, I have to admit, I've always hoped you might decide ordained ministry might be the right path for you."

"You could have said that to me more directly, you know."

"It wasn't my place to do that. You needed to discern it for yourself."

"That's always puzzled me a little bit. The part about discerning what the Holy Spirit wants you to do. How is that supposed to work, actually?"

"I've found a phrase in the New Testament helpful when thinking about that. There's a place in the Book of Acts where the writer says, 'It seemed good to the Holy Spirit and to us.' What does that sound like to you, Joshua Daniel?"

"It sounds like God wants us listening for clues. But, also, that we have to use our own intelligence and common sense."

"Exactly. I'm convinced that's the way the Spirit works in our lives." He began swinging again. "Did I ever tell you about a conversation I had with Pastor Fangmeyer a few years ago, about getting messages from the Holy Spirit?"

"No. Was he getting messages?"

"Well, he had a really strange conversation…maybe confrontation would be more like it…with a fellow who had been walking back and forth in front of our church building, carrying a sign."

"I remember that. I was a sophomore in high school. The sign said 'Just Tell the Truth.'"

"That was the fellow. Anyway, he and Pastor Fangmeyer got into it about how we know the will of God. This gentleman…Cunningham, it seems to me his name was…was of the conviction that when the Spirit leads us into truth, it's a process that leaves you without any doubt, as if you just get divine knowledge poured into your heart, somehow." He chuckled. "Pastor Fangmeyer told me there was a lot of feeling involved in this fellow's theology, but not much intellectual thought."

Josh laughed. "Too bad I missed that discussion. Must have been fascinating."

"The point I want to make, Joshua Daniel, is that the Spirit doesn't lay everything out plainly. You need to use your God-given intelligence to struggle with what you already know, even while you keep yourself open to what God may want to say to you."

"It's that second part that I have trouble with."

Daniel chuckled. "I remember one time, years ago, I told your mother it might be time for me to consider taking a call to a different congregation. She wasn't too hot on the idea. She told me, 'Pray about it, Daniel. And, when you do, make sure it's not just you doing all the talking.' Your mother proved to me that day what a good theologian she really is."

Josh said, "I think I hear the Spirit calling me into ordained ministry. I'm just not sure how to make it work."

"What do you mean?"

"I could go to Dubuque, and ask Sarah to come with me. I understand they've got a trailer court down there now, where married men live while they're in school. It sure wouldn't be like living in the Franklin Avenue house, that's for sure."

"You could adapt, I suspect."

"There are a couple hospitals down there. She could get a job at one of them."

Daniel nodded.

"But, wouldn't it be a lot simpler if I just stayed in Minneapolis and went to Northwestern Seminary? I could practically walk there from the mansion."

"It's the wrong synod, Joshua Daniel."

"Or, there's Luther. Pastor Ward told me we're getting ready to merge with the Norwegian Lutherans. So, in a few years, that would be one of our seminaries."

"But it isn't yet."

"You think I should go to Dubuque?"

"How about coming home on weekends? You wouldn't have to move out of your house. Sarah could keep her job. And you've got your own car now."

"Gosh, Dad, I don't know. That would be a lot of driving."

Daniel nodded. "It would be up to you. But, for my part, I'd feel better about it if you chose one of our seminaries. Besides, if you came home on weekends, you could do some practice preaching from our pulpit."

"You want me practicing on our congregation?"

"Seminary interns do it all the time."

"You and the other pastors pretty much have the preaching covered."

"I preach twice a month. I could give one of those Sundays to you."

Josh grinned. "In grade school I used to sneak up into the pulpit and pretend I was preaching. I had to stand on a stack of hymnals, just so I could see over the top."

Daniel looked amused. But then he turned serious. "Why don't you talk to Sarah? She needs to know what you're thinking about. And she may have some good suggestions for you."

"Dad?"

"What, son?"

"If I do go to seminary, I don't want you trying to get me to come back to Minneapolis and take a call at Saint Michael Church."

"I wouldn't recommend that. People would say we were trying to create a dynasty. And you and I might not even be able to work together."

"It's not that."

"What is it, then?"

"It's just that...I need to be my own person."

"Haven't I let you be that at the free medical clinic?"

"Sure. But if you and I were pastors in the same congregation, I'd be completely in your shadow. Everybody would make comparisons. It just wouldn't work."

"I agree completely."

"Thanks. I was afraid you had other expectations."

"How could I have? I had no idea you were even considering seminary."

"SEMINARY? Really? You?"

"Sarah, don't act so surprised. We talked about the possibility once."

"I know. Back before we got married. I thought you'd given that up."

"I told you I'd give the clinic a few years. Well, I did. I'm feeling differently now. Except..."

"Except?"

"I won't do anything you don't want me to."

"Like what?"

"I really want to go to Dubuque. I really want you to come with me. But, if you don't want to, I'm willing to drive home every weekend."

"It's about six hours one way, isn't it?"

"It would be worth it. If I had to."

"If I moved to Dubuque, we'd have to find somewhere for Grampa to live. He really likes living with us. I don't think he'd want to stay in this big old house all by himself."

"He could move back into his own house. Except that Paul David and James are living there."

She sat thinking. "I like my job here. I've already built up a little seniority. And, even though I didn't think I'd ever say this, I really do love living in this wonderful old house."

"Then I'll come home on weekends."

"Are you sure you're okay with that?"

"Are you sure *you* would be?"

"We'll make it work, Josh."

Chapter 35

The small charter plane circled high over the University of Minnesota, then flew north, along the Mississippi River. It made another circle, above The River's Edge supper club, then headed further north. Somewhere over the undeveloped landscape of rural Brooklyn Park, the plane suddenly began to climb, higher and higher above Hennepin County, as if heading toward outer space.

Finally the pilot, who was alone in the small craft, lost consciousness in the rarefied oxygen. His hand released the throttle and the plane tipped back toward the earth. It plummeted, nose first, thousands of feet, picking up speed as it went. It smashed into the ground in the midst of a farmer's potato field.

The following morning, the newspapers on both sides of the river reported the death of Arnold Elliot. He was described as the 36-year-old proprietor of a local air charter service, whose plane mysteriously crashed on the way back to Crystal Airport. Several of Arnold's high-profile business clients, none of whom had the misfortune of being in the plane with him at the time of the accident, were listed.

Almost as an afterthought, the Minneapolis *Tribune* mentioned that his wife, Sandra, owned a popular local supper club.

SANDRA STOOD in the funeral chapel, across the room from Arnold's open casket, greeting friends as they came through the receiving line. She showed little emotion. In fact, she was still sorting out her feelings. Arnold had been so distant in the past year, and so rarely at home, she had almost become a stranger to him.

The truth of the matter was she was far more emotionally attached these days to Adam Engelhardt, thirty years her senior. She and Adam had become more than friends. Through their regular Wednesday morning coffee visits at the supper club, the two of them had become confidants. Their common experiences of grief had created a bond Sandy found hard to define.

She looked toward the door of the chapel and saw Adam, coming through with his granddaughter. Sarah reached her first. "I'm so sorry, Sandy. This must be terribly difficult for you."

"Thank you," she said, pursing her lips.

When Adam stepped closer, she threw her arms around him and began to sob. She realized it was more out of relief that he had come, than that she had lost her elusive husband in a plane crash.

"Pilots always know they're living on borrowed time," said Adam kindly.

"Yes, I suppose that's true," Sandy replied, dabbing her eyes with her handkerchief.

"I'll be at the funeral tomorrow," he assured her. "Sarah's taking time off to come with me."

"Thank you, Adam. You're such a dear." She smiled and hugged him again. Then she said, "After this is all over, we need to sit down again and sort everything out."

"Wednesday morning at ten o'clock. Your place. It's on my calendar. It always is," he said with a twinkle in his eye.

DANIEL JONAS conducted Arnold's funeral at Saint Michael Church. It was a weekday morning, and most of the congregation was at work or at school. Those who were free to attend, but didn't, had never gotten well acquainted with either Arnold or Sandy. The fact that neither of them had been regular worship attenders was a large part of the reason.

As a result, there were fewer than fifty in the pews when the service began. Daniel took the unusual step of directing everyone to move up to the front five pews, so that they wouldn't feel so lost in the enormous worship space.

Because it was not his custom to refashion funeral sermons as eulogies, the senior pastor focused on the promises of God, especially the words of the Apostle Paul. He reminded the small cluster of mourners, "Whether we live or whether we die, we are the Lord's." Still, he made mention of his recollection of the time Arnold Elliot took him for an airplane ride, over the city of Minneapolis, and how his charter air business had prospered.

He also made reference to the unfortunate death of Arnold and Sandy's two-year-old daughter. Looking at her from the pulpit, he extended to the widow his profound sympathy. She looked up at him with appreciation.

THREE DAYS LATER, Arnold Elliot was the lead story on the front page of the first news section in both morning dailies. One headline shouted:

CHARTER AIR PILOT LED DOUBLE LIFE!

When Sandy Elliot read the story, she thought she might be experiencing cardiac arrest. Suddenly it was almost impossible to breathe. Her pulse was racing. Her brain was pounding. She wondered what it felt like to endure a panic attack, and whether she was now having one.

A reporter for the *Tribune*, and another for the *Pioneer Press*, both working independently, had discovered that the man Twin Citians knew as Arnold Elliot was known to many in a northwest Chicago suburb as Elliot Arnold. Somehow he had managed to establish two separate identities, complete with residences in both Minnesota and Illinois. The name "Elliot Charters" had actually been used in both places.

Even more shocking to Minnesotans who began to devour the story, however, was the revelation that Arnold, or Elliot, also had two wives. And, while his friends in Minneapolis had thought him the survivor of a deceased infant daughter, his neighbors in Park Ridge, Illinois, knew him to be the father of three healthy young children.

"Elliot Arnold," Sandy fumed, throwing the newspaper onto the coffee table. "A better name would be *Benedict* Arnold!" She walked angrily back and forth across the living room carpet, muttering, growling, shouting, shrieking her anger and her pain. There was no one there to hear it.

"That slimy, two-timing, two-faced, lying bastard! How in hell did he think he could actually get *away* with that?"

She stared at the headline again, then grabbed the first news section, crushed it into a missile, and hurled it at a lampshade. The lamp fell across an armchair, the shade dropping onto the carpet.

She went to the picture window and stared out at the front lawn. "No wonder he didn't want kids!" she seethed. "He already had *three* of them! The man was a bigamist! A lecherous, deceiving bigamist!"

ADAM PHONED after he'd read the story. He offered to put off their Wednesday morning coffee conversation. Sandy told him, "Absolutely not. I need a friend right now, more than I ever have. You have to come, Adam. You just *have* to!"

SANDY HADN'T BEEN to the supper club since the scandal had broken. Consequently, Adam had to find her residence, a place he'd never visited. He drove up and down along the north suburban residential lane, looking for the address. By the time he found it, he was fifteen minutes late.

"I was afraid you had decided not to come," Sandy said, ushering him inside. "That would have been just about the last straw. My last friend deserting me."

"Nobody's deserting you," Adam said. "Certainly not me."

"I'm sorry," she said, looking contrite. "I'm under so much stress I just don't know how to behave anymore."

They sat together on her couch, drinking coffee, talking as they always did on a Wednesday morning. But this time, the topic was volatile.

"I've had to hire a lawyer, Adam. I don't even know what I own anymore, much less what that...Jezebel...in Chicago owns. We're trying to sort everything out. Thank God, I never signed the supper club over to Arnold, or gave him joint tenancy in it. That place is mine, free and clear."

Adam's head was spinning. He wasn't sure how to respond.

She continued, "It looks pretty likely that I'll get to keep this house. It's in Arnold's name. The point is, it's in the name of Arnold Elliot, not Elliot Arnold. And, so, it looks like it's going to go to me." She paused and thought about what she'd just said. "Isn't that the damnedest thing you ever heard of?"

Adam shook his head and offered a weak smile. "I have to admit, Sandy, I've never quite encountered anything like this." He said, "Who will take care of those three small children?"

Sandy's face twisted into a scowl. "We've already found out Arnold signed all his insurance policies over to...to that other woman. He had some savings. Turns out, he put about half of it in her name, the rest in mine."

"What about the charter business?"

"As far as I can tell, without the airplane, there isn't much left of it. Arnold rented space at two airports. The plane was insured, but he still owed money on it. And, he was behind on both rents. There may not be much left when the debts are all paid. My lawyer doesn't exactly know who owns the business. At this point, I don't really care."

"So, you're pretty much left on your own."

"I've been on my own for a long time, Adam. I'll get by, believe me."

They sat in silence, listening to the ticking of a wall clock. Finally Adam said, "Do you have any idea, Sandy, what actually happened? I mean, when the plane went down?"

"The investigators say it was as if it was aimed at the ground. Can you believe it? It's almost like Arnold wanted to end his life."

"Maybe things just got too complicated for him to manage anymore."

"Well, he probably figured out that, if I ever caught wind of what he was up to, I might just castrate him in the middle of the night."

Adam shook his head, furrowed his brow, and tried to be sympathetic. "You would never have done anything like that."

She sighed. "No, of course not. I would probably just have thrown the bum out."

Chapter 36

"Thank you for letting me come to visit Alice, Mrs. Feldermann."

Abigail Feldermann looked warily at James Wilson, then stepped aside and let him into the small apartment. She led the way into the living room and said, "Sit down. She'll be out in a minute."

James took a seat in one of the chairs. He studied the tidy but spare room, trying to organize his thoughts. He had not seen Alice since the showdown with their mothers at Saint Michael Church, more than a year before.

When she appeared at the hallway door, he realized she looked exactly as he had remembered her. How, he wondered, was it possible for her to have had a baby, and not show any signs of it?

"Hello, James." Her voice was less tentative than he had remembered it on the train trip to Indiana. The shyness was gone.

She sat down on the couch. Her mother stood in the doorway, until Alice looked at her, signaling it would be safe to leave the two of them alone. Abigail disappeared into the kitchen.

The two teen-agers sat looking at one another. To James it felt as awkward as he had feared it might. He said, "Alice, you never answered any of my letters."

She just looked at him, but said nothing.

"Did you get any of them?"

She nodded.

"I know you probably won't ever be able to forgive me. I guess I've probably ruined your life."

"I'm still planning to have a life, James. But probably not with you in it."

Now it was James' turn to nod silently.

"I had the baby at the end of May," she said. "It was a boy. I didn't get to name him."

"You gave him up?"

"Somebody adopted him. He'll have a good home. Somewhere." There was melancholy in her voice.

He said, "I wish I could have seen him."

"I'm glad you didn't get to. They didn't show him to me either."

Again he was speechless.

"I had him in Wisconsin. I went to live with my aunt and uncle last year."

"You had to drop out of school, right?"

She nodded.

He said, "My mom kicked me out. I don't live at home anymore."

Her expression changed. "So, I lost a year of high school—and you had to leave home. I had a baby that I can't keep." She folded her hands, then unfolded them. "Do you think it was worth it, what we did?"

He didn't answer. Instead, he said, "I'm really sorry for everything. I still want to be your friend."

"Well, that's more than some guys would tell a girl they got pregnant." It was not spoken unkindly. "But I don't think my mom wants us seeing each other anymore."

"Are you back in school now?"

"Yes. Unlike you, I'm still a junior." He heard sarcasm in her voice.

He began to wonder whether coming here had really been such a good idea. "Paul David Engelhardt…that guy that went to the convention as one of the adult sponsors last year…he's letting me live with him. Until I get out of high school." He hesitated. "He makes me go to church with him every Sunday." She arched an eyebrow. He grinned. "It's not so bad. I sort of like it, actually."

"James, I'm not completely blaming you for any of this. I could have said no to you."

"The guy is supposed to look out for the girl. I didn't do that."

"Let's just say we both made a mistake."

James looked at the carpet. He said, "I might not ever get married." He looked up, to see a look of puzzlement and surprise on her face. "But, if I ever do, I hope she's a lot like you."

PAUL DAVID came home from the newspaper office one evening to find the house filled with a tempting aroma. He followed the scent into the kitchen.

"James! You're cooking!"

"Just baking chocolate chip cookies."

"Nobody's cooked anything in here since my grandparents moved out. Where'd you find the pans and mixing bowls and everything?"

"They're all in your cupboards." James shoveled a cookie off the pan and onto his spatula. He gave it to Paul David.

He took a bite, savoring the warm morsel in his mouth. "These are great! Where'd you get the recipe?"

"It's on the bag of chocolate chips. I noticed it when I was in the market one day."

"So, why did you decide to make cookies?"

"Well, I figured your mother's been so good to me, feeding me all those suppers. I wanted to do something to show my appreciation. So, I'm taking these over there for dessert tonight."

"I'm sure my mom will be surprised."

"I don't think so. She's the one who gave me the ingredients."

"THE INGREDIENTS? I don't remember precisely," said Polly Broadman, beginning to clear away the dishes. "It's just some of this and some of that. An old family recipe. I make it a lot."

Rosetta Jonas followed the corporate executive's wife into the kitchen, carrying more of the plates. She said, "Thanks for inviting Daniel and me to your home. It's lovely."

"Well, Harry's been president of the congregation for nearly a year now. I thought it was about time we had you out." She set the dirty dishes down on the counter. "Just leave those. Come on. I want to show you the solarium."

As the women retreated to the sun room, Daniel and Harry relaxed in the executive's private den. "You ever been up to the Boundary Waters Canoe Area, Pastor?" he asked, gesturing toward a paddle fastened to the wall. Not waiting for an answer, he said, "It's like going to heaven. If you like the outdoors, that is."

Daniel smiled and sat down in a plush, stuffed, leather chair. "You have a beautiful home, Harry. Thanks for inviting us out."

"I'm embarrassed it took so long. You know, we could have church council meetings out here once in awhile. Just like we did when the task force met to plan the anniversary celebration. All the meetings were in our dining room."

"The church council wouldn't fit around your dining room table, Harry."

"Wasn't thinking of that. The basement's fully finished. There's a full-sized conference table down there." Daniel arched an eyebrow. "Don't believe me? I could show you."

"No. Don't get up. I'm sure it's as you say. I'm just wondering why you have a conference table down there."

"Because once in a while General Mills has departmental strategy sessions here on the weekend. I hate going into the office on Saturdays. So I bring the office out here."

Daniel shook his head and grinned. "You're one of the most take-charge people I know, Harry. I think it explains how you rose up so high in the corporate structure."

Harry absorbed the compliment. He said, "There's something I wanted to tell you. Something I've done, on behalf of the congregation."

What now? Daniel wondered.

"Your son, Josh. In your presence, I guess I should say Joshua Daniel, since you always do."

"That's actually what we named him, Harry."

"Okay. Anyway, here's the deal. Joshua Daniel is an absolute hit with the congregation. Everybody knew they loved him before he went off to seminary. But now that he's home on weekends, taking his turn in the pulpit, he's almost...not quite, mind you, but almost...as good as his dad. That young man is one fine preacher. And he's not even through his first year yet!"

"We're working hard helping him not to get an expanded ego," said Daniel dryly.

"No problem there. He's got his priorities straight. What I can't figure out is, how come he waited so long to go to seminary? He's a natural for this."

"Well, he didn't know he really wanted to go. I'm not in the habit of pressuring my children to do things they're not ready to do."

"Wise. Very wise. You know, Pastor, if I had kids, I'd want them to be just like your two."

"Harry, not to be indelicate, why exactly don't you and Polly have children?"

"We can't. God knows, we tried. Did all the medical tests, too. It's me, not Polly. Anyway, I think it may have been a blessing. I'm such a driven son-of-a-gun, with the job and everything, I'd probably neglect any kids I ended up having."

Daniel saw the wisdom in Harry's words.

"The worst of it is, of course, unless I adopt somebody, I'm going to have to leave all my money to the church." Daniel wondered if Harry was serious. His host didn't provide much help with an answer. He broke out in hearty laughter.

Daniel said, "If I'm not mistaken, you said you wanted to tell me something you've done, something I should know about."

"Oh. Yes. It's about Joshua Daniel. I, umm, I took the liberty to, well, take a step on the young man's behalf."

"What exactly?"

"You know, Pastor, there's no point in dragging out Joshua Daniel's seminary training. Especially since he waited so long to get started with it."

"Harry, seminary training takes as long as it takes."

"Oh, I know. The classroom part. No shortcuts there. I'm more concerned about the year of internship. Practical experience in a congregation."

"That's required now. Unlike when I was in seminary."

"Well, that's what I thought too. So, I took the liberty of phoning the seminary president a couple weeks ago. I followed it up with a letter summarizing the phone call. We corporate types like to do it that way."

Daniel was getting an uncomfortable feeling. "What did you say to the president of the seminary?"

"Basically, I laid out the argument for getting Joshua Daniel a variance. So he could opt out of internship."

"On what grounds?"

"On the grounds that he's been working in our congregation for several years already—in the free medical clinic. If that isn't on-site training, I don't know what is. And, as far as practice in preaching is concerned, he's getting that right now. Every single month. Exactly like a regular intern would. Except, Joshua Daniel will have three years of it, not just one."

"Harry, I don't want to sound ungracious, as a guest in your home, but I have a feeling you may have overstepped the bounds of propriety."

"Well, the seminary president didn't seem to feel that way. He said the church needed to be flexible when there was warrant for it. And, he said he thought I might have a reasonable case. Of course, they have procedures down there in Dubuque, Iowa, for deciding things like this. It's not really up to me."

"Why do you think it would be to Joshua Daniel's advantage to skip internship?"

"Well, your son told me himself he wished there was a way he could accomplish that. Of course, he quickly added he expected to complete the requirement like everybody else. But I don't think Sarah has any desire to give up her good job at the hospital. And there's that house of theirs. That place is a gem. Somebody needs to watch over it. Then there's the possibility that the seminary could give him an internship assignment in Pittsburgh or Los Angeles or somewhere like that. Would Sarah want to uproot and go somewhere else for a year? She'd lose her job at Fairview for sure. On the other hand, she wouldn't want to sit in Minneapolis for a year waiting for him to get his internship finished. You can't drive home every weekend from the west coast. And, besides, their biological clocks are ticking right along."

"Harry, what does that last part have to do with anything?"

"Sarah told me she has no intention of having children before Joshua Daniel gets finished with seminary. And, if we can cut down the waiting time by a year, you're going to have your first grandchild sooner, not later."

"Harry, this is all leaving my head spinning. I can hardly keep up with your reasoning."

"If it sounds like I'm in a corporate brainstorming session, forgive me. That's the way I get when I'm after something. It's the way I am at General Mills. It's the way I am with the congregation."

"Have you told Joshua Daniel what you've been doing on his behalf?"

"No. That wouldn't be appropriate. It needs to come to him from the seminary, not from me. And, I'm sure you'll understand, Pastor, it shouldn't come from you either."

"Well, I'd be very surprised if anything comes from this ploy of yours anyway. So I'm not even going to worry about it."

"How would you feel, though, if Joshua Daniel were allowed to skip his internship year?"

"Well, like I said, I never had an internship. Although, it probably would have helped make me a better pastor."

"I can't think of anything that would make you a better pastor. Except, maybe, a little less humility." Harry roared with laughter.

"Just between you and me, Harry, if I were the president of Wartburg Seminary, I wouldn't take your suggestion very seriously."

"Well, maybe *you* wouldn't. But I think *he* will."

"Why would he?"

"Because, when I sent the letter summarizing our phone conversation, I enclosed a generous contribution, for the school to use anywhere they might need it the most."

JENNY LANGHOLZ brought her fourth graders to the office of the *Bloomington Avenue News* one morning in February. It was a field trip, designed to show the students how a newspaper gets put together. While Tom

Tozer walked the crowd of youngsters through the intricacies of selling an ad and then laying it out on a page, Jenny stuck her head through Paul David's open office door.

"Hi. Come on in."

"You need a maid. This place is a mess."

"It's a newspaper office."

"It's still a mess." She grinned.

"Just wait until I get James over here. He'll have this place spic and span." He paused and realized the foolishness of what he'd just said. "Come to think of it, James has cleaned this place up about six times. Still looks like a mess."

She said, "You know, I'm really impressed with how you've taken James under your wing. He's really come to life under your tutelage."

"It was just something I wanted to do."

"A lot of men would never have done it." She brushed the hair back from her forehead. "Keep it up and I just may have to revise my opinion of men. Some men, anyway."

"You know what? Hardly any of the men I know are anything like Buzz Winslow."

She decided to change the subject. "How's Alice Feldermann doing?"

"Okay. Back in school. She graduates next year." He paused. "She gave up the baby."

"That had to be hard."

"Listen, you want to have coffee sometime?"

"No. Not really."

"Okay."

"Gotta go. The kids are getting restless."

"Jenny?"

"What?"

"Stop by any time."

Chapter 37

"GRAMPA, are you really going to do it?"

"Sure. Why not? I'm a big boy. I can take care of myself."

"I'm not worried about you. It's just that...well...people might talk."

"Let them talk. What do I care? I'm sixty-six years old."

"That's the whole point. Sandy Arnold is half your age."

"By the way, she's changed it back to Engstrom. She's gotten rid of her married name."

"She's also gotten rid of her wedding band, I've noticed."

"Can you blame her?"

"Well...no."

"Sandy has been through a whole lot. I don't blame her for wanting to get away for awhile. This whole mess with Arnold's death, and the humiliation she got from the newspaper stories, and the lawyers and all of it...no wonder she wants to get out of town for awhile."

"But it sounds so morbid. Driving all the way to Bemidji, just to look at a tombstone."

"To pay her respects to her late father. After all, if it hadn't been for him she wouldn't have the supper club today. She might be out on the street with a tin cup."

"I don't know. I still think the two of you, driving up to Bemidji together, seems a little odd. I mean, what will you be doing while she's decorating her father's grave?"

"Standing right there, giving her moral support."

Sarah shook her head in disbelief. "You're really going to do it, aren't you."

"Yes. I'm really going to do it."

"THIS IS WHERE my parents grew up," Sandy said, steering the Buick onto a side street. My dad lived in this house down here on the corner. My mother lived in the next block. They knew each other from Sunday school and grade school days."

"That's sweet," said Adam. "Sometimes childhood romances just evaporate when kids grow up."

"Not with them. Puppy love turned into the real thing."

"It's a nice town, Bemidji. You don't come here often though, do you?"

"My grandfather had a café here. But my dad moved to Minneapolis and started the Riverside Restaurant. Later he changed it into The River's Edge. I grew up down there."

She pulled up in front of a comfortable old home on a quiet street. "Here's the bed and breakfast. I hope you told your granddaughter that we have separate rooms. We wouldn't want any scandal to come out of this." She listened to her own words. "God knows, I've had enough scandal to last me a lifetime."

After they had checked in, Sandy came into Adam's room and sat down in an upholstered rocking chair. He chose a comfortable couch nearby. They soaked up the antique ambience, admiring the canopied bed with its polished wooden corner posts.

"You know, Adam, I don't think I would have gotten through all the craziness of the last year if it hadn't been for you. It's so good to have someone you can actually talk to, actually trust. Unlike that lunkhead I ended up marrying."

"Sandy, I've been thinking about that."

"Now, don't go taking Arnold's side."

"The man's dead. He doesn't have a side anymore."

She returned a repentant look.

"Now, don't take offense at what I'm about to say. You're too adult for that, okay?" She nodded uncertainly. "It occurs to me," said Adam, "that things might have gone very differently for the two of you if you could have been more flexible at the beginning."

Her mouth was open, words of protest ready to pour out, but he kept going. "I know you wanted to keep the restaurant going. And you were right to do it. But you were so hands-on about everything, it probably threatened Arnold. He had to prove he could be as successful as you already were. You know, a lot of men think their manhood is being threatened if a woman outshines them. It's foolish, but some of them feel that way."

"You think that's the way it was with Arnold?"

"It might have been. Anyway, he gave you all kinds of signals about wanting children. You made it pretty clear that wasn't going to happen. Not for a good while, anyway. And, so, he was ripe for an affair somewhere else."

"So you think I drove him into the hands of another woman?" she replied, testily.

"Sandy, if you're going to take this the wrong way, I'm going to stop talking right now. I'm not trying to offend you."

She took a deep breath.

"I'm only saying, there's a way to explain, and understand, why Arnold ended up doing what he did. Without excusing a single bit of it."

She sat puzzling over what he'd just said. "Adam, you're just an amazing human being. Most people I know would never have waded into a minefield like that. And you did it with such grace, and compassion…and love." She pursed her lips. "I'm so lucky I met you."

"Is it a little bit like getting your father back, maybe?"

"Excuse me?"

"Sandy, I'm thirty years older than you."

"You know what? I've discovered age has nothing to do with friendship. Or love. It's the quality of the relationship between the two people. You and I have struck gold together."

"Well, I'm glad you feel that way about us."

"You are?"

"Sure. Because if you didn't, I'd have a pretty steep account to pay off by now…all those cups of coffee at the supper club I never paid for."

"You are just crazy," she said, laughing. "She got out of the rocking chair, moved to the seat next to Adam on the couch, and put her hand on his arm. "Thank you for coming with me on this trip." She kissed him softly on the cheek. "And thank you for coming into my life."

To her astonishment, he kissed her back—squarely on the lips.

AS SHE STEPPED DOWN from the city bus, a block from her apartment, Abigail Feldermann was preoccupied with what sort of supper to prepare for her daughter, Alice, and herself. Work had run late and she wasn't even sure what was in the cupboard. As she mulled the options, she misjudged the distance from the last step down to the street. She fell onto the curb, sending a searing pain racing up and down her leg.

Passengers who had stepped off just ahead of her saw her go down and stopped to help. They could not get her up. She was weeping pathetically, writhing in agonizing pain. Someone called an ambulance.

At Fairview Hospital she was diagnosed with a broken ankle and torn ligaments. Her lower leg was so swollen, it was hard to tell where the ankle really was.

When Alice got the word, she called a friend, whose parents took her to the hospital to be with her mother. She found something to eat in the public cafeteria and decided to stay the night in the hospital room.

The next day, after she had arrived at school, she called Janet Fenstermacher at Saint Michael Church. She asked if one of the pastors would please come by to visit her mother.

The following Sunday morning, Abigail's name was included in the list of those for whom prayers were offered. Paul David's ears perked up. He looked at James, seated next to him in the twelfth pew, but detected no reaction in particular.

"SO, GRAMPA, how was your weekend in Bemidji?"

"It was just fine, Sarah. We had a good long chat."

"I'd think you would. It takes about six hours to drive up there, doesn't it?"

"The way we did it, it took more like eight."

ON TUESDAY AFTERNOON, twenty minutes after the nurse had left her room, Abigail Feldermann looked up from her hospital bed, expecting to see her daughter. Alice had promised to come right after school. Instead, she found herself looking at James Wilson.

"Mrs. Feldermann, I just wanted to come by for a minute."

"James? Why are you here?"

"I…brought you something." He carried a round, red metal container with a country scene on the lid, to her hospital table and set it down. He'd found the vessel tucked away in one of Elsa Engelhardt's kitchen cupboards.

She looked at him in confusion.

"They're oatmeal raisin cookies. I made them myself." He offered a tentative, almost uncertain look. "They're not too bad. I ate one, just to be sure."

In spite of herself, Abigail grinned. "You made cookies? And you brought them to me?"

"Yes, Ma'am."

"Why would you do such a thing?"

"I found out you had your accident. I'm sorry about that. I wanted to do something just for you."

"Why would you?" She eyed him suspiciously. "Is this really about Alice?"

"No, Ma'am. It's about you."

She looked at the box in bewilderment.

James said, "They told us in Bible class that we're supposed to do good to our enemies."

Her expression changed to astonishment. "James, I'm not your enemy, and you're not mine."

"Well, it's just the way it feels to me."

"I'm sorry," she said. "But you have to appreciate what Alice and I have been through since…"

"I know, Mrs. Feldermann. I'm sorry too. About everything." He furrowed his brow. "Anyway, I'm sure Alice will be coming any minute. I don't want to be here when she walks in. So, enjoy the cookies. And, if you don't like them, the nurses might."

Before she could respond, he was out the door. Abigail lay looking at the container of cookies. She reviewed the anger she'd nurtured toward James over the past several months. She thought about what he'd just said and done. She thought to herself, *I just may have misjudged that young man.*

JOSH JONAS rapped softly on his father's office door. Daniel looked up from behind his desk and smiled. "Come on in."

"You have a few minutes?"

"I should ask *you* that. We're right in the middle of vacation Bible school, and you're running the whole program."

"Yeah. Thanks for letting me do that. I need the experience."

"Well, if we're expected to provide you an internship on weekends and during summer vacations, we need to give you every kind of learning opportunity we can."

"I appreciate that. And the hospital and home visits have gone just great. I didn't realize how much I'd enjoy visiting older people."

"I've always found it one of the most satisfying things I do, Joshua Daniel. Our seniors have a lot of accumulated wisdom. We need to listen to them."

Josh nodded. "Dad, can I ask you something?"

"Of course."

"This business about getting a waiver for a year of internship. When the seminary informed me they were going to let me go through on the fast track, it almost bowled me over. I never asked them to do that, you know."

Daniel wondered how much he should tell his son. So far, he hadn't said a word about Harry Broadman's complicity.

"You may not believe this," Josh continued, "but I actually prayed for the possibility I could find a way to skip internship." He looked tentatively at his father. "I guess prayer actually does work, doesn't it?"

"Joshua Daniel, it always has. But you have to be careful not to conclude it didn't work if you don't get what you think you wanted."

"I know. But in this case, it just seems so amazing. I asked God for something, and I actually got it." He pondered what he'd said. "Dad, you didn't by any chance have anything to do with that, did you?"

"Absolutely not," said Daniel, transparently. "I don't believe in using my influence, whatever it might be, to get favors for my friends or family."

"Okay," said Josh. "Just checking."

ALICE WARD and her children, Elizabeth and James, were at the Detroit River, waiting to board a cruise boat. Her twelve-year-old daughter and ten-year-old son had been eager to get out of their grandparents' house and do something "interesting." Alice had been just as eager to go with them, any excuse to escape the lavish Grosse Pointe house where her husband's parents lived.

"Boy, Mom, I'm sure glad we don't have to come here very often. Grandma is a real pain in the neck. You can't touch anything in her house without getting a lecture. Why doesn't she just turn the place into a museum and put up a 'No Kids Allowed' sign?"

Alice suppressed a laugh. "Just be patient, James. We go home in two more days."

"That's waiting about two days too long," groused Elizabeth. "I wish I'd stayed in Minneapolis."

"Elizabeth, your grandparents hardly ever see you."

"Serves 'em right," Elizabeth grumbled. "Especially Grandma."

The boat arrived, and the three moved toward the gangplank, which had just been lowered onto the dock.

"MOTHER, WHAT WAS SO IMPORTANT that I had to miss a boat ride with my wife and kids this afternoon?"

"Something I need to share with you in private, Aaron. You can tell the rest of your family when you're back in Minneapolis."

"Is it a secret?"

"Not exactly. But I just thought it was only fair to tell you first." She reached to the back of her head, assuring herself that her permanent wave was still holding. "Your father is changing jobs."

"At General Motors?"

"General Motors gave him notice. They've decided to redefine his position. He's 62, you know." She added, with disdain in her voice, "The top brass seem to think they need a younger man in that job now." She scowled. "I guess loyalty and experience don't count for anything anymore."

"They're letting Dad go? Three years before retirement?"

"He could retire early. But we wouldn't get as much that way. So he's been looking for something else."

"Has he found anything?"

"Well, yes. As a matter of fact, a position very similar to the one he's got right now. With a salary increase, if you can believe it."

"He has a solid offer?"

"Solid as the Rock of Gibraltar."

"With whom?"

"With 3M. In St. Paul, Minnesota."

The hairs on the back of Aaron Ward's neck began to stand straight up.

Chapter 38

"James, can you come in here for a minute please?"

The seventeen-year-old set down the stack of archival copies of the *Bloomington Avenue News* he had intended to take upstairs for storage. He walked to the doorway of Paul David's office and stood, waiting.

"Come in. Sit down."

"Am I in trouble?"

"No, I just want to talk to you."

James cleared away the accumulated paper from the visitor's chair and sat down in it.

"I've been wanting to ask you something. I just never seem to do it. So let me do it now." James looked puzzled. "You've been out of high school for three months. You're still living in my guest room. What are your plans?"

The youngster shrugged. "I don't have any. I was hoping I could work here."

"Is that what you want to do for the rest of your life?"

"I don't know. Maybe."

"Why don't you go to college? I could help you find a scholarship."

"You really want to get me out of your hair, don't you."

Paul David smiled. "No. You seem like one of the family. But I don't want you getting stuck somewhere you don't want to be for the rest of your life. Didn't your high school guidance counselors give you any good ideas about what you should consider doing?"

"Not really. They said I could do whatever I set my mind to."

"Well, have you set your mind to anything yet?"

He sat thinking. "I want to wait until Alice gets out of high school next spring. Maybe she and I could…you know."

"She's back in Luther League, isn't she."

"Yeah. And the problem is, now I'm out of high school and probably shouldn't be going anymore."

"There's no rule about that."

"I know. But after high school, kids pretty much stop going."

"How is it with you and Alice now?"

"Well, her mom seems to think I'm safe to have around. I go over there once in a while. Alice doesn't scowl at me the way she used to. I'm trying to figure out if she actually likes me."

"What have you learned so far?"

"She says she wants to stay friends. But she won't let me touch her."

"Really."

"Yeah. Says she doesn't want to get into any more trouble."

"Well, you can't blame her, can you?"

"No." He sighed. "But I just wish she'd give me another chance."

"Maybe you should give her some space. Let her know you want to be her friend too. Do nice things for her. But make your own mind up that, if she's not really interested in you, your life will still go on." He added, "There are other girls out there, you know."

James said, "Yeah. You're right. As usual."

IT WAS THE FIRST TIME members of the Engelhardt family had not eaten Thanksgiving Day dinner at home. Adam had insisted on hosting the meal, in the private dining room at The River's Edge. And so, at precisely twelve o'clock noon, around a festively-decorated table, with Sandy Engstrom's hired staff serving the courses, the clan gathered.

David and Molly sat next to Paul David and James. Across the table, facing them, were Josh and Sarah, who sat next to Adam and Sandy.

Adam offered a toast, thanking his granddaughter and husband for allowing him to live in their home. He voiced appreciation to all of the members of his family for their love and support during Elsa's last years. And, he spoke of his regret that his older son, Jon and his wife, Susan, were too far away, in Columbus, Ohio, to have made the trip back to Minnesota.

Josh was asked to offer a blessing for the meal, after which the food was brought to the table. Immediately, happy chaos broke out. Conversations flew in all directions.

As the meal was ending, Sarah noticed for the first time that Sandy was wearing her wedding band once more. That struck her as curious, but she said nothing about it.

When the dessert had been eaten, Paul David made a move to get up. "James and I are going to shoot some baskets back at the church court," he announced.

But the patriarch of the Lutheran Church of Saint Michael and All Angels stood up first. Adam declared, "I think it would be fitting for us to sing a hymn. You all know the words. Please stand and sing with me."

Members of the family looked at one another. This was not part of the expected ritual. Nevertheless, they did as they were told. Adam began to sing, and the others quickly joined in.

Now thank we all our God
With hearts and hands and voices,
Who wondrous things has done,
In whom this world rejoices;
Who, from our mothers' arms,
Has blest us on our way
With countless gifts of love,
And still is ours today.

Adam said, "Thank you. That meant a lot to me. Now, please sit down. We have an announcement."

We? thought Sarah.

Her grandfather said, "I didn't know how else to tell you this. I didn't want to do it one by one, so I decided to get all of you into the same room." He stopped speaking. There was a long silence. Sarah wondered if her grandfather was perhaps having a seizure. What he was, in fact, having was difficulty putting his words together.

Out of the silence the next sentence came like a thunderbolt. "Last Monday morning, Sandra Engstrom and I were married. It was a private ceremony. We wanted it to be simple and quiet."

Quiet was what hung heavily in the room just then.

"This was not a hasty decision. We've been thinking about it for more than a year." There was palpable disbelief around the table. "We'll be living in her home, just north of here."

The silence was heavier still.

"I realize some of you…perhaps all of you…will be upset with us. I am profoundly sorry about that. But you have to understand, I'm an old man. I'm very lonely. I simply want some companionship to fill the aching hole left when Elsa died."

Nobody knew what to say. Finally, Sandy got up from her chair, stood next to Adam, and said, "We knew this would be difficult. I apologize if any of you are feeling hurt…or betrayed. I hope we haven't completely ruined your Thanksgiving with this. We hoped you would be happy for us."

There was trepidation in her face.

Finally, Josh stood up and said, "I can't speak for any of the Engelhardts. But as a Jonas, I want to wish Adam and Sandy the very best. Congratulations to you both."

All eyes were on the pastor's son. Suddenly he felt as if he'd just committed a capital crime.

But Adam said, "Thank you, Josh. You don't know how much that means to me. To both of us."

"JOSH, HOW COULD YOU stand up and say that?"

"What? That I wish them well? Why couldn't *you* have said it, Sarah?"

He steered the Pontiac south along Lyndale Avenue, toward Franklin, trying hard not to let the rising irritation he was feeling affect his driving.

"Well, he's my grandfather, not yours. And I'm shocked. And embarrassed. And humiliated, if you want to know it!"

"Sarah, why is this about *you*?"

"Why isn't it? Why shouldn't it be? The man is sixty-six years old. She's thirty-six. What kind of marriage is that!"

"Never ask a history major to answer a question like that."

"What's that suppose to mean?" she snapped.

"Throughout history men have traditionally been much older than their wives. In ancient Greece men usually married women half their age. It's only recently that our culture has narrowed the age gap."

"Well, this isn't ancient history. This is now! And it isn't right."

"Sarah, regardless of what you or I think about it, it's already done. They're married. He's moving in with her tonight."

"That's not the point. The point is, you approved it publicly." She was seething. "When you become a pastor, are you going to recommend men in their thirties get married to fifteen-year-old girls? Which, I might add, would only be half the age gap that we're talking about in this case."

"They're mature, consenting adults. They can do what they want. And, as far as I can tell, it's really none of our business."

"Oh!" she huffed, folding her arms across her chest and looking out the side passenger window.

They drove the rest of the way home in silence. When he pulled up in front of carriage house, she jumped out, slammed the door with extra force and marched angrily toward the house.

Josh sat behind the wheel, shaking his head slowly, trying to calm himself. His heart was racing. And, to his surprise, he was angry. With his own wife! He thought, *Well, this is certainly a great way to cap off Thanksgiving Day.*

SARAH HID OUT in their bedroom during the rest of the afternoon. Adam and Sandy came by as the sun was going down. Josh volunteered to help them move his possessions to the trunk and the back seat of her Buick. As they were standing at the curb afterward, Josh said, "Adam, don't worry about your relatives. They'll get used to it."

"Sarah isn't taking this well, is she?"

"She's sulking. She'll get over it. I know she will."

Sandy said, "I guess we just really made a mess of everything, didn't we?"

"How else would you have broken the news?" asked Josh.

"I suppose we could have had a church wedding, and invited everybody. But I was just afraid nobody would come."

Josh grinned. "You're damned if you do and damned if you don't." Adam offered a weak smile. "You two did the right thing. It's going to work out okay. I hope the two of you will be very happy together."

AT BEDTIME, Josh tapped softly on the bedroom door. There was no reply. He opened it and looked in. Sarah was lying on the bed, looking miserable. She had obviously been crying.

When she saw Josh, she sat straight up, pointed an accusing finger at him and shouted, "You can just get out! Go back to Wartburg Seminary and stay there, for all I care!"

He opened his mouth, ready to respond. She ordered, "Out! Do you hear me? I don't want to see you!"

He looked at her in disbelief, then backed out of the room and closed the door.

JOSH STAYED with his parents for the next three nights. He decided the next move was Sarah's. He found himself astonished at the ferocity with which she'd spoken to him, and amazed at how calm he'd remained through all of it. He was irritated with his wife, but mostly sad.

On Saturday afternoon he went to Sarah's parents' home. He told David and Molly the situation with Sarah, and suggested they look in on her. Then he went to Paul David's house. James was out with some of his high school friends, checking out the new Southdale Shopping Center in Edina. So, the two men had the house to themselves.

"My wife is eating me alive over this Adam and Sandy marriage business."

"Well, you have to admit, it was quite a shocker."

"Was I out of line, speaking up at the dinner table like I did?"

"Not as far as I'm concerned. But women react differently. Maybe that's why I've never married one."

"Speaking of women, what does your mother think?"

"Curiously enough, she's happy for Grampa. Maybe because she worries he'll end up lonely at his age. Gramma's death was a lot harder on him than he ever let on. At least, to me."

"I know it was hard. He was a good soldier. But you can't hide the hurt."

"So, what happens now?"

"With what?"

"With you and Sarah. Sounds like she's not going to give you any peace until...gosh, I don't know...until..."

"She's pretty much kicked me out of my own house."

Paul David had a fleeting memory flash of James Wilson, sitting with him at the newspaper office, telling how his mother had thrown him out. He said, "That won't last. The two of you are married."

"Well, let's hope you're right."

Paul David looked at Josh in disbelief. Evidently things were more serious than he'd guessed.

ON SUNDAY AFTERNOON, before leaving for Dubuque, Iowa, Josh phoned the Franklin Avenue mansion. There was no answer. That evening, when he arrived back at the seminary, he tried once more. Again, she didn't pick up.

That evening he wrote her a letter.

Dearest Sarah,

I'm sorry you're so angry with me. There's very little I can say to change things. I'm not going to apologize for what I said to your grandfather and Sandy Engstrom at Thanksgiving. They deserve our support. If you can't agree with me on that, we'll just have to disagree.

As long as you don't want me at home, I'm planning to live with my parents. I'll be back in Minneapolis every weekend, as usual. It's up to you. If you want me back, you're going to have to tell me. I tried to phone you twice. It's your turn.

I still love you. I miss you. I hope you miss me too.

Josh

He was back at St. Michael Church the following weekend, taking his turn in the pulpit. She did not come through the line at the end of any of the four services. He made no effort to track her down.

The same thing happened on each of the next three weekends. He returned to the city, taught one of the confirmation classes, as he had been doing on a regular basis, and then led one of the adult Bible classes on Sunday morning. There was never a sign of her.

At one point he was tempted to drive down Franklin Avenue, ring the doorbell, and talk with her. He had the foolish fantasy that she might have changed the locks on the doors. There was no point, he decided, in finding out, only to be humiliated. Besides, the ball was in her court.

Was he being incredibly stubborn? No, he decided, she was.

DANIEL JONAS took mercy on his son—and himself—on Christmas Eve. He made certain all the worship leadership tasks were distributed among the other pastors, so that Josh and his parents could sit in a pew together for the Nativity Eve Eucharist. The seminary student appreciated his father's gesture, but was feeling increasingly ill-at-ease, realizing he was at worship without his wife.

His parents had arranged to go to the Andreas Scheidt home after church, for a gathering with five of the six founding families of the congregation. They invited Josh to come with them. He declined.

Instead, he put on his winter coat and went walking, alone, in Powerhorn Park. He sat on a cold park bench and looked at the frozen lake. He felt as barren inside as the landscape in front of him. He wondered if his marriage was ending.

He sat there for perhaps twenty minutes, before he saw her. Sarah was coming down the path, her hands plunged into the pockets of her heavy coat, heading toward him. He thought of getting up but, for some reason, decided not to.

She stopped in front of him and looked down into his apprehensive eyes. "We used to walk out here. I figured you might be here."

He didn't reply.

"May I join you?"

"Sure." He showed no emotion.

She sat down next to him and studied the perimeter of the lake. Finally, she said, "I'm doing better now."

"Excuse me?"

"I'm handling it a lot better. Grampa's marriage."

He said nothing.

"You were right. It's his life. I shouldn't have been so judgmental."

Still he was silent.

"I'm amazed how many people in the congregation told me they were happy for the two of them. I could tell they weren't just saying it. They meant it. For some reason, it meant a lot to me, hearing them say that."

He carefully slid his arm around her shoulders, wondering if she'd let him keep it there. She did.

"Thank you for being patient with me," she said.

He looked at her. She was looking repentant.

"Will you forgive me? For shouting at you. And all the other things?"

He smiled. "I love you. I love your strong convictions and your hot temper. Sometimes."

She laughed softly. "What do you want for Christmas, Josh?"

"That's easy. To spend the night in bed with you."

She grinned. "Let's go home."

Chapter 39

Pastor Aaron Ward sat admiring the colored-glass windows in the Reformation Room. Pastor Daniel Jonas came through the door, five minutes late, and sat down across the table from him. "Sorry. Janet Fenstermacher couldn't get the mimeograph machine to work."

"Where's the ink that's supposed to be all over your hands?"

"That's why I'm five minutes late. I finally got it all off. But enough about that. What did you want to talk about?"

"I think maybe it's time for me to put in my name for a call to another congregation."

"What? Why?"

"Have you seen these numbers?" Aaron pushed a sheaf of papers across the table. They were tabulations showing participation in the neighborhood cell group meetings over the years since the program had begun.

"Not as many cells as we used to have," Daniel murmured, studying the charts.

"We started with over 300. We have 120 now. I think that's something to be concerned about."

"The membership is holding steady at 7,000. How do you account for the decline?" Daniel asked, puzzled.

"The best I can determine, people may just be getting tired of attending these small group gatherings. It takes a lot of time and commitment."

"We've had them going for almost nine years."

"Which makes me think they may be outliving their usefulness."

"Oh, I can't imagine small groups ever ceasing to be useful," said Daniel. "On the other hand, we know that programs have a life cycle. This one may be coming to an end here."

"Which makes me believe I should put my name in for call. After all, it was the cell groups program that I came here to manage. It's my primary responsibility."

"We could redefine your call, Aaron."

"There's more."

"Excuse me?"

"I'm really feeling the need to relocate."

"Honestly? I'm sorry to hear that."

"Here's the thing. My father's position with General Motors in Detroit was terminated, effective the end of last year. He's been hired by 3M. My parents are moving to St. Paul in another month."

"That should be good news for your family, I'd think."

"Well, for some families, I suppose it would be. In our case, let me say it this way: My mother can be a real…"

"Trial?"

"My daughter puts it less diplomatically. She calls her grandmother 'a pain in the neck.' Her own grandmother!"

Daniel grinned. "And having them living across town doesn't sound like your idea of a good time."

Aaron returned a rueful grimace.

"Say no more. I understand perfectly." He thought about it. "Suppose your parents move here and discover you're about to leave. Wouldn't they see that as you running from them?"

"Probably. They'd just have to deal with it."

Daniel weighed the comment. "Well, you've been here well beyond the expected three-year minimum. I certainly won't stand in your way, if that's what you'd prefer to do."

"I'm positive it is."

"HOW'S YOUR ANKLE, Mrs. Feldermann?" James Wilson sat nervously on the living room couch. Alice's mother was seated across from him, in a wooden rocker. It was the first time the two of them had been alone in the same room since Abigail Feldermann had gone to the hospital.

"It's just fine, thank you. Completely healed. But you didn't come over here just to inquire about my health. Or did you?"

"No, Ma'am. I wanted to ask your opinion about something. And your advice." With Alice not due home from school for another forty minutes, he figured the two of them wouldn't be interrupted for awhile.

"Well, I'll see if I have any answers for you. What's on your mind?"

"I'm having a hard time figuring out how Alice really feels about me these days. I mean, the few times I've seen her this school year, she's been nice enough. But she's always real careful not to get into much of a conversation with me. I just wondered if she'd rather I'd leave her alone altogether. And, also, whether you would prefer that."

Abigail tilted her head. "I can't speak for Alice. You'd need to ask her directly. As far as my own attitude is concerned, I've rather changed my mind about you, I must admit. You seem like a thoughtful and sincere young man—who happens to have made one bad mistake with my daughter."

He looked contrite.

"Alice will be eighteen in a couple months. She can start making her own decisions. I have a feeling any interest in young men may not be in her plans."

That wasn't exactly what James had been hoping to hear. "Actually, I was going to ask you if she was planning to go to her senior prom later this spring. And if you'd object if I offered to take her."

Abigail looked wistful. "The first date I ever had with my late husband was to our high school senior prom." She gazed off into space for a moment, as if reliving it. She said, "I think it would be a shame if Alice missed having the opportunity to go to hers. But, I can't assure you she'd even want to go, James."

"I understand. But, if I wanted to invite her…I mean, assuming there's no rule against guys who are already out of high school attending, as a guest of a senior…I just wanted to be sure you wouldn't mind."

"I suppose you wouldn't have had to ask my permission to invite her."

"Well, I really think it's the right way to do it. Under the circumstances."

"You'd behave yourselves, I assume."

"Oh, yes Ma'am. Absolutely. We've learned our lesson. At least, I know I have."

"Would you like to wait and ask her? She should be here in a few minutes."

He hadn't expected such an invitation. "Yes. Thanks. I'd like that."

AS THEY GLIDED ACROSS the floor of the high school gymnasium, melodic tones of a popular music group playing in the background, James said, "This is just great, Alice. I'm really glad you let me bring you to your prom."

"Well, nobody else asked me. And I sort of wanted to come."

"I didn't even go to my own senior prom last year."

"Why not?"

"Well, you weren't exactly on speaking terms with me back then. And you were...you know..." From her trim appearance, he still couldn't believe she'd actually given birth.

"Weren't there any girls in your own high school that you liked?"

"Truthfully? No."

The music came to an end. He said, "Would you like something to drink?"

"Yes. That would be nice. I'm going to sit down over here."

As they sat sipping their punch, watching the other dancers out on the gym floor, he said, "What are you going to do after graduation?"

"I don't know. Get a job, I guess."

"You're not going to college?"

"I don't think so. I never planned on it. I've always had a very old-fashioned idea about what should happen after I graduated."

"What's the old-fashioned idea?"

"That I'd meet the man of my dreams, get married, settle down and have about four kids."

He smiled. "Yeah, that's pretty old-fashioned." She looked at him suspiciously. He quickly added, "But not bad. Not bad at all." Her dubious expression faded. He said, "That's sort of my idea, too. I don't want to go to college. I have this really good job at Mr. Engelhardt's newspaper office now. I'm starting to make a pretty decent salary."

"What are you doing there?"

"He taught me how to do bookkeeping. I'm managing the accounts for the newspaper. I found out I'm pretty good at it. It's a great place to work. There's always something interesting going on in a newspaper office. I've even written a few stories that got into print."

She offered a wan smile.

"And now," he continued, "all I need to do is find the girl of my dreams. So we can settle down and...I don't know...maybe have three or four kids."

"Well, I certainly hope you find her," she said coolly.

"So do I." They continued to sip their punch. "By the way, have I told you what a great dancer you are?"

"Yes. Four times already tonight."

He listened, briefly, to the music, then said, "Thanks for letting me bring you to your prom."

"You've said that four times already, too."

"Well, here's something I know I haven't said yet, even once." He looked into her eyes, admiring how they seemed to glisten in the dim light. "I think you're a gorgeous girl. Somebody's going to be very lucky to end up with you." He thought she was blushing. It was hard to tell in the semi-darkness. "And I'm not going to forget this night for a long, long time."

JOSH LAY IN THE DARKNESS, holding his wife close to him. He sighed with contentment. "Another year and three months and we can start having kids." He stroked her hair, then smoothed his hand down along her side to her waist and back again to her neck. "I'm going to be so glad to be done with seminary. The trips to Dubuque and back are wearing me out. And that old Pontiac may not hold up much longer."

"When you get a call, you can buy a better car," she said.

"Yeah. About the time I get this one paid for."

"Josh?"

"What?"

"I'm really glad we found each other."

He chuckled. "I almost lost you before I even found you. To Peter Fenstermacher."

"I know. He told me."

"He did?"

"That time he was in the hospital with the shoulder injury. I went into his room and we chatted briefly."

"Just long enough for him to tell you secrets about me, huh?"

"Well, it was a secret about him, too." It was her turn to chuckle. "He told me when I got tired of you, he'd be waiting in the wings."

"He *what*! That frisky colt. Who does he think he is, trying to steal away my girl?" He buried his face in her neck, kissing her until she squealed.

"Josh! I was just getting relaxed. Now you've gotten me all stirred up."

"I've been all stirred up for a whole week, just thinking about getting back to Minneapolis...and making love to you." He began kissing her passionately.

"And to think we almost broke up last Thanksgiving," she murmured.

"We almost did no such thing," he protested, continuing to kiss her.

"Well, it was touch and go there for about a month."

"We would never have broken up. Never in a million years."

"Did I ever tell you how sorry I was about being so mean to you?"

"Yes. About ten times. Now, are we going to make love or aren't we?"

She whispered into his ear, "We're going to make love."

ON THE DAY after Easter Sunday, Pastor Aaron Ward received a letter of call. He took the document home and showed it to his wife. The two of them spent three days praying about it, after which Aaron informed Daniel Jonas he intended to accept it.

Daniel called the president of the congregation with the news. Harry Broadman agreed to place an item on the next church council agenda, requesting a release for Pastor Ward.

The council responded with a vote of confidence in their staff pastor, commending him for his faithful work at Saint Michael Church, but granting him the requested release.

Within six weeks, he and his family were on their way to Los Angeles.

BECAUSE THEY HAD JOINED Gloria Dei Lutheran Church in St. Paul, Aaron's parents were not privy to the developments at Saint Michael Church. They would have been, had their son done them the courtesy of adding their new White Bear Lake address to the congregational newsletter's extended mailing list. Or, if mother and son had been on regular speaking terms with one another.

Consequently, Rebekah Ward learned of her son's departure only by reading a item in the metro section of theMinneapolis *Tribune*, the day after the moving van had left Minneapolis. She stormed into Daniel Jonas' office, demanding to know why the information had been concealed from her. Daniel told her he'd assumed she and her son maintained normal communication. She assured him that was not the case.

Daniel told her he was sure it must have been an oversight on Aaron's part, even though he knew better. He also suggested she might want to work on better communication with her offspring. That sent her storming out of the room in a huff.

He never saw her again.

Chapter 40

Harry Broadman sat in the senior pastor's office, across from Daniel Jonas. He said, "So, how do you want to handle this pastoral vacancy? The same as before?"

"Not necessarily."

"You don't want to just find a person you'd like to work with, and then have us ratify him?"

"I think we might want to organize a search committee."

"You want to go to all that trouble?"

"There's nothing wrong with taking a look at a variety of candidates, Harry."

"Except, we already have an excellent candidate waiting in the wings."

Daniel returned a look of incomprehension.

"Your son. Joshua Daniel."

The senior pastor shook his head vigorously. "That's not an option. I won't even consider it. Just think how that would look to the members."

"You know, I'm one of the members. It would look just fine to me. And I can think of about a hundred other people who would agree with me."

"No, Harry," said Daniel adamantly. "It's not an option. Joshua Daniel has already told me he'd never consider a call here. Besides, he preaches here once a month. The District Office frowns on a congregation calling someone who's been serving them on a short-term basis."

"Why? We'd know what we were getting."

"It looks too much like we're stacking the deck."

Harry screwed up his mouth into a thoughtful pout. "Technically, we stacked the deck with all three of the staff pastors we called. You picked them, we ratified them, that settled it."

"This is different. He's my son. This congregation should not end up with some kind of 'royal succession' in its leadership."

"You think that's what it would be?"

"It's just not a good precedent, Harry."

"Okay, Pastor," he said with resignation. "But a lot of people are going to be really, *really* disappointed."

WHA-A-A-ANG! The basketball hit the rim, rolled around its perimeter, and then dropped through the net. "Nice goin', Preacher Man!" shouted Matt Horner. The muscular, bare-chested, seventeen-year-old had taken to calling Josh by a nickname of his own creation, ever since he'd learned the seminary student was planning to be ordained in one more year.

Josh felt a river of perspiration running down his bare back. He grinned at Matt and said, "Okay, we're up by four. Let's keep those two renegades at bay for four more points and the game's ours."

"In your dreams," exclaimed Jeff Carter. The eighteen-year-old's tee shirt was soaked after twenty minutes of hard-fought competition on the church court. He took the ball out of bounds and fired it into the hands of his team-mate. Ivan Sikorsky, the only sixteen-year old in the foursome, dribbled hard along one side of the asphalt, stopped and sent a high, arcing shot toward the basket. It fell short.

He shouted out an angry curse. Immediately he apologized to Josh.

The 'shirts' and the 'skins' continued to battle it out, in the heat and humidity of a July Saturday afternoon, until all four were totally exhausted. When Matt sank the winning basket, even the opposing pair seemed relieved.

"Would'a worked better with more guys out here," said Jeff, trying to mask his disappointment for having been on the losing side.

"Bring more of your buddies next time," said Josh, wiping perspiration off his bare chest and midsection. He studied the three teen-agers, admired their energy and their athletic prowess, and wondered whether any of them would ever darken the door of Saint Michael Church. So far, none had. But, he figured, an occasional game of hoops might coax them closer to religion.

"How'd you get so good at this, Preacher Man?" Matt queried, picking up his discarded shirt and drying his underarms. "I never seen a preacher who could sink shots like you."

"Practice," said Josh. "I used to work in that free clinic, right there." He pointed to the building adjacent to the ball court. "It was pretty easy to come out here on break, or at lunchtime, and polish up my jump shot."

"Well, for an old guy, you're pretty good."

"Old guy? I'm 26!"

"That's ancient," said Jeff, chortling.

"You'll be there soon," said Josh. "What do you guys think you'll be doing in ten years?"

Ivan said, "Tryin' to stay outta jail, probably."

The others laughed. "Ivan likes takin' things that don't belong to him," said Matt. "All of us've took our turns with the cops. So far, we've stayed a couple steps ahead of them."

"So that's your goal for the next ten years? To stay out of jail?"

"And not get any girls pregnant," said Jeff, snickering.

"Any of you three planning to get a decent job and try to amount to something?"

Matt said, "Oh, we'll figure something out. As long as it doesn't interfere with our social life."

"You wouldn't want to let that happen," Josh said, with poorly-concealed sarcasm.

"Look, we gotta go, man," Jeff said. "Thanks for a good game. How about Monday afternoon, so we can get even?"

"Sure," said Josh. He watched the three young men pile into a beat-up old Ford and drive away. He pulled on his shirt and headed for the corner. He walked the short half block, to Anderson Avenue, and sat down on the grass in front of the parish house. He wondered if any of the three unemployed high school graduates would ever really amount to anything.

His Pontiac came into view. Sarah pulled up at the curb and he scrambled in on the passenger side. As they headed home, she said, "You stink. You need a shower."

"You're not telling me anything I don't already know. How was shopping?"

"That new Southdale Mall is amazing. The place was jammed today. Everything's under one roof, Josh!"

"So I've heard. How much smaller is our bank account, now that you've been out there?"

"Well, I found you some sexy pajamas. They're sort of silky. I thought maybe you could wear the bottoms—and I could wear the tops."

"Why do we have to wear anything at all?" he growled suggestively.

She looked momentarily confused, then grinned. "Sounds like you're ready to go to bed right now."

"Right after my shower. Okay?"

"It's only four o'clock in the afternoon."

"Does it matter?"
"Obviously not to you."

SHORTLY AFTER the announcement appeared in the parish newsletter, that a search committee was being organized in order to select a new pastor, a petition began to circulate among the members of Saint Michael Church. It requested that the committee not be organized, and that the church council bring the name of Joshua Daniel Jonas to a voter's meeting. Nobody would own up to having created the petition, although it was widely believed that Harry Broadman had secretly authored it.

Within a month, it had collected over 1,500 names.

ALICE FELDERMANN took a job after high school graduation, working in a florist's shop on Cedar Avenue. James began finding excuses to drop by on his lunch break. He would sit on a stool in the workroom, admiring the way she created bouquets, chewing on a sandwich and complimenting her on the arrangements she was putting together.

At first she wondered about letting him into the workroom, but when her employer told her there was no problem, as long as her productivity didn't suffer, she allowed him in.

He would show up two or three times during a work week. He'd tell her funny stories he'd heard, or read her advance copy he knew was about to appear in the pages of the *Bloomington Avenue News*. She always smiled demurely, sometimes giggled, but rarely offered more than ten words of conversation. Still, he felt encouraged by the fact that she didn't ever order him not to return.

One day, in late September, as he'd finished his sandwich and his monologue, he was about to climb down off his stool when Alice unexpectedly picked up a pink carnation, snipped off most of the stem and brought it to him. She pinned it on his shirt and said, "There. Now you have something to make you think of me for the rest of the afternoon."

He thought of her during the afternoon, during supper, throughout the evening and in his dreams.

IN NOVEMBER, the church council voted to dissolve the recently-formed search committee and to call a special meeting of the congregation on the Sunday before Thanksgiving Day. There was one agenda item: a recommendation to call Josh Jonas as a staff pastor for Saint Michael Church.

When Daniel caught wind of the decision, he phoned Harry Broadman. "I'm going to speak against this motion, Harry. You know that, don't you?"

"I know, Pastor. But we have 1,825 names on our petition. We can't just ignore them."

Notwithstanding his father's reasoned and passionate argument to the contrary, the congregation voted overwhelmingly to call Josh. The term was to begin two weeks following his graduation from seminary. Harry Broadman mailed off the Letter of Call to the District Office, along with a personal note to Josh, urging him to prayerfully consider accepting it. The District President sat on it for a week, then sent it to the pastor's son.

Josh mailed it back to the District Office, respectfully declining even to consider it.

"DAD, HOW COULD YOU let them do that? You know what we agreed to, you and I. There's no way I'm taking a call to Saint Michael Church."

"Didn't Harry Broadman tell you how I argued against doing it, right in front of the voter's meeting?"

"Of course not. Why would he include a little detail like that?"

"Well, that should settle it. I think they may have to go back to working with a search committee. They can create a new one at the Annual Meeting in January."

WHEN THE CONGREGATION met in January, the issue of calling a third staff pastor was not on the agenda. But, under new business, Mark Farnan, a member of the church council, arose and verbally reintroduced the identical motion that had been passed the previous November, that Josh Jonas be called as staff pastor. It was immediately seconded.

Daniel did not rise to comment on the overture. It passed overwhelmingly.

JOSH SAT STUDYING the letter of call which had arrived in his mailbox for a second time. Out his dormitory window, Martin Luther, bold and bronze, stood holding a copy of the Holy Scriptures. To Josh, he looked determined and defiant. That was how Josh was feeling. He mailed the letter of call back, with a brief note explaining he had not changed his mind, and was not accepting it.

IN THE MIDDLE OF LENT, James asked Alice if she would go with him to the Palm Sunday afternoon performance of Mendelssohn's *Elijah.* The every-other-year staging of the oratorio had become, years earlier, one of Lillian Fischer's signature musical gifts to the congregation.

He was on cloud nine when Alice accepted the invitation. His spirits were deflated, at least a bit, when she asked if it would be all right if her mother came along with them. There was no good way he could think of to say no.

"THANKS, JAMES. It was nice of you to let my mom come to the concert with us."

"It was fine," he said, shifting on the stool in the florist's workroom. "How did you like the music?"

"Long. Complicated. Sort of amazing. I've never been to one of those performances before."

"Do you like music like that?"

"Do you?"

"Asked you first."

"It's okay." A guilty look crept onto her face. "But, if you want to know the truth, what I really like is the Everly Brothers."

James laughed. "No kidding. I *love* the Everly Brothers. And what about Marty Robbins?" He began to sing softly, "A white sport coat and a pink carnation, I'm all dressed up for the dance…"

Alice grinned. She was obviously enjoying the improptu concert. She said, "Why don't you come over on Saturday? We can listen to some of my records."

"Really?" His eyes lit up. He sobered. "What about your Mom? She'll be there, right?"

"No. She has to work this Saturday."

"Alice, there's no way I'm coming to your apartment when it's just you and me there and nobody else."

"It's okay, James. I already told her I might invite you over sometime. She trusts you now."

"You sure?"

"Absolutely."

ON THE SUNDAY following Easter Day, another special congregational meeting was convened. The same motion brought in January was introduced again, once more by Mark Farnan. Again, the motion carried by a large margin.

Josh, who knew what was in the works, didn't officially learn the results until several days later. He had made a point of staying away. He'd convinced his wife that she shouldn't attend either. So, after the last liturgy, they went home.

As they ate the noon meal together, he said, "By now they've probably voted to call me again. Is this some sort of conspiracy, or what? Whoever heard of getting a call to the same congregation three times in a row?"

She sighed. "Maybe it's the Holy Spirit's way of telling you you're supposed to be a pastor here."

"But I'd be serving with my dad."

"Could you do that?"

"I don't know. I don't want to, really."

"But if the congregation wants you this badly, shouldn't you at least honor their wishes?"

He sat studying the tablecloth. "What would you do if I was pastor here, Sarah? Wouldn't it seem a little weird to you?"

She shrugged. "I'd kind of enjoy it."

He looked at her in amazement.

"It's not as if you and your dad don't get along. You're pretty good friends."

"This might spoil the friendship."

"I don't see why. Anyway, if it didn't work out, you could always take another call after three years and go somewhere else."

He sighed heavily. "What are you really saying?"

"I'm saying it's your choice. But you shouldn't be so bulldog stubborn. Especially if you think this is what the Holy Spirit wants for you."

"I'm not sure it is."

"Are you positive it's not?"

He stared out the dining room window, toward nothing in particular. He sat in silence for almost a minute. Finally, he said, "No. I guess not. I don't know. I really don't know."

Chapter 41

THE ORDINATION of Joshua Daniel Jonas was celebrated on a warm Sunday afternoon in June. The Lutheran Church of Saint Michael and All Angels was filled to overflowing. As Lillian Fischer led the congregation in the entrance hymn, a long procession of robed clergy from area congregations moved slowly up the center aisle, toward pews reserved for them at the front of the nave. The seminary graduate was astonished, and deeply grateful, to see so many ordained pastors on hand. Silently, he named off the ones he recognized: Kenneth Siess, Erik Strand, Henry French, Ron Johnson, Steve Benson, Gary Kierschke, Gordon Braatz, Chris Nelson, Paul Youngdahl, Tim Fuzzey, Steve Cornils. There were still more, whose names he did not remember.

Josh had invited one of his seminary teachers, a professor of historical theology, to preach. His sermon exhorted the young candidate to be mindful of the Christian Church's long history of faithful ministry, often in the face of adversity. He focused on Wilhelm Löhe, the German Lutheran pastor for whom Wartburg Seminary's chapel was named. Josh remembered how his instructor had once extolled Löhe in the classroom, telling how the 19th century churchman stood on principle when the German Lutheran hierarchy tried to convince him to do otherwise. Sitting with the other clergy, in the front pew, he wondered whether he was made of similar stuff, and whether he'd ever be called upon to face challenges such as the Bavarian clergyman once had, more than a century before.

When it was time for the rite of ordination, Daniel Jonas stepped to the center of the chancel and motioned for his son to come forward. The vows which Josh repeated seemed unreal to him. He wondered how he had ended up in this place, standing before his own father, promising faithfulness to God, to Holy Scripture and to the Lutheran Confessions. He marveled that he had received—and accepted—a call to the congregation where he had grown up, and where his father was the senior pastor.

He became aware that the clergy were surrounding him, standing close, laying their hands upon his head, speaking words of blessing and affirmation. Suddenly he was overcome with gratitude, and an unexpected sense of terror. He feared he might prove unequal to his calling.

When he stood and turned to face the congregation, to receive their thunderous applause, tears were streaming down his face.

"JOSHUA DANIEL, I can't tell you how proud of you I am, and how excited I am that you and Dad will be working together."

"Thanks for coming all the way from Pennsylvania just for this event, Sis," Josh replied.

"Are you serious?" Hannah Ruth Baumgartner replied, "John and I wouldn't have missed it!"

"I just hope the congregation hasn't made a big mistake. I gave them three chances to change their mind."

"The Holy Spirit was obviously working through them," she suggested. "Whoever heard of a congregation picking a pastor in such a way?"

"Well, there was Bishop Ambrose, actually," Josh replied with a grin.

Hannah Ruth looked at her brother with astonishment. "You're not comparing yourself to some bishop already, I hope!"

"No. But since you brought up the idea of picking a pastor by acclamation, it so happens the famous Bishop of Milan got into office just that way. In fact, he wasn't even ordained when the people asked him to become their bishop. If I recall, he wasn't even a baptized Christian. They just rose up and swept him into office, pretty much against his will."

Hannah Ruth looked at her brother with mock disgust. "History majors. They always have a story from the dusty past."

"The 'dynamic past,'" said Josh, with a twinkle in his eye. "The past is only dusty if you let it be. I see memorable things happening there. Exciting stories. People of faith and courage." He had fire in his eyes. "Wasn't it great the way Wilhelm Löhe ended up in the sermon this afternoon?"

"I guess," Hannah Ruth said, shrugging. "I'd never heard of him before today."

"Did Hannah Ruth tell you our news?" asked John Baumgartner, taking the chair next to the couch where the Jonas siblings were seated.

"News?" Josh replied. His eyes grew large. "You're finally pregnant!"

"No. Not yet," said John. "First things first. Starting this fall I'm joining a medical practice."

"Where? Here?"

"Well…no."

Josh looked at John, then at his sister, and then again at John. "Not in Philadelphia!"

Hannah Ruth said, "In Columbus, Ohio. With some physicians John met when he was at Ohio State."

"You're not coming back to Minnesota?"

"We'll come back. Every now and then."

Josh looked disappointed. "I suppose you've cleared this with your old pal, Jenny Langholz."

Hannah Ruth returned a guilty look. "Not yet. I will though."

"You know, she always thought you'd be coming back here."

His sister sighed. "I know. She'll probably take it hard. But she's a big girl. She'll get over it."

"JUST GET OVER IT, Jenny!"

"That's easy for you to say. You're a guy. And, anyway, you've never been in a serious relationship." Jenny Langholz glowered at Paul David Engelhardt. Why, she wondered, had she allowed him to take her out to dinner, if this was the way it was going to end up?

Paul David said, "It's *not* easy for me to say. It's difficult. Believe me. I wasn't going to bring it up. I know how painful your relationship with Buzz Winslow was. But, Jenny, how many years ago was that?"

"It still hurts." She looked sternly at her dining companion. In a quiet but intense whisper, she said, "He could have raped me, you know."

"I know. But thank God he didn't." He looked intensely at Jenny. "Here's the thing. I've begun to grow fond of you. I really want us to give each other a chance. But it's not going to happen if you hold onto this ridiculous idea that you can't date guys because some creep in your past ruined things for you. That's not fair—to you, or to me."

"Who said I had any interest in you?"

"Nobody did. But I was hoping you might be willing to consider having some."

"Why would I? I'm single and happy. You told me you were, too."

"Well, I was. I'm just not sure I want to stay that way for the rest of my life."

"So, you took me out to supper to create a sense of obligation in me so I'd agree to start dating you? Was that it?"

"For crying out loud, is *that* what you think I'm doing?"

"Well..."

"Come on. Let's go. I'll take you home."

She stared at him in disbelief. "I thought we were going to have coffee and dessert."

"What's the point? I've upset you. Anyway, I think I've lost my appetite for dessert."

Her expression changed from defiance to contrition. "I'm sorry. I didn't mean to ruin your evening. It's just that...I've never quite gotten this Buzz Winslow business out of my system." She exhaled heavily. "And I've really wanted to. You're the first person to confront me with it, head on. I just wasn't quite prepared for the way you did it."

"Telling you to get over it?"

"Yes. That seemed insulting. But, I've told myself the same thing a hundred times. I really do need to get over it. I'm working at it. It's just taking longer than I wanted it to."

"Well, if I was insensitive, I apologize. But I really would like to help you get past it, if I could."

She played with her napkin, folding and unfolding it. Suddenly she said, "So you think we should be getting serious about each other, huh?"

"I...yeah. I do. I've come to realize, more and more, how much I really, *really* like you. In fact, I'm starting to care about you."

"No kidding."

"You find that so difficult to believe?"

Her face took on an impish grin. "I've never told you this, but maybe this is the right time. Back when we went on that trip with the Luther Leaguers to Purdue University, I remember thinking, 'If I ever did decide to get serious with anybody again, it might just be with Paul David Engelhardt.' I don't know why I thought that back then. Because I didn't know you that well. I just liked your good looks and that sharp beard of yours." She studied his clean-shaven face and grinned "You're just as handsome without it, by the way."

He colored. Did she really feel this way? He was surprised.

She said, "Of course, I was just infatuated with your good looks at the time. But then I saw how you took James into your home, and into your life. That was so...so sweet."

He was feeling uncomfortable, listening to her compliment him like this.

"So, I decided there was probably more to you than most guys. You were so...I don't know...caring, and decent, and thoughtful."

"You're embarrassing me, you know."

She seemed not to hear the comment. "I can understand why you're on the prowl for a girlfriend. I mean, you're going to be living alone again before long."

"What do you mean, 'living alone'? James is still staying in my guest room. He doesn't give any signs of moving out."

"Oh, my goodness. He hasn't talked to you about any of this?"

"Any of *what*?"

"Well, I think it's okay for me to tell you. He asked Alice to marry him. And she said yes. And then Alice asked me to be her maid of honor."

"What! James has said nothing about this to me. Just when, exactly, is this secret wedding supposed to be taking place?"

"At the end of summer. I thought he was going to ask you to walk Alice down the aisle and give her away."

Paul David looked thunderstruck.

"Well, I only heard from Alice a couple days ago. I'm sure James will be talking to you about this before long."

"He'd better be. Or I may just have to take him over my knee."

"I can just see you doing that."

"Jenny?"

"What?"

"Are those two ready to get married, do you think?"

"Why not? They're both out of high school. He has a good job, working for you. She's happy at the florist shop. She said they found a vacant apartment upstairs over that drug store up the street from your newspaper office. They can afford the rent. Both of them can walk to work from there. Sounds like it could work."

"I can't believe it," Paul David mumbled. "That rascal's getting married. And he didn't even consult me!"

"WELL, I WAS GOING to say something to you one of these next days," James confessed sheepishly.

"A fine thing," Paul David said, affecting hurt, "I find out about my house guest's wedding plans while I'm out to dinner with a third party."

"Sorry. I just sort of thought you might have guessed what we were planning."

"How? With extrasensory perception, perhaps?"

"No. I just thought it might be obvious."

"Well, think again, partner. I was blind-sided, thanks to you."

James tried to look apologetic. But then he said, "So, are you happy for us?"

"Happy? Why would I be happy? You're moving out of my house. I'm going to end up a lonely old bachelor after all."

James studied his employer's face for signs he was putting him on. Not sensing any, he said, "I have the perfect solution. Why don't you marry Jenny Langholz?"

"Just like that?"

"Sure. We could have a double wedding."

"Then who would give the bride away? And besides, what makes you think I even *like* Jenny Langholz?"

"Gosh, I don't know. All I know is Jenny Langholz really likes you."

"Says who?"

"Says Alice, that's who."

JOSH JONAS headed down the sidewalk, along the side of the parish house. Crossing the alley, he caught sight of four young men, scrimmaging on the church's asphalt basketball court. He was late for a home visit, but stopped and watched for a moment.

All four appeared to be Mexican, perhaps 18 or 19 years old. Two of them had shed their shirts, and their upper bodies were slick with perspiration. The shirts the other two wore were soaked. The four shouted competitively at one another in Spanish.

Welcome to the United Nations, Josh thought. He waved at one of the four, who returned the gesture, just seconds before snagging the ball, turning and sinking a clean shot through the net.

Forty minutes later, when he was returning from his visit, Josh passed the court again. By now the game was breaking up. Josh walked toward them and shouted cheerfully, "Anybody here speak English?"

"Oh, yeah. All of us do. What can we do for you?"

"Well, just make sure nobody gets hurt, I guess. This is a private court. If any of you four got a concussion, our insurance would have to pay for it."

"No problem, Padré. We would never sue a priest. Or a church."

"Well, I'm a pastor, not a priest. Josh Jonas. Who are you?"

"I'm José Gonzalez. These are my friends…Juan Sanchez, Felipe Garcia and Ferdinand Martinez. Did we need permission to use the court?"

"No. Not at all. In fact, we're happy to have you use it. Just keep it clean, okay?"

"Keep it clean?"

"You know. Watch your language. No fighting. Don't cheat."

"No problem, Padré."

"You four live around here?"

"Yeah, in the neighborhood."

"This is a Lutheran church. Any of you guys Lutheran?"

All four grinned and shook their heads. "We're Mexican. We're Catholic. You know?"

Josh grinned. "Who's your best shot?"

Each of the four pointed to a different companion. Then they all laughed.

"What about you, Padré?" asked José. "You any good with one of these?"

Josh held out his hands. José tossed the ball to him. "How's this?" He sent the ball arcing high, from mid-court. It swished silently through the net.

There were hoots of admiration and applause. "You have to come out here and play with us next time," José said, grinning with approval.

"I'm pretty busy these days. But I'll see if I can fit you guys in."

"We'll plan on it," said Juan. He turned to the others and said, "Come on, losers buy drinks for the winners."

Josh watched them pile into a rusty old Chevrolet and head out. The car needed a new muffler. He wondered what the four of them did when they weren't shooting baskets.

Chapter 42

Sarah Jonas wasn't sure what to think when she looked out through the leaded-glass window of the front parlor, toward Franklin Avenue. A Minneapolis squad car had pulled up in front of the house, and a uniformed officer was climbing out.

Her pulse slowed when she realized it was her husband's high school buddy, Skip Warner. She opened the door and stepped out onto the porch.

"Afternoon, Ma'am," he said in mock seriousness. "Had a report of a domestic disturbance at this residence. Thought I'd better swing by and investigate."

She shook her head, stifling a grin.

He returned a broad smile of his own. "Hi, Sarah. Where's your other half?"

"Making home visits. He'll be sorry he missed you." She thought about Skip's presence on her front porch. "Aren't you supposed to be patrolling up on the north side somewhere?"

"That's why I stopped. Wanted to tell Josh I've been reassigned. I'm working south Minneapolis now."

"Really!"

"Yeah. I have a little seniority. My wife was worried I'd get into some sort of violent encounter up there. North side's getting pretty rough, you know."

"Well, then it's lucky for you, I guess."

"Yeah. I'd say. The normal drill on my new beat is people running red lights and...well...an occasional domestic disturbance." He smiled.

"You want to come in?"

"No. Just tell Josh I stopped. And tell him my good news."

JENNY LANGHOLZ slipped into the seat on the charter bus, next to Paul

David Engelhardt. “Thanks for insisting I come along to this thing,” she said, smiling. “I was going to stay home this afternoon and write letters. But this was something I don’t think I’ll forget for awhile.”

The bus pulled away from the curb near the Minnesota state capitol building and headed back toward Minneapolis. Paul David said, “It’s not every day you get to stand in a crowd of 100,000 Lutherans. That will probably never happen again.”

“How often does the Lutheran World Federation have these big meetings, anyway?” she asked.

“Every few years, I think Pastor Jonas said.”

“Which Pastor Jonas?”

“The older one. It was his idea to charter six buses just for our congregation. I’d say we were pretty well represented over here.”

“They probably won’t have another one in St. Paul, right?”

“We’ll be lucky to have another one in the United States. A lot of these meetings are in Europe. That’s what Pastor…Pastor Daniel…said in the adult forum.”

Jenny reached over and slid her hand into Paul David’s. He did a double take. He had not intended this to be a date. He knew describing the cross-town visit that way to Jenny would have been the kiss of death.

She said, “I really want to you thank you, Paul David.”

“For what?”

“For helping me face up to my demons.”

“Excuse me?”

“That time in the restaurant. When you told me to get over my anger and my fear. I was mad as the dickens at you when you did that. But it was just what I needed.”

He smiled tentatively.

“Guess what. I’m over it.”

“No!”

“I am. Really.”

“Well…I’m very pleased to hear you say that.”

“Paul David?”

“What?”

“Would you like to take me out sometime?”

He looked at her in disbelief. He was speechless, but not for long. He replied, “I thought you’d never ask.”

JOSH JONAS got his first opportunity to provide premarital counseling when James and Alice came to his office door and asked if he would do the honors. "What about my dad?" he asked, only half seriously.

"He's okay," James answered, speaking for both of them. "But you're closer to our age. We'd rather have you do it. If that's okay with you."

And so the young couple came to see Josh for three sessions. He helped them prepare themselves for building a relationship together, and developing skills for dealing with conflict. They listened politely, but then made it abundantly clear to him that they believed everything would be perfect, no matter what. He helped them come to terms with the high probability that things would actually turn out differently, over time.

He asked them whether there was any lingering guilt about their having slept together, and having caused a child to be born out of wedlock. Alice shed some tears, recalling how she had given up her infant boy without ever seeing him. James drew his arm around her and gave her a gentle squeeze. But they assured the young pastor that they had come to terms with the hurt and anguish they had caused each other, and their families.

They talked about the fact that James was now estranged from his mother, in part because of his sexual indiscretion. He assured the pastor that a falling out would have occurred sooner or later. And, he explained, it had turned out for the best, since he'd gained a close friend in Paul David, and had learned a trade in the bargain.

They talked about budgeting money and the importance of keeping Christ central in their lives. The two of them had already considered the importance of both, and showed themselves to be well prepared to move into married life with their eyes open and their feet on the ground.

"Well," said Josh, when the final session was wrapping up, "if all the couples who come to me are as ready for marriage as the two of you seem to be, this marriage counseling business should be a piece of cake."

In future years, he would look back on his shared time with James and Alice as one of his greatest premarital counseling successes.

PAUL DAVID ENGELHARDT had offered to rent a hall and pay for a dinner and dance for the bride and groom, following their wedding, but James had made it clear that he and Alice didn't want him spending that kind of money on them. When his employer offered to make it a wedding present, James suggested that, if he really wanted to do something for the two of them, a down payment on a used car would be more useful.

As the wedding rehearsal was breaking up, Paul David walked the couple to the curb and announced, "I don't know where you're heading on your wedding trip tomorrow night, but you can drive this."

They looked at him, uncomprehending. Before them was parked a very sharp looking, three-year-old Oldsmobile. The sticker on the back indicated it had come from Joe Pavelka's used car lot.

"We…actually were planning to take the bus to Duluth and spend a couple days in a cabin on Lake Superior," James explained.

"Take a bus on your wedding trip? That's crazy!" Paul David replied. "You need some privacy. Take the Oldsmobile to Duluth."

James gulped. "We'll take good care of it. It'll come back to you without a scratch."

"What do I care if it comes back with scratches? I'm giving it to you. Here are the keys. And here's the title." He handed over an envelope.

James pursed his lips, fighting tears. But Alice was not so restrained. She flung her arms around Paul David and kissed him on the cheek.

JAMES AND ALICE were married on a Saturday afternoon in August. Paul David walked Alice down the aisle of Saint Michael Church's enormous nave, the colors in the towering stained-glass windows bathing them in soft light as they moved forward, toward the altar.

James stood waiting, next to Pastor Josh Jonas, at the first chancel step. There were perhaps one hundred in the pews. Alice noted with appreciation that her Aunt Sylvia and Uncle Edmund had come from Eau Claire for the ceremony. It was they who had taken her in during her pregnancy, and had arranged to find a home for the child she could not keep.

While waiting for the bride to come down the aisle, James had scanned the small congregation, half expecting, half hoping not to see his mother in one of the pews. She was not there. It occurred to him there was little chance she would have known about the wedding. It also occurred to him that he had absolutely no idea where she was living now, or with whom.

The women of Saint Michael and All Angels Church hosted a reception for the couple and their guests in the Community Room following the ceremony. Paul David offered a toast to the bride and groom. Raising a cup of punch, he said, "If any two ever deserved to be happy, these two do. Here's to great prosperity, and to a wonderful future for James and Alice."

As the couple drove away from the curb in their "new" Oldsmobile, Jenny Langholz slid her arm through Paul David's and said, "That was a very nice toast. I was impressed."

"James is a great kid," he said. Hastily he added, "So is Alice, of course."
She said, "I know we're getting kind of old for this sort of thing, but..."
"But what?"
"But how about you and me going steady?"
"Bad idea."
"Really?" she said, taken aback.
"Why mess around with that high school stuff? Let's just get married."
"Us? When?"
"I don't know. How soon could you be ready?"

JOSH WAS FINISHING a conversation with Maggie Washington in the free clinic, across the alley from the parish house, when he heard the commotion. Moving to the window facing the basketball court, he saw what appeared to him to be a fistfight among a half dozen neighborhood teen-agers. There was shouting, shoving and profanity.

Then he spotted a squad car at the curb, next to the ball court. There was nobody in it. That struck him odd.

"Excuse me, Maggie, I think I need to check this out."

"Don't get in the middle of anything," she warned. "Things are looking a little nasty out there."

He walked out the door of the clinic and headed for the basketball court, wondering whether he was asking for trouble. He realized that any one of the young men involved in the altercation could probably handle him physically. Still, it was the church's property, and there was potential for somebody to get seriously hurt.

As soon as the combatants spotted him, they all took off running. He realized he'd seen all of them before. Four were white, the other four brown-skinned Mexicans. All had played on the court one time or another, but never all at the same time.

Then he saw the policeman, lying face down on the court. He raced toward him, knelt down and turned him over. His heart began to thump in his chest. It was Skip Warner. There was a deep gash in his neck, and the blood was spurting out, creating a spreading lake of red on the black pavement.

Josh tore off his shirt and tried to tie the sleeve around his friend's neck, hoping to slow the loss of blood. He looked toward the window, where Maggie was looking on in horror.

"Call an ambulance!" he shouted.

"I did!" she yelled back. "They're on the way!"

"Oh, God," Josh pleaded, leaning close to Skip, "Don't let him die. Please. Please. Please."

BY THE TIME the medics arrived, Skip Warner had no pulse. He had lost massive amounts of blood. All attempts to revive him were in vain.

Josh stood by helplessly, watching them load his friend's lifeless body onto a stretcher and carry him away.

He covered his face with his hands, soaking his chin and cheeks and eyebrows with Skip's blood. He sobbed inconsolably, his body shuddering with searing grief.

Suddenly Maggie Washington was standing next to him, circling him with her arms. "Oh, Josh, I'm so sorry." She absorbed the shaking in his tortured frame. "Come on," she said, "Come back into the clinic. You need to lie down."

He tore himself free. "No! I need to go and be with Skip."

She wondered if he realized the policeman was already dead. But she decided not to challenge him. Instead, she said, "Well, before you do that, you have to get this blood off you. Come back to the clinic with me."

He looked at her, wild-eyed. He seemed not to comprehend anything she was saying. But she persuaded him to walk with her.

In one of the examination rooms, she removed his blood-soaked undershirt and washed the blood from his face and neck and chest.

"Wouldn't you like to lie down for a minute or two?"

"No!" he retorted. "Skip needs me!"

"Well, then wait until I call your wife. She'll bring some clean clothes. You can't go without a shirt."

Somehow, that made sense to him. He sat on the cot, watching her go out. He heard her dial the phone. Whatever she said was spoken too softly for him to hear. When she returned, she had a glass of water. "Drink this," she said firmly. "Your wife is coming. While you're waiting, drink this."

He took the glass, drained it and handed it back. She stood watching him. Within a minute or two he was feeling dizzy. He was sure she had put something into his drink. But he was too drowsy to accuse her of anything.

"Lie down," she said. He felt Maggie pushing him down, onto the cot.

And then he felt nothing.

Chapter 43

Josh sat in the den, staring sullenly out the window, toward the street. Since Skip Warner's funeral, he had not left the house. The church council, at his father's suggestion, had given him indefinite leave with pay. And so, each day, all day, he would sit in the den of the brick mansion and brood.

The days had stretched into six long weeks. Sarah had worried, at first, about leaving him alone when she went off to work her shift at the hospital. But each day when she returned, she would find him precisely where she had left him. She wondered whether he might have slipped into clinical depression.

One morning in mid-October, when he was sitting and staring, there came a rapping on the heavy oak front door. The brass knocker sent what sounded to him like hammer blows, piercing the gloomy silence.

It was jarring to Josh. He dragged himself from the leather upholstered couch, walked slowly into the great center hallway, and pulled the door open.

"May I come in?" Karen Warner waited for a response, but got only a dumbfounded stare. Skip's widow stepped past Josh, into the vestibule, and waited for him to push the door shut. Leaning against it, facing her, he found himself unable to speak.

"In here?" she suggested, gesturing toward the parlor. "Can we sit and talk in here?"

He nodded and followed her into the wood-paneled room with its ornate fireplace.

When they were seated, Karen said, "I hate to say this, but I think I'm dealing with Skip's death better than you are." He grimaced. "Not that I'm handling it very well. It's been hell these past six weeks." She sighed heavily. "But I'm getting through it." Josh nodded miserably. "Your father's been a great help. I've been to see him a few times." She studied Josh's drawn face.

"I would have come to you if you'd been available." His expression was now tinged with guilt. "Not that I could have expected that from you. He was your best friend. How could you have talked to me about him...and me...and all of it?"

Josh finally found his voice. "I'm so terribly sorry. I thought I could save him. I really did. But there was just so much blood..."

"It wasn't going to happen, Josh. That knife wound was so deep...and you know it cut the main artery in his neck..." She pursed her lips, fighting tears.

Josh got out of his chair and went to the couch where she was seated. He drew his arm around her. "You've been so brave," he said. "I don't know how you do it."

She said, "It's something you always think about...worry about...when you're married to a cop." She exhaled heavily. "Skip and I talked about the possibility sometimes. And then, when he got assigned to south Minneapolis, I thought, 'At last. Out of the war zone, into a peaceful neighborhood.'" She looked into Josh's eyes. "It just shows how wrong you can be."

At last, Josh felt his pastoral instincts surfacing. "Karen, how are your three beautiful children?"

That was the trigger that opened the floodgates. She broke down and wept in deep, shuddering sobs. Josh pulled her close and tried to comfort her. He waited, perhaps a minute, until her tears were at an end.

"I don't know," she said miserably, "how those little guys are going to get along without their daddy. They're five and three and one. The youngest won't even remember him." She began to sob again.

Josh felt a terrible deep ache in his soul. For the first time since the funeral, it was for someone other than himself. He said, "I was really proud of those policemen. I've never seen so many uniformed officers in one place in my life. It was great they all showed up for the service."

"Skip attended a few of those services himself. He would come home and tell me how hard it was to watch a member of the force lowered into the ground, but how wonderful it was that all those officers turned out for him."

"What can I do to help you, Karen?"

"That's what I came here to ask you," she said, smiling. There were still tears in her eyes. She did her best to dry them.

"I think we've both helped each other," Josh said.

"You know who's helped the most?" she asked. He shook his head. "Pete Fenstermacher. He's on the force in northeast Minneapolis, you know."

Pete's cocky announcement, back in high school, that he was going to make a play for Sarah Engelhardt, had been the impetus to convince Josh to go after her himself. In a perverse sort of way, he'd always thought he owed Pete something for having spurred him into action.

"What sort of help has Pete been?"

"He's been coming by. He plays with Eddie and Luke. They like him. I think he's good for them. I know it's a big help to me."

"Karen, how are you getting along…financially?"

"Okay. For now. Eventually I may have to go to work."

"With those three little guys at home?"

"I know. It's going to be hard. But you do what you have to do. You know?"

"Now I'm going to ask you something that may be indelicate. So, if you don't want to answer, just don't."

She looked at him, puzzled.

"Did they ever…you know…figure out what happened on the ball court? I mean, whose knife it was, for example."

Her face turned somber. She said, "It turns out, one of the white boys had a switch-blade. But one of the Mexican boys did too. They were facing each other down when Skip pulled up to the curb. He tried to separate the two of them. Skip was just in the wrong place."

"So they don't know exactly who killed him."

She shook her head. None of the boys who were there will testify. Everything was happening so fast." She sighed. "What difference does it make, really?"

"Well, justice may never be done. That doesn't seem right."

"Josh, Skip is dead. That doesn't seem right either." She had a hurt and angry look on her face. "They should just let it go. Because nothing is ever going to bring him back. And that's all that matters to me."

THE CHURCH COUNCIL was ready to discuss new business. Chairman Bill Fredell looked around the table and asked whether anyone had anything for consideration.

"Yes. I have something," said Harold Kurtz. "We're wrapping up our 30th year as a congregation, and we haven't even taken the first step toward celebrating."

"Most congregations don't do much with their 30th year," said Tim Marburger. "Some of us are still recovering from that big shindig we had five years ago."

"Well, I have a suggestion," said Harold. "I know the year is almost over, but we can at least take the first step before Christmas rolls around."

"What did you have in mind, Harold?" Bill asked.

"I think it's time we did something about that confounded basketball court on the other side of the alley. I did some research in old council minutes, and I discovered that, once upon a time, there was talk about building a gymnasium on that site. The congregation was saving money for the 25th anniversary, so they compromised and covered the area with asphalt. But nobody can control who goes in there and we've had an increasing number of neighborhood...I hestitate to call them gangs, but you know what I mean...young roughnecks, maybe...anyway, they show up and act like it's their turf and if some other group wants to use the court, they fight."

He paused dramatically. "I don't need to tell the rest of you what tragic results we had last summer. Which leads me to believe we could solve a lot of problems by building a gymnasium on that site, and then hire a manager to regulate who uses it. We could have neighborhood teams compete. Maybe even a south Minneapolis league of some sort. The players wouldn't have to be church members. It might be a good way for us to show hospitality. And who knows? Maybe a few of them would end up joining the congregation."

It was quiet around the table.

Jon Chapman said, "How much money are we talking? And where would it come from?"

"That's a good point," said Tim. "Lillian Fischer has already put the congregation on notice that there's a new hymnal about to be published—next year sometime, I think she said—and she intends for us to be one of the first congregations to put them in the pews. That's going to take some money for sure."

Harold was not to be deterred. "The hymnals will pay for themselves. People can put bookplates inside the front covers, telling who paid for them and who they want to honor with them. And, as for the cost of the gymnasium, I'll bet you we'll get every nickel we'd need in pledges within three months."

"Why would we?" Bill asked.

"Simple," Harold replied. "We tell the members it's going to be called the Sanford 'Skip' Warner Memorial Gymnasium."

ALICE WILSON put down the letter she had just opened. She said, "James, my aunt and uncle from Eau Claire are coming to Minneapolis. They want to take us out for supper."

"Great. Where shall we have them take us?"

"My aunt says we're supposed to find a really nice place. Do we know any?"

"Sure. The River's Edge. Paul David says it's a dandy place to go."

"Have you ever been there?"

"He took me there a few times, back when I was living at his place. His grandfather's married to the owner, you know."

"So that would be a good place to suggest to Uncle Edmund and Aunt Sylvia?"

"I think they'd like it. I know I'd like going back up there."

THE MEAL WAS over and the plates had been cleared. Alice's uncle said, "This is a wonderful restaurant. We don't have anything like it where we live."

"I hope it wasn't too expensive, Uncle Edmund."

"Nothing's too good for our niece and her husband," he said, smiling.

"Well, thanks to both of you," said James. "We don't go out to restaurants much, you know."

"If we may ask, just how are the two of you doing…financially?" asked Sylvia.

"We're doing fine," James replied.

Alice's aunt returned an uncertain look. She appeared to be sorting her words before she spoke them. Finally she said, "Alice…James…your Uncle Edmund and I have some…well, some news to share."

Alice looked at her aunt in puzzlement. Why didn't she just come out and say what was on her mind, she wondered.

Sylvia said, "This is very awkward…and difficult for us to talk about."

"Is anything wrong?" Alice prodded.

"Well, yes and no. Yes, because we have a confession to make. And no, because it could all turn out for the better."

James offered a thoughtful frown. He didn't understand the turn in the conversation. A quick glance at Alice indicated she wasn't comprehending things much better.

"Alice, when you gave birth to your child, in the hospital in Eau Claire…"

"You know, Aunt Sylvia, that's in the past. James and I have come to terms with it. We really don't want to open the subject up again."

"I know, dear. It was a painful time. And giving up the child must have seemed cruel…"

"Aunt Sylvia, really..."

"But we need to talk about that."

"Why?" Alice demanded.

"Well...because...things have changed."

"What things?"

Sylvia took a deep breath and exhaled slowly. To Alice, her aunt looked as though she were on trial for something. The older woman said, "When we told you we gave the baby to an adoption agency, we...sort of..."

"We told you a story," Edmund interrupted. "It wasn't exactly a lie. We really did give the baby for adoption. But not through an agency."

"What!" Alice and James exclaimed together.

Sylvia nodded. "We didn't have the heart to give him up to strangers."

James was getting impatient. "What happened to him, then?"

Sylvia continued. "Your Uncle Edmund has a nephew in Wausau. He and his wife were never able to have children. We knew they'd make wonderful, loving parents. We told them they could raise the child...if they never told you."

Alice was wide-eyed. "Aunt Sylvia! You had no right! That means you get to watch our baby grow up and we don't even know where he is."

"Please be patient," Edmund cut in. "There's more." He cleared his throat. "My nephew's wife contracted a rare blood disease last year. She's not well. Not well at all. She can't take care of the little fellow any longer. They wondered if they should give him up to an agency for a proper adoption. But, well, naturally we thought..."

"Oh, Uncle Edmund! Could we have him?" There was pleading in Alice's eyes and voice.

"Well, we were sort of hoping you might...that is, if you thought you could afford to take care of a child."

"Are you kidding?" James blurted out. "I'm trying to get Alice pregnant right now!" Immediately he looked around the supper club. The words had come out loudly enough that he was certain people all over the room must have heard. Nobody was looking his direction. He lowered his voice and said, "We're his parents. Our home is where he belongs." He looked at Alice. Her eyes were full of hope and wild excitement.

Sylvia said, "We were hoping you might feel that way. Edmund's nephew and his wife can't take care of him much longer. He's only two years old, but he's a handful, considering his foster mother's condition now."

"When can we have him?" Alice begged.

"When will you be ready?"

"Right away!"

James asked, "Should we drive to Wausau to get him?"

"No," said Edmund. "I think it would be better if we brought him to Minneapolis. Maybe he could be this year's Christmas present for the two of you. Would that be soon enough?"

"We'll fix up the extra bedroom. We'll get a crib. I'll quit my job at the florist shop. Christmas will be perfect."

Edmund heaved a sigh of relief. "I'm really glad this is working out. We were worried it might not. But it looks like it's going to be just fine. Just fine." He smiled and sighed. "I feel so good about this I think I'm going to order some dessert."

James looked at Alice. She was having a hard time containing her joy.

"What was I thinking?" Edmund said. "Desserts for everybody!"

Chapter 44

In the spring of 1958, copies of the new red *Service Book and Hymnal* arrived at the Lutheran Church of Saint Michael and All Angels. The worship book had been designed by a committee whose members came from a half dozen Lutheran church bodies. Lillian Fischer taught her choirs the new liturgies as soon as the books were unpacked, so that on the first Sunday they were put into use, the congregation was able to find their way through without too much confusion.

Lillian made it clear that, as far as she was concerned, the new book was a cut above the old *American Lutheran Hymnal,* which it was now replacing. Soon the congregation was singing hymns they had never heard before. Lillian's accompaniments were so confident—aggressive, a few members suggested—that she carried the congregation along with her, in spite of themselves.

IN MAY, Sarah Jonas revealed to Josh that they would be welcoming their firstborn sometime in the fall. He told her that, if it was a boy, he wanted to name him Daniel Sanford, in honor of his father—and in memory of his fallen friend, Skip Warner.

A MONTH LATER, on consecutive weekends, two weddings were solemnized at Saint Michael Church. Daniel officiated at the first, for Paul David Engelhardt and Jenny Langholz. Hannah Ruth Jonas flew from Columbus, Ohio, to be part of the bridal party. The newlyweds flew off to Seattle for a week, then settled in at Paul David's home on Anderson Avenue.

The next weekend, Josh presided at the marriage of Pete Fenstermacher and Karen Warner. It was an emotional service, and Josh found himself choking up several times, thinking about Skip. But Karen's reassuring glances helped him get through the ceremony successfully.

AT MIDSUMMER, construction began on the new Sanford Warner Memorial Gymnasium. The funds had been raised during the previous six months, guaranteeing the building would be debt-free on the day of its completion.

IN THE FALL Adam Engelhardt announced to his family that he and Sandy were planning a tour of Europe. They expected to visit England, then Sweden, where her ancestors were buried, and finally Germany. Since there was no easy passage into the eastern part of the country, run by a Communist government, they would spend Reformation Sunday in Augsburg, in south Germany, the city where the Lutheran princes read a statement of faith to the Holy Roman Emperor in 1530.

When asked who would run The River's Edge in her absence, Sandy replied casually, "Others can do that. I'm not getting any younger. It's time I saw the world."

THE SAME WEEKEND Alice Wilson gave birth to her second child, Ellen, Sarah Jonas went to the hospital to deliver a set of twins, Elsa Rosetta and Daniel Sanford. Josh had been congratulating himself on having been so well prepared for the blessed event, only to discover that he was one crib short. The day after the deliveries, he went back to the furniture store and purchased a second one of identical design.

The day he brought Sarah home from the hospital, Josh told her, "It's about time we started filling this place up. The two of us have been rattling around in here for far too long."

"I wasn't exactly expecting to double the size of our family in one day," she said, a look of happy resignation on her face.

"We'll figure it out. How hard can it be to change two sets of diapers?"

"I was planning to nurse," Sarah replied. "I hope I have enough milk."

"I can't figure this out," he said. "We put off having kids all these years so we could earn some money, and then so I could get through seminary. After waiting so long I wasn't even sure we could make it happen anymore. And so what do we get? Twins!"

"I wasn't worried about us having children, Josh. After all, I'm named for a woman who gave birth when she was about ninety years old."

Josh thought about the Bible story. How in the world had Abraham and Sarah managed, he wondered. "Well, we don't want to stop with two. Let's just keep on going."

"Wait! We have twins. That's enough for now."

"Oh, I wasn't planning on getting you pregnant tonight."

"You'd better not have been. Anyway, how many do you think we really need to have?"

"In this big house? I'd say about a dozen."

"Joshua Daniel, get a grip! I'm not having a dozen kids."

"How many, then?"

"Haven't we ever discussed this?"

"Not as far as I can remember."

"How about three, altogether?"

"How about seven, like Luther and Lillian Fischer?"

"Four. That's my final offer. Take it or leave it."

ONE DAY in the spring of the year, Josh looked up from his desk at Saint Michael Church to see a young Mexican he judged to be about twenty standing in the doorway of his office.

"May I help you?"

"My name is Juan Sanchez. Do you have time to talk to me?"

Josh had been working on a sermon which didn't seem to be going anywhere. He said, "Sure. Come on in." He joined the visitor on the other side of his desk where two chairs were facing one another. "Sit down," he said. He thought he might have met the young man, but couldn't place him.

"I was wondering if you knew of any jobs in the neighborhood. I'm looking for work."

Josh tried to think. Nothing came to mind. "Not at the moment. Sorry."

Juan frowned.

"We have a community newspaper. They have advertisements for jobs most weeks. Have you seen copies of the *Bloomington Avenue News*?"

"I'm…not a very good reader."

Josh thought, *What sort of job will he be able to hold if he can't read?* "Have you asked around at any of the businesses in the area?"

"People don't like to hire Mexicans."

"How do you know?"

"Believe me, I know."

Josh wasn't surprised to hear the comment. He furrowed his brow. "You know, Juan, if I took some time to think about this, and maybe ask a few people, I might be able to come up with something." He studied the athletic-looking young man. "You could probably do a lot of day labor jobs, right?"

"Anything. I'm not afraid of hard work."

"Do you live around here, Juan?"

"Yes. Up on the other side of Lake Street."

"What have you been doing? I mean, to pay your bills?"

"Nothing much. I live with my parents and my brothers. We rent…my folks rent…a big old house. But my mother says if I don't find work I have to move out. She's tired of feeding four sons who are old enough to pay their own way. I think we're eating her out of house and home."

Josh grinned. "What was your last job?"

"Like I said, it's hard to get one. And when I do, I'm the first one fired. I think they don't like the way I look. Or the way I talk. I don't sound 'American,' I guess."

"There's nothing wrong with the way you talk."

"I have a pretty heavy accent, you know?"

"Lots of people have accents. That shouldn't make any difference. Of course, it probably does to some people, doesn't it?"

Juan grinned. His white teeth contrasted with the brown skin of his face.

"So if you can't find work, what do you do with your time?"

"Bum around. Try to stay out of trouble. Get into games."

"What sort of games?"

"Football. On vacant lots. Basketball, when we can find a court. Half the time the Yankees…you know…guys with white skin…"

"People like me, right?" Josh tried to suppress a smirk, but failed.

"Well, not all white-skinned people are the same. You're different. But some of them, you know, guys my age…who want to play basketball…they try to chase us off the courts."

Josh got a sudden uncomfortable feeling. "Juan, didn't you play with some of your friends on our basketball court…before we built the gymnasium?"

The young man looked at the pastor with uncertain eyes. "Yeah. We did sometimes."

Josh was tempted to pursue the discussion, but thought better of it. "So what sort of work would you most like to do, Juan?"

"Anything. Yard work. Janitor work. Anything."

"Well, we don't need a custodian around here. Or a gardener. But I'll keep my eyes and ears open."

Juan sat in silence. He nodded in appreciation. Then, as if to change the subject, he said, "That's a nice looking gymnasium you have over on the other side of the alley."

"You ever been inside it?"

"No. I figured I had to be a member here. I'm supposed to be a Catholic, you know."

"Supposed to be?"

"Yeah. Mexicans are supposed to be Catholics."

"But they aren't really?"

"Well, you know. We're born that way." He offered a sheepish grin. "Some of us don't go to Mass very much. I haven't been to confession for about five years. So I guess I shouldn't go to communion. Anyway, I don't."

Josh nodded. There were plenty of Lutheran young people, he realized, who didn't take their own confirmation promises seriously. It seemed to him to be a growing problem in the church.

"Well, I'll tell you what. Let's take a walk over to the gym. I'll show you around. Maybe you and some of your friends would like to play in it sometime."

Juan said, "You have a key?"

Josh grinned. "I'm one of the pastors here. I have a key."

"OKAY, JUAN, here's the ball. Let's see what you can do."

The visitor stood at center court and lofted a high arcing shot toward one of the baskets. The ball hit the rim and fell off to the side. He walked after it, picked it up, and fired it back to the pastor.

Josh stood at the same spot, took careful aim, and pushed the ball into the air. It swished silently through the hoop.

"Holy Jesus," Juan said, almost reverently. "You're really good, man."

"I get lots of opportunities to practice."

Juan said, "Does this place get used very much?"

"We were supposed to organize a neighborhood league, with different teams coming in here to play against each other. That never really happened. Our Luther Leaguers...those are our high school kids...have organized some teams that play against each other. That's about all."

"How about little kids from the neighborhood? I know lots of them, around where I live. They don't have much to do. Maybe they should have a league of their own."

"The baskets are pretty high, don't you think?"

"Yeah. They are. Too bad there aren't some that are lower down. Maybe you could get some of those."

"You trying to organize a little kids' league, Juan?"

"Just making a suggestion. It might be a good thing for the church to do. You know, for the neighborhood."

"We'd have to find somebody to organize something like that."

"I could do that."

Josh looked uncertainly at Juan. "How would you do that, exactly?"

"I'd go around in the neighborhood and sign up the kids. I'd make up a schedule, and put it up so every team knew who they were playing on which days. We'd have a chart showing who had won and how many times. At the end of the season, we could have prizes for the best teams. We'd need referees. And coaches. And rules. No breaking the rules. No bad language."

"You've got this all figured out, haven't you?"

"It's a beautiful gymnasium. You really should be using it more."

"ARE YOU GLAD you married me?" Paul David asked, rolling over in bed to embrace his wife.

Jenny snuggled close to him and smoothed her hand across his bare chest. "Positively. I don't know why I waited so long."

"Neither do I," he said, rubbing his nose affectionately against hers.

She laughed softly.

"When are you and I going to have kids?"

"I don't know," she murmured. "We agreed not for a while."

"I know you love teaching fourth grade, but if we wait too long, you won't want to have them at all."

"I just don't want to give up my teaching career."

"Those little rascals really love you, don't they?"

"Fourth grade is such a perfect age to teach. They're full of questions and eager to learn. I just love that in them."

"What about Hannah Ruth. You've been staying in close touch with her. Is she planning to have kids?"

"I don't know. She has her music career. She's teaching at Ohio State, you know."

"She could have her career and still have kids. Look at Lillian Fischer."

"This isn't about Hannah Ruth, is it? It's really about me."

"Why do you say that?"

"You want me to admit I can have kids and a career at the same time."

"Well, since you brought it up…"

"I didn't. You did."

"We're driving my parents crazy, you know."

"What do you mean?"

"They want more grandchildren."

"Tell them to have some patience."

"The weird thing is, James and Alice, who are years younger than you and I are, already have two of their own."

"And neither of them went to college either. So is that such a great comparison?"

"No, I suppose not. I just wish we had some little Engelhardts running around here so I could spoil them."

"Why don't you just spoil me?" she replied impishly, flattening her hand against the bare skin of his back.

"What did you have in mind?"

"Do I have to spell it out?"

Chapter 45

"OKAY, JUAN, here's the deal. The church council approved buying basketball hoops on moveable stands, low enough for young kids to shoot at. And they're okay with me hiring somebody to organize and manage a little kids' league. But the coaches and the referees have to be volunteers. And the person we hire has to answer to me."

Juan looked hopefully at Josh.

"Are you still interested?"

There was a broad grin on his face. "Is the pope Catholic?"

"I guess you'd know the answer to that one."

"When could we start this?"

"Aren't you even going to ask what we'd pay you?"

"I know you'll be fair."

"How do you know that?"

"I just know. It's the way you are."

Josh wasn't sure how to respond. He said, "Oh, there's one other thing. The members of the council have a requirement you'd have to meet."

"What's that?"

"You have to get involved in a church somewhere, and worship there on a regular basis."

"I don't really have a church right now. I've been staying away from the Catholic Church."

"Any reason for that?"

"Yeah. But I'd rather not say."

"Well, you decide. You'd need to get involved somewhere. Is there somewhere you'd like to belong?"

Juan looked around the pastor's office, as if looking for a favorite framed picture. Then he looked at Josh. "What about here? Could I worship here?"

Josh brightened. "Of course. Why not?"

"I don't think you understand what I'm asking you."

"What do you mean?"

"I mean, what would happen if I came to worship here? I'll bet you don't have any Mexicans in this church. Of course, I don't really know."

"You think our congregation wouldn't welcome Mexicans at worship?"

"It wouldn't be the first place that didn't."

"Maybe they would." Josh realized he didn't really know.

"But, see, here's the deal. If I came, I'd bring my brothers along. All five of them."

"Really?"

"Yeah. I wouldn't feel so outnumbered that way."

Josh tried to visiualize five Mexican men and boys, all sitting in the same pew at worship at Saint Michael Church. He said, "I'll tell you what. You give me a month to get people prepared for the idea that you'll be showing up. Then let's try it."

"You think a month would be long enough? I'll bet it might take about a year for people to get used to the idea."

"Just leave it to me. Okay?"

"Okay. But if it doesn't work, don't say I didn't warn you."

THE FOLLOWING WEEK an essay, written by Josh appeared in the parish newsletter. It described the new program to reach out to unchurched neighborhood youth by organizing a kids' basketball league. It explained that a coordinator had been hired and was organizing teams in the area.

On the Sunday following the appearance of the story in the newsletter, Josh was scheduled to preach. For once he decided not to use the Scripture readings assigned for the day. Instead he preached on a text which he had selected. It was from the Letter to the Galatians, and declared that there is no longer male or female, slave or free, Jew or Gentile, but that all are one in Christ.

In his sermon he expanded the concept, saying, "If Paul had lived in our world, he would also have said, 'There is neither white skin or black skin or brown skin. We are all one in Christ.'"

He studied the faces of the congregation and said, "Almost two-thirds of our members now live in the suburbs. Our membership in the near neighborhood, here in the blocks surrounding the church building, is fewer and fewer with each passing year. It's to our credit that we have never talked about closing this building and moving to Edina or Golden Valley or Eden Prairie. But if we're going to remain in this location, we have a responsibility to serve the people who live around here, whether they're members of our congregation or not."

He took a deep breath. "You may have noticed that there is a growing number of Mexicans in this part of our city. You will also have noticed that none of these people are members of Saint Michael Church, and none of them are sitting in our pews."

There was no visible reaction from the congregation.

"Now, I want to ask you a question. How many of you would disagree with the Apostle Paul, who says there is no longer a difference between Jew and Greek? Keep in mind that was a radical idea for him to put forth." His listeners seemed impassive. "Raise your hands if you disagree with Paul about that." No hands went up.

"Now, how many of you would disagree with the idea that, in Christ, there is no difference between white-skinned people and black-skinned people and brown-skinned people? Raise your hands."

There was no response.

"One more question. How many of you would have a problem if a half dozen Mexicans...brown-skinned people...walked into church some Sunday and filled up half a pew? Raise your hands." His pulse was racing. He fully expected some hands to go up. None did. He decided to try a different approach.

"Raise your hand if you believe it would be a good thing for a half dozen Mexicans to come to worship here." He studied the vast throng. Nothing happened. At least not at first. Then a few hands tentatively went up. Then more joined them. Soon nearly all the hands were up.

"You all passed the test," he said. "The Apostle Paul would be mighty proud of you if he were here today." He cleared his throat. "I wasn't asking the question just to make you squirm, or as an empty exercise. The reason I asked you what you might do if a half-dozen Mexicans came to worship here is, we have about that many from the community who have asked whether it would be all right for them to come here and worship with us. I told them I thought so, but that I'd share the possibility with you first."

There were murmurs in the pews. "I believe you've given me your assurance that we would welcome them when they come."

He had said *when*, not *if*. He wondered if the congregation had noticed.

The parishioners who shook his hand coming out of worship made no mention of the reference to Mexican visitors. But, in the week following, comments and conversations flew back and forth. Was the pastor planning to turn the congregation into a haven for Mexicans? Was this his way of making them feel guilty for not having welcomed such people before? Didn't he realize a lot of the members were already driving past six or seven Lutheran congregations on the way to Saint Michael Church and could very easily transfer their membership to one of those?

Did young Pastor Jonas realize he might be playing with fire? And, what did his father think of all this?

DANIEL JONAS stood solidly behind his son's initiative. He took it upon himself to say so, both from the pulpit and in print. That seemed to settle the matter for many in the congregation. But there were rumblings among a few who were not so sure that "those kind of people" really belonged in a "white church."

On a Sunday morning in March, Juan Sanchez walked into the nave with his four brothers, all with jet black hair, dark brown eyes and unmistakably brown skin. There was an awkward moment. They were not sure where to sit, so took a pew halfway between the door and the altar. There was no way they could have known it was the pew traditionally used by one of the most generous, and most well-fixed, families in the parish.

When the Gingerich family arrived, all six of them, they paused significantly at "their" pew, where plenty of room for all of them still remained, albeit further into the row. Then they walked, dramatically, to another pew and relocated themselves.

That left the Sanchez brothers sitting conspicuously by themselves. Until crusty old Alma Feuerbringer got out of her ordinary seat, marched defiantly up the aisle and sat down next to Juan. She made a point of conversing with him, thanking him for coming, and promising to help him find his way through the Lutheran liturgy, if he needed any assistance.

The Sanchez boys made the same pew their own from that Sunday on, and Alma took to sitting next to them. On occasion, Maggie Washington would join them, seated at the other end of the pew.

Nobody noticed for awhile, but it became clear within a month that the Gingerich family was no longer at worship. Someone who was in a position to know reported they had begun to attend services at a congregation in Minnetonka.

AS THE YOUNGSTERS raced up and down the basketball court, passing the ball or dribbling their way from one goal to the other, Juan Sanchez sat on the sideline watching the action. Josh had come by to observe some of the activity.

"You've gotten things launched very nicely, I'd say," the young pastor observed.

"These kids love playing here. It beats competing for time on a cement court in one of the city parks, or not getting to play at all because they can't find a place."

"How many teams do you have in the league now?"

"Eight already. Maybe twelve by summertime."

"Nice work, Juan."

"Thanks. And thanks for the job. I really appreciate having a steady paycheck."

"Your folks happy with what you're doing?"

He laughed. "Heck, yes. Now I can actually pay them rent."

They watched the youngsters running up and down the court for a few minutes. Finally Josh said, "I've been wanting to ask you something, Juan."

"What's that?"

"You told me you were staying away from the Catholic Church because…I don't know…why was that again?"

Juan didn't reply. Josh wondered if he'd heard the question. Finally the young man said, "I couldn't go to confession anymore. So, that means, I can't take communion in the Catholic Church."

"Tell me more about that."

"About what?"

"About why you can't go to confession."

Juan was silent again.

Josh said, "You can tell me, Juan. I won't share the information with anyone."

"Will you condemn me if I tell you?"

"It's not my job to condemn anyone."

"If I tell you, you might want to."

"All right. I promise not to condemn you, no matter what it is you tell me."

Once again, Juan was silent.

"Is this the wrong place to be having this conversation?" Josh asked.

"Yeah. Maybe so."

"Then let's take a walk, you and me. Come on."

AS THE TWO MEN walked through the neighborhood, Juan said, "You remember that time when a bunch of guys were playing ball on the basketball court where the gym is now?"

"There were lots of times like that."

"Well, this was the time when the white-skinned guys were playing, two-on-two. Four of us Mexicans showed up. We wanted to challenge them to a game. So, guess what? The white boys told us to...well, I can't say it in polite company. The point was, they thought they had some sort of claim to the court, even though none of them belong to your church or anything.

"So, we figured we'd stand our ground. We had as much right to play there as they did. It started to get ugly. They started calling us names, racial slurs, insults. Unfortunately, we started doing the same thing.

"Pretty quick, it turned into a fistfight."

Josh felt the hair begin to rise along the back of his neck. He knew what was coming next.

"So one of them white guys suddenly pulls out a switch-blade and snaps it open. Turns out, I had one too. So there we were, facing off with switch-blades, while all the other guys were yelling at us to go after each other."

Juan paused. He stopped walking and turned to Josh. "I was scared out of my skin. I figured he was gonna kill me sure as anything."

He started walking again. "So then this squad car pulls up and a cop climbs out. He heads toward us, shouting for us to put the knives away. Well, we did. But then the white guy suddenly pulled his out again, and lunged toward me. The cop was right between us. He got it in the neck. Everybody panicked. They all ran."

Josh thought his heart was about ready to explode in his chest. He tried calming himself before he said, "So you had a knife but you had put it away before the policeman got to the scene."

"Yeah. Right."

"Who was the guy who stabbed the policeman?"

"I didn't know any of them guys. I couldn't tell you who he was."

They walked in silence for an entire block. Finally Josh said, "Okay, so here's what I don't get. Why is this something you can't confess to your priest?"

"Isn't it pretty simple?" asked Juan. "I pulled a knife. I could have killed that guy."

"But you put your knife away. He's the one who killed the officer."

"It doesn't matter. I wanted to kill him. I really *wanted* to. I hated him in my heart. That's a sin. That's as bad as killing him."

"But you didn't do it."

"But I *wanted* to. And I've never been sorry about it. I'm not sorry about it to this day. If I can't repent in my heart, how can I repent to a priest?"

"Do you still wish you'd killed that guy, Juan?"

"Yes. But I wish I didn't feel that way."

"You can control your feelings, you know."

"I've never been able to control *these* feelings."

They stopped walking again. Josh turned to Juan, put his hands on the younger man's shoulders, and said, "Make your confession to me."

"How can I?"

"Say this: 'Lord, I believe. Help my unbelief."

Juan repeated what he'd heard.

"Now say, 'Lord, the good I want to do, I don't do. And the evil I don't want to do, that's what I do.'"

Again, the younger man repeated the words.

"Now say, 'Lord, I'm sorry for the evil I feel in my heart. Take it from me.'"

Juan hesitated. But finally he repeated the words.

Josh said, "Juan, in the name of Christ, I declare you forgiven and absolved of your sin. Go and sin no more."

His companion pursed his lips. His eyes were flooding. His lower lip was quivering. He said, "Thank you, Padré. Thank you so much. Thank you."

Chapter 46

The year 1960 was a benchmark for Saint Michael Church. The congregation's business manager announced that, for the first time in its history, the membership had declined. After its high-water mark, at 7,200 baptized members, the parish now counted 6,900. The statistical report, which appeared in the parish newspaper, explained that deaths, removals due to inactivity and transfers to other congregations had outnumbered members added by new births, transfers in and new members from the community.

The news had a sobering effect on Daniel Jonas. He discussed the report with his wife Rosetta over dinner, the night after the report became public.

"I know I shouldn't take this as an evaluation of my effectiveness, but it really makes me uncomfortable. We're simply not growing anymore."

"Daniel, we're one of the largest congregations in the denomination. What difference does it make if the totals are a little lower once? God never promised you everlasting success in your ministry. There are bound to be some bumps."

"But it's never happened before. It makes me feel…I'm sorry, Rosetta, but I need to say this…it makes me feel inadequate."

"Oh, for heaven's sake, Daniel. There's nothing inadequate about you. People fall all over themselves to sing the praises of your ministry. I even hear people describe it as 'powerful,' although I've never said that to you. I know how you feel about false praise."

Daniel was silent. When he spoke again he shifted the focus of the conversation. "I've been thinking about this for a good long while. I really think my continuing at Saint Michael Church is a hindrance to Joshua Daniel's ministry here."

"He seems to be doing just fine. I know he once worried about ending up in your shadow, but those concerns seem to have evaporated."

"How do you know that?"

"Very simple. I asked him."

Daniel marveled that he had never bothered to do the same thing himself.

"But," said Rosetta, "I would never stand in your way if you wanted to step down. The trouble is, you have seven years before you can retire. What would you do?"

"Take a small, struggling congregation that needs some love. Do you remember how satisfying it felt, back in the early days of this congregation, when we worked with just a handful of members?"

"You want to do that again?"

"Well, no. But there are lots of smaller congregations looking for pastors. I could serve one of those for seven years. It would be a good way to slow down."

"You'd get a reduction in salary. You know that, don't you?"

"Would that be a problem for you?"

"No. Our children are out of the house. We have no debts. But…"

"But?"

"But would you be happy doing that?"

"There's a little congregation in Columbus, Ohio, that's looking for a pastor. The Ohio District president told me about it at the last national convention. He was actually asking me if I knew of anybody in Minnesota who wanted to relocate to Ohio. I told him no. But I've noticed that congregation is still vacant."

"Columbus, Ohio? Hannah Ruth and John are there."

"That's right. And they're finally about to give birth. We could be near our new grandchild."

"And leave four of them behind, here in Minneapolis. To say nothing of all our friends."

"What's fair is fair, Rosetta. Joshua Daniel and Sarah have had us close to them all these years. Why shouldn't Hannah Ruth and John get a chance to see us more often? Besides, we could see our relatives in Fremont without making a major effort to get there. They're starting to die off, you know."

Rosetta looked at Daniel and offered a wan smile. "Do you remember all the times we talked about leaving this congregation, but never did?"

"Do I ever. One time I wanted to go and you didn't. Another time you thought it might be time, and I wasn't so sure. Maybe this time we both actually agree on this."

"Shouldn't we be asking what the Holy Spirit wants us to do?"

"I've been doing that. I think the Holy Spirit is telling me to go to Ohio."

"THE HOLY SPIRIT will make things clear. We have his promise."

Sarah Engelhardt looked dubiously at the two young men standing at her front door. She'd hesitated to open to them, having seen them through the parlor window, coming up the walk. But they were both well-dressed and well-groomed. And, with the twins down for their nap, she wanted to open the door to avoid having the visitors set the door chimes ringing, which might awaken them.

So here she was, talking with two young men fresh out of college, intent on convincing her that the Church of Jesus Christ of Latter Day Saints was the bearer of God's true and final revelation.

Tired of standing and listening to their well-rehearsed recital, she made a decision she hadn't thought she would make. She invited them into her house.

As they sat talking, the young man whose name badge identified him as Caleb said, "Thousands...no, millions...of people have read the Book of Mormon and become convinced that it is the true revelation of the Holy Spirit, given miraculously to Joseph Smith, our prophet."

Sarah was tempted to tell Caleb that her husband was a Lutheran pastor. But she decided to let them talk a little longer. She'd never heard a member of the Latter Day Saints religion explain his beliefs.

The badge on the other young man identified him as Lehi. Sarah had a feeling that name came straight out of the Book of Mormon. He said, "Isn't it exciting to think that an angel led an uneducated young farm boy to dig up the golden plates with the truth about God? What other religion can claim such a thing?"

Sarah had serious doubts about the claims Caleb and Lehi were making. Suddenly she had an idea. She realized it was probably unworthy of a pastor's wife to inject fiction into a serious conversation, but she suspected that was what the young Mormons were doing now, whether they realized it or not.

She said, "Now, let me get this straight. God told Joseph Smith where the golden plates were buried. And then God told him how to translate them, from reformed Egyptian hieroglyphics into English. But nobody except Joseph Smith ever saw the plates. And, after he buried them again, the angel Moroni took them back to heaven."

"That's right," said Caleb, nodding confidently.

"How do you know that Joseph Smith was really listening to God and not to a false angel?"

"Oh, the Holy Spirit makes the truth known to all who ask him to do so."

Sarah felt her pulse increase. Should she say what she was thinking? She decided to go ahead with it. "It might interest you two young men to know that I also receive messages from the Holy Spirit. They come to me very clearly, quite distinctly. They're not dreams. I'm usually wide awake when they happen. One of the messages revealed to me that my uncle was in great danger. A few days later we learned by means of a letter which he had written, that I had correctly perceived the truth, to the day, the hour and the minute of its happening."

"What was the danger?" asked Caleb, looking dubious.

"He's a forest ranger. A tree fell on him. There were broken bones, but fortunately nothing more serious." Lehi's mouth was open, but before he could speak, Sarah continued, "On another occasion, I received a message that the man I later married was in great distress. After awhile a letter from him confirmed, once again, that I had perceived his peril at exactly the moment he was experiencing it."

Lehi said, "Could those things have been coincidental?"

"Well, that's what I wondered when I first read the Book of Mormon." This part was a lie. She had never seen a copy of the Mormon scriptures before. "I wondered whether Joseph Smith had perhaps imagined what he later claimed was the truth, instead of having an encounter with an angel."

"So you're familiar with the Book of Mormon then," said Caleb.

She didn't reply. Instead, she said, "That caused me to ask the Holy Spirit for guidance, just as the message in the front of the book instructs I should." She only knew there was such an instruction because Caleb had told her so ten minutes before. "And the Holy Spirit told me in a clear and unmistakable message—as clear as the other two I received—that Joseph Smith was really nothing more than a creative writer of fiction with an incredibly rich imagination. I was told not to listen to anything he said in his book, because it was nothing but a pious myth. And that's pretty much what I believe about the Book of Mormon."

"Well, that must have been a false angel you were listening to."

"How can you be so sure?"

"Because the Holy Spirit promised us he would lead us into the truth."

"But that's what the Holy Spirit promised *me*."

Caleb and Lehi looked at one another. It was clear they had never heard this line of argumentation before. Suddenly Caleb glanced at his watch and said, "You know, Lehi, we're going to be late for our meeting."

They both stood up. "Thank you Mrs....I'm sorry, I didn't catch your name."

"That's because I didn't toss it your direction," she replied, smiling.

They excused themselves and moved to the door. She watched them head for the curb, shaking their heads. Along with the feeling of euphoria which was surging over her, Sarah felt guilt—that she had undoubtedly broken the Eighth Commandment. She whispered a silent prayer, asking God to forgive her. In spite of her best attempt at contrition, however, she could not shake a feeling of smug satisfaction because of the way she had handled herself in the presence of the two young Mormon missionaries.

DANIEL'S ANNOUNCEMENT came in the form of a letter to the congregation. The response was swift and impassioned.

Members of the church council told him they felt blind-sided and disappointed. They would, they assured him, have tried to change his mind. That, he told them, was precisely why he had shared his intentions using the method he had chosen.

Members of the congregation at large told him clearly, at the door of the church as they departed worship the following Sunday morning, how unhappy they were with the news. A few told him they were now in grief, just contemplating life at Saint Michael Church without him. He assured them that the congregation was far more than one person, and that other capable leaders were still in the congregation's future. Those assurances seemed not to satisfy many.

Harry Broadman was especially disappointed. He did what he always did when he wanted to make a point forcefully and convincingly. He invited Daniel to lunch at the Minneapolis Club. As they sat eating, Harry said, "I suspect this is your way of getting even with me. Am I right?"

"Harry, I don't have the first idea what you're talking about."

"Of course you do. I was the one who convinced the seminary that Joshua Daniel's internship should be in our congregation. I was the one who started that petition to have him called here."

"Harry," said Daniel, genuinely surprised, "nobody ever told me who started that petition. I rather suspected it *might* have been you."

"Well, it was. Who else would have done it, for crying out loud?"

Daniel grinned. "Harry, this has nothing to do with you. In fact, one of my greatest regrets about leaving Minnesota is going to be moving away from you and Polly. Your friendship has been incredibly important to Rosetta and me."

"Then don't go," said Harry. "There's still time to change your mind."

"I'm not changing my mind. I've been here for thirty-three years. That's longer than most pastors ever stay in one parish."

"You're not most pastors. And this isn't an ordinary parish. This is the place you founded."

"All the more reason to step down before they carve my statue and set it up in the courtyard."

"We may do that anyway," said Harry, grinning.

"Over my dead body."

"That's pretty much when a lot of statues are erected," he said, grinning more broadly than before.

"When I'm dead and gone, you can start a fund-raiser for a statue. But you'd be violating the First Commandment, I'm sure you understand."

"What? Worshiping other gods?"

"No. Bowing down before graven images."

Harry looked dubiously at Daniel. Then he broke out in his trademark belly laugh. "We're gonna miss that sense of humor of yours."

"Sounds to me like you're already getting used to the idea of my leaving."

Harry frowned. "I know we can't stop you from doing what you think you should do."

"Harry, I truly believe this is also what *God* wants me to do."

"Okay. I won't argue with that. But just because your mind's made up, doesn't mean we have to like it." Daniel nodded, smiling. "So, we'll have you until next spring. At least, that's what your letter said."

"Yes. You'll have about ten more months of me."

Harry frowned. He grumped, "Well, at least we'll still have your son in our pulpit."

"Yes. Unless, of course, Joshua Daniel feels called to go somewhere else."

"That's not going to happen."

"You're pretty sure about that, are you?"

"Your son is in love with history. He's got a whole house full of it up there on Franklin Avenue. He'd never move away and leave that amazing old fireplace behind."

Daniel shook his head in disbelief. "You don't know my son very well, do you, Harry?"

"Oh, I think I know him very well. Very well indeed."

Chapter 47

In 1960, the American Lutheran Church merged with two other church bodies. Combining with a smaller Danish Lutheran denomination and a larger Norwegian one, the new entity decided to call itself The American Lutheran Church. The old ALC lost its headquarters location and its publishing house in Columbus, Ohio. The new church established its center in downtown Minneapolis, a few dozen blocks north of Saint Michael Church.

The constituting convention was held at the Minneapolis Auditorium and Central Lutheran Church. One event in the week of celebration was a festive choral concert, in which a massed choir sang a new composition, "Una Sancta."

As David Engelhardt sat in the midst of the vast audience, listening to the surging four-part harmony, he marveled that his former church, with three colleges, had suddenly more than doubled in size, and now had eight schools. He studied the program, reviewing the names of the institutions whose choirs were represented. Distinctive choir robes set each group apart, even as they stood shoulder to shoulder: Augustana College, Sioux Falls, South Dakota...Capital University, Columbus, Ohio...Concordia College, Moorhead, Minnesota...Dana College, Blair, Nebraska...Luther College, Decorah, Iowa...St. Olaf College, Northfield, Minnesota...Texas Lutheran College, Seguin, Texas...and, the school to which Saint Michael Church had sent so many of her sons and daughters—Wartburg College, Waverly, Iowa.

He marveled that Augsburg College, just blocks away, was not included on the list. The school's denomination, the Lutheran Free Church, had decided, in a close vote following a fierce debate, not to join the new denomination. Two years later the tiny Norwegian holdout would reverse itself.

David leaned over and whispered to Molly, "It's exciting to see how large this new church is now. But it's sad to see how my folks' home state of Ohio has lost so much influence with this merger. Not only that, I wonder how you can tell when a church body has become too large."

Molly said, "Quit worrying about it. Just listen to the music. Isn't it glorious?"

He nodded. "Yes, dear. Glorious is exactly the word for it."

IN THE CLOSING MONTHS of Daniel Jonas' long ministry at Saint Michael Church, an animated discussion broke out among the members. How could the congregation best honor its founding pastor? What would seem most fitting? All kinds of suggestions surfaced, including naming the parish house for him, establishing a scholarship in his name and commissioning a new stained-glass window in his honor. As the months went by no consensus was reached.

At the annual meeting in January of 1961, the question of a fitting tribute was on the agenda. Daniel took the speaker's stand and announced he would be uncomfortable with any such tribute, certainly while he was still serving the congregation.

That seemed to end the discussion.

ADAM ENGELHARDT and Sandy Engstrom had enjoyed their tour of Europe so much, they decided to make a return visit. Shortly after Easter they flew off to Sweden, to visit the Engstrom relatives. Sandy had been fascinated, on their first visit to rural Malmø, to discover the parish church cemetery where so many of her ancestors' names were carved on tombstones. They visited the churchyard for a second time.

As they walked among the markers, she said, "I feel a real connection to this place, Adam. Isn't that strange?"

"Not strange at all," he said, squeezing her hand affectionately.

A week later, they were back in England. This time they kept a promise they had made to themselves on their previous visit. They took the train to Cambridge and listened to the famous boys choir sing. They explored the university campus and walked together through the streets of the old city.

On the morning they were scheduled to head back to London, Sandy left Adam at their hotel, while she went shopping for gifts for friends in Minnesota. As she walked from a gift store, burdened with bags filled with newly-purchased treasures, she experienced a momentary lapse. Thinking like an American, she forgot on which side of the street traffic moved in England.

She looked the wrong way, then stepped off the curb directly in front of a fast-moving taxi. The driver had no time even to sound his horn. She fell to the pavement, her packages scattering on the street.

By the time the news reached Adam, she had been transported to the nearest hospital. She had suffered a concussion and lay unconscious, barely breathing. As the doctors worked over her, he walked the hospital halls, tortured with panic and dread.

After two days she suddenly stopped breathing. The doctors and nurses were unable to revive her.

ADAM FELT PARALYZED. He phoned his son in Minneapolis. David offered to fly to England to be with his father. But, in the course of the conversation, Adam experienced a moment of clarity. He said, "David, don't come over here. There's no need. I already know what I'm going to do. I can handle this. All right?"

HE HAD HER body transported back to Sweden. Within a couple days he had secured a burial plot, adjacent to some of the Engstrom graves. He knew no Swedish and would have felt strange attending a service among people whom he did not know. Instead, he asked the priest of the parish church to hold a graveside service for her. He and the local Lutheran clergyman were the only ones at the grave.

That same afternoon he took a train to Stockholm for a flight home.

DANIEL JONAS' last Sunday at Saint Michael Church was freighted with emotion. He preached a sermon full of gratitude and hope. He reminded his congregation, at each of the four worship services, to keep their eyes and hearts focused on the Gospel of Jesus and the promises of God. He reminded them that the congregation had grown because the Spirit of God had called, gathered, enlightened and made holy the members who had joined the huge fellowship over the span of the past thirty-three years.

He reminded them that a Christian congregation was never to be identified with one individual, unless that person was Jesus. And, quoting the words of a familiar hymn, he urged the congregation to remain "fervent in spirit, serving the Lord."

He closed with an old text used during the congregation's first year, when members had been worshiping in the living rooms of a handful of families.

The words were a sort of benediction, traditionally shared by founding member Frieda Stellhorn. He read the words, first in German, and then in English translation:

Oeffne, Gott, meine augen und mein herz, fur dein erscheinen.
Ich sehe wie du mich liebst. Du bist da.

"Open, O God, my eyes and my heart for your coming. I see your love for me. You are present to me."

His last words from the pulpit at Saint Michael Church were these: "God is always present to us. We are never alone. In the Holy Spirit we have his power, for doing what is good and honorable and right. Let us continue to be the people God intended us to be. And may God's holy angels surround and keep us, this day and always. Amen."

There were audible sobs in the congregation as he finished and stepped down from the elevated pulpit. At the church door, while he greeted the departing congregation, many eyes were red.

At a farewell banquet in the parish house, the congregation presented Daniel and Rosetta with a finely-detailed line drawing, picturing the exterior of Saint Michael Church and its adjoining parish house. It had been executed by a local artist, Ray Johnson, and was enclosed in a finely crafted wooden frame.

The following Tuesday Daniel and Rosetta were on their way to Ohio.

TWO DAYS after his parents left the state, Josh Jonas sat down with the other two pastors, intending to discuss with them how to restructure the congregation's pastoral ministry. Suddenly the congregation was without a senior pastor, and he was unsure how to proceed.

The meeting with his colleagues provided anything but clarity. Both of the other men surprised him by announcing they intended to submit their resignations to the congregation and to seek calls elsewhere. Pastor Fangmeyer explained, "I like you very much, Josh. But I was called to work with your father, and I don't feel comfortable staying on here now that he's gone. Besides, I'm fairly confident it's only a matter of time before the congregation calls you to be its senior pastor. You would want to pick your own pastoral partners."

Josh was astonished. He said, "Martin, we have 6,700 members in this congregation. I've been out of seminary for exactly three years. You're going to leave me here alone? Maybe we should all resign, and let the congregation have a clean slate on which to write."

Martin smiled. "I can't stay, Joshua Daniel. That should be obvious to you. As to what you should do, I can't speak for you. But I'd be very surprised if this congregation would let you go without a fight."

Josh realized Martin was right on both points.

AT ITS NEXT MEETING, the church council voted without dissent to call a special congregational meeting at midsummer, and to recommend that Josh be called to serve as senior pastor. They also voted to ask the congregation to authorize the hiring of a team of interim pastors for the short term, and to organize a call committee to replace the three clergy who were leaving.

Josh was the only clergyman in the room when the actions were taken. He accepted them without comment.

IN NOVEMBER Americans elected the first Roman Catholic president in the country's history. There were murmurings among some members at Saint Michael Church that the Vatican might become the state department for the federal government. Most, however, took assurance from John F. Kennedy's remarks, made to Texas clergymen during the fall campaign. He had told them, "I'm not the Catholic candidate for president. I'm a candidate for president who happens to be Catholic."

AFTER SIX MONTHS of mourning for his dead wife, Adam Engelhardt made a momentous decision. He put The River's Edge supper club up for sale. In spite of the fact that the business was thriving, and had a reputation for exquisite cuisine, he felt a growing discomfort owning the commercial property he had unexpectedly inherited. He found it impossible to go to the restaurant. Whenever he did he sensed Sandy Engstrom's presence. It always drove him into deep melancholy.

The realtor he hired was 56-year-old George Kleinhans, one of the founding members of the congregation. Within a week George had a buyer for the business. Adam accepted it with alacrity.

In the weeks and months that followed, Adam moped about the empty house in which he and Sandy had lived since their marriage. He was at his wits' end, not knowing what to do with himself. Finally he went to see Maggie Washington.

"I need something to do. You always need volunteers. What can I do to help out?"

"Adam, you're a godsend," she replied. "Our tutoring program is always short of teachers. You could help some of the neighborhood kids with their reading skills."

"Me? A tutor?"

"You'd be great at it, Adam. You could start with just one youngster. If you liked it you could take on more of them. It would be up to you. And if it didn't like it, or if it just didn't' work out, you could back out of it."

He thought about it. "I'm an old geezer, Maggie. Would little kids let me be their tutor?"

"You're about as old a geezer as I am. I do it. They love working with older people. We're so wise and smart, it practically bowls them over." She looked soberly at Adam, but then broke into the familiar throaty laugh by which everybody knew her.

Adam smiled. "Okay, Maggie. Sign me up."

GEORGE KLEINHANS took Adam to lunch a month after the supper club had been sold. The realtor said, "You ever wish you hadn't given your old house on Anderson Avenue to your son?"

"Absolutely not. He and Jenny love the place. Besides, they're having their first child in a few months. They'll have that house full of kids before long."

"Really? I didn't know Jenny was pregnant."

"You never go to the same worship service they do. You probably never talk to them."

"Well, I had a reason for my question."

"Which is...?"

"I think you should consider moving closer to the church."

"Why?"

"Because you're way up there on the north side, and all your old friends are down here. Do you realize all of us who organized this congregation are still living in the same houses we were in back in 1927? Everybody except you."

"Well, I've been through two wives since then. Times change."

"Exactly. And your situation has changed. I'll bet that house would bring a great price right now. And you could get out from under all the maintenance that goes with owning a place like that."

"So this is really about you getting a second sales commission out of me, right?" Adam said with a twinkle in his eye.

"Heck, I'd manage the sale commission-free if that was what it took to get you back into the neighborhood."

"Well, swapping one house for another wouldn't save me doing homeowner's maintenance, George."

"No, but moving into a maintenance-free property would."

Adam eyed the younger man curiously. "You have a place in mind?"

"Lots of older people are selling their homes now, and moving into condominiums. They own a share in the building, but an association takes care of upkeep. It's perfect. You can travel or do whatever you want, and not think about mowing the lawn or shoveling snow."

Adam realized that was an appealing concept.

"I've got this idea, Adam. I want to get you in on the ground floor. Here's the deal. The houses across the street from the church building are in pretty bad repair. They make a sorry streetscape for people coming to visit our church, or even for people coming out the front door. They're all owned by the same absentee landlord. He's been neglecting them for years. Now their value has deteriorated, and he wants to get out from under them. I've been talking with him. He'd be ready to let them go for a pretty decent price."

"And what would you do with them?"

"Andy Scheidt's construction company and my real estate firm are talking about putting up a new condominium complex on that side of the street. We've got plans drawn. They'd look very sharp. Bay windows, gabled roof line, secured entrances, underground parking. It would be a great place to live."

"And you want me to buy one of these units?"

"All the rest of us are thinking about it. You should too."

"The 'rest of us' being...?"

"The Scheidts...the Bauers...the Langholzes...the Stumpfs...and Polly and me, of course."

"But you people are all still in your fifties. You'd want to give up your homes for a condominium complex?"

"Our kids are all out of the house. We're getting tired of all the upkeep. Besides, Andy Scheidt will be 60 next year. The rest of us aren't far behind."

"Kind of like getting the old gang all onto the same block, sounds like."

"Exactly. And we're saving a unit for you. If you want it."

"When would this project begin?"

"There'll be twelve units. Whenever we get financial commitments from six, we can move ahead. You'd make six."

"I think I'd want to see the plans, George."

"They're right here in my briefcase."

The realtor signaled the server to clear away the table. Then he spread out the drawings. He explained everything to Adam. After twenty minutes, the older man said, "Only if I can sell my house."

"Well, let's not sell it until this complex is completed."

"Oh, no problem there," Adam deadpanned. "I'll just move in with you and Polly for the duration."

It took George Kleinhans a moment to realize Adam was pulling his leg.

Chapter 48

By 1962 the ordained leadership at the Lutheran Church of Saint Michael and All Angels was back to full strength. Four pastors were once again in place, with Josh Jonas at the helm. During the triple vacancy, the senior pastor had made a strategic decision to change, once for all, the pronunciation of his last name. He explained in the congregation's newsletter that he no longer wished to have the J in his last name sounded in the German fashion, as a Y.

He had consulted with Sarah about the change. Together they had agreed it might not be helpful to saddle their four children, the twins, two-year-old Andrew and baby Ruth, with a last name that required endless explanation.

The ones with whom Josh had *not* consulted were his own parents. He knew they'd read the article he wrote for the congregation. He also knew that his father would ignore his wishes and continue to use the older pronunciation, just as he insisted always on addressing his son formally, as "Joshua Daniel."

AT EASTER TIME Josh received a curious letter from Columbus, Ohio. His father had enclosed an "invoice" which he had typed out himself. It explained that Josh owed the sum of one dollar, which would pay in full the cost of the older pastor's vacation home on Lake Saint Michael. In the note that came with the invoice, Daniel explained he and Rosetta were too far away to make good use of the property any longer, and that they wanted Josh and his growing family to enjoy the lake-front home. He also indicated that he and Rosetta expected to be invited to use it from time to time.

A MONTH LATER Luther Fischer stopped on his way out of worship to talk briefly with Josh at the church door. He told the senior pastor that his third son, Michael, was enrolling at Wartburg Seminary in one more year. Josh was delighted to hear the news. "Tell him to come see me during Thanksgiving vacation," he said. "I'd love to talk with him."

AT MIDSUMMER, demolition began on the row of houses across the street from Saint Michael Church. Week by week parishioners watched with interest as the old structures came down and the foundation was prepared for the promised condominium complex. A builder's sign, posted at the corner of the property, pictured the proposed facility and announced boldly that it was to be called "Saint Michael Village." A temporary placard, fastened to one corner of the board, explained that only two units remained to be sold.

MICHAEL FISCHER stopped by Josh's office at Saint Michael Church during Thanksgiving vacation. The congregation's lead pastor and the Wartburg College senior discussed life on the Waverly, Iowa, campus where both had attended, traded tales about the foolish things that college boys are prone to do and speculated about the future of the newly-formed American Lutheran Church. Josh jokingly suggested to his music director's son that he might want to consider opening himself to call at Saint Michael Church in four years. The college student replied, "I've made a firm commitment never to accept a call to a congregation that's named after me." Josh got a good laugh out of that.

ONE DAY IN FEBRUARY Josh decided, without warning, to go home for lunch with his wife and children. It had not been his usual pattern but he thought he'd surprise Sarah for a change.

When he walked into the front hallway, he discovered flames dancing in the fireplace. Sarah, who was tending the blaze, was startled when he spoke her name. She turned around and looked uncomfortably at him.

"A fire in the middle of the day?" he queried, puzzled.

"I...just felt like burning something."

"Not my old love letters to you, I hope."

She laughed. "Never."

"What then?"

She hesitated. "Sit down," she said. When they were seated next to one another on the couch, she said, "I was doing laundry this morning. So I went through stuff in the closets, looking for things that should go in the washer. I found a box, back in the corner, with...oh, my gosh, should I even be telling you this?"

"You found somebody *else's* love letters?" he said, attempting humor.

She shook her head. "That old, bloody tee shirt you were wearing the day you tried to save Skip Warner's life."

"You still had that thing?"

"For the longest time I thought I could get the blood out of it. But I never could. So I…I don't know why I did it, but I just put it in a box and left it in the closet."

"You're burning that old shirt?"

"I just did."

"It's just as well," he said, sighing. He hadn't thought about Skip for years. He didn't like the feeling he got now, resurrecting the memories.

She watched the flames begin to die down. "There was another reason I kept the shirt."

"What was that?"

"Something I never told you."

"Can you tell me now?"

She sat in silence for a full half-minute. "Three times before that awful day when Skip was killed, I had one of my…what?…visions, I guess. It was just like the other times. I was wide awake."

"And…?"

"Well, I knew in advance something terrible was going to happen. I had this vision of you, weeping. You had blood on your hands and on your face. I couldn't tell whose blood it was. I was afraid it might be your own."

"You saw a vision of that before Skip died?"

"Three days in a row."

"You never told me. Not even afterwards."

"I was afraid."

"Of what?"

"I was afraid it would frighten you. And then afterwards I was afraid to admit I had kept it from you."

"Oh, Sarah," he said kindly. He wrapped his arms around her. "But that still doesn't explain why you kept the shirt all these years."

"I had this foolish notion that, if I kept it, I wouldn't have any more visions. I thought hanging onto it might make them stop."

"Why would it?"

"I don't know. It makes no sense. I realize that now."

"Have you had any…messages…since then?"

She sighed and smiled. "No. So maybe keeping it actually did the trick."

"Well, I'm glad you burned it."

She watched the fire descend to ashes. "So why are you at home in the middle of the day?"

"Because I'm hungry. Will you feed me?"

"The kids and I are having tomato soup and grilled cheese sandwiches," she said, getting up. "I think we can find some for you too."

"Sounds like a feast," he said, following her into the kitchen.

ON THE FRIDAY before Thanksgiving the nation was suddenly plunged into horror and despair. The president of the country was murdered while riding in an open convertible in Texas. Americans went into a weeklong period of mourning.

The next weekend, Michael Fischer came to see Josh. The senior pastor had handed off the Sunday morning preaching assignment to one of his colleagues, so found himself with time for a conversation with the first-year seminary student.

They sat in Josh's office and exchanged stories about student life in Dubuque, Iowa. Michael explained that he was experiencing significant spiritual growth, both in his classes but also through daily chapel and in community life on the close-knit campus.

Then the seminarian paused, as if sorting his thoughts. When he spoke he was focused and serious. "I'm experiencing something of a faith crisis, I think."

"Excuse me?"

"My New Testament course is...well...really making me rethink a lot of things."

"Such as?"

"How much can we really know about Jesus, for example."

"How much do you think we need to know?"

"I'm not even sure I can trust that the four Gospels are telling us what he actually said."

"Why is that?"

"Well, the textbooks we're reading argue that, since Jesus never wrote anything down, we have to depend on what his followers said about him."

"That's not such a bad thing, is it?"

"Well, no. But what if they didn't write down what he actually said?"

"Do you suspect that's what happened?"

"Think about it. The first three Gospels sound a lot alike, but they're actually quite different in some pretty important ways. And the fourth Gospel sounds nothing like the first three. So, where did John get all the stuff in his version? I mean, he has Jesus saying things none of the other three report."

"He wrote his version last, you know."

"Sure. I know. But why wouldn't he say pretty much what the others did?"

"Perhaps he wanted to tell the story of Jesus in a different way."

"But then, which version is authentic? In Mark's Gospel Jesus gets arrested in the Garden of Gethsemane and dragged off to a trial. The whole thing sounds like he's a victim who can't defend himself. He even begs God not to make him go through with it, unless it's truly God's will."

"Yes. A very human picture of Jesus."

"But in John he practically has to command the soldiers to arrest him. He sounds like he's in control of everything. He almost takes charge of the trial before Pilate. He looks a lot more…I don't know…powerful."

"John gives us a picture of Jesus that shows his divinity. That's his main point. Jesus is in charge."

"But that's the problem. I have these two pictures of Jesus, and I don't know which one to believe. Somebody has to be making something up…don't they?"

"You never noticed these differences in Sunday school, or high school, or college?"

"No. I just assumed everything fit together, that the writers agreed about everything."

"Well, we really do have four different pictures of Jesus. That's for sure. There's also Paul's picture in his letters. And who knows how many other pictures were floating around in the early church that never got included in the New Testament?"

"So, what are we supposed to do with all that stuff?"

"What does your professor say?"

"He just says it's our responsibility to figure it out. He's not telling us what to believe."

"Would you want him to?"

"Well…no…but a little help wouldn't hurt."

Josh grinned. "I made the same discoveries when I was in seminary. I had to figure it out for myself, too."

"What did you decide finally?"

"Think about it like this. There was a terrible lynching up in Duluth many years ago. Some black men were ambushed and falsely accused of things they didn't do. A big mob made sure they were strung up. That was a terrible tragedy. But how did people report it?"

"I can't guess. I didn't really know that story."

"A lot of Minnesotans don't. And those who do want to forget it. But here's my point. The Duluth newspaper reported it one way, the Minneapolis papers in other ways, the St. Paul papers in still other ways. The people who were there reported it in a lot of different ways too. Which version is true?"

"Did the stories contradict each other?"

"Oh, I suspect some of them did."

"Then how would we ever know?"

"Well, in one way, all of the versions are somehow true. Because everybody who experienced what happened knew something about it. And then there's another whole question—what did the event *mean*?"

"I'd say it meant there were some real bigots in Duluth in those days."

"That's one thing. It also means the community may have been complicit. There were a lot of people who weren't even on the scene, but should have been. They could have stopped it."

"I'm getting lost in all of this," said Michael. "What does that story have to do with the four Gospels?"

"This is what I think is true. Four different writers all knew something true about Jesus. They told stories about him to explain what they knew. The stories didn't come out identically."

"But they can't even agree about how Judas Iscariot died, for example."

Josh took a deep breath. "The people in the first century seem to have had a different idea about history. They didn't worry about getting all the historical 'facts' documented. They may not even have known all of them. But they knew what they wanted to teach the church. Mark tells us Jesus was a suffering servant. Matthew says he was a teacher who did God's will in righteous obedience. Luke tells us Jesus was a compassionate lover of poor people, who prepared us for living in the Holy Spirit. And John teaches us that Jesus has the power to deal with—and overcome—all God's enemies. All four messages are true. But you may not be able to make the four Gospels fit together 'factually.' Their stories weren't created to interlock perfectly with each other."

Michael sat thinking. "Did you and your dad ever discuss any of this?"

"No. I don't think he would have appreciated my thoughts, or what the seminary was helping me to discover."

"Have you preached any of it?"

"Actually, yes. But not in the way you and I have just discussed it."

"Well, it would have helped me if you had, you know."

"It would also have upset a lot of our members if I'd suggested the Gospel writers have differences."

"Wouldn't people figure that out for themselves, sooner or later?"

"Well, you didn't. Until now."

"So what's a pastor supposed to do with what he learns in seminary. I mean, when he gets into a congregation?"

"Begin by loving the members. Be their pastor. And their friend. When they're ready…if they're ready…help them to go deeper into Scripture. And always make sure they understand you love this book."

"And what if the members are never ready to go deeper?"

"Tell them the truth the best way you can. Don't ever lie to anyone. But don't feed people meat and potatoes when they're on a milk and cereal diet."

Michael nodded. "This biblical studies stuff is more complicated than I expected it would be." He exhaled. "But you've been a big help. Thanks. Thanks a lot."

Chapter 49

Five-year-old Andrew Jonas awoke with a start. He thought he was dreaming when he first heard the voice. But now he was wide awake, and he was still hearing it. He sat perfectly still and listened hard.

Nanny Annabelle, where are you? It was a small boy's voice. But where was he?

Andrew crept from bed and walked to the door. Opening it, he peered into the hall. There was no one there. He went to the closet and looked in. He could see nothing but his own clothing, hanging on hooks and hangars. He got down on his knees and peered under the bed. There was nothing there but dust.

He decided he had imagined the voice. Crawling back into bed, he pulled the covers up over himself again and lay as still as possible.

Nanny Annabelle, where are you?

Andrew sat up again. The morning light was seeping in, around the edges of the closed bedroom curtains. The room was bright enough to convince him there was nobody else there.

He felt a chill run down his spine. He was not liking this at all. Getting out of bed a second time, he hurried from the room. Down the hallway to his parents' bedroom he went. He knew he was not supposed to enter without permission, so he stood outside the closed door and said, in as brave a voice as he could muster, "Mommy? Can I come in?"

There was no reply.

"Mommy? It's Andrew. I need to come in."

Silence.

He opened the door, stepped into the room and walked silently across the carpet to his mother's side of the bed. He whispered urgently into her ear, "Mommy! Wake up!"

Sarah Jonas opened her eyes. When she saw her third child standing so near to her, she smiled and reached out to touch his cheek. “It’s Saturday morning, Andrew. Mommy and Daddy are still tired. Why don’t you stay in bed for awhile.”

“I can’t sleep.”

“Aren’t you still sleepy?”

He shook his head pathetically. “I’m scared of my room. Can I sleep in here with you and Daddy?”

Sarah pulled herself from bed, took Andrew’s hand, and walked with him to the nearby upholstered rocking chair. Lifting him onto her lap, she said, “This is Daddy and Mommy’s room. You have your own room. That’s where you belong.”

“It’s scary in there.”

“Why is it scary, Andrew?”

“There’s somebody else in there.”

She looked at him in puzzlement. “Who else is in there?”

“I don’t know. I just hear him.”

“What does he sound like?”

“I can hear a little boy. Like me. He says he wants his nanny.”

“ADAM, I’M REALLY GLAD you bought one of these condominiums. You can sit here and watch people going in and out of the front door of Saint Michael Church. And it’s such a comfortable place. You look like you’re right at home here.”

“George Kleinhans was right. I really needed to get out of that house up on the river. It was a wonderful place, but it was just too big. And too full of memories of Sandy.”

Josh Jonas sat looking at Sarah’s grandfather. For a seventy-seven-year-old, he thought Adam looked incredibly fit. He knew the congregation’s patriarch walked twenty blocks every day, ate sensibly and kept himself active. He was assisting five children in the after-school program, and kids waiting for a tutor were all preferring him to anyone else.

Adam had steadfastly refused to purchase a television set. “I watched enough of that stuff at Sandy’s place. It’s brain poison,” he’d told Josh. So he busied himself by reading one book after another. He would frequently polish off a fat novel in the space of a week.

“What did you want to talk about this afternoon, Adam?”

“I have an idea, Joshua Daniel, and I need your help.”

“Okay. What’s the idea?”

"I made a lot of money selling the supper club. Sandy had no heirs, you know, and the court ruled that Arnold's 'other wife' down in Chicago wasn't entitled to any of her property. So it all came to me. I also did very well when selling the house up on the north side. I bought this condominium for cash, and had a fair amount left over from the sale of the house."

"Of course there were those outrageous sales commissions you had to pay to George," Josh said, joking.

"He barely charged enough to make a profit on those deals. How does he expect to make a living, doing business like that?"

"Plenty of other people pay his full commissions, believe me. So, anyway, what's all of this extra cash got to do with your idea?"

"I want to establish a scholarship. I want kids in the tutoring program to be eligible to get money to go to college. If they finish high school, that is."

Josh nodded appreciatively. "Good idea, Adam. But...you want to limit the awards to kids in the tutoring program?"

"They're the ones who need it most. *Your* children won't have any trouble getting financial help for college. You probably didn't either. But these kids, Joshua Daniel..." He sighed. "I work with them every day. I see what's happening in their lives. Some of those kids are going to end up stuck in dead-end lives if somebody doesn't help them take a different path. I have one sixth-grade boy who's sharp as a tack. He loves to read. He has an eager mind. He wants to learn everything he can. But he's in a home where the parents have no interest in education. He's in the tutoring program because his public school teacher wants him there, not his parents. I don't want to see a young fellow like that slip through the cracks and get lost."

Josh said, "Perfect. The idea is just perfect. I'll take it to the church council. Better yet, why don't you come to the next meeting and lay it out yourself?"

"Okay. I'll plan on it. Now, on to other important topics."

"Such as...?"

"Such as, how are my beautiful, wonderful, delightful great-grandchildren?"

"The same as they were when you asked me last week, Adam."

"How's that little rascal, Andrew?" He smiled and sighed. "Oh, to be five again."

Josh furrowed his brow. "You know, there's something going on with him."

"With Andrew?"

"Yes. He's…I don't know exactly what this is about, but…"

"But what?"

"He doesn't want to sleep in his own room anymore."

"Why not?"

"He says he's afraid of it. He has this odd notion that there's somebody else in there."

Adam nodded and smiled. "When I was five years old, I had imaginary animals. I herded them around the house. My mother told me I even took them into the bathtub with me. Whenever I splashed the water out onto the floor, I blamed it on the animals."

Josh said, "I don't think this is exactly like that. Andrew says he isn't imagining this."

"Tell me about Andrew's 'visitor.' What's he, or she, like?"

"Well, it's a little boy. He only says one thing."

"And what's that?"

"It really makes no sense."

"Just tell me."

"He says…" Josh wondered if he would sound credible to Adam. But he plowed ahead. "He says, 'Nanny Annabelle, where are you?'" Josh let out his breath slowly. "Sarah and I have tried to figure out whether that's a name from a story we might have read to him. It doesn't make any sense."

Adam sat thinking. He had a focused, intense look about him, as if he were remembering a deeply-hidden secret of some sort. Finally, he said, "Of course. Why didn't I make the connection earlier?"

The pastor stared at him, not comprehending.

"I was trying to remember, ever since she moved into this complex, exactly why I should know her. I never could. But now I think I have it figured out."

"Adam, I'm lost. What are you talking about?"

"The condominium on the other end of the block, the last one to sell, was purchased by a seventy-year-old woman. She'd been renting over in St. Paul, somewhere. Said she'd saved her money and could afford to buy one of these units. She saw the sign when they were still selling them. She'd been going into the church fairly often. Liked to go in there on weekdays for meditation."

He looked at Josh. "I'm not one to pry. She told me all of this one day, when one of our association meetings was breaking up. I was just trying to be friendly."

"Stick to the point, Adam. What about this woman?"

"Do you remember Pastor James Darnauer?"

"Sure. He was called to serve with my dad. I was just a kid. He went off to New Guinea as a missionary after the Second World War."

"He's still there. But he told me, once upon a time, that his first counseling session at Saint Michael Church was with a woman whom he discovered crying inside the church. She was sitting in the Children's Chapel, looking at the stained-glass window showing Jesus with the children."

"You have an amazing memory, Adam. That was over thirty years ago."

"That window has a replica of a five-year-old boy, sitting at Jesus' feet."

"I know. Michael Morgan-Houseman, Jr. He died when a delivery truck hit him, over on Bloomington Avenue. His father gave the congregation five million dollars, which is how we got the church building we're in now."

"Exactly. But that youngster didn't just walk in front of a delivery truck. He was riding a streetcar with his nanny. He had a rubber ball, a birthday gift from his father. It bounced away from him. He ran after it, off the streetcar. His nanny didn't react quickly enough to stop him. She always blamed herself for his death."

"And Pastor Darnauer…?"

"He found her sitting in the Children's Chapel years later, weeping. She'd come back to ask the boy in the window to forgive her."

"Pastor Darnauer told you all this?"

"I never forgot it. Unfortunately, I seemed to have forgotten her name. Until just now. It was Annabelle. Annabelle Sorensen."

"Nanny Annabelle," said Josh, whispering the words almost reverently.

"And here's the kicker," Adam continued. "Annabelle Sorensen is the seventy-year-old lady who lives in the condominium at the other end of this block."

THE ELDERLY WOMAN sat primly in the parlor of the Franklin Avenue parsonage, studying the stone lions that adorned the historic old fireplace. She said quietly, "It's just as it was. The lions are still there." She looked at Josh and Sarah, seated across from her. "Mr. Morgan-Houseman used to like to sit in here, with the fire blazing, drinking brandy. He'd be thinking up some new way to make more money."

Sarah said, "Thank you for coming, Ms. Sorensen."

"Call me Annabelle."

"All right…Annabelle."

"Your son, Andrew. May I say hello to him?"

Josh got up from his seat. "He's in the playroom. I'll bring him down."

After he had gone out, Sarah said, "At first I thought Andrew was imagining things. But he's not one to make things up. He's never lied to us."

Annabelle smiled. "Five-year-olds can tell fibs. Sometimes they don't even know they're telling them. But I'm sure this was no fib he told you."

The youngster came into the parlor, holding his father's hand. "Andrew, this is Annabelle Sorensen. She used to be a nanny when she lived here."

Andrew's eyes grew wide. "Somebody in my room is looking for you, I think," he said, in a mysterious voice that carried all the charm of a five-year-old's credulity.

She got up from her chair. "Could you show me your room, Andrew?" Josh and Sarah got up with her. Annabelle said, "It might be best if just Andrew and I went up." She smiled. They nodded and sat down again.

As the elderly woman and the small boy climbed the stairs, she said, "Little Michael used to stand up there at the top of the stairs and shout, 'Nanny Annabelle, I need you!' And I would stand down at the bottom and say, in my impatient, adult voice, 'Michael, is there a fire in your room? Is there a burglar in the house?' He would say, 'No, Nanny Annabelle'. And then I would say, 'Then please use your indoors voice, Master Michael.'"

Andrew looked at her and grinned. "You were a pretty good nanny, I'll bet." Annabelle returned a look of regret.

In the upstairs hallway Andrew stopped in front of one of the bedroom doors. "This is my room."

Annabelle looked at him with a mysterious countenance. "This was Master Michael's room."

"Do you want to go in?"

"Yes. May I?" Andrew nodded. "May I go in alone, please?" He nodded again. "You wait right here. I won't be long." She stepped into the room and closed the door.

Andrew leaned his ear to the door. He heard nothing. He waited for what seemed to him a very long time. Finally, tired of waiting, he sat down on the hallway floor and leaned back against the wall.

Twenty minutes later, the door opened. Annabelle came out. Andrew scrambled up. "Did you hear him? Did he talk to you?"

"Let's go downstairs. I can explain it to you and your parents at the same time."

Sarah invited them into the paneled dining room. She had coffee and a freshly-baked coffee cake ready. There was a glass of milk at Andrew's place. Josh lifted him onto his booster seat and pushed him in.

When they were seated, Annabelle said, "Andrew, you were a brave little boy to stay and listen to the voice."

"Did you hear it?" he demanded impatiently.

"Yes, I did."

"What did he say?"

"He said, 'Nanny Annabelle, where were you? I wanted to tell you goodbye.'"

Josh and Sarah returned looks of astonishment. The pastor said, "After all these years, he was waiting to tell you goodbye?"

She nodded. "He seems to have felt comfortable calling out to me through another five-year-old. I told him how sorry I was that he had gone away so early in his life. He told me not to worry. He said he was in a wonderful place. He said he was glad another little boy, just like him, was living in his room."

Her eyes were pooling. She continued, "He told me he loved me." She almost choked on her words. "And then he said goodbye." Her lower lip was quivering. She found a handkerchief and dried her eyes.

She looked at Andrew and said, "I don't think you'll have to worry about hearing the voice again." She smiled at the five-year-old who had given himself a milk moustache.

He smiled back, then turned to his mother. He seemed not to notice the tears in her eyes as he asked, as politely as he knew how, "May I please have another piece of coffee cake?"

Chapter 50

Josh and Sarah sat together on the parlor couch. The children were all in bed. The lights were low. A dying fire glowed in the fireplace, casting strange flickering shadows onto the chins of the stone lions, staring at them from the two ends of the mantel.

Two emptied wineglasses sat on the low table in front of them.

As he pulled his wife close to him, Josh said, "I can't remember who said 'May this house be safe from tigers,' but if any ever showed up here, I think our lions would chase them off."

"You're so goofy sometimes, I can hardly believe you're a pastor," Sarah replied, punching her husband playfully in the midsection.

"Why can't pastors be goofy once in a while?"

"As long as it's just when you're around me, it's fine, I guess."

He squeezed her shoulder. "Back in high school, did you ever in your wildest dreams think you'd end up living in some millionaire's fancy house?"

"I thought I was going to marry Tommy Sullivan and end up an architect's wife."

"Whatever happened to him, anyway?"

"His family moved to Vermont. Why does anybody move to Vermont?"

"You and I should go there sometime," he said.

"Sure. We could check up on Tommy."

"Are you kidding? He's probably living in New York City by now, designing skyscrapers."

"I'll bet he doesn't have twins," she said with smug satisfaction.

A log crunched down in the fireplace. Sparks flew up, then burned themselves out.

"Sarah, remember back when I was in seminary and you threw me out of the house?"

"That was so stupid of me. What was I thinking?"

"You were thinking I was insensitive…that I should have taken your side and not your granddad's."

"We're never going to let that happen again. I still can't believe I did that to you."

"I thought maybe our marriage was going to be over before it even got started."

"Josh?"

"What?"

"Are you glad you married me?"

"What kind of a question is that?"

"You never really dated anybody else."

"Maybe I should have run around more in high school. Is that what you think?"

"No. It's just that…well, you know how so many of the kids in high school were trading off all the time? By the time some of my friends got to graduation, they'd had six or seven boyfriends."

"A few of them got pregnant out of wedlock, too. And a few more of them got divorced after getting stuck in unhappy marriages, as I recall."

"Times are really changing, aren't they?" She sighed. "Back when my folks were dating, if you got pregnant outside of marriage your life was pretty much over."

"Well, your Mom seems to have survived it."

"You know about that?"

"My dad told me. How that guy…holy Toledo! The guy who used to sit in this room and drink brandy!…how he took advantage of her when she was working for him. What a creep he must have been!"

"A creep who gave five million dollars to Saint Michael Church."

Josh remained silent.

"Would you have taken his money, knowing all of that?"

"Well, my dad didn't really know the whole story when he took it."

It was Sarah's turn to remain silent.

"Do you think I should stick around here much longer?" He asked.

"What do you mean?" She straightened up and looked at him.

"Maybe I should open myself for a call."

"Why?"

"Because things aren't going as well as they might at Saint Michael Church. Think about it. My dad had the membership up to 7,200. We're just over 6,000 now, and we might be going down even further. People keep moving out to the suburbs. We have maybe twenty percent of our members living in the neighborhood around the church now. Some of the ones who've moved further out are finding other churches to join. I can hardly blame them, not wanting to drive all the way into south Minneapolis. And with the neighborhood changing the way it is, some of them are a little skittish about coming into the city anymore."

"None of that's your fault, Josh. The city isn't the same as it was. The numbers are bound to go down some."

"And then there's the problem with the Mexican people. I guess we're supposed to call them Hispanics now. But they're all sitting in one section at the early service, and nobody else goes near them. I don't know what to do about that."

"Be glad they're even there. Most Lutheran congregations can't get Mexicans...Hispanics...to walk in the door."

"And the Luther League. Remember how many there were in it when you are I were in high school? About two hundred, I'd guess. Now we're down to...what...sixty? They don't even want to call themselves 'Luther League' any more. Now it has to be 'Teens for Jesus.' What's the matter? Are they ashamed of Martin Luther, or what?"

"It's happening everywhere. Quit beating yourself up about it. It's not anybody's fault, really."

He sighed. "I know. But I'm getting weary of some of the stuff I'm having to deal with. Last week I had a couple come to me for premarital counseling. When we got to talking, they almost bragged that they were sleeping together already and having really great sex. And I'm supposed to sanctify their marriage? I was really insulted."

"Are you going to have the service for them?"

"Only if they agree to stop sleeping together until after the wedding."

"Are they going to?"

"They haven't decided yet," he said sarcastically.

"That's pretty sad, isn't it?"

"The world's going crazy, Sarah. And I'm supposed to do ministry in it."

"It could be worse. What if we were living in East Germany? The Lutherans over there can't even have their kids confirmed without taking big risks. It's a wonder their church is surviving at all."

"Maybe a healthy dose of that would be good for the American church about now."

She snuggled up to him again. "Don't get so morbid, Josh. You know good and well that, if you took a call somewhere else, you'd have the same thing going on there."

He studied the glowing embers of the dying fire. "You're probably right." He kissed her hair. "Anyway, there are some good things happening at Saint Michael Church. I should focus on those."

"Like Harry Broadman donating his fancy hunting lodge up by Grand Rapids, so the congregation can have a retreat center? That's a pretty neat thing," she said.

"And," he continued, "the fact that we now have a dozen of our kids heading to seminary is pretty amazing."

"Michael Fischer gets ordained next June. That should be an exciting day for the congregation. His mother will probably pull out all the stops on that pipe organ."

"Did you know I once told him he should consider coming back to serve at Saint Michael Church?"

"He's not going to, is he?"

"Well, it depends on what seems good to the Holy Spirit and to him. But he already told me he wasn't open to the idea."

"That's what *you* told the congregation once—about yourself."

"I think Michael really means it."

They sat listening to the crackling fire.

She said, "My granddad really likes that condo he bought, across from the church."

"All six founding families are over there. Who would have guessed that would have happened?"

"They've been the best of friends for almost forty years. It just makes sense."

Josh said, "Did you know Adam's been having coffee a couple times a week with Annabelle Sorensen?"

"Oh, no. Really?"

"Is that bad?"

"That's the way it started with Sandy and him."

"Well, Annabelle is only a few years younger than he is. Besides, I don't think it's leading anywhere."

"We didn't think so the last time either."

"I think he and Annabelle are good for each other."

Sarah was silent for a moment. "Well, I must admit, she was really good for Andrew. Ever since that time she came over here, he's never heard another strange voice. I'm really thankful for that."

"I'm still trying to figure out what that was all about."

"It's simple. Michael Morgan-Houseman, Jr. couldn't leave this place until he told her goodbye. So he waited."

"For forty years?"

"Maybe it's like Annabelle said. Little Michael was waiting for another five-year-old to show up in his old bedroom. I don't claim to understand these things, Josh."

"I still don't understand those messages *you* used to get, Sarah. Especially the ones about me."

"Neither do I. And, just between you and me, I hope I've had the last of them. They're not all that much fun."

"They don't make you feel sort of...powerful?"

"No. They make me feel apprehensive, and power*less*—because they're always about something that's about to happen, that I can't do anything about. And most of the time I end up with a blazing headache after I've experienced one of them."

"There are so many things I don't understand," he murmured.

"Want to know something else I don't understand?" she whispered.

"What?"

"I don't understand how I got so lucky, ending up with you. You are just about the best husband a woman could have. You're great with the kids. You're great with me. You're great with everybody." He smiled with appreciation. "A cut way above your father, that's for sure."

He looked stupefied. Had she really said that?

"I mean it. The congregation may be smaller than it was, but you're an even better pastor that your dad was. I'm convinced of it."

"You're embarrassing me."

"Can you see your dad playing basketball with a bunch of neighborhood kids who didn't even belong to the church, and maybe never would? But you do stuff like that all the time. And those years working in the free clinic. Can you imagine your dad ever having done anything like that? I can't."

"You're warming me up to ask a favor, right?"

"No. I really meant what I just said."

"You've never said that to me before."

"Well, you were sounding a little down this evening. And I was waiting for the right time to say it. This seemed like the right time."

The fire was dying. Its light was growing dim, so that the two lions, and the rare stone inlays, along the top and the sides of the fireplace, were fading into the shadows.

Josh got up and walked to the stereo. He found a 78 rpm disc and put it on the turntable. As the melody began, he said to Sarah, "I used to play this song, over and over, back when I was a student at Wartburg College. When I was feeling lonely and thinking of you, I would fantasize that you were there with me, and we'd dance together, to this song."

She smiled. She'd heard the tune on the radio, frequently, a dozen years before, but had never realized Josh had liked it.

"Come on," he said, beckoning to her with open arms. "Come step into my fantasy, and dance with me."

She got up off the couch and went to him. As the music softly played they moved together on the ornate carpet, in the near darkness. The vocalist sang a ballad of separation from his loved one, and of his longing to be near her.

Oh, my love, my darling, I hunger for your touch
A long, lonely while.
Time goes by so slowly, and time can do so much,
Are you still mine?
I need your love, I need your love,
God speed your love to me.

He held her close, and offered up a silent prayer of thanks—for every blessing which had so richly shaped his life, and the life of the amazing congregation he had been called to lead. He had no idea what lay ahead. But he knew, with certainty, that the future would be full of hope and promise. Because God was waiting there.

Faithful Reader,

The Glory and the Wonder is the second in what is intended to be three consecutive novels in "The Saint Michael Trilogy." The story traces the life and ministry of the members of The Lutheran Church of St. Michael and All Angels over the span of 75 years, from 1927 until 2002.

Fifteen percent of revenues received from sales of these three volumes, when copies are sold through its office in Minneapolis, Minnesota, will be contributed to *Metro Lutheran,* America's only independent pan-Lutheran newspaper.

If you enjoyed and appreciated reading this book, and especially if you are a friend of *Metro Lutheran* and would like to help assure its future financial success, please encourage your friends to purchase their own copies. They are available from *Metro Lutheran,* 122 W. Franklin Ave., # 214, Minneapolis, MN 55404. Please make your check payable to *Metro Lutheran.* Because of the nature of the sale—in order to maximize the benefit *to Metro Lutheran*—credit card purchases are not available.

Copies of the first book in the Trilogy, *In the Presence of Angels,* continue to be available from *Metro Lutheran.* For more information, call 612/230-3282.

If the planned progression is not interrupted, the third and final book, *A Rehearsal of Praise*, will be available for purchase in late 2006.

Thank you for purchasing and reading this book. I hope it has been a blessing to you as you seek purpose, meaning and direction on your daily path.

Michael L. Sherer
The Feast of St. Michael and All Angels
29 September 2005

Printed in the United States
47267LVS00005B/90

9 781424 120642